I0761303

DEATH IN THE PALACE

Also by Barbara Hambly
from Severn House

The Silver Screen Historical Mysteries

SCANDAL IN BABYLON
ONE EXTRA CORPSE
SAVING SUSY SWEETCHILD

The Benjamin January Series

DEAD AND BURIED
THE SHIRT ON HIS BACK
RAN AWAY
GOOD MAN FRIDAY
CRIMSON ANGEL
DRINKING GOURD
MURDER IN JULY
COLD BAYOU
LADY OF PERDITION
HOUSE OF THE PATRIARCH
DEATH AND HARD CIDER
THE NUBIAN'S CURSE
MURDER IN THE TREMBLING LANDS

The James Asher Vampire Novels

BLOOD MAIDENS
THE MAGISTRATES OF HELL
THE KINDRED OF DARKNESS
DARKNESS ON HIS BONES
PALE GUARDIAN
PRISONER OF MIDNIGHT

DEATH IN THE PALACE

Barbara Hambly

SEVERN
HOUSE

First world edition published in Great Britain and the USA in 2026
by Severn House, an imprint of Canongate Books Ltd,
14 High Street, Edinburgh EH1 1TE.

severnhouse.com

Cover and jacket design by www.us-now.com

British Library Cataloguing-in-Publication Data
A CIP catalogue record for this title is available from the British Library.

ISBN-13: 978-1-4483-1488-1 (cased)
ISBN-13: 978-1-4483-1900-8 (paper)
ISBN-13: 978-1-4483-1487-4 (e-book)

All Severn House titles are printed on acid-free paper.

Typeset by Palimpsest Book Production Ltd., Falkirk, Stirlingshire, Scotland.
Printed and bound in Great Britain by TJ Books, Padstow, Cornwall.

The manufacturer's authorised representative in the EU for product safety is Authorised Rep Compliance Ltd, 71 Lower Baggot Street, Dublin D02 P593 Ireland (arccompliance.com)

Praise for the Silver Screen Historical Mysteries

"Exciting adventures and thorny mysteries"
Kirkus Reviews on *Saving Susy Sweetchild*

"Outstanding . . . Showcases the author's wit and her compassion for the underdog"
Publishers Weekly Starred Review of *One Extra Corpse*

"Everything feels just right: the characters are abundantly human, the mystery is beautifully constructed, and the Hollywood milieu is vividly realized"
Booklist Starred Review of *One Extra Corpse*

"This splendid romp is sure to win Hambly new fans"
Publishers Weekly Starred Review of *Scandal in Babylon*

"Exhilarating, exasperating, and dangerous . . . A sparkling series launch featuring Hollywood hijinks and a clever sleuth"
Kirkus Reviews on *Scandal in Babylon*

"Emma feels fresh: not merely another flapper-era amateur sleuth, but rather a vibrant, intelligent woman with whom readers will enjoy spending time"
Booklist on *Scandal in Babylon*

About the author

Barbara Hambly, though a native of Southern California, lived in New Orleans for a number of years while married to the late science fiction writer George Alec Effinger. Hambly holds a degree in medieval history from the University of California and has written novels in numerous genres.

www.barbarahambly.com

For Steve, Mark, and Tony

Special thanks to Ruth Judkowitz
And to
Laura Frankos
For assistance above and beyond!

ONE

Mr. Clark Dexter
Dexter Consolidated Industry and Finance
Dexter Building
East 47th Street
New York, NY

November 7th, 1924

Miss Camille de la Rose
Foremost Productions
Sunset Boulevard
Hollywood, CA

re. Proposal of Marriage

Dear Miss de la Rose:

Will you marry me? I am twenty-four years old, in good health, and the head of a conglomerate of mining, banking, and holding companies worth in excess of $800,000,000. My personal income is in the neighborhood of a million per year.

I have long admired your work in motion pictures, and I will give you, free and clear, $50,000 if you will marry me for the space of one week. After one week, I will give you grounds for divorce (terms to be agreed upon by contract in advance), and you may return to Hollywood or remain in New York, as you so choose, without prejudice. You may keep the ring.

I will arrange for your train fare (California Limited to Chicago and Twentieth Century Limited Chicago to New York) and your accommodation in New York before the wedding. We can be married within days of your arrival in New York, and you may arrange whatever publicity you desire for the ceremony itself. I ask only that you do not discuss this offer with a lawyer or with any representatives of newspapers or magazines until we have had a chance to talk in person. I will pay for your wedding ensemble, and all expenses for the divorce itself.

This is a serious offer. Please consider it, and accept.

My heart pines for you, and I hope to hear from you soon.

Yours faithfully,
Clark W. Dexter

"Frank would take on just *dreadfully* if I accepted this." Kitty—Camille de la Rose, to the adoring movie-going public—frowned doubtfully. Frank Pugh was co-owner and studio head at Foremost Productions, whose central quadrangle lay just outside the three gauze-curtained French windows of the dressing room in which she—and her tall, thin sister-in-law, Emma Blackstone—sat on that bright, mild morning in November. Emma was drinking tea; Kitty, her usual morning cocktail of coffee, cream, sugar, and gin (Prohibition notwithstanding). It was Emma's job to make sure Thermos bottles of all ingredients were packed and ready to go the moment Kitty rose from her make-up table at home in the morning, along with the latest issue of *Modern Astrology*, half a dozen phonograph recordings, and Kitty's three exquisitely groomed Pekinese.

A recording of 'It Had To Be You' half obscured the noise of extras in police uniforms being marshalled in the quadrangle outside: evidently, Larry and Jerry, the studio's two resident wielders of the slapstick, were due to be pursued through Griffith Park yet again.

"Even if it *is* only for a week," Kitty went on. "He'd probably tear up my contract, or put me in some awful social drama about laundresses in Sweden. And I *do* make more than fifty grand a year here, so it wouldn't be worth it, even if it *did* make Darlene Golden tear her hair out and spit blood . . ."

Then her delicate brow cleared. "Oh, but it sounds like just the thing for *you*, darling!" She held the letter out to her sister-in-law, her smile dazzling.

Emma studied the page: tall and a little lanky beside her sister-in-law's fragile voluptuousness, her light-brown hair and gray eyes a quiet contrast to Kitty's black storm-cloud curls. "Does he mean it?"

"I have no idea, darling. I've never met him in my life. But it's good money. And we're going to *be* in New York on the twenty-fifth. I could tell Frank I need to go visit my grandmother on the day of the wedding, if she's still alive. She may not be. And anyway, Frank doesn't know they disowned me. And after that, I'm sure I could get away to do the filming. The studio's in Queens . . ." She ticked off a mental schedule on her delicate fingers. "Oh, but we'd have to make sure nothing leaked out to the screen magazines."

"You're not seriously thinking of taking this man up on his offer?"

"Well . . ."

"No," said Emma, horrified—and even more horrified to hear how much she sounded like her Aunt Phyllis.

"It *is* only for a week . . ."

"*No!*" Emma was aware as she said it that it wasn't her place. Kitty was three years her senior (twenty-nine, though she had been claiming twenty-two for at least four years), and moreover had brought her to Hollywood, California, after four dismal years as the ill-paid companion of a wealthy manufacturer's widow in Manchester. Her duties—as Mrs. Pendergast's butler would certainly have pointed out to her—were simply to brush, feed, and exercise Chang Ming, Buttercreme, and Black Jasmine, to care for Kitty's expensive wardrobe, to balance the primal chaos of Kitty's checkbook, and to find lost earrings, stockings, champagne glasses, and invitations in the untidy welter of Kitty's belongings. And, principally, to provide Kitty with respectable companionship so that the film magazines would not label her an unmitigated tart. (*Miss de la Rose shares the modest elegance of her home in the Hollywood Hills with her widowed sister-in-law, whose husband sacrificed his life defending democracy in the fields of Flanders*, was how *Movie Weekly* had put it.)

Putting her foot down about marrying unknown millionaires was not part of it.

But Kitty only looked discontented, as if Emma had reminded her that more than one chocolate bon-bon would show up on her chin line in the next set of dailies. "I'd at least like to find out what the deal is," she coaxed.

"Whatever the deal is," returned Emma firmly, "it stinks like rotten fish. Just because a man claims to be the head of a business conglomerate making a million dollars a year doesn't mean he's actually doing so. Or that he won't sell the story of your marriage to *Photoplay*—with pictures—the week after the divorce."

"Hmm." Kitty sighed. "Or sell the negatives back to me for a lot more than fifty thou. I suppose you're right. And a divorce would take just *months*, even in Nevada." She glanced at the dressing-room clock. Mr. Pugh had gone to great expense to have clocks installed in the dressing rooms of every star on the Foremost lot. The only reason Kitty had arrived at the studio fifteen minutes before the initial fitting of her costumes for the new film *Shining Bright* was that the young man with whom she had spent much of last night (*not* Mr. Pugh) was an extra in *Peril Under Paris*, currently being filmed on Stage Two, who had to be on the set at seven. At ten minutes to midnight the previous night, Emma had received a telephone call instructing her to bring not only the usual coffee, gin, gramophone records, and dogs to the studio in the morning, but fresh clothing and shoes.

Kitty would meet her there . . .

Now Emma gathered up the Russian-leather leashes for the three Pekes, an exercise that caused Chang Ming and Black Jasmine to dash to her side, plumed tails threshing, and Buttercreme to bolt for concealment beneath the daybed. With the same firmness she had shown Kitty, Emma knelt and hauled forth the six pounds of unwilling pale-blonde fluff, and clipped the leads onto collars set with six-carat diamonds, while Kitty wrapped herself in an extravaganza of cut velvet and monkey fur. Crossing the quadrangle to the studio "street" that led to Wardrobe, Emma marveled again at the mild sweetness of the autumn sunshine. She had been in Hollywood for just over a year, and well recalled the damp cold of Manchester, the rainy gray streets, and the bitter chill of her unheated room at the top of Mrs. Pendergast's house.

Even in Oxford—where her parents had lived, where she herself had grown and gone to Somerville College (and had met, and loved, and married Kitty's tall, quietly smiling brother when the American troops had arrived in 1917) . . . even Oxford had been gray and cold, compared to this strange Mediterranean paradise on the Pacific. Τὰ πάντα ῥεῖ καὶ οὐδὲν μένει, Heraclitus had said . . . her scholarly father had said, long ago in that other life. *Everything flows, and nothing stands still.*

She wondered what New York would be like.

There was a sort of conference room attached to the wardrobe department at Foremost, across the "street" from the three-story monolith of the properties building. The table that usually stood in the center of this room had been moved into a corner, and Millie Katz and her "ladies" had set out carafes of commissary coffee, a platter of donuts, and a dish of the penny candy that Mr. Pugh devoured with such relish. Emma smiled, touched that the head of wardrobe had thought to include a small red teapot for her, and a dish of water, set under the table, for the dogs.

Frank Pugh, an obese bear of a man with thick black hair and eyes like green jade, turned from gobbling peanut chews and Tootsie Rolls to greet Kitty with a handclasp that Jane Austen would have described as "speaking," but which gave no further evidence of the fact that they'd spent the earlier hours of last night together. (The young gentleman over in Stage Two had picked Kitty up only minutes after Pugh had deposited her at that "modestly elegant" house in the Hollywood Hills that he'd purchased for her with studio money. Emma suspected that the young gentleman had been waiting in the darkness of Ivarene Street for the studio head's car to pull away.) Mrs. Pugh—the fourth wealthy woman to bear that title—was in Los Angeles, and, studio gossip surmised, Mr. Pugh was being careful.

Conrad Fishbein, equally rotund but fair-haired, with a face like an oleaginous Kewpie doll, crossed the room to shake Emma's hand. As publicity chief for Foremost Productions, he had reason to be grateful to a respectable British war widow who acted as chaperone to the entrancing Camille de la Rose. "May I get you a donut?" He bent, puffing, to ruffle the red-gold Chang Ming, who had already lain down at his feet and presented his fluffy belly to be rubbed. Tiny Black Jasmine placed a white-tipped sable paw on the fat man's wrist, as if returning the greeting. Buttercreme, whom Emma had picked up before she'd entered the room, uttered a soft, disapproving yap at the whole assembly from the safety of Emma's cardigan. Buttercreme had small use for studio bigwigs.

"Thank you," said Emma, and Fishy escorted her to the chair closest to the refreshment table and the dogs' water dish. Head scenario writer Sam Wyatt lounged over to her at once—a slim, medium-sized man with slick dark hair, a perpetual cigarette, and an expression of watchful amusement.

"Congratulations, Duchess. I hear you got the job doin' the script rewrites back East." He nodded in the direction of Neil Bandog, whose ownership of a chain of motion-picture theaters allied with Foremost would ordinarily have put him far above such mundane tasks as reviewing wardrobe details for an upcoming project. "This one's a big deal."

Bandog, trim and forty-ish, with a neat dark mustache, was having his shoes licked (metaphorically) by Gordy Graves—Emma had no doubt that the activity would have been literal had Gordy been called upon to perform it. Gordy was generally in charge of line producing the studio's lesser projects. Both he and Ken Elmore, the handsome six-footer slated to play Beau Sharpless, the hero-turned-highwayman of the romantic epic *Shining Bright*, were laughing ecstatically at one of Bandog's collection of off-color "darky" jokes.

"I suspect that has more to do with Mr. Pugh wanting to save money on train fares," surmised Emma. "I think I'd have been going in any case, since Kitty can't bear to be parted from the celestial creamcakes"—she smiled down at Chang Ming, prostrate already on Wyatt's shoes and gazing adoringly up into his face—"and the poor things would starve to death without someone to look after them . . ."

"And her," Wyatt reminded her, and Emma laughed.

"I doubt Kitty has ever missed a square meal in her life. And that was unfair of me. She would make sure they were fed. Only it would be at the expense of something else: making it to the set on time, for instance, or keeping appointments that Mr. Fishbein arranges with photographers and reporters."

"Or spending a romantic evening with certain persons . . ."

Emma followed the scenarist's glance to Pugh, who had conducted Kitty to Bandog and was watching her possessively as they exchanged trivialities. On camera, Kitty might not be able—as the Americans said—to act her way out of a wet paper bag, but her balance of non-flirtatious friendliness with Mr. Bandog while radiating subtle enslavement to Mr. Pugh's intoxicating personal charms (!) was breathtaking to say the least. *Let no one ever say my sister-in-law is not one of the greatest actresses in the business . . .*

"I thought Mr. Pugh was staying in Hollywood."

"He will be as long as Mrs. Pugh's in town with her lawyer," returned Wyatt, taking a drag on his cigarette. Studio gossip had it that the screenwriter had run guns to the Arabs during the war, had driven a taxicab in El Paso, and had operated a saloon on Zanzibar, yet he had about him the indefinable air of long-ago dancing classes and ivy-covered halls. "The minute he thinks the coast is clear, he'll hand the whole show over to Willie"—Eando Willers was Pugh's assistant—"and be burning up the eastbound rails. And speaking of persons who'll be burning up the rails . . ."

He held out a manila folder containing what looked like several dozen yellow telegraph forms, and five or six letters, each letter three or four typed pages in length. "All yours, Duchess."

Emma groaned. "Drat the man . . ."

In the course of several months of working with Wyatt on the scenario, she had heard all about the letters, telegrams, and long-distance telephone calls he had received from Devon Kingsley, author of the best-selling novel *Shining Bright* (*Soon to be a major motion picture . . .*).

"I thought Mr. Kingsley lives in Savannah?"

"He does." Wyatt added the blue-covered bulk (517 pages—Emma had read it, conscientiously, twice) of the novel itself to the folder in her arms (*. . . with her dazzling beauty and family fortune, Summer Fairisle lacked for nothing—except love . . .* stated the back of the dust jacket. *A heart-lifting saga of courage and faithfulness against the bloody world of . . ." ". . . with love and hope as her only weapons . . .*). "The minute he hears the filming's going to be in New York, bet me he'll be pounding on the studio door wanting to make sure you don't screw up his story."

Emma sighed. "Oh, joy."

"Hey, if anybody can do it, Duchess, you can . . ."

Further comment was cut short as Mr. Bandog turned suddenly, the adoration in his eyes as he beheld Darlene Golden—framed dramatically in the doorway that led to the dressing rooms—rivaling Romeo's upon first sight of Juliet: *O, she doth teach the torches to burn bright!*

And so, admitted Emma, she did. Had the artist Botticelli been called upon to illustrate Mr. Kingsley's best-selling novel, he could have found no model more perfect for the incarnation of its heroine: a fragile angel in layers of white gauze, maize-blonde curls tumbling in enchanting disarray on ivory shoulders.

Bandog—recently introduced to Miss Golden by Frank Pugh as a means of further incentivizing the theater owner's investment in Foremost Productions—stepped toward her, one hand held out, his face that of a man who beholds a vision.

“Oh, Mr. Bandog,” whined the vision in a pronounced drawl, “do I gotta wear this thing?” She cracked her chewing gum. “Kitty gets all the pretty dresses in this picture. If I’m the star, how come I get stuck in an old flour sack like this?”

TWO

Before Millie Katz could point out that the fairy-like confection that more or less (mostly less) enveloped Miss Golden's slim form had been the height of fashion in the early phases of the Napoleonic Wars, against which background *Shining Bright* took place, Mr. Bandog turned indignantly on Pugh. "Yeah," he scowled. "I thought Darlene's supposed to be a duke's daughter. That thing looks like a nightgown, and a pretty cheap one at that."

(*France disguised as Austria, wraps herself in a rag*, the French had screamed when Marie Antoinette had been painted in a gown considerably less simple and "Grecian" than that one. Emma reflected that Mr. Bandog had obviously taken no notice of the meticulous sartorial research that had gone into *Shining Bright*.)

To the wardrobe mistress's patient explanation that (a) Summer Fairisle would have been far more fashionably attired than any other woman in the ballroom in 1797, and (b) such a garment was specifically described in the ballroom sequence in Chapter Fifty-Three, Bandog only replied, "I don't like it. If she's a duke's daughter, she should be the most gorgeous woman in the room." He turned back to Pugh. "Change it. You know, like the ladies in the museum pictures, with those big dresses with all the jewels and flowers, and the big hair." His manicured fingers sketched the extravagant "poufs" (as such hairdos had been called) worn by French Court ladies—most of whom had been beheaded by Chapter Fifty-Three. "Paying customers don't want to see wispy little shit like that, and neither do I."

Mrs. Katz opened her lips, probably, thought Emma, to point out that $35,000 had already been spent on Directoire-style wardrobes for Kitty, the matronly Margaret Mackenzie, and six other featured players in the film, but Pugh silenced her with a glare. "Change it."

"Should be easy to do," declared Bandog cheerfully. "We'll be in New York, fer Chrissake. There's a high-class costume rental every other block, downtown. It's the reason Foremost has purchased the MBQ studio in Queens." He raised his voice importantly, silencing the chatter in the room. "Three hundred thousand square feet of production space, two acres of backlot, two of the biggest stages in the business."

His sweeping gesture took in the actors who would be boarding the California Limited at noon on Thursday, as well as Gordy Graves, assistant wardrobe chief Carrie Drebbett, and by implication the studio's top cameramen (currently engaged on Stage Two). "You can only do so much out here," he went on, addressing the room like a politician the week before an election. "New York is set up around Broadway. In New York, we'll have access to costumes, sets, lighting, production labs . . . Paramount and Metro were working with the big Broadway supply houses when Griffith was still shooting guys riding around the Hollywood Hills with a Brownie. *Shining Bright* is going to be a production to rival the best that Broadway has to offer, a show that will outstrip even the gorgeous work that's been done here at Foremost in the past ten years." His momentary pause seemed to wait for applause. "A show that will make America sit up and take notice of motion pictures as a serious medium! As the new literature of the twentieth century!"

Darlene Golden cracked her gum again. "We won't have to take the streetcar all the way out to Queens, will we? You'll give us cars?"

"A fleet of them," he proclaimed, his heart in his eyes, "my—" He just stopped himself from saying *darling*, and finished with an awkward, "My word on it."

She stopped chewing long enough to look deeply gratified.

Having demanded the ostentatious acreage of 1770s high fashions to set off Miss Golden's charms, Bandog saw nothing incongruous about keeping (for budgetary considerations) the gaudier examples of the narrow-cut, clinging Directoire wardrobe for Kitty and the other women of the cast. Nobody suggested to Mr. Bandog that this would cause "Summer

Fairisle" to appear grotesquely out of place at the ball at which the defiant heroine reappears in Paris society to shine down her conniving nemesis, the evil Comtesse de Palogneux.

Mr. Pugh said nothing. In addition to owning major stock in a chain of medium-sized theaters across ten Midwestern states, Neil Bandog's banking and financial interests underwrote a number of Foremost projects, including—since shortly after the moment he first laid eyes on Miss Golden—*Shining Bright*.

One glance from Mr. Pugh's cold green eyes was enough to make the silence general.

"It will be simple enough, Mrs. Katz assures me," sighed Emma, an hour later, "to find costumes in the proper historical range once we get to New York." She perched on a corner of a wooden hand truck laden with three coffins in a quiet corner of Stage Two and sipped her tea, while the lighting chief, Doc Larousse, and his minions shifted Kliegs, spots, and reflectors for Scene 571 of *Peril Under Paris*. "But I'm afraid that will entail moving the entire story back before the Revolution, which will mean cutting Napoleon out of it entirely."

"Nah." Zal Rokatansky—shaggy rust-colored hair and beard sweat-beaded from the heat of the Klieg lights despite the chill morning outside—polished the sweat from his glasses with one of the dozen clean white handkerchiefs he habitually carried to keep his camera lenses spotless, and turned his near-sighted brown gaze towards the mysterious brick arches of the set. "For one thing, most people won't know the difference. Big dresses and lots of jewels equals scheming aristocrats, and that's all most of them care about. The trick'll be to find costumes in New York that'll blend the two looks. Carrie can do that. You've seen how in something like *Foolish Wives*, or *Manslaughter*, some of the women dress like it's 1921, and the older ones—or the ones who're supposed to be rich bluenoses—still have skirts down to their ankles, and it's hard to tell what year it's supposed to be. Is Carrie taking anyone else to New York to look after the custom-made stuff, or do they have someone lined up when you get there?"

"I think they have someone there."

In the Paris sewers—which seemed, Emma observed, to have impinged on the Catacombs, to judge by the number of skulls and bones scattered near the sunken water tank stage left—director Madge Burdon was instructing hero Seth Ramsay in the routine of his climactic battle with the evil Colonel Poilu. Burdon—stout in her linen skirt, work boots, and white cotton shirt—pointed to the precise camera angles she wanted in the scene: Ramsay shook his head violently. He swept his arm toward the tall stunt double, Brad Marsden, whose dark hair had been dyed blonde to match the star's and whose athletic figure almost exactly duplicated that of the younger man. Judging by the director's gestures, Emma could guess that this was not the first time she'd explained to Ramsay that all he had to do was spring out of the water tank, sword in hand, and lunge forward under Marsh Sloane's blade in a classic passata sotto, but that the camera had to be close enough to see his face as he did so. It was also fairly clear that this was not the first time that Miss Burdon had explained that the chances of his foot slipping in water dripped from his clothing—causing him to impale himself on his opponent's blade—were less than negligible.

Marsden, still soaked from the previous shot (Seth's costume and hair were bone-dry), though two inches taller, was a near-duplicate of Ramsay from the back, or at a distance of thirty feet in carefully arranged lighting. But at some point, Emma was well aware, the audience would have to see that it actually *was* Seth Ramsay (or "Gaston") taking on the wicked "Colonel," no matter who then went on to perform spectacular feats of swordplay in the master shots.

Long familiar with Ramsay's reluctance to put a hair of his own head in danger, Zal continued to gulp down the two hot dogs Emma had brought him from the commissary. The argument in the Catacombs didn't look to be ending any time soon, and filming, Emma guessed, having bypassed lunch, would prolong itself far beyond dinner without a pause.

"Have you ever heard of a millionaire named Clark Dexter?" she asked after a time. "Or of Dexter Consolidated Industry and Finance?" And when Zal paused, frowning in half-recognition of the names, she went on to describe that morning's extraordinary billet-doux. (She hoped it was extraordinary, anyway, and wasn't going to turn out to be a commonplace of Hollywood life.)

"I know Dexter Consolidated owns I don't know how much of the War-horse Copper Mine in Arizona," he said after a time. "They have about six mines in Arizona and Colorado, plus, I think, coal in West Virginia. There was a hell of a strike there in '16; their 'private detectives' killed three men on the picket line. Probably other holdings in things like railroads and city property. Big family corporations like that spread out to control whatever they can get. But why he'd want to marry Kitty . . ." He shook his head. "Knowing ahead of time he's going to want a divorce a week later makes sense, if he reads the fan magazines, but—"

"Beast." Emma flicked him on the back of his shoulder, like a schoolgirl. "I'm not saying you're wrong—"

"Don't get me wrong." Zal wiped his fingers with a paper napkin before reaching out to squeeze Emma's hand. "I love Kitty like a sister. I'm just saying I know her. You might want to ask the folks in town who work mostly in the New York studios: the Gish girls, or Gloria Swanson if she's in town. Or maybe one of the Talmadge sisters. Tom Ince worked in the New York studios back before the War. So did Mary Pickford. New York's different from Los Angeles, Em. There's a lot more going on: Broadway and vaudeville as well as the movies; publishing and banking and newspapers. Big-time law firms and shipping from literally every port in the world. Rich kids coming in from Long Island looking for kicks, French artists and British earls, and guys who make their fortunes off canned soup and cars."

He nodded towards the set, where Emily Violet's stand-in, clothed in a copy of Miss Violet's artistic deshabille, now crouched against a pile of bones while Doc Larousse adjusted reflectors and spots. "Out here, everybody's in the movies. You go to a party, and they don't talk about anything else. In the nightclubs on Broadway, or up in Harlem, sooner or later you're going to cross paths with everybody and hear pretty much everything. I'll ask around . . ."

"No." Emma rose from her macabre perch on the coffin cart, as Zal gulped down the last fragment of hot dog and got to his feet as well. She put her hands on his shoulders, and he rested his on her waist, his stocky strength giving her, despite the three-inch disparity of their heights, a feeling of reassurance. Of safety. "If we're leaving Thursday, I doubt you're going to have time to sleep, let alone search for expatriate New Yorkers."

Madge had stepped to the chalked line on the stage floor that marked the edge of the frame, peering out past the blazing lights in quest of her first cameraman. Beside her, Ramsay was going into detail about a friend of an uncle's who had been killed by slipping in a puddle on his kitchen floor.

"I'm sure I can keep Kitty from doing anything silly—"

Zal turned his head sharply. Following his glance, Emma saw Frank Pugh striding the length of the darkened stage building. A small, sturdy-looking woman walked behind him, in what—as they came closer—Emma recognized as a very expensive lavender Chanel suit and a staggeringly Parisian lavender hat.

"Don't bet on it," murmured Zal.

A thin, stoop-shouldered man with a briefcase followed the pair, sporting what would have been a mustache had there been more of it. By his gestures, the studio chief was showing them the towering sets under construction for *Message from Beyond*, but when his eye fell on Madge Burdon, he altered course and made directly for the lights, sewers, and bones.

"You going to have this wrapped by Wednesday night?" he asked the director, motioning Zal to join the discussion. His cheery tone of voice deceived no one: there was only one answer permissible.

"It'll be a stretch," confessed Burdon. "We've got the escape through the flooded sewers scheduled for Sunday and Monday, and the guillotine's set up in the back lot for Tuesday and Wednesday. We can do the prison-cell sequences Tuesday night and Wednesday night."

Zal stepped back and murmured to Emma, "And if you believe that, I have a real nice bridge to sell you." He nodded wearily at the still-fussing Ramsay, visibly waiting for his chance to pounce on Mr. Pugh concerning the perils of swordplay and water puddles, let alone flooded sewers.

"I know you can do it." Pugh thumped Miss Burdon companionably on the shoulder, and turned to deliver a similar slap to Zal's back. To the woman—and the man with the briefcase—he explained, "Zal here is the best cameraman on the lot. He's one of two I'm sending to our new eastern facility next week—Manhattan-Brooklyn-Queens Studios. Good camera work is one thing we can't take chances with, and several of the top-flight New York men—like Bill Stuart—are booked through the New Year. Once the principal shooting is done here, we can have Alvy Turner and Sim Braxton do the second unit work—rain pouring down, water rushing through the labyrinth of the Paris sewers, that kind of thing. It'll be a pinch," he added, with the grin of a man who hasn't had to work seventeen hours a day for many years. "But our team are troopers. Zal, Madge," he added, gesturing toward his guests, "I don't know if you remember Mrs. Pugh?"

Hands were shaken all around, and Emma noticed that neither she nor the gentleman with the briefcase were introduced. (She learned later from Vinnie Lowder on the switchboard that he was Mrs. Pugh's lawyer and his name was Gwinnett Doughty). Pugh and his guests moved on, but the interlude had given Madge Burdon the opportunity to lay hold of Zal and pull him back onto the set. Mechanically, Emma tidied up the detritus of paper napkins left by what would probably be the cameraman's only meal until well after midnight, and tried to picture herself telephoning Lillian Gish (*Is she still in Hollywood or has she gone back to New York?*) to ask about Clark Dexter. On the set, Ramsay continued to delay shooting with his protests against immersion in the eighteen inches of water that represented the sewers of Paris.

It was, Emma guessed with a pang of pity for Zal, going to be a long night.

Peggy Donovan might know about Dexter, she reflected, as

she made her way back to Wardrobe. She'd been introduced to the director Tom Ince once at a party . . .

The Pekes greeted her happily, having been penned into the conference room while Kitty was being fitted for costumes suitable for 1799 and Darlene Golden was hastily measured for the most spectacular ballgown of some fifteen years earlier. But Peggy, Kitty's closest friend in Hollywood, was, Emma recalled, away on location in the mountains of San Bernardino County, and she knew Mr. Ince would have no recollection of their meeting. And there were few other stars she could think of whom she felt able to telephone out of the blue. And Kitty, once released by Mrs. Katz's "ladies," was too busy blithering with indignation over the presence of Mr. Pugh's wife on the lot to be of much help.

"Why couldn't the old bat stay in Chicago where she belongs?" she asked, as she climbed into her car at the studio gates. "She can get a divorce from there as easily as in Los Angeles . . . Or go to Reno like everybody else? Oh, did I tell you, darling Peggy Donovan tells me that Charlie Chaplin's getting married again. Only it's a secret, but I bet I know who it is . . . Catch *Frank* keeping *his* marriages a secret! But at least"—Kitty took a cigarette from her handbag and slammed her foot on the accelerator of the immense yellow Packard, leaping like a racehorse out of the Foremost lot's gate—"it means Frank isn't going to see me this evening, so I've phoned Bill . . . You remember Bill Powell, don't you, darling? That *gorgeous* creature who played the villain in whatever film it was from Cosmopolitan last year?"

She fitted the cigarette to an amber holder accented with diamonds, darted across two lanes of oncoming traffic to turn left onto Sunset Boulevard as she did so, then gently lifted Black Jasmine from her lap as they roared eastward into the gathering autumn dusk. "No, darling," she addressed the Pekinese, "I can't let you drive the car until you get your license . . ." She whipped deftly around a yellow streetcar—the tiny dog kept his paws insistently on the steering wheel, wind streaming his silky black ears back. "Anyway, Bill's coming to pick me up at six . . ." It was five forty-five, and Emma had no doubt they'd be at Kitty's house by the time Mr. Powell put in his appearance.

"And speaking of Cosmopolitan"—Kitty lit her cigarette and dodged between a van and a truck full of lumber—"they've signed a deal with Tom Ince to produce pictures at his Culver lot starring Marion Davies, and Frank's going to be up at Tom's tomorrow. I thought it would be a good place for me to meet up with Frank, but I need you with me, in case that *septic* lawyer of Mrs. Pugh's puts a detective on my tail. Can you come?" She blew a line of smoke. "You'll have to dress like me."

Emma said, "I would be delighted." *I should be able to wangle ten minutes of conversation with our host . . .*

Kitty slewed the Packard into another left-hand turn against the Sunset Boulevard traffic, and gunned the car up Vine Street and into the velvet darkness of the hills. "Dearest, you're a *life-saver*! *Thank* you! I don't see what business it is of Florrie Pugh's *who* Frank takes out to dinner—"

Dinner, Emma was certain, was *not* why Mr. Pugh had bought Kitty the house on Ivarene Street.

"It's not like she lives in Los Angeles or anything! And why *anyone* would live in a place like Chicago . . . I spent nine months in Chicago, and I swear it was like being stuck on a two-bit vaudeville gig in Kickapoo, Kansas! And since poor Zallie's going to be shooting people splashing around in water from now until six o'clock Thursday morning, you won't be missing out on a night of frenzied passion or anything . . . Will you mind lying down on the floor on the way up to Tom's? I just *know* I'm going to be watched."

THREE

Other than dressing in a frock similar to Kitty's black-and-red Poiret—complete with a scarlet cloche hat and a red wool jacket of military cut—and curling her awkward height on the floor of the Packard's tiny rumble seat, the drive along Sunset Boulevard the following afternoon, and thence up Benedict Canyon, wasn't bad. (*I should have guessed Kitty had some ulterior motive when she bought me an outfit so similar to one of her own*, Emma sighed, some six days later, to Zal, on the train to New York.) Last week's rain had laid the dust where the pavement of Sunset Boulevard petered out, but hadn't been enough to generate much mud.

They left the "boulevard"—originally a cattle trail—to follow its erratic course through the hills, and proceeded up Benedict Canyon, where stars like Douglas Fairbanks and John Barrymore, and directors like King Vidor, had mansions on the wooded slopes. There, they could keep horses, ride in the hills, live like characters in their own films, and drive conveniently down to the studios to work.

One of these demi-paradises was Dias Dorados, the home of director/producer Thomas Ince, a mile up from Sunset Boulevard.

To Emma's unending gratitude, Kitty drove circumspectly up the dirt road and then along the oak-bordered drive to the house itself. ("I don't want to lose the detective, dearest. He's got to see *you* drive home wearing that outfit and tell Mrs. Pugh that it's me.") More oaks clumped before the house itself: Kitty halted the Packard where they would block any view from the road. "He'll probably have binoculars." Kitty gave Emma a hand getting from the rumble seat, and turned her "ambrosial" smile (as Homer would have described it) upon the young Mexican who came forward to take the vehicle onto the flats where several other cars already stood. "But he can't see anything from that distance."

She reached back into the car as she spoke, and brought out one of her own coats, though the November day was mild. This she handed to Emma: dark blue, not red, and slightly longer than the hip-length scarlet garment that Kitty (and Emma herself, for the moment) wore. If thirteen years on the Broadway stage and before the cameras had taught Kitty nothing about acting, she had gained a comprehensive knowledge of how to mislead suspicious observers.

Emma obediently shed her own red jacket and red cloche, donned the blue coat, and carried the more vivid garments draped, inside out, over her arm as she followed Kitty across the tiled entry plaza and into the house itself.

If there was not precisely a party going on, a number of guests were scattered on the patio of that beautiful Spanish hacienda. Emma recalled that the director had just signed some sort of agreement with newspaperman William Hearst's film company, Cosmopolitan. Reason enough for festivities. Ince had a large studio in Culver City, she remembered, and Hearst had a lovely mistress, the sprightly former chorus girl Marion Davies. In the immense main hall of the house itself, Kitty cried, "Oh, excuse me, darling, there's Mr. Bandog—" and flitted off, leaving Emma to relinquish their coats to a grave Japanese houseman.

"Mrs. B–Blackstone," said a voice, and Emma turned to see the aforesaid Miss Davies emerge from the enormous patio room opposite. "Well, isn't that j–j–just like our Kitty," the actress said, and crossed to her with a hand held out and a smile that combined warmth and exasperation. "Leaving you standing in a t–total stranger's house—"

"I actually don't mind." Emma gazed around her at the hewn oak of the floors, the painted rafters overhead, and the Mexican statues in the niches. "So *beautiful* . . ."

"Yes, isn't it?" Miss Davies followed her eyes. "Tom c–collected art and furniture for years, before he s–started building. Have you met T–Tom?" she added, with a quick touch on Emma's elbow to lead her toward the doors of the patio room. The patio itself was visible beyond, through floor-to-ceiling windows, and behind that the velvet brown of the hills just beginning to flush with the first grass of California's rainy season. At twenty-seven, like most actresses Miss Davies looked younger, a smooth, innocent face with a sparkle of mischief in her bright-blue eyes. Like Kitty—another former Ziegfeld dancer—she moved with a grace that Emma, at five feet ten, profoundly envied. When Emma paused beside an old refectory table, her attention drawn by a pottery dish of fruit, the actress glanced a question that smiled as she understood: "You d–don't have those in England, do you?"

"I know avocados." Emma moved her hand toward the aptly nicknamed green-black "alligator pears." "I think I even saw one, once, back home. My Aunt Phyllis said they were purely ornamental and inedible."

Miss Davies laughed, "I b–bet they were, in England! It would never get hot enough to ripen them over there, would it?"

"It was a revelation," agreed Emma wholeheartedly. "I love them—like butter! And those orange ones are . . .?"

"P–Persimmons. I'm sure Tom'll give you a couple—he has a whole orchard of them, those and avoc–cados. Not those, though," she added. "They're hard as rocks. The b–best time to eat them is when they're so ripe they're almost squishy. They're just disgusting to touch, and Ch–Charlie—"

Meaning Chaplin, Emma guessed . . .

"—said persimmons looked like what the audience would throw at them in small-time vaudeville . . ."

"Like medlars back home," agreed Emma. From her expression, it was clear her companion had never heard of these. "They're about so big, and brown. You have to wait until they get mushy—my husband was horrified when I gave him a ripe one." And the memory of Jim's face at that moment, under the medlar tree in her parents' garden in Oxford, was still an untouched smile of delight.

Jim . . .

Jim had been dead, somewhere in Flanders, three weeks after that smile. But his laughter and the scents of fruit and cut grass and the bay rum he used after shaving still flooded her memories, like the echo of sunlight before darkness closed in. *Momentary as a sound*, says Lysander in *A Midsummer Night's Dream . . . swift as a shadow, short as any dream . . .* After six years, she still woke in the night, asking herself, *How could he be gone?*

After six years, she still sometimes, lying in Zal's arms, wondered, *How could I betray him?*

Gently, she set the memory aside, as she had learned to do—set it on the shelf with the voices, the faces, of her parents, her brother, her aunts, all dead in the influenza—and listened with genuine delight to Miss Davies's account of Charlie Chaplin's first encounter with some of the more vehement varieties of Mexican peppers.

"One can scarcely blame him," Emma laughed, remembering the first time Zal had taken her to El Cholo on Western Avenue. Or, for that matter, her first experience of dining in Chinatown . . . "It's funny: when I came to the United States, I never even thought about it in terms of eating foods that I'd never heard of—"

"Like cafeteria chili?"

"Oh, is that supposed to be *food*?"

The two women were still giggling as they stepped out onto the patio, and Marion said, "Oh, there's T–Tom! And Kitty, too—"

Emma had seen the director at studio parties, tall and sturdy, athletic despite the beginnings of middle-aged fleshiness to his face. A man who radiated vitality. Something about the way Kitty stood near him, her fingers on his bicep, the way he put a hand on her shoulder, drew her closer, made Emma groan inwardly (*Not another one!*). But as she approached, she heard Ince say, "Don't answer it, Kitty. Don't have anything to do with it. Or with him, when you get back there."

Kitty flipped her hand as if tossing away a spent match. "Oh, nobody cares about a little thing like scandal—"

"I'm not talking about scandal, Kitty. I'm talking about—" He looked quickly around him, as if checking who else was on the wide patio (nobody close: Frank Pugh in conference with Charlie Chaplin in the shadow of a fig tree half denuded by autumn, another Japanese servant offering a tray of drinks to a burly gentleman whom Emma half-recognized as a producer, and a very lovely girl who looked far too young to be out without a chaperone). "I'm not joking, Kit. Stay away from it. Stay away from *him*. I—"

A woman emerged from the house, still beautiful in her forties and with that same graceful carriage that seemed to announce, *Actress*. She called out, "Tom!" and Ince turned—and Kitty took an instinctive step back.

Marion whispered, a little drily, "Nell Kershaw—Nell Ince. Tom's wife," as the woman strode forward. But at the sight of the tall, powerful-looking man who followed her, the actress melted into a beaming smile and almost skipped like a child to meet him. "Bill!"

Emma recognized the wide shoulders, unsmiling face, and steely eyes of the owner of Cosmopolitan Studios (and of twenty-eight newspapers, two news services, a major publishing syndicate, thousands of acres of land in California and Mexico, a half-built Spanish castle in northern California, a yacht, and huge resources of timber and mines): William Randolph Hearst. Hearst's arm went possessively around Marion's waist, and after a quick kiss, he called out, "Happy Birthday, Tom! Just stopped by to invite you: the *Oneida*'s cruising up the coast this weekend. I thought maybe you could join us"—his arm tightened around Miss Davies—"and celebrate your birthday while we work out the terms of those films."

Kitty and Zal had both told Emma on a number of occasions—when the rumors of the Cosmopolitan–Ince contract were discussed (and Zal was right, Emma reflected, in Hollywood most of the talk *was* about movies)—that nobody in their right mind turned down invitations from Mr. Hearst. Particularly those who wanted a picture deal. Ince beamed, left Kitty standing, and made for the millionaire's side. "I'll phone you when I get back to town, Kit!" he called back over his shoulder.

With visible regret, Kitty wrote to Mr. Clark Dexter of Dexter Consolidated the following day (or, rather, told Emma to write, though she signed the letter herself), thanking him for his obliging offer and expressing her regrets at having to refuse. Emma walked down to the mailbox on Vine Street to make sure the letter wasn't stopped by later second thoughts.

"Tom said not to even get in touch with Dexter when I get to New York," said Kitty, after she'd waked up Sunday and had three cups of coffee, two cigarettes, a glass of gin, and a bath, in that order. "He talked like the guy had a wolf's head like in that creepy French movie." With gentle deftness, she dusted Pompeiian face powder on her cheeks, worked Djer-Kiss Persian Rose onto her cheekbones with one hand, and picked up her glass with the other, without taking her eyes from the mirror. "Maybe it's for the best. But since Frank has to stay here in LA and pretend he doesn't even know me, I just *know* I could get married and at least *file* for divorce without his catching on. Fifty thousand clams is a lot of cabbage."

She dipped a finger in a tiny dish of water, dripped a single drop onto the mascara cake and carefully stirred it into an ink-like syrup with the brush.

"I still think it sounds like a good deal for *you*, dearest—"

"I have no desire," said Emma, as she gently combed through Black Jasmine's sable petticoats, "to wake up and find myself married to a gentleman with a wolf's head, even if he does live in a palace." After changing the blue coat for a red one, donning the red cloche hat, and driving back to Ivarene Street with a detective on her trail ("Be sure not to lose him in traffic on Sunset, darling," Kitty had cautioned), she felt she had done sufficient service to Kitty's love life for one day.

"And," she added, "what would you do if notice of the marriage somehow got into the newspapers? Or if Mr. Pugh found some good excuse to come to New York before your week is up?"

"It would have to be a doozy to get around Florrie and her lawyer. Those detectives were still outside the house when the studio car dropped me off at three!"

"And how would you explain to Mr. Pugh the six months you'd have to be in Nevada?"

"Oh, darling, I'd go to Mexico! Or I'd send my lawyer—you don't even have to be there yourself. Or I'd go to Paris. It's a lot more chic, and you can get a divorce there in two weeks, and I could do some shopping at the same time . . ." She frowned thoughtfully. "Although that Callot Soeurs dress I got there last year cost more than a divorce would have . . . But it would be no trouble for you, I promise. I'm sure Zallie would understand."

"No."

Nevertheless, Kitty had still not given up the idea by Tuesday morning, when Emma came down to make breakfast and discovered a five-color brochure for the S.S. *Cassiopeia*, New York to Le Havre, and eastbound transcontinental train schedules on the kitchen table at the place where Emma usually sat. But the dream of assisting her sister-in-law to brief and lucrative secondes noces ended abruptly later that morning, when Kitty came flouncing into her dressing room at the studio—where Emma was puzzling over rewrites on the *Shining Bright* scenario that would accommodate more elaborate costumes—fizzling with righteous indignation.

"The nerve of that gold-digging floozy!" Kitty threw herself into the chair before her banquet-sized dressing table. "After all her 'Oh, that's a wonderful idea, Mr. Bandog!'"—with deadly accuracy, Kitty mimicked Darlene Golden's simpering Texas drawl—"'Ah've nevuh felt this way befo', Mr. Bandog . . .'" She placed a finger to her cheek as the blonde actress habitually did in the presence of gentlemen, and fluttered her eyelashes. "And laughing at his stupid jokes . . ."

"What did she do?"

Good heavens, did she try to vamp any of the four extras with whom Kitty was currently betraying Mr. Pugh?

Did she try to vamp Mr. Pugh? *She couldn't have, not with Mrs. Pugh and her lawyer snooping around . . .*

Or the wealthy Mr. Crain, who owned half the oil wells between Santa Paula and Long Beach . . . and whose bouquet of pink-and-white orchids currently graced the dressing table?

"That greedy little round-heels is going to accept Dexter's proposal!"

Emma blinked, startled. "How did she . . .?"

"He sent her the same letter he sent me, the four-flusher!"

Kitty gestured with one delicate balled-up fist. "Serve him right if she *does* marry him! After all her"—again the nasal drawl—"'Mr. Bandog is just waiting for his divorce to become final—'"

Emma refrained from pointing out that Mr. Pugh was in the same situation vis-à-vis Mrs. P. and her lawyer, and said, "You can't let her. Mr. Ince warned you—"

"Hide and watch me!" Kitty dug a gold-tipped Sobranie and her diamond-dotted holder from the dressing-table drawer, and scratched a match on the side of the box. "And anyway," she added, more calmly, "if I told her I got a warning that the man was a creepy French werewolf, she'd tell me I was just making it up because I was jealous. She'd pull my hair out, first." She glared wrathfully at her line of blown smoke.

Emma sat in silence for a time, remembering the grimness in the director's voice. The way he had grasped Kitty's shoulder. *I'm not talking about scandal, Kitty—*

"We don't know what that warning is about," she said at length.

"Whatever it is, she won't listen to me. She's been rubbing my nose in Mr. Bandog this and Mr. Bandog that . . ."

"Then *I'll* talk to her."

Kitty gave her a smoldering sidelong glance, but said nothing.

"Whatever it is, it's serious."

"How serious could it be? It's not like he's going to strangle her on their wedding night."

"We don't know," said Emma. "Mr. Ince worked in New York for years. And as Zal said the other day, in New York one talks to people outside the film business. He clearly heard something. Something he felt he had to warn you about. We can't not at least pass that warning on."

"She isn't going to listen."

"That's not our business."

"Oh, all right." Kitty drew another lung-full of smoke and almost visibly put aside the daydream of seeing Darlene Golden strangled on her wedding night by a French werewolf.

She sat up then, and her eyes brightened at the prospect of dire secrets. "She'll just say I'm jealous . . . But I wonder what it is? Tom did sound scared, didn't he? And he doesn't scare easy. Maybe Clark Dexter really *is* a werewolf . . ."

She sounded pleased at the thought.

The headline of Wednesday morning's newspaper said:

MOVIE PRODUCER SHOT ON HEARST YACHT

FOUR

For four days east on the California Limited to Chicago, Emma descended at every stop for newspapers as well as to supervise Chang Ming, Black Jasmine, and Buttercreme on what Zal inelegantly termed the Piddle Patrol. Then for another twenty hours, from Chicago to New York: the *Chicago Daily News*, the Gary, Indiana *Post-Tribune*, the Toledo *Times*, and the Syracuse *Evening Telegram.*

Kitty said, "What the fuck?"

By Wednesday evening, it was as if that morning headline had never existed. Every newspaper in Los Angeles had instead recounted the unfortunate death of film producer Thomas Ince from heart failure, at his home (although some said that he had taken ill at Hearst's home at San Simeon)—("But he went down to San Diego the same afternoon we saw him," protested Kitty. "That's two hundred and fifty miles in the opposite direction."). By the time the California Limited reached Albuquerque, New Mexico, on Friday afternoon, Ince's body had been cremated.

"But Peggy Donovan told me she'd heard from her gardener that he'd been shot." Kitty crumpled last night's *Santa Fe New Mexican* down into her lap, as the flat, green acres of the Kansas plain streamed past the windows of the parlor-sleeper car. "He said Charlie Chaplin's chauffeur saw Ince's body taken off Hearst's yacht bleeding from a bullet to the head." Kitty had spent a good portion of Wednesday (while Emma was doing the packing) on the telephone with various friends in the studios, and everyone had heard something, one way or another, usually through the gossip of servants. "Nell Boardman told me that Elinor Glyn—who was *on* the yacht!—told her that nobody's ever going to know what happened because Hearst paid off everybody on board to keep their mouths shut. Does that sound like something someone would do if there *wasn't* something fishy going on?"

"Does that sound like something someone would say about a kindly, well-loved man like Mr. Hearst?" countered Zal, with grave sarcasm. The newspaper mogul was one of the most soundly hated men in the country, particularly among those in the film and newspaper industries who had felt the crush of his well-financed opinions in the newspapers he owned.

Kitty subsided, with an expression of discontent. Everyone else in the small "drawing room" of the lush Santa Fe car had been turning over rumors about the events on the yacht *Oneida* for two days now, trading what their valets or gardeners (or their neighbors, in the case of the two cameramen, who had curtained bunks in the sleeper car elsewhere on the train) had said they'd heard. Hearst had shot Ince because he'd found the director in a clinch with Marion Davies. Hearst had shot Ince because he'd found Charlie Chaplin in a clinch with Marion Davies, and by the time he'd run out and gotten his pearl-handled revolver and come back, he'd mistaken Ince for Chaplin (Ince was seven inches taller, with hair many shades lighter than the comedian's gypsy-dark curls). Hearst had poisoned Ince and bribed the coroner. Hearst had hired an assassin . . .

"I won't say that he doesn't deserve to get his ass bit by rumors," Zal added after a time, leaning back in the tufted red plush of his chair and stroking Buttercreme as the little dog lay in his lap. "I'm a believer in Fate. Given the stories every Hearst newspaper in the country spread about poor Roscoe Arbuckle—who lost pretty much everything he owned even after he was acquitted of raping that woman—I'd like to see Hearst get pointed at and whispered about for the rest of his life. But Hearst murdering Tom Ince because he made a pass at Marion Davies sounds a little . . . a little too much like the kind of thing everyone would like to see on the front page of the *Police Gazette*."

Emma looked up from shifting the mahjong tiles around the marble surface of the table between them, and recalled one of her scholarly father's favorite observations, quoting Marcus Aurelius: Ότι πάν υπόληψις. *Everything is opinion* . . .

"However—and whyever—it happened, we are left with the

question: What do we tell Miss Golden? Whatever Mr. Ince meant by warning Kitty away is now exactly like the information we have about his death: nothing but rumor and speculation. And fairly sensationalistic, at that."

"She'll just say I'm jealous," repeated Kitty, and dropped the newspaper into the wicker bin beside the little group of chairs. ("You done with that, Kit?" immediately asked Gordy Graves, rising from his pinochle game on the other side of what the Santa Fe Railroad liked to call a "drawing room.") (And prudently bringing his cards with him.)

"I'm certainly done with *this*." The queenly Margaret Mackenzie—scheduled to be beheaded as Summer Fairisle's mother shortly after the company's arrival in New York—returned from her conference with the pinochle coterie, trailed by a uniformed porter bearing a tray of what was allegedly perfectly alcohol-free lemonade and ginger ale. She handed Gordy a folded copy of the *San Bernardino Sun*. "Terrible load of tosh. To hear them, you'd think Mr. Ruth's batting average was of greater concern to the public welfare than the League of Nations, and the plans of Cecil DeMille more important than those of Mr. Mussolini. Always supposing anyone in Hollywood knows who Mr. Mussolini *is*. This one's yours, Zal," she added, taking a drink from the tray and offering it to the cameraman. Meaning, Emma guessed, that it hadn't had anything illegal added to it in transit from the dining car. "And a pot of tea for the Duchess. Thank you very much for your trouble, Mr. Travers." She placed a coin on the tray as the porter straightened up from arranging the teapot and a cup on a corner of the table, and the man beamed.

"And thank *you* for 'washing the tiles,' Duchess," she added, gently lifting Black Jasmine from one of the red plush chairs. "Yes, yes, my poor wee darling, I'm afraid you shall have to make way for your social inferior . . . Shall we build the Great Wall of China?" She set the black Peke on Kitty's lap.

At the same moment, Emma saw Neil Bandog enter the "drawing room," dapper and sleek on his way through to the barbershop car. She rose from her seat. "Perhaps Black Jasmine could play this hand for me?" The tiny "sleeve" Peke, who had been watching the preparations for the game with proprietary interest, appeared perfectly willing to do so.

Mr. Bandog's presence meant that Darlene Golden would probably be alone.

Zal didn't glance up from carefully stacking tiles in a hollow square. "Lotsa luck," he said.

The so-called "Seven-two" cars on the California Limited (for nearly ten dollars on top of the regular sleeper fare) consisted of seven sleeping compartments and two "drawing rooms"; by tacit consent, one of these drawing rooms served as a sort of day room for the Los Angeles principals in *Shining Bright*. The other was generally left as a private bower for Darlene Golden (née Dorcas Spitz) and Neil Bandog, whose two sleeping compartments lay closest to that end of the car. (The "rude mechanicals" of the party, as Shakespeare would have termed them—the two cameramen, their respective assistants Herbie and Sy, Carrie Drebbett and her assistant from Wardrobe in charge of the custom-built costumes, Gordy Graves's assistant Boothe Sellars, and the maids of Darlene and Margaret Mackenzie—were relegated to Pullman sleeper bunks further down the train and expected to entertain themselves in the public lounge car.)

Thus, Emma came upon the fair-haired star—fully made-up but clothed in an exiguous negligée and a dressing gown of gold-stamped blue velvet (it was past one in the afternoon)—sipping coffee and gazing at the fragile green stems of new-sprouted wheat bending like ocean waves beneath the sweep of prairie wind. Distant islands of trees marked homesteads, achingly isolated in this huge land. What is it like, Emma wondered, to live there, half a day from anyone but your family?

"Do you have a moment?"

Miss Golden looked her up and down, the twitch of her beautiful nostrils an unspoken *Oh, Jesus, who wears skirts like that anymore?* "Can't it wait? I'm having my coffee, and Mr. Bandog"—she emphasized the name as if waving a copy of the man's bank statement—"will be back in a minute . . ."

"It's why I wish to speak to you alone," replied Emma evenly. She had already heard, from various sources, Miss Golden's remarks about Zal "trying to get on Pughie's good side by fucking Kitty's sister-in-law"—interspersed with occasional accusations of helping herself to the contents of Kitty's bank account. But compared with the behavior of her former employer, Mrs. Pendergast and her son, these were pin scratches. *Fustibus et lapidibus ossa mea confringent*, her father would declare grandly when told of small schoolroom gossip: *Sticks and stones may break my bones* . . .

Miss Golden heaved a great, ill-done-by sigh, and waved an impatient hand at her Filipino maid. "Well, what is it? Here, Olivia, put this away—" She held out to the woman a velvet jeweler's box containing an aigret of emeralds and peacock eyes: not closing it and holding it to make sure that Emma could see. "Neil is *so* generous—"

Emma waited until the maid was gone. "It's about Clark Dexter's proposal of marriage."

Miss Golden's whole slim body stiffened. "How did you . . .? My goodness, that's the silliest thing I ever heard of!" While not as unconvincing before the cameras as Kitty was (the same could have been said of Brownie the Wonder Dog), Miss Golden was no Bernhardt. "I mean—I don't know what the fuck you're talking about. Who's . . .?" But her cheeks blazed with angry color—outstripping her rouge—when Emma explained that Kitty had received an offer before she had.

"I never *heard* of a letter like that. And Kitty saying I had is . . . is just *jealousy*, because she knows Pughie's never going to leave that battle-ax, no matter how much time she spends on her knees. Why would I want fifty thousand smackers"—Emma had not mentioned the sum involved—"when the man I love—the man who just *adores* me!—is going to come across with a ring the minute the court gives him his judgment? Much less that I'd take *her* sloppy seconds . . ."

"The reason she turned him down," Emma continued doggedly, "is because she received a warning from Mr. Ince. Mr. Ince was in New York. He told her to have nothing to do with the offer—"

"Oh, and how convenient that he's dead! What is she, scared I'll accept? What a—"

There followed a monologue on the subject of Kitty expressed in terms that Emma hadn't heard since she'd transported wounded Army mule drivers from the Oxford train station to the nearest hospital during the War, concluding with, "And she doesn't even have the balls to pitch me this load of hooey herself. I thought you had more class than to run that kind of errand for her, Duchess. Tell her to fuck herself."

"She told me what you'd say," replied Emma, her own cheeks burning in spite of herself. "But I felt it only fair to let you know."

"Fuck her. And fuck you." But as Emma turned to go, Darlene sprang from her chair and caught her on the way to the door. "And don't you dare tell anyone about me getting that letter—I mean about you *hearing* that I'd got that letter, which I didn't. I never heard of it." The lovely blonde actress released Emma's wrist long enough to plunge across the little parlor to where her handbag lay on a chair, and came back with a wad of bills which she shoved into Emma's hand. "Don't you tell a soul."

Emma handed the money back, noting the depth of the other woman's panic by the size of the numbers she glimpsed. "I won't. But Kitty heard it—"

"From who?"

"I have no idea. So you should know the rumor is out there."

Darlene swore again. Though her vocabulary on the subject was small, she used what she knew many times in any given sentence. The mule drivers had been much more original.

Emma returned to the larger drawing room.

"Told you so," said Zal.

FIVE

New York was, as Zal had promised, a world very different from Los Angeles.

The stars of *Shining Bright* were all given suites at the Plaza Hotel, which looked out onto Central Park; the "rude mechanicals" had rooms at the Bayrose, a few blocks away on Fifty-Seventh Street.

Having passed through Grand Central Station the previous year, on her way from Manchester to Hollywood, Emma recalled the epic confusion of the seemingly mile-long underground platforms, the immensity of the concourse, and the multiple ramps and stairs, and made sure to take the Pekes on a final platform promenade at the Twentieth Century Limited's last-but-one stop in Harmon. Cabs awaited them on Vanderbilt Avenue, to take cast and crew to their assigned quarters. "I'm astonished Mr. Pugh thought to provide for the crew," remarked Emma quietly to Zal, as they followed the legion of porters through the slanting columns of light in the concourse. One hand she kept firmly on her handbag, and the other gripped the handle of Black Jasmine's wicker carry-box.

"He didn't," said Zal, suitcase in one hand and Chang Ming's wicker carrier in the other. "Margaret Mackenzie telegraphed Checker Cabs from Chicago when she heard Bandog and Pugh had just ordered cabs for the 'Talent.'"

Kitty, cradling Buttercreme in the luxuriant bosom of her chinchilla coat ("She's so sensitive . . ."), followed on the arm of her long-time admirer, the silver-haired millionaire Ambrose Crain. "Did anybody think he would?" she sniffed now.

Old Mr. Crain (whose passion had endured for over a year—a long time, for Kitty) had met them on the platform, with a legion of porters and an armload of pink-and-burgundy orchids.

Emma exclaimed, "*Honestly!*" and Zal grinned.

"Hey, fifty cents is two meals at the Automat. Three, if you skimp on the vegetables." He stepped quickly ahead of the little group to open the portals of bronze and glass, and held them propped with one shoulder as Emma, then Kitty and her enamored escort, passed through. At one end of the rank of cabs, a shining Packard limousine waited, a uniformed driver hastening to open its door the moment they came in sight. At the other end of the cab rank, Mr. Bandog was just handing Miss Golden—a pastel symphony of golden finger waves and pink-dyed monkey fur—into a cream-colored Duesenberg the size of an ocean liner, while his chauffeur, a willowy Adonis in a cream-colored uniform, stood respectfully by.

"Will your little friends be comfortable in the back seat?" asked Mr. Crain, as his driver took Chang Ming's carrier from Zal.

Kitty placed a hand on her bosom and managed to smile endearingly up at Mr. Crain in spite of the fact that he wasn't much taller than she was. "They'll be OK if I snuggle up tight against you. You don't mind?"

"I shall endure the discomfort for their sake," returned the old man, a gallant twinkle in his eye. "Oh, please," he added, turning to Emma as the driver relieved her of Black Jasmine's carrier, "I hope you'll ride with us to the hotel, Mrs. Blackstone? You don't mind sitting up beside Hwang, do you?" He nodded at the driver. "It would be a shame to burden poor Mr. Pugh with the cost of an extra cab."

Emma privately reflected that without her sister-in-law actually in the vehicle, Pugh would undoubtedly stick her companion—or, it seemed, Mrs. Mackenzie—with the fare.

"I'll come to the Plaza when I'm done checking over the luggage." Zal squeezed Emma's hand. His fingers were warm, even through the two layers of glove between them—the wind snapped cold through the canyon that divided the terminal itself from twenty-six stories of the Biltmore Hotel. Beside them, Ken Elmore—soon to ride the midnight highways of England as Summer Fairchild's masked lover—helped Margaret Mackenzie into a cab, and a little further down the ranks, Nick Thaxter tipped the army of porters who had brought out his five trunks, three train cases, and customized portable make-up box.

"I'll take both you ladies out tomorrow night for supper," Zal went on, a little awkwardly, "if Kitty doesn't have other plans—"

"I'm sure she will." Turning her head, Emma caught uncertainty in his eyes and smiled. "And if you were the kind of man who would take a lady friend to dinner on his first night back in town, rather than go see his mother—"

Startled that she'd guessed, Zal laughed, and his shoulders relaxed. For a moment, there was silence between them. Then he said, "She's not going to like you, Em."

"She'll like me just fine," replied Emma serenely, "should we ever meet, when I casually mention how I weep into my pillow every night with loneliness for my sweetheart Howie back in Los Angeles."

His grin returned at the choice of the name. Mr. Pugh regularly suggested that Emma be seen in the local nightspots with he-man actor Harry Garfield, to quash the fan magazines' suggestions that Garfield (real name Howie Mellnick) much preferred the company of his long-time friend Roger Clint. She suspected that Foremost generally paid for the dinners as well.

"Nah," said Zal. "I'm the only son, so she suspects every woman of having designs on me."

You'll have to tell her one day, her eyes said to his, in the beat of silence that followed.

I know, his replied.

The pain of the letter she'd gotten from Jim's parents, when, in her desperation after her own parents' death, she had written to them for help, lay on her heart like a fresh-made burn; she had early understood Zal's willingness to postpone any discussion of marriage—or even cohabitation—between them.

That Zal loved her, she knew to the marrow of her bones. And to the marrow of her bones, she knew that they would be part of each other's lives for as long as those lives lasted.

But she had felt like that about Jim. And even without the pain of his Orthodox parents' angry horror, the wound of Jim's loss still bled, sometimes unbearably.

Zal would have to face what Jim had faced. Maybe not to the extent of Jim's—and Kitty's—rabbi father, but the shadow was still there. Jim had wed a shiksa, taken unto himself an "impure thing" (as his father had written to her). "*For you, he betrayed the blood of his fathers,*" the old scholar had written. "*Had it not been for you, he would have returned in time to me, and to the ways of his fathers. That betrayal I cannot forgive.*"

She had always wondered whether they had written such cruelties to Jim in those last weeks of his life, in the scrawled Yiddish script of their own early homeland. Waking sometimes in the night, she had wondered whether he had died quickly, torn to pieces by machine-gun bullets. Or had those words returned to him as he bled out in the mud of the Forest of Argonne?

Please, no . . .

Neither spoke of it, but she knew Zal understood: that while she waited for her heart to heal, he also waited, for the right time, the right occasion, the right words.

"I'll leave the matter entirely up to you," she said lightly, as if they were only speaking of that night's plans. "At least—I hope!—your mother doesn't have a daughter whose scandalous example she can throw in your face along with her suspicions," and Zal laughed again—genuine laughter this time, though tinged with bitterness. He, too, had heard Kitty's tales of how her parents—Jim's parents—had thrown her out of the house when she had refused to be what they expected of a girl.

"God, I love you, Em!" And he kissed her, as another pack train of trunks spewed from the station doors, and cameraman Chip Thaw waved imperatively. "Whatever time I get back, I'll take you out for cheesecake. The best in town. That's a promise."

Kitty had not yet returned from dinner at the Ritz with Mr. Crain when Zal arrived at the service door of Suite 1202 at the Plaza at ten. Sleepy as she was, Emma made sure that the Pekes were comfortably bedded down, then put on her coat—the night was bitterly cold—and followed Zal downstairs, for a fifty-cent cab ride to Lindy's on Broadway.

Zal was right about the cheesecake.

And Broadway was lit up like a film set, as crowded as Broadway in Los Angeles at two o'clock on a Saturday afternoon.

He had also been right, Emma sensed immediately, about the difference between New York and Los Angeles. At this hour, pretty much everyone in Los Angeles was home in bed; the only late-night festivities were private parties at someone's mansion, or in one or two nightspots like the Café Montmartre or the Coconut Grove.

But the crowd at Lindy's reminded her of the liveliest of Hollywood parties, in its noise level and in the energy that seemed to crackle in the air. Only it wasn't film people all talking of contracts and new cars and how many takes some imbecile director had demanded. Fragments of talk flicked her ears as Zal steered her among crowded tables and chairs, to a couple of seats at the counter: men arguing about horse races and card games with the sharp specificity of professionals. Men speaking of shipments from China or France clearing customs, or complaining about cops confiscating the book receipts and selling them to competitors. Girls, still in the over-bright make-up designed for stage lights, complaining about men who flashed a roll that turned out to be one C-note wrapped around a wad of aces. Gamblers griping about some damn fink calling the bulls when he started losing, or about horses with four left feet that somebody had sworn they'd seen beat Man o' War in training. Agents calculating percentages with their clients and producers calculating how many girls you'd need to fill a stage ("Are you talking ponies or real show-girls, Sam?"). Out-of-town Texans and Cincinnati manufacturers marveling over the reviews of *George White's Scandals* or nodding eagerly at a sleek gentleman's assurances that a poker game that evening would be "just a good time, plenty of girls an' decent whiskey . . ."

Men who sat quietly at corner tables and held court for a steady stream of tough and sleazy-looking men who left paper-wrapped packets, quickly slipped from one briefcase to another.

Cheesecake like the food of the gods.

"Theaters have just let out," said Zal. Behind the thick lenses of his glasses, his eyes sparkled with the pleasure of a man who has come home. "It's quieter here in the daytime. The dark-haired lady who just came in is Mary Ellis—she can knock down walls in opera, but she's on Broadway now in *Rose-Marie*. The gent over there with the hair"—the identification was obvious: a black, thick mass that stood up like a fright wig—"is George S. Kaufman the playwright; the fat gent with him is Alexander Woollcott—"

"The critic?" Emma had gotten Kitty to subscribe to the *New York World* for the sake of the man's sardonic reviews.

"In the flesh—and plenty of it. And the quiet guy on Woollcott's other side is, believe it or not, Harpo Marx. That geezer in the white fedora who just came in with that girl in the hair ribbons is Daddy Browning, the millionaire who just got divorced from a girl he married when she was sixteen . . ."

"I see Mr. Chaplin has some East Coast competition."

"More than I like to think about. Browning's supposed to be advertising in the newspapers for a girl to be a 'sister' to his two little daughters."

Emma wrinkled her nose. "That isn't legal, is it?"

"Neither is that champagne they're drinking. Every nightclub on the street is paying off the police—and paying off the gent at that table over there in the corner, too. It's another world, Em." He laid his hand over hers, half smiling, but his eyes were grave and a little sad. "The cheesecake is great—but watch your step."

Si fueris Romae, as Saint Ambrose had once advised a parishioner, *Romano vivito more; si fueris alibi, vivito sicut ibi* . . .

After nearly five years in Manchester following the death of her family—reading aloud to the sour and demanding Mrs. Pendergast or fetching her glasses of milk at two in the morning—Emma had found Hollywood bizarre, sometimes frightening, sometimes simply appalling. She felt now as if she had stepped back through Alice's Looking Glass, to find herself diverted into yet another world, equally strange—as if she had left Oz and ended up not back in Kansas, but on Barsoom.

Stars of their own, Virgil had written of Elysium, *and their own suns they knew* . . . There was certainly nothing here of the planet on which she'd grown up. The world on which she had expected, in her girlhood, to spend a peaceful life.

It wasn't as if every philosopher from Socrates on didn't warn me . . .

The first week at the Plaza, she barely saw Zal. Twice she accompanied Kitty—and the inevitable Pekes in their diamond-studded collars—out to the former MBQ Studios in Queens, a semi-rural suburb on the east side of the river where a number of film companies had their film stages and production facilities. Manhattan island itself, as Mr. Bandog had boasted, was studded with such establishments, as well as costume houses, film laboratories, and rental companies that catered to both the film business and the literally hundreds of theaters and nightclubs that enlivened the city's dark hours. Most of the larger studios in Los Angeles were in fact merely subsidiaries of the New York production companies: Paramount, Biograph, Fox, and Warner Brothers were all headquartered in New York or New Jersey, along with a dozen smaller outfits that had begun by filming stage shows or vaudeville.

The week was occupied with costume fittings not only for the principals but for the hundreds of extras who would feature in crowd scenes, three ballroom events, and a climactic reprisal of the Battle of Waterloo to be filmed near an old Army embarkation center at the far end of Long Island. Stand-ins were found for all the principals, hired to sweat under the blazing violence of the Klieg lights in duplicate costumes as the lighting was adjusted. Kitty's stand-in, though she shared her doppelganger's trim voluptuousness, was fifty, a grandmother, and still performed regularly in vaudeville as Princess Laura (with her Peerless Pachyderms) (and ran a pinochle game among the extras when not on duty on the set). Darlene's, on the other hand, exactly mirrored the star's fairy-like beauty, and once she'd dyed her hair to match her principal's, could barely be distinguished from her if the lights were positioned properly.

There were consultations with New York cameramen,

gaffers, prop departments, and grips; there were negotiations to procure the services of hundreds of horses (and early-nineteenth-century saddles). ("And What's-Her-Name better be able to ride," shrilled Miss Golden, who refused to remember or use young Miss Haley's name, "because I'm not getting on no horse!") The cast had met the director, a melancholy-looking, aristocratic Englishman named George Blakeney whose show on Broadway had closed unexpectedly, leaving him in need of work. The remainder of the week, Zal said, he'd be back and forth to the studio and the various locations on Long Island, working out the physical logistics of the filming itself.

"I shouldn't worry too much about the costume anachronisms, Mrs. Blackstone," the director had said, bowing slightly over Emma's hand. "In films, practically no one notices, and most of your audience can't tell the difference between a farthingale and a fedora. You should see what they have the Empress Josephine wearing as she bids Napoleon farewell before Waterloo."

Emma drew breath to protest that even Mr. Kingsley, the author of *Shining Bright*, knew that Her Imperial Highness had been dead—and certainly long divorced from the Corsican emperor—by the time Waterloo rolled around in Chapter Fifty-Eight. Then she caught the resigned amusement in Mr. Blakeney's eye and only shook her head.

"I expect I shall. Mr. Rokatansky tells me that a Broadway revue called *I'll Say She Is* contains that very scene. I shall study it with interest."

While Zal, Chip Thaw, Carrie Drebbett, and Gordy Graves (and their respective assistants) trundled around Long Island in the bitter cold ("All I got to say is, they better film Waterloo before it starts to snow," remarked Zal), the "talent" of the picture, as they were called (clearly, reflected Emma, by someone who had never seen either Kitty or Miss Golden on film), were left to their own devices in New York.

Never one to waste the red wine of the present moment, Kitty quickly made herself at home in any number of the nightclubs and speakeasies that populated Broadway: the El Fey and the Club Durant, the High Wire and the Opal, the

Chicken Club and the Silver Slipper Cabaret. A one-time dancer in the Ziegfeld chorus, she re-established old friendships, and in addition to dinner and dancing with Mr. Crain, she was often squired by the gentlemanly owner of the High Wire Club, Mr. Shakespeare Malone, and by a vaudeville star named Chico Marx. (Pronounced "Chicko," Kitty insisted firmly, not "Cheeko".) These gentlemen came and went from the elegant Suite 1202 at the Plaza, and on those evenings that Kitty was at the High Wire, Emma was instructed to tell Mr. Crain that she was at the MBQ Studio late and would not be back in New York until after midnight.

The first time that she produced this lie—sounding as convincing as she could over the telephone, and hating herself, because she liked Mr. Crain—the old man said wisely, "I see. Then—do *you* like opera, Mrs. Blackstone? Dearly as I love Miss de la Rose—and I do love her, you know—"

"I know," said Emma softly.

"—I also dearly love Rossini. Might I convince you to join me this evening for dinner at Marguery, and a performance of *The Barber of Seville*?"

It was better than a thousand parties, and any amount of jazz music, bright lights, and bootleg champagne. Emma felt as if after years of starvation, she had supped her fill on boeuf marchand de vin.

"Darling, I'm *so* glad!" cried Kitty the following morning. "Sometimes I feel so *guilty* about Ambrose, because I know he likes that opera stuff, and champagne and dancing are just *wasted* on him. Besides," she added, pouring them both a cup of coffee in the chilly forenoon sunlight of the suite's living room, "that'll be one in the eye for Darlene. I just *know* she's sending the most *vile* rumors to Frank about me and Chico . . . and me and Mr. Malone . . . and about what happened the other night at the Chicken Club, and I didn't start it either. *Way* worse than *anything* I've sent to Frank about *her*!"

It was Kitty—one night when she convinced Emma to come with her to the popular El Fey Club—who pointed out her disappointed suitor Clark Dexter on the other side of the dance floor. "I honestly thought he'd be handsome or debonair or *something* interesting, darling," she said, indicating the tall, weedy young man who was attempting to insert himself into the line of scantily clothed dancers gyrating for the entertainment of the patrons. The two young ladies who'd come into the club with him were attempting—laughing—to disengage him from the chorus line. From the by-play between them and the girls in the line, it was clear (if their make-up and the cut of their frocks wasn't proof enough) that they were in the chorus-line business somewhere themselves.

Dexter had clearly drunk himself to the point of admiration for his own wit and prowess. Tortoiseshell glasses askew, he pulled back when his lady friends tried to tug him away, and persisted in his quest for one of the ostrich feathers worn by the nearest El Fey chorine. "Hey, hey, hey, Floppy," drawled the blonde mistress of ceremonies, strolling onto the dance floor to intercept his fumbling hands. "Give the poor kid a break! Them feathers don't grow on trees."

She hooked her arm through Dexter's, drew him against her side with a friendly smile, and tweaked the collar of his extravagant pink-striped shirt. "They grow on big, mean, nasty birds," she went on, leading him back toward his table, "that'll gang up and kick you to death if you're not careful. Why not pick on them, if you want a feather, instead of a poor little girl from Kenosha?"

Dexter—"Floppy" was evidently his nickname—blinked owlishly at the blonde, and his face worked suddenly with the facile remorse of the inebriated. "Jeez, Texas, I'm sorry," he whispered. He tried to turn back to the chorus, who had resumed their prancing and singing behind Lolly LeJeune's sprightly rendition of "Alabamy Bound," but Texas Guinan was clearly stronger than she looked. She returned him firmly to his table and commanded his fair companions to keep him there while she sent drinks over to the three of them—"Oh, on the house. He'll fall asleep if he has another and then you gals can get him in a cab . . ."

Prohibition? mused Emma. *Volstead Act?*

Both girls, of course, immediately turned their attention to a couple of well-dressed young men at the next table the moment the hostess retreated in the direction of the bar, but Floppy made no move to return to his feather hunt. Thanks to four years of dealing with Mrs. Pendergast's son, however, Emma remained obliquely conscious of the young man as a potential source of trouble—not that half the men present weren't in the same condition, and just as likely to come over and make a scene with Kitty. (*Heaven only knows which ones she's been keeping company with so far . . .*) Thus, she was aware of it when he startled, turned—

For a moment, she thought he was going to come over to their table—Kitty had broken off her story about the latest scandal to horrify New York society (". . . married her in the *teeth* of his father's objections . . .") to bat her long eyelashes at a comely waiter—but in fact his attention was on the doorway of the club. Texas Guinan called out her usual gay greeting—"Hello, suckers!"—to the men of the party, but it was the delicate, fair-haired woman in their midst that clearly riveted young Dexter's attention.

For an instant, Emma thought it was Darlene's stand-in, Mila Haley, clinging to the arm of the hard-faced, deadly man in the striped suit and wide-brimmed hat. But no, she realized a moment later.

That really was Darlene Golden.

SIX

The light in the club wasn't good—the flashing mirror ball above the dance floor had the effect (possibly intentional) of making identification difficult. But Darlene's golden-haired stand-in could never have afforded that Lanvin extravaganza of gold silk tulle and crisscrossed burgundy ribbons, or the glitter of garnets and diamonds at the woman's throat. Emma could not keep herself from wondering who'd paid for them.

Darlene's stand-in also did not habitually chew gum.

She saw Darlene sweep the crowded dance floor with a glance, while her grim-faced escort was trading jokes with Miss Guinan. Saw the delicate head on its greyhound neck halt for the smallest moment, as her eyes locked with Floppy's.

Then she turned with a gay laugh to lean against the grim man's shoulder, to place a coy finger to her cheek as she raised an adoring gaze to his face. Floppy, manufacturing a sigh that would have made Harry Langdon appear subtle, turned with elaborate unconcern to gaze at Lolly Lejeune and her simpering chorus line.

Oh, dear . . .

To Kitty, she whispered, "Who is that with Darlene?"

"Darlene?" Kitty turned from her own budding romance with the waiter and blinked as if, dazzled by love, she were trying to remember if she knew anyone named Darlene. Then her eyes flared wide and a moment later narrowed. "Well, *she's* playing with fire. That's Angel-Eyes Taralla!"

She spoke as if Emma had failed to recognize Abraham Lincoln—always supposing that Kitty herself could have picked America's sixteenth President out of a line-up.

And when Emma did not gasp with recognition, she urged, "Angel-Eyes Taralla! He runs whiskey in from Canada for Killer Madden! Frank'll spit blood when I tell him—what a pity Zallie isn't here with his camera! Though I expect"—regret tinged her voice—"Taralla's boys would shoot him if he tried to take a picture. I wonder if I could tell old Bandog—?"

"*No*," Emma reminded her patiently. "You *want* Darlene to stay in love with Mr. Bandog"—*if one can call it love*—"Better than having her stuck to Mr. Pugh like a piece of chewing gum."

"Oh, I suppose so . . . Oh, Chico!" She half-rose from her chair, waved joyously to another party that had come in after Mr. Taralla, Darlene, and (evidently) Mr. Taralla's two grim-looking "boys." "Over here!"

These four newcomers maneuvered their way past Darlene, Taralla, and the two thugs with him, and through the tables, to gather around Kitty with exclamations of delight. All four were just on the right side of "nondescript," except for the bright, wicked sparkle of their eyes. The bespectacled one, whom Kitty introduced as Groucho, kissed Emma's hand like a gigolo and asked, "What's a nice girl like you doing in a place like this?" and immediately turned to kiss Kitty's. "And what's an iniquitous tart like you doing in a respectable place like this?" With a glance at Emma, he said, "You'd better watch who you're seen with, Kitty, or people will get the wrong idea about you."

"Nah," objected Chico, pausing in the act of kissing Kitty's hand, wrist, and arm all the way up to her shoulder. "Nobody in this place has any ideas." A third brother (they all had the same last name) was kissing his way up Kitty's other arm; Chico shoved him away, and the would-be suitor immediately squared off as if prepared to fight.

"Now, knock it off, boys!" admonished Miss Guinan, laughing.

Both men laughed, too, and turned back to Emma. "Don't pay no attention to my brother," said Chico, taking Emma's hand in greeting. "He gets wrong ideas about every woman he meets."

"He keeps trying to get them to get the wrong ideas about *him*," added the youngest (and handsomest . . . *Zeppo*? Emma tried to sort them out. In the bad lighting of the club, he would have been Groucho's double except for the glasses). "It kills him that they never do."

"What sort of wrong ideas do you want women to get about you, Mr. Marx?" asked Emma, genuinely curious.

"That he's single," cracked Zeppo immediately.

"That he's funny," added Chico.

"That I'm an only child," returned Groucho, pulling up a chair and mounting it backwards like a horse. "Say, I didn't come here to be abused," he added, jerking his thumb at his brothers. "I've got a wife waiting at home to abuse me."

"Does she do it well?" Emma inquired, with great seriousness, and the gray eyes behind the steel-rimmed spectacles twinkled with appreciation.

"She could be a professional. And that's not the only thing she could do professionally. Why, in Kansas City, I met a lady who . . ."

He was interrupted by the arrival at the table of Angel-Eyes and his "boys," effervescing with steely bonhomie as the gangster shook hands and slapped shoulders with Chico and Zeppo (both of whom appeared to owe him money), embraced Kitty, and called for champagne all around. "And if that champagne came from France, then so did I," remarked Groucho sotto voce.

The fourth brother, having finished his interrupted osculatory progress up Kitty's arm, leaned over to Emma and asked, "Can I get you anything from the bar, Mrs. Blackstone? The beer here isn't bad."

"Compared to what?" retorted Groucho. And then, "Beer for me, too, Harpo. And he's right," he added to Emma, momentarily abandoning the flashy wise-crackery of the stage. "Straight down from Canada—Texas deals with the best crooks in town."

"Beer, then, please." Emma smiled her thanks as Harpo vanished into the crowd. The song had finished, and several ostrich-feathered ladies came to join the group at the table. The taller of Taralla's "boys"—a heavy-shouldered man with a broken nose—put an arm around the girl whose feathers had attracted Floppy Dexter's attention. The "poor little girl from

Kenosha" smiled pertly, giggled as he pawed her buttock, but as she turned her head coyly aside, Emma caught the disgusted contempt in her eyes.

The next moment, as the men who'd gathered around the other chorus girls shifted, between them Emma caught a glimpse of diamonds, flashing in the light reflected from the mirror ball. It was (as she had suspected) Darlene Golden, making her way with elaborate casualness past Floppy Dexter's table. The blonde actress only checked her steps for a moment, but Emma saw her pick up something from the table's top—*A note?*—and slip it into her jeweled handbag.

With drunken impulsiveness, Floppy seized her fingers and brought them to his lips. Darlene yanked her hand away, glancing as she did so over her shoulder in the direction of the scrimmage of gangsters and gamblers around Kitty and the Marxes. Then she set off with a sort of *Who? Me?* flounce in the direction of the ladies' powder room.

Oblivious to who might have been watching, Floppy turned in his chair and followed her with his gaze.

And Angel-Eyes Taralla did likewise. But while Floppy gawped after her with near-sighted adoration, the gangster's eyes had a glint in them like hot steel.

Filming began the following day.

Shining Bright's indoor sets were still being built at MBQ Studios in Queens—jaw-dropping extravaganzas of marble, gilding, with copies of Vigneé-Lebrun and Fragonard on the walls (rented from Klugman's Theatrical Supply on Fortieth Street)—so every day began with two hours and ten minutes on the Long Island Railway. Emma had her suspicions that this schedule had as much to do with the advance of winter rainfall as it did with the construction of French ballrooms and sinister English tavern interiors back in Queens.

A palatial mansion aptly named Versailles, three miles beyond the Port Jefferson railway station on the island's fashionable north shore, had been rented to represent Fairisle Hall. This was chiefly because of the acres of pine woods that encircled it, and the open meadows to the east that would eventually do duty as the Belgian countryside between Brussels and Nivelles, where the Battle of Waterloo had been fought a hundred and ten years previously. Surrounded by its overgrown gardens, the mansion overlooked the Long Island Sound from the top of an escarpment of about twelve feet, which on Long Island constituted a cliff.

"Why can't they just shoot the ballroom and library sequences here?" Emma asked, gazing around her in wonder at the glittering ranks of windows, the white-stucco walls, and encircling wings of the mansion, which did indeed resemble Le Vau's monument to Louis XIV's ego. "Surely Foremost can pay the family to move into one wing for the duration of the shoot—"

"Family doesn't live here." Zal huddled his scruffy tweed coat around him, against the chill mists that lingered among the trees. Above the muted swish of the waves below the cliff, the voices of the prop men and porters sounded loud in the stillness, and looking around her, Emma saw that he was right. What she'd at first taken for thickets of holly and chokeberry encroaching from the woods were in fact neglected gardens in front of what would have been the "ministers' wings" of the original palace. Half hidden from the graveled expanse before the house by a belt of trees, the low bulk of another complex of buildings loomed through the fog—*The stables*? Emma wondered—separated from the house by another tangle of hedge and feral roses, dotted with empty pedestals and a few dilapidated statues. Even at this distance, she thought she recognized Donatello's Perseus and the inevitable copy of Michelangelo's David. (*Did they rent those from Klugman's as well?*)

"The place has a hundred and eight rooms, and thirty-five bedrooms," Zal went on, as he and Emma followed the little groups of assistants, make-up artists, property handlers, and a whole string of box-toting porters towards the eastern wing. "I hear the man who built the place blew out his whole bank account trying to get it finished in time to have his daughter's wedding here . . . which happened to fall just about the time the country went into the post-war slump. You folks got hit with that in England, didn't you?"

"We did." Emma shivered at the memory. She felt Zal's quick sidelong glance, but before she could explain the awfulness of that time, a smallish man in an expensive coat blocked George Blakeney's approach to the east wing's door and waved his arms for attention.

"My name is Jefferson Blair," he called out, in a forced, thin voice. "I represent the owners of this property. Just because your film company has rented this property, do not think it can be treated like some sort of backdrop, to be altered as you please." He brandished a sheaf of papers. "Please understand that *no* employee of Foremost Productions is permitted to enter either the main block of the chateau—"

"He really thinks it *is* Versailles," whispered Zal.

"—or the western wing, or the kitchen wing, or the cellars, or the upper floor of the eastern wing. You are not to alter any of the plantings in the gardens—"

Another whisper, "*What* gardens?"

"—or cut any foliage, either in the gardens or the woods. Adequate space has been contracted in the east wing for necessary dressing rooms, make-up room, and costume storage, but under no circumstances are other rooms within the east wing to be utilized, altered, marked, or entered, nor are any rooms or indoor spaces in the stable buildings"—Mr. Blair waved with the contract towards the white walls of the compound to the west—"to be entered or utilized for storage or filming or for any purpose whatsoever . . ."

While Californians and the extras and artists alike shivered in the courtyard, Mr. Blair, like a stunted pillar box with his round, chinless face framed in the astrakhan of his coat collar and the black fur of his Russian-style hat, continued for another ten minutes with his list of contractual restrictions. No food to be consumed anywhere in the chateau except those rooms contracted for, etc., etc. No rooms whatsoever to be used for immoral purposes ("I think we've just been insulted, Em"). Only the temporary toilets constructed by Foremost to be used . . . "And the police will be summoned," concluded Mr. Blair, "if any alcohol is found on any Foremost Productions personnel, either within the chateau or anywhere on the Versailles grounds."

With that, he grudgingly handed Blakeney the keys and stepped aside from the east-wing door, frowning upon the cast and crew as they filed past him.

"For God's sake, somebody switch on the fucken heaters!" Marsh Sloane's bronze-and-velvet baritone boomed in the long, empty room within.

"And those animals"—Mr. Blair glared at Emma—"are contractually restricted to Miss de la Rose's dressing room. Any damages will be charged against Foremost Productions' account."

Black Jasmine barked at him. (*Sez you!*)

The Foremost properties department had been dispatched to Versailles the previous Thursday, to construct four toilets at the western end of the "Italian garden," to set up a gasoline-powered generator sixty feet from the building (the plant original to the house had long since decayed into a Pompeii of rust), and to string lights in what had been the servants' dining room. This room, fifty feet by fifteen, like every other room in the "chateau," had been plastered but never finished. Icebox-cold and reeking of mold, the mere smell of it—and the stink of three electric heaters warming up—brought back to Emma the piercing recollection of her days in Manchester during the "post-war slump" as no words could.

The room itself had been roughly furnished by an advance party from the nearby hamlet of Brookhaven that morning. Trestle tables bore Thermoses of coffee, and—a homely and welcome contribution—plates of cookies, chocolate brownies, and donuts. (*Do the wives and daughters of the local farmers make extra money doing this?*) Collapsible racks along the walls held the silk polonaises, Directoire frocks, and peasant chemises of the French sequences of the epic, and sinister English robber togs, all of which would be hauled back and forth, pre-dawn, every morning from Brookhaven as well.

"For God's sake, doesn't anybody have any gin?" demanded Margaret Mackenzie. Kitty obligingly dug into the pocket of her chinchilla coat.

"I am not getting into that costume until the room warms up!" declared Darlene, as one of Carrie Drebbett's assistants shook an extremely décolletée confection of silk free of its wrappings and held it out invitingly. Above clouds of monkey fur and fringe, Darlene's head with its "pouf" rose in incongruous glory: a garden of roses, lace, and ostrich plumes, deliberately downplayed to emphasize her innocence at this point in the tale. All the women of the company had been coiffed on the train—and painted insofar as the jostling of the private make-up carriage would permit. As brighter electric lights blazed forth, the extras sorted themselves into their places at the portable make-up tables, and the principals—Miss Golden, Kitty, Margaret Mackenzie, Ken Elmore, et al.—retreated, cookies and coffee in hand, to the assortment of pantries, storerooms, silverware rooms, wine rooms, and linen rooms that would serve as their private dressing facilities.

"See you ladies at the Bastille." Zal kissed Emma—warm hands, warm lips—gave Kitty a brisk military salute, and was gone.

But his words re-echoed in Emma's mind as she followed Kitty, slowly, down a short hall to what had been the butler's pantry. The blotched plaster, the water-stained ceilings, made her realize how patchy were her memories of the year 1920: images out of order, as if she had moved in and out of a haze of disorientation and grief that at times had amounted to physical pain. The world had experienced the "post-war slump" in that year, but for Emma, the years 1918–1920 had been something else. Widowhood. The worldwide epidemic of influenza. The deaths of her parents, of her three aunts and their husbands, of her brother. Waking in the hospital to the knowledge that she was alone.

In Manchester—where the hospital had arranged to find her an employer—Mrs. Pendergast had complained constantly of times being hard and there being no money, but Emma herself had been conscious of this only distantly. She'd understood even then that England's situation was not nearly as bad as what was happening in Germany. But even in Manchester, she had seen men begging on street corners, or sleeping in doorways—something she had never seen before the war or even during it. Yet it was as if it were merely a part of having nowhere to go herself.

Kitty switched on the heater, the sound of it bringing Emma back to the present, and she smiled. Her room at Mrs. Pendergast's had not had such a thing—and the one in the servants' hall at her employer's house had been coin-operated. Her predecessor, she had been given to understand, had been sacked for circumventing the timer mechanism with a magnet.

Beyond the uncurtained windows, Emma could see handlers bringing a beautiful painted carriage—complete with hammer-cloth on the coachman's box—around from the stables, four matched gray horses puffing steam like dragons. (*Don't tell me someone on Long Island has a matched team in this day and age*!) She wondered if Mr. Blair had a clause in the contract about dung on the driveway.

Turning, she saw that two huge vases of orchids—lavender, white, and pink, in a foaming cloud of baby's breath—flanked the mirror on the make-up table: Ambrose Crain's favorite offering. Emma wondered who the millionaire had paid to bring them out here. More practically, a bottle of high-quality Canadian rye decorated the table itself—Kitty had mentioned last night Shakespeare Malone's connections with the distilleries of Toronto and Montreal. And Gordy Graves—or someone—had placed three little dishes in a row close to the heater, a larger dish filled with water, and three fluffy towels marked *Plaza Hotel*, for the dogs.

They filmed on Long Island for almost two weeks, before the murder.

Emma had assumed that once filming started, Kitty would have less to write in her misspelled reports to Frank Pugh concerning Darlene Golden's conduct—addressed discreetly to Conrad Fishbein, in view of Mrs. Pugh's continued presence in Hollywood (Peggy Donovan and the incurably gossipy Millie Katz kept her apprised of that situation). But Darlene—like Kitty herself, as well as Ken Elmore, Margaret Mackenzie, Marsh Sloane, and Gordy Graves (who really should have known better, Emma thought)—succumbed like schoolgirls to the kaleidoscope delights of Broadway. Once the six o'clock train pulled into Penn Station, the Hollywood contingent, like the dozens of New York extras, returned to their quarters only long enough to change clothes—if that—before sallying forth to speakeasies, nightclubs, theaters, or floating crap games as their natures dictated. By Monday, Darlene, Kitty, and Ken were all taking bright silks or snappy cufflinks and ties along in their luggage on the morning train, and hailing cabs straight from the station to take them to the El Fey or the High Wire, or up to the Cotton Club or the stylish black-and-tans of Harlem.

Emma returned to the Plaza, fed the dogs, and went to bed.

Neil Bandog—with a wife and an apartment in the Alwyn Court building—found reasons to turn up at Versailles every day that week, jealously watching the filming and holding long conversations with Darlene while Zal, Chip, and the New York lighting man Tony Ransom and his crew adjusted reflectors and camera angles around the lovely blonde Mila Haley. Mr. Blair came to the set nearly every day, snooping around to make sure nobody violated the terms of the contract, examining the unfinished floors for signs of "damage" by the dogs and the more remote rooms of the chateau for signs of "immoral activity" ("Not unless somebody rigs a heater up there!" complained Kitty. "We nearly *froze*! He listens at keyholes, too.")

Bandog, on the other hand, came to Emma—and to George Blakeney—daily, with suggestions for close-ups and camera angles that would further showcase Miss Golden's extraordinary beauty, and Kitty started paying Zal's assistant Herbie Carboy to keep count of how many close-ups Darlene had per scene. Twice, the enamored financier suggested adding whole scenes, with no other purpose than to demonstrate what a gracious and tender soul Summer Fairisle was.

"Like she hasn't been out every night with Angel-Eyes Taralla," sniffed Kitty, sipping coffee with one hand and smoothing on her stockings with the other, while outside the windows of Suite 1202's little kitchen, the early-morning sky was moonless and black as pitch. "I saw her at one in the morning at the Chicken Club with him—"

(*And what were you doing at the Chicken Club at one in the morning?*)

"—and the night before at the Eldorado dance hall with Joey Saylor. He's a dancer," she added, and touched up her lipstick—she was fully made-up though her black hair was tousled and every brush-stroke of powder, mascara, and rouge would be replaced by camera make-up the moment she boarded the train. "Mila Haley tells me he just got his big break, in *Ripples of 1924* at the Palace. He'd better be careful, though." She scooped a gold-and-turquoise Paquin from the end of her bed, slithered into it with practiced speed while Emma glanced at the clock and mentally calculated how she'd get Kitty out to Brookhaven if they encountered so much as a single adverse traffic signal and missed the train. "Angel-Eyes is jealous as hell. You should see how he watches her, and mutters to that awful stooge of his . . . Bronco Burnett? The one with the broken nose? She's playing with fire." She shivered—*Not*, reflected Emma, *that Kitty hadn't toyed with proverbial blow-torches of her own* . . . "So's Bandog, I understand—"

She stepped into turquoise-and-gold pumps, caught up her chinchilla on one arm and the leashes of the celestial cream-cakes with the other hand, headed for the door.

(*If we miss the elevator, we're not going to make the train* . . .)

"And one of these days, that *snoop* Blair's going to fink about the rumors he picks up from the extras . . ."

And what might Mr. Pugh's reaction be to news of Kitty closing out the High Wire Club? Or "painting the town red," as the saying was, after the theaters closed, with Chico Marx?

At least the owner of the High Wire Club—Mr. Shakespeare Malone—did not appear to be the jealous type. And though Emma suspected that, as gentlemanly as he was, he might be operating a bootlegging ring of his own, he didn't have henchmen with names like Bronco Burnett and Knuckles Gracciola. Two nights previously, the camera crew had (for once) been able to return to New York on the same six o'clock train from Port Jefferson, and Zal had celebrated the event by taking Emma to dinner at the Maison Arthur. Afterwards, they had gone to hear one of Zal's favorite singers—a Black woman named Bessie Smith—who was appearing at Malone's Mardi

Gras Club in Harlem, where they had encountered Kitty and Chico. Malone had come over to their table with what seemed to be perfectly affable greetings—a tall, slender, sandy-haired man with sleepy golden-hazel eyes and a thin slip of a Continental mustache. He'd congratulated Chico on his win on the Alabama–Georgia football game, kissed Kitty's hand, and, on his way out to return to the downtown High Wire Club, had given instructions to his (white) maître d' to supply the table with whatever they wished, on the house.

Leaving the club after Smith's first show, at a more or less decent hour ("I'll be along soon," Kitty promised, from her perch on Chico's knee), Emma had caught a disturbing glimpse of young Zeppo Marx, with Darlene on his arm, just getting out of a cab on Seventh Avenue . . .

Not another one!

Or is that Mila Haley? From across the street and in poor lighting, it was hard to tell.

Before she could speak, the couple had disappeared into the crowd outside the Club Hot-Cha, and Zal was signaling to her from their cab.

But Kitty's words remained in her mind, and that Saturday morning, while Kitty was having the inevitable French Court wig fastened to her head in the Long Island train, Emma took her tea and moved down the dining car to the table where Miss Haley sat with three of the extras: like her, Emma guessed, chorines filling in between jobs on Broadway.

She'd exchanged words with the girl once or twice on the set, so when she said, "Do you mind if I join you?" they moved their chairs to make space at the table for her. One of the extras—a Black girl named Monette—pushed the sugar bowl and cream pitcher in her direction. "I heard a rumor the other day that rather disturbed me," Emma went on, as the girls scooped the litter of cards aside. Monette and the other girls—Sugar-Pie and Ginger—played servants or peasants, their hair in simple braids. Mila's coiffure was a reasonable facsimile of Darlene's "pouf," and her make-up (which, like most extras, she did herself) was expertly applied to heighten her resemblance to the golden-haired star. "It occurred to me that since you live and work in New York, you might be able to tell me. Have you ever heard of a man named Floppy Dexter?"

Mila's blue eyes widened as her friends flung up their hands in exasperation. "Don't tell me he's proposed marriage to *you*, honey?"

Floppy Dexter, it appeared, made a habit of approaching actresses with offers of matrimony. "I played one of the other hookers last year when Gloria Swanson was shooting *Zaza* over at Astoria," provided the brunette Sugar-Pie. "Miss Swanson said she got a letter from Floppy offering her fifty thousand dollars if she'd marry him for, like, a week, and then get a divorce—"

"Who *is* he?" asked Emma. "A . . . A friend of mine in Los Angeles got a letter like that—"

"Actress?" inquired Mila, and Emma nodded. "What's she make a week?"

Without waiting for a reply, Ginger—a snub-nosed, red-haired "pony" without the perfection of figure that would have gotten her hired at the top-tier Broadway revues—provided, "Everybody in town knows Floppy, Duchess. His daddy owned about half the state of Arizona and banks from here to San Francisco; he's worth I don't know how many million dollars. But he's all wet. Dumber than my dog and drunk every time I've seen him. He got kicked out of the Mardi Gras Club the other night for trying to sneak into the girls' dressing room."

"I heard from a friend of mine he tried to get Jobyna Ralston to marry him, too." Mila gathered up the cards and shuffled them with the same deft swiftness Emma had seen Kitty employ when she was getting ready to deal off the bottom of the deck. "I think he also tried to get Dorothy Dalton . . . Was it Dorothy?" She turned inquiringly towards Sugar-Pie, who shrugged. "She did a couple of those society romances for Zukor at Famous Players, anyway. I hear that's why Swanson just tore up Floppy's letter. She said it stank to hell."

"Why?" asked Emma. "I mean, why is he trying to pay women to marry him? Wouldn't it be cheaper to . . . well . . . I'm sure there are less expensive options all up and down Broadway."

"Like he needs to go cheap," Mila scoffed, and Emma had to admit she was right.

"He's movie-crazy." Sugar-Pie waved a dismissive hand. "I hear he's got a screening room at his mama's place in Stony Brook and another in his apartment in town. He has his own projectionist and spends the whole day watching movies, then goes out and hits the clubs at night. If you ask me, I think he writes those letters when he's drunk. He'd wet his pants if one of those ladies ever turned up on his doorstep saying 'I do.'"

No, thought Emma, remembering the way Mr. Ince had put a hand on Kitty's shoulder, the urgent note in his voice. *I'm not joking, Kit. Stay away from it. Stay away from* him.

Seeing again how that gawky young man in the pink-striped shirt had watched Darlene walk away from him, after picking up whatever it was he'd put on the table.

SEVEN

Rain had started at about three o'clock the previous afternoon before Mr. Blakeney had been able to get a single take of the monumental confrontation between the beautiful Summer Fairisle (Darlene) and the evil Comtesse de Palogneux (Kitty) that both Neil Bandog and Devon Kingsley—author of *Shining Bright*—approved of. Mr. Kingsley—a tall, stout man whose voluminous mustache seemed to have been made up from hair that had fled the barren territory above his ears—had arrived on Friday morning from Savannah overflowing with joy that *Shining Bright* was being produced as a high-quality, nine-reel feature—joy that had quickly evaporated when he realized that the necessity of condensing 517 closely printed pages of sub-plots, family history, and backstairs intrigue into just under two hours had involved the excision of four major characters and two whole storylines (not to speak of alterations in everybody's wardrobe). By the time Blakeney had been able to return to filming, storm clouds, literal as well as metaphorical, had gathered over the plaster of Paris "druid ruins" in the pine woods, with the result that there were no "dailies" to be viewed on Saturday in the small room that would have been devoted to the cleaning of the Versailles silverware. Thus, Zal, Chip, and their assistants were again able to return to New York with everybody else on the six o'clock train.

Following an excellent dinner at André's, Zal, Emma, and Kitty took advantage of the tickets Chico had provided to go to the Casino Theater and laugh themselves sick watching Chico and his brothers in a revue called *I'll Say She Is*. After the show, Kitty disappeared with Chico, and Zal and Emma returned to the Plaza for much less sleep than either of them would had if they had been alone.

In the dining car on Sunday morning, just as the train pulled away from its stop at Jamaica Station, and Kitty departed to be coiffed and supplied with an under-painting of Motion Picture Yellow, Emma told Zal of what Mila and her friends had said. "Does that sound like something a man would do if he was drunk? But Mr. Ince sounded as though he knew what he was talking about . . ."

"Ince was smart," agreed Zal. "He worked at Famous Players in New York before the War, but he kept up his connections here when he went to California. California has nice weather, but New York is where the money is. Hence, Darlene sneaking off last night for a little nookie with Bandog." Saturday's early conclusion of filming had prompted the banker to make arrangements with the star for dinner at the Colony and an evening of romance in one of his several apartments in town—an itinerary that Darlene had not hesitated to compare to Kitty's plans for "an evening of vaudeville and hot dogs."

"It looks like he wasn't the only one she sneaked off to meet." Emma unfolded that morning's Sunday *Times* on the little table before them, to display a rather grainy photograph of Darlene in the arms of what was unmistakably Floppy Dexter, sans glasses but still resplendent in his pink-striped shirt, on the dance floor of a crowded club. "When Kitty gets picked up at the house by some handsome saxophone player fifteen minutes after Mr. Pugh drops her off, she has the good sense to go someplace where they won't be photographed by every journalist in town. I daresay Kitty's already bought her own copy of this, to send the picture to Mr. Pugh."

Zal studied the shot with a photographer's practiced eye. "Won't do her a lot of good. Darlene's three-quarters turned away from the camera. She could argue it was some other girl in two hundred and fifty dollars' worth of Lanvin. Looks like Darlene might not really believe Bandog's song and dance about just waiting for his divorce to come through."

Emma sighed. "At least Kitty doesn't believe Mr. Pugh, when he says that. But why would Mr. Dexter even believe that a cinema star—much less the 'Goddess of the Silver Screen'"—she quoted the title that *Screen World* magazine had bestowed on Kitty back in April—"would marry him at all, much less let herself in for the nuisance of a divorce? He can't be that desperate for . . . well . . . feminine companionship. Not if his company at the El Fey last week was any indication."

"I think he does it to upset his mother."

Emma looked around, startled, at this new voice, to see a girl standing beside their table, a copy of that morning's *Times* clutched to her thin chest.

At the same moment, Zal lowered the paper, exclaimed, "Becca!" and looked immediately down the length of the dining car toward its door. Emma caught a glimpse of a dark-clothed woman there, her hair covered by the sort of scarf that Kitty—and Millie Katz back at Foremost—had often pointed out to her as traditionally required of the more conservative Jewish women. The woman, like the girl beside them (and like Zal), wore thick-lensed steel spectacles, and her iron-gray, full-cut skirt reached her ankles. Zal, clearly taken by surprise, started to lift his hand in greeting, but the woman turned and disappeared through the door.

"We've got seats two cars down," explained the girl Becca. "Ruthie thinks movie stars are going to kidnap me and force me into slavery in Hollywood. But how much would it cost for slave stealers to drag me to Hollywood? Wouldn't it be cheaper to kidnap some poor Mexican girl who's already out there? Oh!" she added, as Chang Ming and Black Jasmine, roused from their nap by Kitty's departure for the make-up tables in the parlor car, emerged from beneath Emma's chair to sniff the newcomer's shoes. Her thin, beaky face transformed by delight, Becca knelt to caress the Pekes, and raised her eyes to Emma's.

"Oh, these are Miss de la Rose's dogs, aren't they? Zallie told us about them when he came for dinner!" She stood, quickly and self-consciously, dropped her newspaper (and the cardboard box she also carried), and nearly knocked her head on the table's edge in bending to pick them up. "Oh, there's another one!" she added, as Buttercreme's shy little face peeked from behind Emma's ankles. "Aww . . . And what's your name, hintele?"

She seemed for a moment undecided whether to crouch all

the way down and pat Buttercreme, then stood, smoothing her unflattering, too-long skirt and hand-me-down coat. She too wore a headscarf, though it didn't cover her hair as uncompromisingly as her chaperone's did. Thus, Emma observed that her hair was a few shades more ginger than Zal's; her nearsighted eyes, behind their thick spectacles, like his, were brown and kind. "I'm sorry," Becca stammered, and Zal, who had already risen, brought a chair around for her and picked up the dropped impedimenta.

"That's Buttercreme," Zal introduced. "And, Mrs. Blackstone, please allow me to introduce my sister Rebecca Rokatansky. Rebecca, this is Mrs. Blackstone, who writes film scenarios and takes care of Miss de la Rose's dogs. The big guy's Chang Ming, and the little guy's Black Jasmine. It's Mrs. Blackstone's job to beat them every day. Can I get you some coffee?"

"Oh, yes, please," said Becca. "We had to get out of the house while it was still dark, to get to the station—we live in Brooklyn," she added, turning, a little shyly, to Emma. Emma guessed her age at about fourteen, rail-thin and pale with a tendency to freckle (Jim would have surmised the presence of a Cossack in the woodpile somewhere in the family tree). "When he had dinner with us last week, Zal said he'd be filming pretty much every night, but that I was welcome to come out to the set one day. And Mrs. Tappan—I help clean Mrs. Tappan's house most afternoons and Sunday mornings—is out of town this week, so Mother said I could, if Ruthie—that's my sister—came with me."

"That was very kind of your sister," said Emma, as Zal threaded his way among the tables in the direction of the galley. "I'm sure she would be welcome to join us."

Becca shook her head. "Ruthie wouldn't. She's been lecturing me since we got on the train about actors and painted women and people who lure girls into . . . into immoral ways." She leaned forward in her chair, to stroke Chang Ming's head as the red-gold dog stood to put his forepaws on her knee. Not to be outdone, Black Jasmine stood up beside him, both gazing into her face like transformed fairy-children, plumed tails threshing, pleading for her love as if neither had ever had such a thing in their lives. (Nor buttered toast either . . .) "Can I pick them up, Mrs. Blackstone?"

"I think they will die of anxiety if you don't. Are you and your sister Mr. Rokatansky's only siblings?" She observed how carefully the girl lifted the fragile Black Jasmine, and bent, herself, to hoist the more robust Chang Ming onto her own knees.

Becca nodded. "I was only eight when Zal left home, but he writes to us every week," she divulged. "He tells us about everybody at the studio, and the other studios. It's better than a film magazine. But Mother says he doesn't tell us all the wicked things that go on there. And in the film magazines, it sounds like she's right. Not you," she added quickly. "You're Miss de la Rose's sister-in-law, aren't you? From England? Whose—"

She just stopped herself, clearly, from blurting, *Whose husband was killed in the war?* and changed it to, "Who goes out with Harry Garfield?" And her eyes shone with admiration at the mention of the handsome star.

"Sometimes." Emma gave what she hoped was a maidenly smile as if to deny that she'd ever in her life had her picture appear in *Screen World*, being passionately kissed by Harry Garfield on the sidewalk outside a Hollywood nightclub. "The film magazines try to pretend we're engaged, but it's nothing of the kind. He's just a dear and trusted friend." This was true. Though ordered by Frank Pugh to be seen together, both Emma and the heroic-looking Harry enjoyed their evenings out, and Harry's boyfriend, Roger, invariably bought Emma corsages for these occasions.

Becca turned Emma's copy of the *Times* to view the photograph. "Is that Darlene Golden? Did I hear you say—I'm sorry, I was standing right next to you, and I didn't mean to eavesdrop—that Floppy Dexter proposed marriage to her? *Film Fun* said last year that he proposed to Gloria Swanson, and it was in *Cinema World* and *Screen World* and *Screen Stories* that he proposed to Dorothy Dalton . . . and to Dorothy Gish, it said in the *Herald* two years ago. That was even in *Town Topics*! Only—"

She cast a quick glance towards the door, reddish brows puckered with sudden concern. "Only please, if I can ask you, don't mention it if Ruthie comes here."

"Of course not."

"Mother lets me go to the pictures once a month, if it's something my brother worked on. I go with Ruthie. But Mrs. Tappan—the lady I clean house for—really loves the movies, and she has all these magazines in her house. When she's home, she and I talk about the movies, and the stars, and what glamorous lives they lead, although Zal says there's a lot of hard work making pictures, even for the stars. And she gives me five cents above what she and Mother decided on, and lets me off one afternoon a week to go to the pictures instead of working. I–I don't tell Mother that." She looked quickly down at Black Jasmine's smooth, round head and silky ears. "Or Ruthie. It doesn't hurt anybody—"

"And it isn't Mom's business." Zal, balancing tableware like a waiter, set two cups of black coffee, a cup of tea, and a plate of crullers on the table, and took the chair beside his sister. "I take it this is Mom's contribution to your journey?" He raised the lid of the shoebox. "Day-old pumpernickel and two hard-boiled eggs," he informed Emma. "Why am I not surprised? So why do you say Floppy Dexter wants to get up his mom's nose by offering movie stars money to marry him?"

Becca giggled guiltily at the slang expression—Emma had heard Zal use worse and had heard Kitty use considerably worse.

"He's engaged to Beatrice Schuyler," the girl disclosed. "It was in the article in *Town Topics*. Her family's related to the Schermerhorns and the Vanderbilts and all those people who have mansions out on Long Island. His mother's from some snazzy family in Charleston, and I've heard from Mrs. Tappan—she's a hairdresser and knows lots of things about rich people—that it drives Mrs. Dexter crazy, that ever since Floppy—Mr. Dexter, I mean—inherited the family business, all he does is get drunk in nightclubs and run around with Broadway chorus girls and watch movies, while the Board of Directors runs the holding companies and the banks and the mines. And Beatrice Schuyler," she added, her brown eyes suddenly sharp behind their spectacles, "is on about seven committees for moral reform, and is the spokesperson for the local Anti-Saloon League, and is in the Long Island branch of the WKKK."

When Emma looked blank at this last, Zal explained quietly, "That's the Women's Ku Klux Klan. The gang Griffith made the heroes of *Birth of a Nation*," he added, seeing Emma's puzzled frown. "They really exist. Their main goal is to keep Negroes—and Jews, and Catholics, and immigrants—from voting, or marrying white people, or going to college, or taking the jobs that pay halfway decently that they think white people should get."

"Oh," said Emma, her voice dry. "That sort. My uncle David tells me one encounters the breed in India as well. I think much better of Mr. Dexter now."

"Well," Zal went on, "since the Dexters could buy and sell Foremost Productions, and probably already own stock in Neil Bandog's bank and theater chain, I'm guessing Darlene had better cut her losses and get what she can out of Bandog. It sounds to me like the Dexters are never going to let old Floppy come up to scratch in the marriage market. Or if Bandog doesn't come through, she'd probably better hang on to Pugh. But don't tell Kitty I said so," he added. "And here she is!"

And he sprang to his feet and went to intercept Kitty, who had emerged, with a tiny water mill and a few miniature orchard trees arranged amid the roses and swagged lace of her towering coiffure. Probably, reflected Emma with a sigh, to warn her that for purposes of conversation with Becca, he and Emma were "Mr. Rokatansky" and "Mrs. Blackstone," and Just Good Friends. (*Shiksa*, Jim's father had written in that final letter. *Creeping abomination . . .*)

While young Miss Rokatansky gazed in star-smitten adoration at Camille de la Rose (née Chava Blechstein), Emma turned the *Times* around again and studied the dim features of Floppy Dexter's thin countenance: beaky nose, mouth open in a vapid grin, peering myopically at the face of the woman beside him.

Stay away from it. Stay away from him . . .

If it was just a matter of being dropped by the wealthy Mr. Bandog and the useful Mr. Pugh, she thought—not to speak of the lithe Joey Saylor and Angel-Eyes Taralla and goodness knew who else—she would have shrugged.

But something whispered to her that Darlene, objectionable as she was, was in waters deeper than that.

What had Mr. Ince known, or heard, about Clark Dexter, all the way out on the West Coast?

And from whom?

She only hoped that despite the warning, Kitty wasn't in clandestine communication with Floppy Dexter as well. (Though how she could be, between Chico Marx and Shakespeare Malone . . .)

Becca is quite right, she reflected. *There* is *a great deal of hard work involved in making pictures*.

As it happened, Neil Bandog getting hold of a copy of the society pages of the Sunday *Times* turned out to be the least of Darlene Golden's problems.

"Frank!" squealed Kitty, as she stepped out of the studio limousine in the cobbled outer court of Versailles. Emma always admired her sister-in-law's acting ability when the stakes were real: instants before, as the vehicle negotiated the last curves of the unpaved road through the woods, she had been describing the studio head as "a conceited truck-load of whale-blubber" and expressing her astonishment that Mrs. Pugh hadn't started divorce proceedings years ago. "This one has to hold the record for putting up with him . . ."

But at the sight of that tall, pear-shaped figure emerging from the east wing's doorway, her face transformed with ecstasy, and she scampered across the courtyard to throw herself into his arms. "Oh, Frank!"

Πολλάς αν εύροις μηχανάς, γυνή γαρ εί, Emma's ancient colleague Euripedes had written, of women's "machinations" to get what they want—having presumably, thought Emma, seen a great deal of this sort of behavior in Periclean Athens.

Pugh embraced Kitty—imperiling laces, roses, miniature water mill and tiny trees embedded in the shellacked monument of her hair. But as he did so, he glanced up and met Darlene's eyes as the blonde star emerged from her limousine. It was too far to read expressions clearly, but Darlene's whole body seemed on the point of exploding with passion at the sight of him. She pressed her hand to the haystack of pink-dyed monkey fur at her bosom, and her whole form cried, *It's you. It's always been you . . .*

In the words of Aesop: Πυρ, γυνή και θάλασσα. *Fire, woman, and the sea.* Elemental powers which cannot be resisted . . .

Not by Frank Pugh, anyway . . .

Neil Bandog strode past Pugh and descended upon Darlene with arms outstretched. Though she turned to him with an almost palpable sob of desire, her eyes remained on the studio head's (*Zal must be right about Mr. Bandog not coming through . . .*) until the final second. Even at that distance, it was clear that Mr. Bandog's kisses were of the sort described as "a big ol' smackeroo."

Well, both of them are *actresses . . .*

Zal had briefed Kitty on the Just Good Friends scenario between himself and Emma, and Kitty—as the daughter of Jim's parents—understood this to the marrow of her bones. She, or Zal, must have talked to the other members of the Hollywood contingent, and Zal's sister was accepted with the friendly tolerance they extended to other visitors to the set who knew enough to stay out of everybody's way. While the cameras were rolling, Becca accepted Emma's invitation to join her in what she always thought of as Kitty's "base camp," the circle of folding chairs, make-up tables, portable gramophone, and dog carriers to which Kitty retreated while her stand-in shivered in the ring of light stands and camera getting ready for the next shot. Ruthie kept her distance on a make-up stool with the shoebox of day-old pumpernickel and hard-boiled eggs on her lap, and frowned whenever her sister tripped on a chair or dropped an astrology magazine.

In fact, Emma's only regret concerning Becca's presence was that it made it impossible for her to unobtrusively flee the approach of Mr. Kingsley.

Through the previous two days, the author had clung

doggedly to his delusion that a scenario writer—much less an assistant scenario writer who was only "doctoring" what had largely been written by Sam Wyatt back in Hollywood—could interpret the events in a story exactly as she chose. ("Yes, Mr. Kingsley, I understand that eighteenth-century noblemen did not shoot their own peasants for sport." "No, Mr. Kingsley, they've already rehearsed this scene and arranged for sets and properties for a Druid stone circle; it can't be changed now without re-shooting four other scenes . . ." "I am an historian, sir, and I do know that a priest could not refuse to baptize a child simply because he suspects the child of being illegitimate . . .")

He also seemed to be under the impression that if he pointed out his objections to the writer frequently enough—and loudly enough—the writer would cheerfully abandon the producer's orders, alter the action accordingly, and order re-shoots.

Yesterday, when she had sought shelter in the sprawling maze of the Versailles stables, he had pursued her ("Those guys'll never notice the difference, Mrs. Blackstone!" "You can't disregard the true facts of history!") (*Where is Mr. Blair when you need him?*), until, in exasperation, she had descended from the maze of tack rooms and loose boxes into the underground maze of what had been intended as quarters for grooms, chauffeurs, gardeners, and grounds staff. It had taken her a quarter-hour to find her way back to the stairway, by the shaky illumination of Kitty's cigarette lighter which she'd had in her pocket (Mr. Blakeney had objected to the villainous Comtesse caching the implement in her bosom).

Today she had taken the precaution of packing a "flashlight" (as Americans termed electric torches) in her satchel of notes, school exercise books, and previous drafts, along with a ball of kitchen string and a less-than-classical stick of chalk.

Facilis descensus Averno, Virgil had written: *It is easy to descend into the Underworld. Sed revocare . . . hic opus, hic labor est.* As Zal (or Odysseus for that matter) would have put it, *Getting out is the tricky part.*

On the dozenth take of the carriage pulling up in the woods (the driver was a local man who looked after the Roosevelt stables in Cove Neck) as the disheveled Summer stumbled from the trees, Emma spotted Mr. Kingsley's mustard-yellow coat and red-striped scarf moving purposefully through the trees from the direction of the house. She said, "Drat the man," and thrust everything back into her satchel. Becca looked at her inquiringly, and all three Pekes leaped hopefully to their feet. "Shall we go for a walk?"

They made a wide circle around the east side of the stables, avoiding alike the Druid ruins (snugly wrapped in prop department tarpaulins) and the remains of the "Italian garden" (with makeshift out-houses now behind bad copies of Apollo Belvedere and Venus de Milo) between the stable compound and the eastern wing. It was a tribute to Mr. Blakeney's directorial skill that no shot in the past five days indicated that all the action—whether in "England" or in "France"—was taking place within a hundred yards of the sea, though its constant, soft murmur on the pebbles made a background to the whispering of the pines.

"It's so beautiful here," sighed Becca, as they emerged from the trees a dozen yards from the miniature cliff. Stunted oaks and beach cabbage grew right to the edge of the escarpment, but from the occasional granite tusks of a ruined balustrade, Emma guessed there had been a pathway there at one time. "I guess if you're that rich, you can afford to live someplace beautiful."

"I understand the builder of the house couldn't," remarked Emma, and related to her Zal's story about the unfortunate results of the crash of 1920.

"I remember that." Becca tugged Chang Ming away from a promising clump of beach grass. "Mama and I both lost our jobs at Mr. Goldstein's factory, and the bakery where Ruthie's husband Yakov worked closed. They had to move in with us for nearly a year." She shook her head, remembered darkness clouding her eyes. "Before that, Mama used to send back the money Zal sent us from California—he left town so he wouldn't get drafted during the war, you know. And she said he probably earned part of it working on the Sabbath. After that, she had to take it."

"And from what Za—Mr. Rokatansky"—Emma corrected herself—"has told me, your mother accompanied each acknowledgment of receipt with a long letter demanding that he reform his way of life." She spoke gravely, but lifted her eyebrows at Becca, who laughed as she let the memory of hard times go.

"She did! And she'd tell me all about the evils of Hollywood at supper every night, and moan that he should come back and find work here—when Yakov couldn't even get a job mopping floors, and Zal was making good money in Hollywood! Are those steps going down to the beach?" The girl hurried toward the cliff edge, almost tripping over Chang Ming's leash.

"I doubt there's much of a beach." Emma lengthened her own stride as Black Jasmine and Buttercreme tugged to follow. But in fact, the weathered stairway down the cliff face ended at a strip of gravelly sand studded with rocks of various sizes. By the look of it, a much grander stair had been planned, its foundations half constructed a few yards further east and overgrown now with sea grass and shrubs. Black Jasmine darted out to the end of his leash (*I'm going to be brushing sand out of his fur for the rest of the evening . . .*), while Buttercreme cringed fastidiously back at the mere thought of sand in her silky toes.

Emma laughed, picked her up, and followed Becca the short distance to the water. As each wave of the Long Island Sound withdrew from the shore, Black Jasmine and Chang Ming threw themselves at the shore birds who ran out after the retreating water to peck at the sand crabs ("*And Nimrod was a mighty hunter before the Lord*," Emma quoted from Genesis, which again made Becca laugh). Both dogs—like the birds—then dashed frantically from the next incoming wave, terrified they'd get their feet wet.

"Those are sanderlings," Becca informed her. "And the little ones are—"

Chang Ming turned suddenly, lunged inland to the full extent of his leash, barking.

And Emma turned, in time to see two men among the rocks and scrub of the clifftop, looking down at them.

Although she only saw them for a moment—at a distance

of about fifty feet—she was almost certain that they were the two men—the burly Bronco and his cadaverous partner—that she'd seen some ten nights previously at the El Fey Club with Angel-Eyes Taralla.

EIGHT

"What can you tell me about Floppy—Clark—Dexter?" Emma set her fork down and looked a trifle apologetically across the white linen of the Hotel Brevoort's tablecloth at Ambrose Crain. From the Port Jefferson station that afternoon, Kitty had telephoned the offices of Crain Consolidated with a tale of filming at MBQ that night because Margaret Mackenzie had been suddenly called away and a vitally important scene had to be completed . . .

Emma, keeping a weather eye out on the platform for Frank Pugh, had hoped that Kitty would clear this fiction with Mrs. Mackenzie, in case the queenly Scotswoman was also going to the "Met" and encountered Mr. Crain in the lobby.

"Of course, darling!" she had heard Kitty exclaim. "She would be *delighted*! She'll meet you at the Brevoort at six . . . I'm in *agonies* to miss the opera, but Emma *loves* music . . ."

Presumably, Emma reflected, this was what Darlene Golden went through every other night as she shuffled her romances with Mr. Bandog, Joey Saylor, Zeppo Marx (if that was Miss Golden he'd been seen with), Angel-Eyes Taralla (Emma shivered at the recollection of Bronco and his partner on the clifftop that morning), and now, evidently, Frank Pugh if she could get him away from Kitty. And if it weren't for that note in Mr. Ince's voice when he'd warned Kitty of danger, she would have smiled, recalling those precisely timed sketches in *I'll Say She Is*, with one Marx disappearing under the Empress Josephine's sofa at the very second another stepped through the door (clothed as Napoleon, no less!).

On the other hand, while Kitty spent at least part of her evening proving her love to Mr. Pugh, she, Emma, would be watching a spectacle that she had never thought to see again, bathed in the exquisite music of Mascagni and Leoncavallo.

She sipped her glass of $200-a-bottle French Pinot Noir (which the Hotel Brevoort had thoughtfully purchased back in November of 1919, they claimed) and watched the shadow of sadness pass across her companion's eyes.

"It's a rather painful story," said Mr. Crain at last. "I am grieved by Clark's conduct over the past few years, but I can't say I'm surprised."

"Do you know the family well?"

"Not terribly." The old man stirred his consommé, gray eyes gazing—as Emma had seen her former employer's butler gaze, sometimes—back across the years, an exile seeking sight of a world that was now as unreachable as Fairyland. "He and my son"—his voice stuck at the mention of the young man who had followed up a career of bad debts and impulsive investments with embezzlement, falsified documents, forged signatures, and finally an attempt on his father's life to prevent his peculations from coming to light. Timothy Crain was still in jail awaiting trial. Part of the reason Mr. Crain was in New York was to help the investigation into whether the young man's mother had been in on the scheme as well.[1]

Neither Emma nor, she was fairly certain, Kitty had asked the old man about the progress of the case. Kitty might be bird-brained, but Emma knew she was neither stupid nor insensitive.

After a moment, Crain managed a smile and sipped at his soup. "Well, before the war, Clark misbehaved himself no more than a thousand other young men of his class. His father and I were both members of the Scroll and Key at Yale—Griswold Dexter was Class of '91; I was about ten years ahead of him. I fear I always found the man unpleasant—cold-hearted and avaricious, and with a streak of cruelty in him." He shook his head. "The older boy—Spencer—my son Tim's friend—dealt with him pretty well. But Clark retreated from his father's bullying, first into books and then into movies. Griswold was one of the major backers of Biograph, and I'm sorry to say he used the studio as a personal harîm. But when Clark started

1 See *Scandal in Babylon*.

to develop—I think the word these days is a 'crush'—on some of these same young ladies, his father forbade him to ever visit the studio again."

"Did he know Tom Ince?"

The waiter came and set fish and sweetbreads, petits pois, and asparagus in hollandaise before them, and topped up Emma's wineglass.

Crain frowned again, placing the name, then nodded. "I gather Ince was a sort of Dutch uncle to both boys. Spencer was in college when the United States got into the war; he had missed over a year through contracting rheumatic fever in 1915, and it left him with a weak heart. Clark joined up—he was seventeen—and his father evidently pulled strings and greased palms with the War Department, because I don't think Clark ever got off Long Island. Then, in 1920, shortly after he got out and returned home, Spencer and the boys' two sisters were killed in an automobile accident near Westbury."

Emma recalled the young man who'd staggered into the chorus line at El Fey in quest of ostrich plumes. Who'd written to Kitty—and Darlene—and apparently several others: *My heart pines for you . . .*

When, in fact, he was pining for someone—something—entirely different.

Like a palimpsest, that memory was overlain by that letter from Jim's colonel. *It is with deep regret that I have to inform you . . .* And her own sense that there had to be some mistake. That it was—it *had* to be—some other James Blackstone he meant. That the real Jim—*her* Jim—would come home when the fighting was over . . .

And the months of numbness that had followed.

"Oh."

Crain sighed. "Clark idolized his brother; they both adored the girls. Their mother hoped Clark would 'snap out of it' a year later when his father died—would 'straighten up' and step in to take over the family holdings—but it hasn't happened yet. They have good men on the Board of Directors, but it isn't the same, and Rosemary Dexter knows it. She adored Spencer also—everyone did—and I gather she lives in terror that Clark's going to do something stupid with the investments. I don't think she needs to worry. He doesn't even look at the quarterly reports, much less tamper with the running of the businesses. She rules the Board—and Clark—with a rod of iron."

He shook his head and gently prodded the ris de veau à la financière with his silver fork. "Sorry to go on like that," he apologized. "Kitty said the boy was at the El Fey the other night, making a fool of himself. And, of course, every gold digger on Broadway has her sights on him like a deer hunter after a fifteen-point stag. I'm surprised he hasn't turned up at Versailles to watch the filming. Or has he?"

By the twinkle in his eyes, Emma knew he assumed it was why she'd asked after Clark.

"He's harmless, you know," he added. "And I think he's doing what everyone does, who has something they want to forget."

Forget Timothy Crain, thought Emma.

Forget Jim Blackstone . . .

Stay away from it, Tom Ince had said, back in the mild autumn sunlight of California. *Stay away from* him.

He had clearly heard *something* from his years—or his friends—in New York . . .

But nothing she could point to and tell Darlene, *You're in danger . . .*

There is nothing you can do about any of it tonight, she told herself. So she let herself be immersed in the beauty of make-believe, watching tenors murder one another on the stage. Like the audience of the play-within-a-play of *Pagliacci*, not quite knowing whether the tears, the blood, and the passion were genuine or not.

"I'm going to kill that bitch!" Kitty flounced into the Versailles butler's pantry, still resplendent in the rose-and-burgundy Patou frock she'd had on yesterday while phoning Ambrose Crain from the Port Jefferson train station. Her hair was disheveled as if with the caresses of an infatuated studio chief, but every square centimeter of her make-up was fresh and intact. (*Did she carry Djer-Kiss and Persian Rose with her when Mr. Pugh swept her away last night?*) "Oh, my tiny sweetnesses," she cooed, dropping to a crouch to caress the dogs who came crowding to her ankles. "Did you miss your mommy?" She gathered them, one by one, into her arms, while Emma set about preparing a cup of coffee dosed with equal parts cream and gin.

"I take it you mean Miss Golden?"

"Of course I mean that snake-hipped pocket twister! I had to spend just *hours* last night crying and swearing to Frank that Chico only takes me to nightclubs now and then because I was a friend of his cousin Polly, and Polly made him promise to look after me, and that anyhow he's too busy chasing floating crap games all over Manhattan to lay a *finger* on me . . . And Frank giving me all this 'I heard . . .' and 'People tell me . . .' and I had to say, 'Which people? Who says?' Of course, it's that witch Darlene!"

"Kitty!" Emma turned from the coffee Thermos she'd brought in her picnic basket, cup in hand. "Now, that's a *terrible* thing to say about witches!"—a remark that made her sister-in-law dissolve into giggles. "And so unfair! I trust you were able to bring Mr. Pugh around your thumb?"

"Me?" Kitty put on an expression of innocence and batted her black-enameled eyelashes. "But it took me all night, and I'm just *ruined* . . . I didn't get *any* sleep. D'you think the commissary tent has any ice, honey? Could you go check? Are my eyelids swollen? Frank wanted to make love *all* the rest of the night, which is fine for *him*; *he* can sleep on that cot they brought in for him the other day . . . *God*, I hope it rains again today!"

At that point, a young lady from the make-up crew tapped gently at the door. Filming, Emma had gathered, had been delayed for an hour already, thanks to a fuss raised by Mr. Blair about two journalists from the local Hearst papers (the *Mirror* and the *American*) sneaking into the woods near the set. When she and Kitty arrived in the dining-room-cum-make-up-hall, they found a dozen elaborately costumed extras, an equal number of peasants in rags and filth, and Mila Haley, angelic in a copy of the pillaged finery Darlene would wear in that day's scenes.

The moment the watchdog's back was turned, the journalists reappeared and pounced on Mr. Bandog and Darlene Golden as they, too, crossed the courtyard. Miss Golden, like Kitty, wore the same dress she'd had on yesterday (the rhinestone-sprinkled gold-and-burgundy Lanvin). Like Kitty, she was subtly disheveled, and leaning on Mr. Bandog's arm, tinkling with silvery laughter at his jokes. ("Get it? Get it? Two thirty . . . *Tooth hurty*! A Chinaman goes to the dentist . . . Get it?") His slender little chauffeur followed and intercepted the Fourth Estate before they could snap any incriminating pictures. Bandog was still arguing with them (the bank he worked for belonged to Mr. Hearst) as Darlene sauntered into the make-up hall, one hand arranged on her hip to best display a new ten-karat diamond ring.

It wasn't on her engagement finger, so Emma deduced there was no divorce yet, but even without being a pledge, it must have cost thousands of pounds. (She tried to calculate the value in dollars, and failed.)

A few moments later, Mr. Bandog followed, ostentatiously dusting his hands, as a comic actor would to mime, *Well, I sure took care of* them*!* He paused to give Miss Golden a lingering kiss—Miss Golden carefully holding her hand to one side to give Kitty a good look at her ring—then approached the doorway where Emma still stood and removed his hat. "May I have a few words with you, Mrs. Blackstone?"

"Of course." She turned back into Kitty's little dressing room; Chang Ming immediately rolled on his back before the newcomer, recognizing him as a long-lost father. Black Jasmine followed the banker to one of the folding chairs with the air of an accountant about to deliver a Stock Market report, and Buttercreme hid in her carry-box and barked at him like a little rubber toy.

"Would you care for some coffee?" Emma shifted the gin bottle out of sight. "What can I do for you?"

What she could do, it transpired, was rewrite at least eight sequences in the scenario of *Shining Bright* to emphasize Summer Fairisle's virtue while she was living in the slums of Paris and later in the sordid hideout of the Bethnal Green Gang of highwaymen. (*Does that diamond ring have anything to do with this?*) "Of course, we all know Summer never yielded her virtue to either Graignor Barbu"—he named the Parisian bandit chief who had once been Miss Fairisle's groom—"or Brute Cobbleigh"—the head of the Bethnal Green Gang—"but that point is made, you know, between the lines in the book. I think it's something that a film audience needs to *see*: Miss Fairisle standing up to Graignor, maybe even fighting Brute—" He grinned, picturing the scene. "Breaking a bottle over his head, you know, or pushing him down the stairs or into the fireplace. Something that'll get the point across and showcase that Summer's a girl who can take care of herself in a pinch!"

Since Summer Fairisle spent 517 pages being repeatedly ravished and fleeing into the arms of any number of male rescuers (strangers for the most part) after running through rainstorms which were apparently the constant state of weather in the late eighteenth century, Emma could only nod and say, "I'll see what I can do, Mr. Bandog." This would add, she estimated, a good thirty minutes of screen-time to Darlene's performance (more, counting close-ups)—time that would almost certainly have to be cut from the villainous machinations of the Comtesse de Palogneux.

Kitty, she guessed, would have something to say about that.

"I'll have to clear it with Mr. Pugh, of course," she added, and Bandog waved his hand.

"There should be no problem. I'll speak to him. It will make *Shining Bright* a better, stronger film."

But as Petronius, another of Emma's ancient colleagues in the brotherhood of writers, had pointed out in the first century, there is little point in expecting much of one's projects when Fate has projects of her own.

Whatever Kitty might have had to say about Miss Fairisle's relationships with Parisian bandit chiefs or English highwaymen, she was beaten to it by Devon Kingsley.

Emma managed to avoid Mr. Kingsley for much of the morning by concealing herself in either the stables' box rooms and lofts, in the maze of the house's kitchen quarters (also hiding from Mr. Blair), or the gloomy labyrinths below both. The white chalk she had brought made navigating in the underground tunnels easier: she had found a passageway leading from the chateau's wine cellars some two hundred feet across the "Italian garden" to the sub-equine realms, and another stairway down from the garden itself, concealed in a niche in the stable wall behind a florid statue of Hercules slaying the Nemean lion. The flashlight showed her that some, at least, of these chambers and tunnels pre-dated the mansion itself: ruinous brickwork and antique masonry, old wells and moldering doors, alternated with the plaster and timber and level brick floors of the later excavation.

Only the knowledge that some members of England's aristocracy had devised even more Gothic accommodations for their hirelings kept her from shaking her head in disbelief. *And someone expected his servants to* sleep *down here?*

Unnervingly, also, she had found that some previous Theseus had marked the walls, as she did with her guiding arrows drawn in white chalk: arrows in blue chalk, and straggly lines at barely the height of her hip, in pink. *Leading where? Who had been hiding there from whom?*

She had been glad, after an hour or so, to return to the surface and sneak back to Kitty's base camp, which today had been set up near the gazebo in what had presumably been another garden on the west side of the house. With infinite patience, Mr. Blakeney was walking Kitty through a minor scene with one of the Broadway actors—the Evil Comtesse hiring henchmen to ambush the blameless Miss Fairisle in the first reel . . .

She saw no sign of Mr. Kingsley's bald pate or red-striped scarf, and had opened the most recent of her exercise books on Kitty's make-up table when a voice behind her boomed, "What's this I hear about you *completely rewriting* scenes from my book?"

"I certainly didn't agree with the idea, Mr. Kingsley." Emma turned and set down her pen. Kingsley reached across her and turned the exercise book around so that he could see it.

Graignor—I saved you from the flics; I don't do things like that for nothing. (Seizes her arm, drags her towards him)

Summer—And I kept my brother from killing you . . . (That particular sequence had not yet been written, let alone filmed.)

"I never wrote anything of the kind!" Jupiter Tonans would have quailed at the thunder in the writer's tones. "Oh, this is absolutely outside of enough!"

"Believe me, sir," Emma went on, in the calm tones that had worked well in dealing with Lawrence Pendergast, "I prefer the sequence as you wrote it. I'm not a writer. I know how to put words together, but please understand that I have to write what I'm told, or risk dismissal. I fully intend to speak to Mr. Pugh about this before I take anything to final form . . ."

"You can save yourself that trouble, Madam!" Kingsley scooped the draft from the folding table where she sat, and looked around to spot Frank Pugh, who stood gazing with an expression of deep satisfaction as Kitty came down the gazebo's steps . . . "I shall see to this myself!"

Emma settled back in her canvas folding chair. Mr. Kingsley, she was certain, would be much better in the role. Mr. Pugh was always readier to listen to a man than to a woman.

Except, of course, when that woman was beautiful, young (*well, twenty-two going on thirty . . .*), and throbbing with passion in his arms . . .

Everyone in the Pullman parlor car hired from the Long Island Rail Road by Foremost Productions heard the row. Early-December darkness had settled on the woods and shoreline of Long Island; through the trees flashed occasional glimpses of the lighted windows of the mansions of the "Gold Coast" or the flare of lanterns on private docks. Smaller "parlors" at either end of the coach had been allocated to the film's two major stars, but Emma had gone into the larger "double parlor" in the center of the car to play pinochle with Margaret Mackenzie and two of the Broadway bandits. Blakeney, Gordy, and the entire camera crew had remained yet again at Versailles to view yesterday's dailies. Kitty had retreated to her own private parlor at the eastern end of the west-bound car.

"I'm dying for a nap, darling, but be sure to come let me

know if he makes so much as a *move* towards that peroxide alley cat . . ."

But Mr. Pugh, entering the car, went straight to where Darlene sat—temptingly close to the open door of *her* private parlor—and said, "I want to talk to you."

They had closed the door, but very quickly—even over the thrumming of the wheels—the shouting could be heard.

". . . told you to keep him on a string, not break up his marriage!"

And, ". . . wife'll take him for every cent he's got! We need that money to finish the picture!"

And, "See if I care! That Haley bitch looks like you and I bet she can act as well as you can . . ."

Mila—part of the crowd now occupying the "Darlene" end of the central parlor—stiffened at this description of her, but Emma saw her eyes light up at the possibility.

Had Kitty been the recipient of Frank's wrath—instead of one of the twenty avid auditors within earshot of the door—she would have melted into tears of submission, as she had presumably done the previous night. She had often remarked over breakfast that a post-coital Frank was much easier to manage.

Fatally, Darlene lost her temper. She had a voice like a steam whistle and the vocabulary of a longshoreman. Emma heard a few words that even she didn't know, which was something, after living in the same house with Kitty for a year. (After a particularly descriptive outburst, Margaret Mackenzie murmured, "Fook me," in admiration.) When the door handle began to move, the crowd of listeners barely reached seats in the "Kitty" end of the parlor in time. Kitty herself, however, halted in the aisle, as if she had just entered the room, her hand raised to her lips and tears flooding her eyes. (Her sole claim to cinematic talent was the ability to weep on cue.)

Thus Frank beheld her, as he stormed out of Darlene's private sanctum, and everyone in the central parlor bent their heads studiously over books, newspapers, and games of solitaire. Kitty, like one who has just emerged from her own door to hear the tail end of incomprehensible shouting, met his eyes with melting sympathy and whispered, "Oh, Frank, dearest—!"

He strode to her, seized her around the waist with one beefy arm, and thrust her ahead of him back into her private bower.

Margaret Mackenzie returned to the table where the half-played pinochle hand still lay, picked up her cards, and murmured, "I guess our girl doesn't get her nap."

Whatever took place on the LIRR, Frank returned Kitty to her suite at the Plaza at a startlingly early hour that night—just short of ten. When Chico arrived thirty minutes later, she was sound asleep under a pile of Pekinese. "Ah, let the poor kid sleep." The oldest of the Marxes leaned a shoulder on the door frame of the dimly lit bedroom, his voice low as he and Emma peeped inside. Kitty had clearly changed her dress and renewed her make-up in preparation for the second assignation of the night. Her dark hair strewed the pillows around her, and the single shaded lamp in the parlor caught reflections in five golden eyes as the three dogs raised their heads. (Black Jasmine, like many Pekes, had suffered eye damage as a puppy and had had one removed before he had come into Kitty's life.)

Emma glanced across at the man beside her, hearing a tenderness in his tone unlike his usual attitude of a brassy Broadway Don Juan.

Then, either from embarrassment at showing that he actually felt affection for one of his flings or from force of habit, the piano player resumed his cocky grin and added, "Could I interest *you* in coming out for a drink, Duchess?"

"I think I'll stay here." She returned his smile. "But thank you."

He gave her a wink. "Tell her I'll call her tomorrow, OK?"

In fact, it was just as well that she, as well as Kitty—and later Zal, who arrived around midnight—remained in the suite. For just as Emma was clearing away the dishes from room-service coffee and rolls the following morning in the rainy dark before sun-up, a knock sounded on the door.

The three looked at one another, startled. Buttercreme darted for the safety of the bedroom, and the two male Pekes sat up to attention, ears cocked.

"Frank?" surmised Kitty—who, despite the earliness of the

hour and the fact that she would be made-up for the camera the moment she stepped on the train, was fully painted for the journey from the hotel to Penn Station. She glanced at the rain-streaked windows. "You think shooting's canceled for the day?"

"Frank would have phoned." Zal slipped into his coat to give the impression that he'd just stopped by to escort the ladies downstairs.

Emma crossed to the door to confront a tallish, unshaven man in a rain-spattered trench coat and a decrepit fedora. He held up a wallet containing a badge and a card that identified him as Detective Second Grade Joseph Smith, of the New York City Police Department. "This where I could find Camille de la Rose?"

"I am Camille de la Rose." Kitty stepped forward, speaking in the smoky accents she usually reserved for the Press. "This is my sister-in-law, Mrs. Blackstone."

He bobbed the rain-speckled fedora and half bowed. "If you ladies don't mind, I have a couple of questions for you."

Emma glanced at the elegant clock with which the Plaza had furnished the suite. "Zal, could you please telephone Mr. Pugh?" *Oh, dear, what kind of trouble has Shakespeare Malone involved Kitty in?* "Tell him we may miss the train and will take the next one—"

"He knows you'll be late, Ma'am," said Smith. "I'd just like to know what time Miss de la Rose came in last night."

"Ten o'clock." Emma glanced at Kitty. "She was sound asleep by ten fifteen, and I was here with her"—her eyes went to Zal, who nodded slightly—"all night."

"I was here from midnight on," said Zal. He held out his hand to the detective. "Zal Rokatansky. I'm one of the cameramen for Foremost Productions."

"Pleased to meet you." Smith had the dry, flat baritone of a man who has trodden entirely too many city streets and asked entirely too many questions in his life. "I take it all of you knew Darlene Golden?"

Emma said, "*Knew?*"

NINE

The first headlines were on the street before the Plaza Hotel kitchens delivered coffee to the meeting assembled in Suite 1506.

MOVIE STAR MURDERED
DEATH IN THE PALACE
SCREEN GODDESS FOUND SLAIN
MURDER ON BROADWAY

The body of Darlene Golden had been discovered at twelve fifteen that morning, Tuesday, December sixteenth, 1924, in the backstage area of the Palace vaudeville theater at 1564 Broadway. The cleaners had departed about an hour previously, following the evening performance. The night watchman had been in the outer of the theater's two marble-paved lobbies when he'd heard three shots; he had searched the auditorium briefly before going backstage. The backstage door, leading to a small yard and a private alley, was closed but not locked. Miss Golden had been shot once in the back and twice through the head.

"Sorry for kickin' down your doors first thing in the morning." Detective Smith, notebook in hand, surveyed the "Talent" assembled in the parlor of a vacant suite on the fifteenth floor that the Plaza's management had placed at the disposal of the police. "But the Captain figured if we tackled you while you were all in the same place, instead of chasing you the hell out to Long Island and screwing up your filming, it would be easier all around."

Frank Pugh, in a blue plush chair beside the window, didn't look as if he thought so. He sat, chewing on his cigar and glancing around him, first at the telephone, then at the door, then back to Detective Smith, like a man who expected . . . *What*? When Emma, Kitty, and Zal entered the suite, Kitty had hastened towards him with arms held out and tears in her eyes, which had not been there during the conversation with Detective Smith in her own suite. One of the two uniformed policemen in the parlor had intervened.

"We're asking that none of the witnesses confer before we've had a chance to question everyone, Miss."

Kitty had clasped her hands to her bosom and directed a heart-rending look at Frank, who only bit his nails and glowered at the cop. Emma noted that the studio head's shoes and the bottom foot and a half of his trouser legs were damp, as if he'd been outside in the drizzle that had begun shortly after four. Kitty whispered despairingly, "Oh, Frank!" and allowed Zal to guide her to one of the suite's two sofas, like Iphigenia going to the sacrificial altar at Aulis.

"We're just trying to establish some preliminary facts," Smith continued, his tone of voice echoing the five thousand times he had explained procedure to panicky witnesses over the years. "So we would appreciate it if everyone kept to themselves, until we've talked to everybody."

Pugh removed the cigar and cleared his throat loudly, his glare sweeping the room. *You say one goddam word about me and Darlene, and I'll can the lot of you.*

"The hotel's sending up coffee and donuts," the Detective added, and consulted his notebook again. "Miss de la Rose?"

When the coffee arrived, Zal fetched cups for himself, Emma, and Margaret Mackenzie. "Nonsense," declared the Scotswoman, and went to the telephone. To the policeman who looked as if he were about to protest, "If we are not here as prisoners, young man, we are here as your guests, and coffee at this hour does not agree with my constitution." She picked up the instrument, dialed the hotel operator, and said, "Please send up a large pot of India tea—Do you prefer India or China, Mrs. Blackstone?—India tea, to Suite 1506, right away. Preferably Assam. Yes, ask your chef what that is . . . Lemon or milk, dear?—I quite agree, lemon is not something I can face at this hour . . . Please send a pitcher of milk with that."

She hung up. "Heaven only knows what their 'donuts' will be like."

"This is the Plaza," pointed out Emma. "They're probably quite good."

"A 'quite good' dog biscuit," replied Mrs. Mackenzie, "is still unfit for human consumption. Oh, be quiet, young man; we're not comparing evidence." She returned to her place on the sofa and withdrew a pack of cards from her handbag.

Silence reigned then, save for the dry rustle of shuffle and deal. When the hotel waiter arrived with the tea ("Pah! Pure Lipton's!"), Emma tipped him well. Dealing with Mrs. Mackenzie, he probably needed it. Mr. Pugh, she noticed, in between scowling at one or another of the actors who had been in the parlor car of the Long Island railway yesterday evening, fidgeted in his chair, gnawing his cigar to wet mush and continuing to glance at the telephone.

He's scared, she thought.

As well he might be, given the number of people who might mention his quarrel with the murdered actress—

Darlene.

To her own astonishment, Emma felt her eyes burn with tears.

Memories of the angelic beauty included off-hand remarks about "family parasites" and "feathering her nest," and on two occasions, the blonde heroine of *Temptress of Babylon* and *Girl Without Fear* had employed private detectives to prove Kitty's unfaithfulness to Pugh. (These efforts had cost Kitty nearly seventeen hundred dollars in counter-bribes.)

And yet she felt grief.

She didn't ask herself why. Petty heckling of that sort merited a hair-pulling, not a bullet through the head.

Not being dead.

All she'd wanted was what Kitty wanted: money, more close-ups, the choicest roles, a powerful protector.

And who could blame her?

Dead was forever.

Stay away from it. Stay away from him . . .

Why the Palace Theater?

And where did Mr. Pugh go after dropping Kitty off at the unwontedly early hour of ten p.m.?

"Mrs. Blackstone?"

She carried her teacup with her to the suite's bedroom, passing Kitty in the doorway. Smith said, "Not a word to anyone, Miss de la Rose," and Kitty—who had been preparing a thousand-watt expression of purest martyrdom for Mr. Pugh—gave the Detective a glare that would have taken the veneer off a mahogany table. She stalked to the chesterfield that Emma had just vacated and sat down with a flounce.

"Anybody got any gin?"

Mrs. Mackenzie opened her handbag. "This was a gift to me," she informed the armies of the Law, "from my poor husband in 1918." She held out a silver flask.

Detective Smith closed the door. He had taken Mrs. Mackenzie's measure and clearly knew all about picking one's battles.

Emma shook her head. "I understand that in America these days, gin and donuts constitute breakfast in the best circles."

A slow smile quirked the corners of the big man's mouth. "Only thing I ever ate until Prohibition went through. Are you the Mrs. Emma Blackstone they call the Duchess at Foremost Productions?"

"I am."

"You a real duchess?"

"The only one that I've ever actually met," said Emma, "makes me glad that I'm not." She seated herself in one of the bedroom chairs. "I assume I am called that because I drink tea." Smith grinned again and flipped to a new page in his notebook.

"I'll start out by saying that we already know your boss Mr. Pugh had a shouting match with Miss Golden on the train back from Long Island yesterday. We're just filling in details here."

Emma wondered if he had already spoken to Mila Haley, or to either of the Broadway actors who'd been in the car the previous afternoon. *At five o'clock in the morning?* If she recalled correctly, Princess Laura and Mrs. Mackenzie's stand-in had been in the car also . . .

"In fact," she said, "Mr. Pugh is not my boss, except when

I 'doctor' scenarios for films. I work for Miss de la Rose, who was my late husband's sister. I look after her checkbook and her dogs, and run errands for her on the set."

And rein her in from temporarily marrying drunken millionaires?

She thought back on the events of the previous day, wondering again who else the police had already interviewed.

"As I understand it, Miss Golden has worked for Mr. Pugh at Foremost Productions in Hollywood since he took over the studio in 1917. This past summer, Mr. Neil Bandog—the financial representative of a chain of theaters that distributes most of Foremost's output—became acquainted with Miss Golden and insisted that she star in the Foremost production of the film adaptation of the novel *Shining Bright.*"

"How'd Pugh take that?"

"I cannot, of course, speak of that from my own knowledge," she replied. "In my opinion, he encouraged the . . . friendship"—she stopped herself from saying *liaison*, but saw the word glint in the Detective's eyes—"and as far as I could tell, it did not affect his . . . friendship . . . with Miss de la Rose."

She took another breath, sorting out events as if tidying up a hand of cards.

"Just before leaving Los Angeles for New York, Miss de la Rose received, in the mail, a proposal of marriage from a millionaire named Clark Dexter . . ."

"Oh, God." Smith made another note. Emma wondered if one of Floppy's previous prospects had been spooked enough to mention the matter to the police . . . or if the dry distaste in the detective's tired eyes had something to do with whatever it was Ince had known. When she hesitated, he only sighed. "Go ahead."

She did, describing the subsequent proposal to Darlene, and from there going on to detail everything she could remember of the overheard conversation on the Long Island Railway the previous day. Smith's pencil scratched over page after page of his notebook—she wondered what kind of information he'd gotten from Kitty.

"I say this," she concluded, "because when Kitty—Miss de

la Rose—spoke of her letter to her friend, the director Tom Ince, before we left Hollywood—"

His head came up sharply at the name.

"—Mr. Ince told her, in no uncertain terms, to stay away from the proposal. He said, 'I'm not kidding,' or words to that effect. 'Stay away from him.' He was called away then but said he would call her—presumably to explain—when he came back from his birthday trip on Mr. Hearst's yacht."

"Yeah," said Smith drily. "I know all about the trip on Mr. Hearst's yacht—as much as anybody knows."

"I say this to put what went on between Miss Golden and Mr. Pugh in context. I doubt anyone murdered the poor man to protect some dark secret, but clearly he knew something about Clark Dexter's affairs that made him feel that a warning was in order. After the argument yesterday, Mr. Pugh and Miss de la Rose retreated to Miss de la Rose's private parlor compartment, and Miss Golden remained in her own private parlor compartment until we reached New York. Mr. Pugh had a car waiting at the station for himself and Miss de la Rose—she told me this morning that they had dinner at the Lambs Club—"

Smith nodded, as if that agreed with Kitty's story.

"—and Miss de la Rose returned to her suite at the Plaza at about ten. From the station, I had returned there already with her dogs. I saw to their dinner at the hotel's dog-feeding rooms, and sent for a sandwich from room service for myself. About half an hour after Miss de la Rose came in, her friend Mr. Chico Marx—I believe his actual name is Leonard—arrived, but Miss de la Rose was sound asleep, and we did not wake her. After he left, my . . . friend . . ." She felt her cheeks heat with a blush.

"Mr. Rokatansky was there with you all night?" By his tone, he could have been asking if the room-service sandwich had been made with white or brown bread. Emma didn't know whether to feel comforted or insulted.

She managed to say, "Yes," in a level voice. "Mr. Rokatansky and the rest of the camera crew had remained behind at Versailles on Long Island to look at the footage that had been shot on Sunday. But he can testify that Miss de la Rose was in bed and asleep when he got there at midnight, because we looked in on her then."

Smith nodded and checked through his notes. "Miss de la Rose own a gun?"

Emma reminded herself that this was the sort of question a policeman had to ask, and replied, "Yes. A Colt Police revolver with a four-inch barrel. I believe it's a thirty-two. It's in the drawer of her room here, if you'd like to have a look at it."

He only nodded again and made a note so short that Emma guessed Kitty had admitted possessing the firearm and had made the same offer.

"You know if Pugh has a gun?"

"No," she said, "I don't."

"You know where Pugh might have gone after he brought Miss de la Rose here?"

"I assume he returned to his own room here," said Emma, feeling as if the big man's damp shoes and trouser legs were projected in close-up, like the footage of the "dailies," on the wall beside her head. "But I honestly have no idea."

"Thank you, Mrs. Blackstone." Smith rose and moved toward the door. Then he paused, turned back, and asked, "You wouldn't happen to know how I could get in touch with Miss Golden's stand-in, would you? A Miss Haley?"

Through Emma's mind flashed Frank's words: *I bet she can act as well as you can . . .* And the combination of rage and determination on the blonde chorine's face.

Darlene, she assumed, had threatened to quit.

And what possibilities did that *trigger in Mila Haley's mind?*

"I don't," she said. "I know she worked in the choruses of several of the big reviews, so Mr. Ziegfeld's offices, or George White's, should probably know how to get hold of her agent."

She considered for a moment mentioning Mila Haley's friendship with Sugar-Pie, Monette, and Ginger on the train, but decided that discretion was called for. She had no idea how any of that information might be used—nor of what sorts of things those three young ladies might themselves be trying to keep from police or newspapermen.

Smith nodded—Emma guessed that he knew already to ask

Mila's agent and had merely been trying to save himself another round of telephone calls—and opened the door for her. One of the police officers signed to him as he did so, and picked up a couple of notes from beside the parlor's telephone. The detective crossed the room and read the notes without change of expression.

Then he turned to face the assembled Hollywood "Talent" and asked, "Any of you folks know how to get in touch with Miss Mila Haley? She ain't at her apartment, and I guess she didn't come in last night."

TEN

At the request of the police—reiterated by Frank Pugh—neither the "Talent" nor the small Hollywood contingent of camera, wardrobe, and make-up personnel went far from their quarters that day. Even before Detective Smith finished questioning everybody, Neil Bandog appeared, with a smooth-faced, white-haired New York lawyer at his side. This Mr. Morris accompanied both Bandog and Pugh into what Kitty and Zal referred to as "the back room"—the bedroom of Suite 1506, which the Plaza had rather grudgingly permitted the police to use for their interviews.

When the forces of the law had departed, the Pugh, Bandog, and Morris triumvirate cautioned those present not to speak to "anyone" about either the investigation or the progress of filming, and encouraged everyone to order room service rather than patronizing any of the Plaza's four public restaurants. Since neither Pugh nor Bandog offered to pay for this service, however—and because pretty much everyone was sick of being cooped up in Suite 1506—Zal, Kitty, and Emma followed most of their colleagues downstairs, to discover a lobby filled with journalists from every newspaper and film magazine in New York.

The management of the Plaza, after a brief conference with Mr. Bandog, graciously offered the hotel's Fifty-Eighth Street Restaurant—usually reserved for the hotel's long-term or permanent residents—to the Foremostians, and stationed hotel detectives in the lobby to repel unauthorized invaders. Elevator operators were instructed to demand room keys before giving anyone service.

Further headlines screamed from the lobby's newsstands:

FILM STAR SHOT
MYSTERY SUSPECT SOUGHT

"How about '*New York World* Reporter Slugged'?" Zal asked a representative of that publication, as he thrust past him into the oak-paneled dining sanctuary.

Halfway through some excellent sandwiches, Gordy Graves, fair-haired and flustered, appeared like a waiter beside the table with the news that Mr. Pugh wanted to see all three of them in his own suite, Suite 1403. Zal seemed on the verge of signaling the nearest house dick to eject the line producer for pestering a diner, so Emma said in her most ladylike voice, "Please tell Mr. Pugh we'll be right up, as soon as we're finished here."

"And if you wait for us," added Kitty sweetly, since Graves looked as though he was going to, "we'll just sit right here and won't finish until you're gone." She removed the napkin from her lap, laid it beside her plate, and folded her hands on it.

Graves left and was immediately ambushed by reporters in the corridor.

"Well, keep looking," Pugh growled into the telephone receiver as Emma and her friends came into the smoke-fogged parlor of Suite 1403 some forty-five minutes later. "Ask Marx. He jumped into it quick enough when Darlene tried to get her fired. And send somebody out to Long Island. She may be shacked up someplace out there. You know anything about that Haley bint?" he added, as he slammed the receiver onto its hook and turned to Emma.

"Only that she was in the Ziegfeld Follies last year, and in a revue at—I believe it's called Albee's?—this past spring. And that she was on the train from Long Island yesterday evening."

Pugh glared at her for a moment as if he suspected some double meaning about his quarrel with Darlene, but Emma, as usual when dealing with the studio chief, did her best to look purely informational.

"Don't know anything about any girl buddy she mentioned? These chorus bimbos all know each other."

Emma shook her head, and Pugh grunted, and nearly jumped out of his skin when the telephone rang again. He grabbed it as if it were a firehose at a three-alarm blaze, and for a moment she saw the angry red of his cheeks blench. "Yowp?" Then the tension relaxed from his shoulders, and he said, "God damn it," and settled himself to listen.

The white-haired Mr. Morris, evidently feeling that social amenities were in order, brought Emma a chair and asked if she would care for a cup of tea. She thanked him and asked, "Miss Golden tried to have Miss Haley fired?"

"That was most unfortunate." The lawyer sighed and glanced to the other side of the room where Neil Bandog, haggard and shaken himself, was leaning close to Pugh as if to listen to what the party on the other end of the line was saying. "I regret to say that yesterday was not the first time that Mr. Pugh spoke—in jest, I gather, on that occasion—of replacing Miss Golden with Miss Haley, joking that the audience would not be able to tell the difference. This led to a confrontation at the El Fey Club on the night of the eleventh—this past Thursday—when Miss Golden encountered Miss Haley and high words were exchanged."

He glanced again at Bandog, now deep in whispered conversation with Pugh and whoever was on the other end of the telephone line. "Miss Golden"—he lowered his own voice—"who was accompanied by Mr. Bandog, demanded that he tell Mr. Pugh to fire Miss Haley. I believe the exact phrase—according to one witness at the El Fey—was 'uppity' . . . um . . . lady. Miss Haley's companion, a popular vaudeville actor named Herbert Marx—"

"Zeppo?" asked Emma, startled. *So that must have been Miss Haley we saw with Zeppo that night, not Miss Golden . . .*

Morris's lips pinched. "I fear I do not patronize the vaudeville and could not tell one Marx from another."

A valid point, reflected Emma. At first glance, the two younger Marxes, though ten years apart in age, would have been virtually doubles save for Groucho's glasses. In fact, without Harpo's curly red wig (and calmer demeanor off-stage), the two older brothers were nearly identical as well. According to Kitty, there was a fifth brother somewhere, who sold raincoats.

"Mr. Marx sprang to Miss Haley's defense, and a very vulgar scene was only averted by the appearance of Miss Guinan—the hostess, you know"—distaste for Miss Guinan oozed like an oil leak from his very pores—"who reminded Mr. Bandog that reporters also frequented her establishment and that both Miss Golden and Mr. Marx were well-enough known by sight to attract adverse publicity.

"Miss Guinan prevailed upon Marx and Haley to leave, but—"

"The problem is"—Frank Pugh's deep, rough voice cut across the lawyer's discreet murmur—"I'm guessing somebody tipped Haley off that Darlene was murdered. So everybody who said 'Boo' to her since she got to town is automatically John Wilkes Booth and Lucky Luciano rolled into one. But we've got a picture to finish."

The telephone rang again, and Pugh spun as if at a gunshot.

"Certainly not," declared Bandog into the receiver. "We will hold a meeting for the press tomorrow if the police permit it, and any attempt to question any of our people before that time . . ."

With a perfectly steady hand, Pugh took his cigar case from his pocket, bit the end off a Vilar y Vilar, and lit up. Only the faintest flare of Mr. Morris's nostrils indicated his opinion of tobacco smoke.

"We've shot eighty thousand feet of film," Pugh went on in a lower voice. "That's just about all the exteriors. And we've laid out ten grand so far to rent Versailles, and that's not even counting the horses, carriages, the generator to keep everybody from freezing to death in that place, on top of two hundred thou for the book. It's rained twice, and it'll rain more. *And*"—his glance shot sidelong to Bandog, still arguing with a reporter on the phone and at the same time reading six notes the porter had handed to him—"certain investors are of the opinion that Darlene's footage should stay in the picture."

Emma recalled Zal's words on the number of close-ups demanded by Darlene—and Bandog—of Darlene's emotional reactions: to her first sight of Ken Elmore's manly chest, to her grief at being told by Marsh Sloane that under no circumstances would she be permitted to marry a mere Captain of Cavalry, manly chest or not, and of her horror at being pursued through the woods by bandits in the pay of the Evil Comtesse de Palogneux—all in loving, interminable detail. Emma could sympathize with the studio chief's attitude.

"What I want you to do—what I *need* you to do, Duchess"—the studio chief poked at her with two chubby fingers and his cigar—"is go through and rewrite the rest of the exteriors with as little footage of Summer What's-Her-Name in them as possible. If we can track down Haley in the next couple of days, and pay off the cops so they don't scare her into blowing town before we wrap—"

"Pay off the—?" Emma recoiled in shock. "Surely they don't think—?"

She ain't at her apartment, Smith had said. *And I guess she didn't come in last night.*

And indeed, if Darlene had tried to get her double fired . . .

"How the hell do I know what cops think?" The big man's face flushed dangerously again. "All I know is, they're sure not going to arrest a kid worth eight hundred million clams. I don't even know if Haley can act or not. But we need to get as much filmed as we can before the weather changes. I'm counting on you, Duchess. You gotta help me save this picture."

He flinched again at the jangle of the telephone. Morris went to answer it. "No, the police have no leads yet . . . No, I'm not at liberty to say. Everyone at Foremost is shocked and horrified . . . All the major scenes of her final picture, based on the best-selling novel *Shining Bright*, have already been filmed . . ." (A blatant lie.) "Yes, a terrible tragedy. I understand the work she did in *Shining Bright* is superb, her best . . . No, I have no knowledge of that . . ."

Pugh, listening also, didn't shudder, but again his pendulous cheeks went pale as swiftly as they'd crimsoned.

And again Emma thought, *He's afraid.*

The cold green eyes returned to her, under the black shelf of his brow. "Can you do it? Can you get us something we can shoot tomorrow, and for the next couple of days? I'll get on the horn to Blakeney, get him down here tonight to talk to you . . ."

"Coffee." Gordy Graves came in from the hall, pushing a

room-service cart. "The donuts are pretty good. The hotel didn't have any Tootsie Rolls, Mr. Pugh, but they said they'd get you some . . . Anybody remember to call Darlene's parents?"

Nobody had.

There was a "General Assembly" the following morning. Extra chairs crowded the parlor of Suite 1403, but space had been left at one end of the big room, near the piano, which Mr. Pugh, flanked by Messrs Bandog and Morris, used as a sort of podium. Detective Smith was present also, slouched in a corner, smoking Lucky Strikes and making notes.

A sleepless and harassed Frank Pugh announced to actors, extras, and crew members that filming at Versailles would resume the next day—Thursday, December eighteenth. "And I expect everybody to be on that six-fifteen train out to Long Island ready to put in a full day's work the minute it's light enough to shoot. We've lost two days already. Scenes two-fifteen to two forty-seven, three-seventy to four hundred, and nine hundred to nine-fifty have been rewritten to shoot around Darlene's absence."

No mention, reflected Emma resignedly, *of who stayed up until four o'clock this morning roughing in the outlines of those scenes* . . . Zal laid his hand over hers.

Calling what she had done so far "rewritten" was taking an optimistic view of her progress, to say the least. She would, she knew, be working far into the night again, while Zal, Chip, and two of the MBQ editors sorted through those endless close-ups and discarded takes to find usable footage.

Pugh glared out over the assembled cast and crew: Gordy Graves and Neil Bandog's secretary had spent most of the evening telephoning the New York actors at their apartments, scattered from Greenwich Village to Washington Heights and on across the river into Brooklyn. "And if any of you hears anything of how we can get in touch with Mila Haley, come to me, or to Mr. Morris—"

He paused, and, in his corner at the back of the room, Detective Joe Smith only sat with his long hands folded over his middle, eyes half shut.

"If you hear from her, tell her that we really need to talk to her."

"Yeah," murmured Zal. "Like *that's* going to happen."

The previous evening, while Emma and George Blakeney had worked over scenes 215–247, 370–400, et al., Kitty had gone out on the town with Mr. Pugh in the admittedly vain hope of encountering Mila Haley in a speakeasy or club. ("As if anybody with half a brain would be out drinking if the bulls were after them," had said Kitty. "Oh, except Bottles Findlay," she had added, naming one of her ex-boyfriends. "Or Blinky Livingston." She recalled another. "Or . . ." She counted several more on her fingers.) Zal had remained loyally in the suite, rubbing Emma's shoulders, feeding the dogs, and ordering coffee, tea, and sandwiches from room service.

Most of the scenes in question had been simply outlined, and notes made with the director's advice, so after the General Assembly and another hasty lunch at the Fifty-Eighth Street Restaurant, Emma returned to the suite to put the first half-dozen into a form which could be filmed on the following day. She was thus engaged—Kitty had retreated to her bedroom for a nap, preparatory to another evening trawling nightspots with Mr. Pugh—when the front desk phoned with the news that a Mr. Karl Marx was there to see Miss de la Rose.

"What'd old Pugh have to say?" asked Chico, dropping onto the sofa. He, too, looked as if he'd spent a sleepless night, though, in his case, Emma guessed it had more to do with high-stakes pinochle than a murdered woman or a missing stand-in. Chang Ming rushed from the bedroom to roll adoringly on his back at their guest's feet. "Cops have any theories yet?"

Emma shook her head. "Filming starts again tomorrow at Versailles. After giving us all a lecture about being on the train on time, Mr. Pugh kept back all the female extras who were approximately Miss Golden's height and build, and looked them over like a Sultan auditioning to fill vacancies in the harem. None of them could pass for Miss Golden in a close-up—"

Her voice caught, when it returned to her, again, as it had

a dozen times during the night, that she was talking about a young woman who was dead. A very beautiful young woman whose vanity, spite, and ambition had been annoying, but who was *dead.* A woman she had known and talked to.

Like the young men Emma had driven from the Southampton wharves to the hospitals of Oxford. Someone who would never laugh again. Never cry, never make love . . .

A young woman who had been murdered. Shot in the head, lying in a messy splatter of blood among the flies and ropes and sandbags of a theater's backstage . . .

"What was she *doing* backstage at the Palace Theater anyway?" she asked. "At midnight . . . How did she even get into the building?"

"Oh, that's easy." Chico waved the difficulty aside. "The whole basement of that side of the Palace is dressing rooms. There's a private alley leading off Seventh Avenue. Folks who maybe want a little nookie with somebody they're not supposed to be seeing—" He spread his hands innocently. *Not* me, *of course, I wouldn't have any knowledge of that . . .*

"Hot-sheet hotels on the Bowery are a dollar-fifty a room, with cockroaches thrown in. Plus whatever it costs to bribe the house dick. Half the girls who work the chorus get keys made"—he produced a key from his pocket—"in case lover-boy doesn't want to deal with the management."

Or with a more formidable boyfriend? The harsh face of Angel-Eyes Taralla flashed across Emma's mind, and the look in his eyes as they'd followed Darlene across the crowd at the El Fey.

Like a little arrow, Black Jasmine darted out of Kitty's bedroom and made straight for Chico, plumed tail a sable banner of excitement. "Hey, boychik, wadda ya know?" Chico scruffed the tiny dog's mane. But he was rising as he did so, for Kitty had entered hard on her celestial guardian's heels. Kitty was in one of her most spectacular négligées, but fully (and freshly) made-up. Emma often marveled at how she did it.

There was a brief pause in the conversation while Kitty and Chico embraced as if rehearsing for Anna Karenina's meeting with Count Vronsky. After what seemed like the length of a honeymoon, Kitty asked, "What's up?" and glanced at the clock. "Don't you have a matinee—?"

"Just got out," said Chico. "My brothers'll kill me if they knew I came this far uptown between shows. I just heard, from one of the girls in the chorus, Angel-Eyes Taralla's got four witnesses say they was with him all night at a floating crap game in Harlem, Monday night. He wasn't. I lost thirteen hundred dollars in that game, and Taralla was noplace around. But the cops gotta accept the story. Two of these guys are stiffs from Muncie, big losers. I don't know if Angel-Eyes paid off their markers or threatened to tell their wives, but they're swearing now he was there. And your friend Bandog's wife and the accountant at his offices—and the accountant's wife, too—are all swearing they were having dinner together that night in Queens and playing parcheesi into the small hours."

"Midnight on a work night?"

"Hey." Chico spread his hands again. "Life is short. Who am I to question what happens when the dice are hot? All I know is, it's a matter of time before your boss"—he nodded at Emma and Kitty—"puts the word around that somebody better step up and say they was with him Monday night or the lot of you is gonna get fired. You ever find out where he was Monday night, after he left you here?"

Kitty and Emma looked at one another, then shook their heads. "But he was outdoors at some point," said Emma quietly. "It rained that night. Zal . . ." She hesitated, wondering in spite of herself why she felt shy of admitting that Zal had spent that night in her bed . . . Admitting it to Chico Marx, of all people! (*Mother would faint* . . .) "Zal got up at about four, to make coffee, because we were all expecting to have to catch the six-fifteen train. It was raining then. When Mr. Pugh came into that first meeting at . . . whatever it was—just after six, I think . . . his coat and his trouser legs were damp."

"He said at dinner he had to put a call through to Al Spiegelmann in Los Angeles," provided Kitty. Spiegelmann was the lawyer at Foremost Productions. "I figured he would do that from his suite."

"Well, he didn't," said Chico. "I asked one of the housekeepers here. She says the cops asked her, too, and had a look through the place, Tuesday morning. She says the bed hadn't been slept in, and the toothbrush was dry. The razor, too, and he's got one of those beards where you have to shave most of your cheeks. No mud on the carpet. Like he'd never been there at all."

Emma and Kitty looked at one another again.

"All the way back after his fight with Darlene," Kitty said slowly, "he kept grousing about her betraying him. That he'd told her to string Bandog along, keep him putting money into the picture. But he was mad at her already, 'cause I guess Bandog was telling him—Frank—how to run the studio to make Darlene a bigger star. And I guess Darlene hit him up for another picture here in New York, like she thought she deserved to star in big-deal stuff like Marion Davies is getting from Hearst. Stuff that gets shot in England or France, or that gets rose scent blown into the theater at every showing with electric fans, for cryin' out loud . . ."

"But that wouldn't be enough for him to *kill* her over," Emma protested.

Kitty only looked at her. After a time, she sank down onto the couch, lifted Black Jasmine onto her lap, and stroked the little dog's ears without looking either at him or at the man beside her. "Frank gets mad," she said at last.

Mr. Pugh's temper was notorious throughout Foremost Productions. But still Emma stared at her, speechless.

"And I don't know what else she said to him," Kitty continued, her small voice almost like a scared child's. "I know he was mad. I don't . . . I don't *think* he did it." She raised her eyes for a moment, and added, "I think he *could have*."

"Where would *he* get a key to get into the Palace?" asked Chico practically. "Kill her slapping her around, maybe, in the middle of a fight, if he was drunk. She falls, she hits her head . . . That kind of kill. That could happen to pretty much anybody, I hate to say it. That happens all the time. But set up to meet someplace where he can wait for her with a gun? That kind of kill? And in the Palace Theater for Chrissake?"

Kitty lifted her head at that and seemed to relax. It occurred to Emma that Kitty—who, in the competition for Mr. Pugh's lucrative attentions, had suffered more of Darlene's malice than she herself had—had been very quiet about the murder.

"Dexter—" began Emma.

"Was at the Mardi Gras Club in Harlem," said Chico. "He was at midnight, anyway. Chasing one of the girls around and getting thrown out trying to get backstage. Everybody in the place saw him. It's about sixty blocks down to the Palace, even if he didn't get mugged wandering around looking for a cab."

"Oh," said Emma doubtfully. "Do you know where Darlene went, Kitty, after she got off the train Monday evening?"

Kitty thought about it. "I know she must have got into a cab," she said after a moment. "Bandog is pretty careful about sending a car for her, since his wife lives in town—though he has the most *divine* chauffeur. He can . . ."

"Whether he did or whether he didn't," cut in Chico, "you know Pugh's gonna line up witnesses, just like Taralla and Bandog did, swearing they was with him. The one who can't line up witnesses is my brother. Zeppo."

The two women looked at him. *A confrontation at the El Fey Club*, Mr. Morris had said. *Mr. Marx sprang to Miss Haley's defense.*

Hesitantly, Emma began, "Surely your brother—"

"Oh, hell—" Chico slashed the air with his hand. "Zepp wouldn't hurt a girl. It ain't like Mila was going out with him. That night last week when he yelled at Darlene, he'd gone to the El Fey 'cause he's seeing one of the girls in the chorus. Mila was there while the show was on, so he goes to sit with her. They been friends for years. He'd had a couple drinks, and it pissed him off to hear Miss Screen Goddess tryin' to get her fired. But you know cops." He took a second look at Emma and added, with a seriousness strange to him, "Or maybe you don't, Duchess. But *I* know cops. They know they gotta arrest *some*body."

"And where *was* your brother Monday night?"

"That's just it," said Chico. "He won't say. The cops went over him pretty good, too. See, back when we lived in Chicago,

Zeppo hung around with some pretty shady characters and owed money to half the gangsters in town. So the bull in charge, that Detective Smith, he's looking at him close. I guess he got it from Zepp's regular girlfriend that Zepp wasn't with her Monday night—and it's not like Zepp can't smell trouble. I take oath he didn't do it." He raised his right hand as if doing so. "Why would he? But cops don't think that way. Thing is, Zepp *knows* all this. And he still won't say where he was."

Kitty said quietly, "Well, shit."

ELEVEN

For the next week or so, the armies of Napoleon and Wellington met in battle.

Emma's later recollections of Christmas week, 1924, were a kaleidoscope of "cross-cutting" (as Zal termed it) of the twentieth century and the nineteenth, the blood and confusion of the Allied army camp mingling with ostrich plumes, sequins, and glitter, and with the dank darkness of the unfinished North Shore chateau.

Increasingly nervous about the weather ("That's why the actual battle was fought in June, Mr. Pugh . . ."), Pugh turned the Waterloo sequence over to Gordy Graves and a half-dozen New York Paramount cameramen—veterans who had served under Griffith and DeMille on battlefields from Jericho to Flanders—while the scenes of Miss Fairisle's heroic labors in the infirmary tents on the Brussels road were left to the more nuanced skills of Mr. Blakeney. There was, Emma pointed out to both Mr. Pugh and Mr. Kingsley, only so much one could do with the efforts of a heroine who could only appear on-screen from the back.

With poignant memories of lost love—and eighty thousand feet of shot film in the can—Neil Bandog would not hear of re-casting and re-shooting *Shining Bright*. He gave orders for Kitty and Mr. Pugh to haunt the nightclubs and speakeasies of Broadway and Harlem in the hopes of catching a glimpse of the fugitive Mila Haley and luring her back to work (cost what it might in bribes), and for Emma to rewrite all sequences that advanced the plot without actually showing Summer Fairisle on-screen. Most of the thousands of feet of close-ups of Miss Golden's every expression of grief, rapture, or terror included court hairstyles and costumes inappropriate for an army camp on the battlelines twenty-odd years after the Reign of Terror and the fall of the Bourbon regime. The young woman who most closely resembled Darlene Golden from the back—a slim, cheerful extra named Betty Cheviot—unfortunately did not look a thing like her when seen from the front.

Emma did what she could. But clear images remained in her mind for years of the Duke of Wellington, mounted on his famous steed Copenhagen (who for a wonder was actually portrayed by a chestnut horse with one white foot), gravely consuming a commissary hotdog, a towel wrapped around his neck to protect the blood splatters and powder stains on his uniform from stray mustard. Of Napoleon smoking a cigarette and reading *Variety* under a bare tree. After seeing *I'll Say She Is*, Emma kept wondering why the French Emperor did not look like Groucho Marx.

At least it did not rain. ("Betcha Pugh's been buying virgins off the boat at Ellis Island and sacrificing one a day to the rain gods," surmised Zal. "How would you list that on your income tax?" inquired Kitty. "Business expenses," said Zal.)

However, whether or not Mr. Blair was on the set, it was now simply too cold to retreat to the tangle of rooms below the stables to avoid Mr. Kingsley. On the first day back at the chateau, Emma tried, and found, in addition to two more secret entrances, another evil-smelling well and a padlocked door with a large blue X chalked on it, and a stack of issues of the *Police Gazette* and "eugenics" and "health culture" magazines featuring naked women in positions that Emma did not consider at all healthful. But even with a pair of cut-up wool socks on her hands, the moist cold was brutal, and she resigned herself to taking her chances above ground for the duration of the Napoleonic Wars.

Then, too, in the darkness, her mind kept returning to the fact that a woman was dead. A woman whom she had known—ambitious, grasping, and obnoxious as she may have been.

Stay away from it, Tom Ince had said. *Stay away from him . . .*

But what was "it"?

And what did it have to do with a half-drunken young man consumed by old grief?

She emerged from the darkness via a small passageway that

opened into a beach cave, near where she and Becca had walked the dogs the week before. From there, she could hear the distant rattle of musket fire, in the open ground to the east of the chateau, and now and then Gordy Graves's distorted voice shouting through his megaphone. She guessed that was where Mr. Kingsley would be, waiting for a break in the fighting to point out to the director that the battlefield at Hougoumont did not resemble Long Island in the slightest and that they should be filming in June, not December. Thus, like the Three Wise Kings in the Bible, she "returned by another way" and took the long way back to the chateau where she had left the dogs.

George Blakeney, she knew, would be in the thick woods near the house, guiding Kitty through the last retakes and close-ups of her "Meeting with the Highwaymen" scene. She could hide herself—and maybe even get some work done—in the tents of the Allied camp, just out of sight on the other side of the stables . . .

And coming around a tangle of laurels, she saw Shakespeare Malone, gazing towards the little cluster of cameras around the gazebo with a pair of binoculars.

Automatically, she stepped back out of sight. He was turned three-quarters away from her but was unmistakable, though instead of his usual tailored cream-colored suit, he wore rough tweed trousers and a Norfolk jacket over a shaggy pullover. His head was bare, and the smooth, sandy hair and elegant cheekbones could belong to no one else.

When she peeked through the foliage again to make sure it was he, and not a mirage, he was gone.

"I can't imagine what he was doing there," said Emma, that evening, as she sipped Château d'Yquem from a bubble-fine glass—Mr. Crain was well known to the management of every eating place in town for his generosity. "And I can't imagine how he would have been connected with Miss Golden's murder, *if* he was . . . But it does occur to me that a man of Mr. Dexter's wealth could hire someone to do his dirty work for him. And in spite of Mr. Malone's lovely manners and sophistication, I have the impression that he would know—well—people who could be hired."

"He does." Old Mr. Crain's face darkened with concern. Emma recalled again that Timothy Crain, in his attempt to murder his father, had been proven to have worked through some of the New York gangsters—who often enough operated nightclubs that doubled as speakeasies.

She began to apologize for bringing the subject up, when Crain went on, "That's what Shakespeare Malone is, you know. And he's more dangerous because he doesn't look like a thug."

Emma was silent. Obedient to Messrs Pugh and Bandog, Kitty had canceled her dinner plans with Mr. Crain in favor of another tour of the nightclubs with Chico Marx. Curious, thought Emma, that Pugh would designate a substitute, particularly in the light of Chico's reputation with women. Pugh's excuse was that he—and Bandog, and the cameramen—had gone to MBQ Studios to comb through twenty thousand feet of close-ups looking for shots suitable to insert into the new scenes Emma was supposed to be writing, but according to Zal, this wasn't necessary. ("Hell, *I'll* take Kitty around the nightclubs while you go keep Crain busy!" he had offered, and kissed her.)

At length, now, she asked, "Would Malone be watching Kitty for Dexter? And . . . and *why*?"

"I don't know." Crain set aside his own wine glass as the waiter brought two cups of excellent coffee. "Versailles belongs to the Dexter family—it was built, you know, by Clark's uncle, Jefferson—"

"Jefferson *Blair*? That tiresome little man who's been pestering poor Mr. Blakeney about keeping the extras out of the chateau?"

"Jefferson Blair," agreed Crain. "His wife Violet is Clark's mother's younger sister."

"Good Heavens!" Was it Clark Dexter—playing there as a child—who made those blue chalked arrows, those uneven pink lines?

"Mr. Blair doesn't still live there, surely? The place is unfinished inside. He clearly doesn't want the film company there . . . Does he still own it?"

"Legally—technically—I think so, though it's part of the Dexter Trust." With grave care he tonged a cube of sugar from the table's silver bowl. "Old Griswold Dexter never liked his wife's sister or her husband, and regarded the whole idea of its construction with contempt. When Jefferson Blair went bankrupt in 1920, Griswold Dexter did nothing to help him. And, no, Blair never lived in the house."

"Zal said trying to finish the house destroyed him financially—"

"Well, not the house alone. Blair made some extremely poor investments and traded on his brother-in-law's wealth, and he had—well—expensive hobbies. Since Blair went bankrupt, he and his wife have lived at Abbottsford, the Dexter mansion—if you can call the place a mansion. It's a handsome old house, but in spite of additions and renovations, it's still basically a large farmhouse. Nothing compared to anything else along the North Shore. And for all their wealth, Rosemary Dexter lives there very . . . modestly. Griswold Dexter took over Versailles to keep it from being taken up for taxes; he and his wife have always treated Blair like a caretaker."

He frowned, as another thought crossed his mind.

"Griswold Dexter was a hard man," he went on after a moment. "A robber baron, they used to call them in the '90s. He was friends with people like the Morello Gang and Arnie Rothstein, who controlled crime in New York even before Prohibition made a joke of law enforcement. Of course, his wife Rosemary—who is a good friend of . . . of my own wife"—his voice halted a little on the words—"says that she never knew anything about the connection and always thought Mr. Rothstein was a very charming gentleman."

"The thing is," said Emma hesitantly, "that wasn't the first time I've seen gangsters out near the set. There were two men near there the day before Miss Golden was murdered, men I'd seen with Angel-Eyes Taralla. Bodyguards, or . . . well . . . thugs."

"In which case," surmised the old man, "Mr. Malone may have simply been checking on what *they* might have been doing. There is a very deadly rivalry between Malone and Taralla."

He shook his head and finished his coffee. Crain's chauffeur,

Mr. Hwang, would be waiting for them on Forty-Third Street in front of the restaurant, and there was no telling what the traffic would be like near Carnegie Hall. (Neither of them felt up to dealing with a modern opera about infanticide sung in Czech, which was the offering at the Met that evening.)

"But if that were so, wouldn't he have sent some of his own henchmen? He was watching the set. Watching Kitty."

"She is very watchable." He smiled as he helped her from her chair. "Would you like to meet them?"

"Meet them?" For a moment, Emma had a dizzy hallucination of being introduced to Bronco Burnett and Knuckles Gracciola.

"The Dexter family—or what is left of them. Clark's cousin Arabella—my wife's god-daughter—married very well, to an importer who owns controlling stock in railroads and oil. It's his birthday tomorrow, and there will be one of those appalling society parties at their mansion, Cypress Cove. I was planning to miss it—I understand there will be three dance bands and a young lady jumping out of a cake. But if you would like to have a look at the family, and possibly meet Clark as well, I would be pleased to escort you."

"If it won't . . ." She hesitated, not sure what one would even call it, when a man turned up at the house of his wife's god-daughter with the sister-in-law of his Hollywood mistress on his arm – much less know how to appropriately respond. "If it won't cause you awkwardness . . ."

His eyes twinkled. "My dear, Mrs. Crain considered Arabella Blair's marriage a shocking mésalliance and wouldn't dream of setting foot in their house. No one there will know who you are," he added kindly. "Half of them will be hangers-on who weren't invited anyway. And even if they knew your connection with Kitty, I doubt that anyone in that crowd would raise an eyebrow."

Kitty was refreshing her make-up when Emma let herself into Suite 1202 at eleven thirty; the profusion of pots and jars, of Pompeian face powder and Persian Blush, of tiny brushes, mascara, Mitsouko, and kohl, amply announced that there was another gentleman on his way. Emma shook her head. She had understood her sister-in-law's unflagging staying power in the days when Kitty had kept a vial of "pick-me-up" in her dresser drawer. But since she'd sworn off cocaine nearly a year before, Emma merely stood in awe of her energy.

"Darling, I'm glad you're here!" Kitty swiveled in her chair. "I was afraid I'd have to write all this in a note, and Shakespeare will be here any minute . . ."

"Did you know he was out on Long Island this morning?" asked Emma. "I caught a glimpse of him, watching you through binoculars in the woods. That seemed—"

Kitty looked startled for an instant, the mascara brush poised in her hand. Then she shrugged. "He could have been out scouting for a place to bring in a boat from Canada. They do, you know: the bootleggers. But there isn't a paved road for miles along the North Shore at that point . . ."

"He was looking in the direction of the set," said Emma. "Not out to sea."

"Well, he probably didn't want to come any closer for fear of meeting Frank." Kitty returned her attention to the mirror and the dark cake of mascara. "Or that nasty little fuss-pot Blair. I'll ask him about that. Darling, Frank asked me to ask you—can you go down to the Eighteenth Precinct station tomorrow morning? It's down on Forty-Seventh Street . . . Darlene's parents finally got in touch with Frank."

She finished the line of darkness below her right eye, turned again on the padded velvet make-up stool to regard Emma. "Well, their lawyer did, anyway. Darlene's father is a dentist in Fort Worth. The lawyer called, asking did Darlene leave a will? And would the rest of Darlene's salary from Foremost be paid to her, and was Foremost contractually obligated to pay the rest of the contract's salary? He'd like to see a copy of the contract. Frank was just about foaming at the mouth."

"I daresay." Emma did not ask whether the studio head's rage stemmed from fury over this parental callousness or the possibility that he'd have to pay out over a hundred thousand dollars from the remainder of Miss Golden's three-year agreement. She had her theories.

"Olivia—Darlene's maid, you know—cleared out her suite last night and all her things are in the second bedroom of Frank's suite, since he wouldn't pay the hotel to store them. But you know that cheap bastard Spitz"—this was Darlene's (née Dorcas) true name, unless, like Kitty, she'd had a few husbands since entering show business—"is going to want an inventory." (Olivia had been put on the train back to Los Angeles—second class—that morning. Emma marveled at Mr. Pugh's generosity, and wondered who had paid for the cab to the station.)

She took a deep breath and let it out. She'd contributed to the collection cameraman Chip Thaw had started, which had raised several hundred dollars from the Hollywood crew and most of the New York extras, to help the woman with her rent when she got home.

In a conversational tone, she said, "Well, I do hope they find that Miss Golden left all her earnings to Olivia."

"Fat chance. Doctor Spitz said go ahead and bury her here. The lawyer asked about storage fees in the hospital morgue and said he'd have to talk to Doctor Spitz if Frank wanted reimbursement. Frank said Spitz gave them a budget limit for the funeral, and I bet they negotiate about *that*. Dr. Spitz has a medical conference to go to Saturday, but he says he and Darlene's mom and brother will come out here after that. The mom and brother won't travel on Sundays, he said."

She stood up, shed the flamboyant kimono that had protected her black silk Premet frock—netted over with a fishnet of rhinestones—from stray molecules of powder, and readjusted the silk bandeau that held back her tempest of dark curls. "Since Frank doesn't have to see this shyster until tomorrow at four, he's taking me sailing in the morning on Jimmy Walker's yacht—"

Emma refrained from mentioning that their whole problem in New York stemmed from Mr. Ince going sailing on somebody's yacht.

"—so Frank told me to ask you to go down to the Eighteenth Precinct and pick up the jewelry Darlene had on Monday night. I guess they're keeping her clothes in the evidence lockers until after they try somebody, but Frank's lawyer got on the phone with the chief of police and Mayor Hylan, and said as how he didn't trust the police not to steal the stuff. Frank must have given her close to a hundred thousand worth over the years"—she let her glance stray to the two bands of diamonds that lay on her dressing table, and smiled a tiny smile—"not counting that *vulgar* diamond ring—which is *not* an engagement ring, Olivia told me. It was just a gift, she said, because Bandog's wife is putting up a fuss about the divorce and Bandog—"

"The murderer didn't take it?" Emma recalled the glitter of the Darlene's jewels in the wild light of the El Fey.

And if she hadn't been murdered for the jewels she wore . . .?

"Oh, no, darling. Well, I don't know about the ring. But he—or she—the killer—must have known the watchman would be on the way. A gun would make just an *awful* racket in a space like a backstage. And, of course, what's really eating Frank is he's afraid Doctor Spitz is going to include Darlene's jewelry in the inventory, so he can get his mitts on it. I think Bandog phoned the Mayor and all them as well. Would you be a—shit," she added, as the telephone rang.

Emma picked up the receiver—the suite had an extension in the larger bedroom, though not the one assigned to her—and a deep, creamy voice inquired, "Is this the Goddess of the Silver Screen?"

"This is the temple charwoman," replied Emma and turned to Kitty. "Mr. Malone."

She heard him chuckle as she passed the telephone over to Kitty.

After swearing that she would be "down in a minute" (Emma had heard her swear the same oath while dripping wet and wrapped in a towel), Kitty tucked stray curls into her bandeau, with its diamond-studded aigret, and slid her wrists into the diamond bracelets. She then squatted on her heels to stroke and kiss Chang Ming, Black Jasmine, and Buttercreme, with instructions to "be good for your Aunt Emma . . ."

"And thank you, darling." Rising, she clasped Emma's hands. "Did you have a good time at the philharmonic? You look *so* much better with Ambrose at shindigs like that than I do. I bet all those snooty women don't look down at *you* when you go up to his box! Frank's going to pick me up at nine tomorrow morning . . ."

And catching up her chinchilla coat, she darted across the living room and out the door of the suite in a flouncing glitter of jewels and fringe.

Emma sighed and considered herself in the mirror. Would this tea-length, dark-blue dress that she wore to the evening's concert be suitable for an "appalling society party" at a Long Island mansion? (What *did* one wear to an orgy of gatecrashers guzzling bootleg booze?) Margaret Mackenzie would probably know, and might be prevailed upon to lend her something. (*And what would Miss Mackenzie be doing with a dress that would pass muster at such a gathering*?)

The thought led her back to Darlene Golden, and the gold-and-burgundy Lanvin that she'd been wearing on the night she died. Two hundred and fifty dollars, Miss Golden had frequently boasted. "I bet Frank never got anything like that for *you* . . ."

And her father wanted it as part of the inventory of her possessions, when he could finally be bothered to come to New York, not to claim his daughter's body ("go ahead and bury her here") but to put in his claim on whatever money she'd left.

Was Dr. Spitz's tight-fistedness the memory of some enormity of Darlene's conduct, she wondered—or had Darlene been who she had been in reaction to that sort of home?

Darlene slept tonight, as she had for the past two, in the cold-storage morgue at Bellevue Hospital, waiting whatever funeral Frank—or Mr. Bandog ("fat chance," as Kitty would say)—would be willing to pay for. *I'll have to talk to Zal about starting a collection . . .*

She sank down onto the make-up stool and viewed the mess of expensive pots and jars. Diamond earrings and discarded pearls, which she knew she'd be expected to clean up (*and take down to the hotel safe!*) before she herself went to bed. At least Kitty said "Thank you," and had bought her this lovely dress to go out on the town ("Darling, you can't go to parties dressed like somebody's maiden aunt!"). *Darlene . . .*

The dogs gathered around her feet, and she felt Black Jasmine's wet pink tongue lick her ankle.

Mr. Bandog—eager as he was to retrieve that monstrous ring and whatever else he'd given Darlene in the way of diamonds—would probably argue that he could not be seen to contribute so much as a dime to the funeral of a beautiful woman he wasn't supposed to be sleeping with, lest his wife cause further trouble.

Preachers liked to refer to Hollywood as Babylon. But she wondered if Nebuchadnezzar in all his glory would have treated people like Frank and Bandog did.

(*Well, he* did *throw them into fiery furnaces and dens of lions . . .*)

She went to bed sad.

And dreamed of Shakespeare Malone, in the brown woods of Long Island, watching Kitty from a distance through binoculars.

TWELVE

Detective Joe Smith turned over to Emma a small parcel wrapped in brown paper the following morning: one pr. earrings (rubies, diamonds, pearls); one bracelet (rubies, diamonds, pearls); one necklace (diamonds, rubies); one gold lipstick; one gold powder compact. (*No ring? Well, even if Kitty was right about the watchman, Darlene would hardly have worn such a gift from one suitor to a rendezvous with another . . .*) One gold chain handbag containing a hotel-room key, five dollar bills and $1.65 in change, a clean cotton handkerchief, and a discreet Bakelite container holding a rubber cervical cap and a tube of Vaseline. Emma could imagine a grim-faced New York policewoman sorting through the handbag and noting this intimate detritus of a dead woman's life.

Smith turned the typed sheet around on his desk for her to sign. As she did so, her eye fell on the separate inventory of items kept as evidence: one gold-and-burgundy silk dress embroidered with rhinestones; one pr. women's high-heeled shoes, gold; one slip; one pr. step-ins; one brassière; one pr. silk stockings; one fur wrap.

"It's not a lot, is it?" she said quietly, thinking of the things she'd taken from the pockets of all those young men she'd knelt beside in the hallways of Bicester Hospital, waiting for a surgeon—or even a nursing sister—to see them. Things she'd packed up in little parcels like this one—less expensive than bracelets of diamonds and rubies, but infinitely more precious. Signet rings. Letters blotted with blood. Sometimes a girl's handkerchief, folded small.

"It never is." And for a moment, she saw the reflection of her own experiences in his eyes. "Her family coming to get her?"

"Their lawyer sent instructions to Mr. Pugh that she should be buried here," responded Emma in a level voice. "They'll be here sometime next week, to sort out whether she left a will."

Smith glanced at the packet she held, said, "Nice folks," and walked her downstairs to the station-house door.

There were, as promised, three dance bands at Brad Farmer's birthday party that night. Cypress Cove—the Gold Coast mansion Mr. Farmer's father had purchased with money made from oil wells and silver mines in Mexico—was lit up like a Christmas tree. Emma estimated there were several hundred people there, whose primary occupation seemed to be drinking to excess: Kitty appeared to have been quite correct about Canadian whiskey coming in on Long Island. And, as advertised, a scantily clad young lady did jump out of Mr. Farmer's birthday cake, scattering dabs of pink icing in all directions.

Petronius—the author of the Roman classic *Satyricon*—would have felt right at home. Emma half expected to be offered a platter of dormice in honey sauce before the end of the evening, and to encounter a procession of singing boy-slaves.

Dozens of people came up to greet Mr. Crain, many of them young men who thumped him on the back, exclaimed over how good he was looking, and tried to sell him shares in Gibraltar Mining, Patton Northwest Land and Cattle, Bellweather Development, Venture Shipping Lines, and a score of other "sure things" that were guaranteed to quadruple in value over the next two years. The man was, after all—as the management of Paillard's had clearly taken into account on Thursday night when they brought out illegal wine—a millionaire.

Crain introduced Emma as his god-daughter from England, a role substantiated by the becoming but modest frock of multi-hued green satin that Margaret Mackenzie had helpfully "borrowed" for her from the wardrobe department at MBQ Studios that afternoon. ("With a bit of luck, no one will recognize it as the one Jobyna Ralston wore in *Touch All the Bases . . .*") The matronly actress had also provided her with necklace and earrings from her own jewelry box:

"They have to be real, dear. Those people can spot fakes across the room."

Thus, she was able to meet Clark Dexter's Aunt Violet, and be greeted with new respect by Jefferson Blair, who was clearly impressed by the tasteful, slightly old-fashioned cameo and pearls. "I do apologize if I've been brusque or . . . or hurried, out at the chateau. I had no idea . . ." He turned her hand a little as he shook it, to surreptitiously estimate the price of her bracelet. "So many of those film people are so rude!"

She forbore to mention the time he'd gone to Mr. Pugh and demanded her dismissal because he'd seen her "trespassing" near the stables, and gave him a smile Queen Mary might envy.

Like his son-in-law Brad Farmer, Mr. Blair seemed bent on conversing with every millionaire in the room. These were easily identifiable as the men around whom the eager young stockbrokers clustered like bees at queening time, and she later heard that two of these gentlemen had discreetly inquired of their hostess about her financial prospects from her "godfather." Despite (according to Mr. Crain) four years of insolvency and dependence on his sister-in-law for a roof over his head, Blair himself wore a tuxedo of the newest and smartest cut, and cufflinks that flashed in the electric blaze of the lights. Violet Butler Blair, tall and wide-shouldered with a round paunch like a man's, looked with approval upon the wardrobe department's version of a high-society gown, and when Emma followed her into the "breakfast room" later in the evening, greeted her with a tired smile.

"Come for a little air?" Floppy Dexter's aunt sat on a cushioned window seat, the casement at her elbow open a few inches to admit the smell of the sea and a whisper of near-arctic chill. A fair-sized silver platter of oysters Rockefeller—a dish Emma had not encountered outside of Hollywood—rested on the seat beside her, and another, already three-quarters full of emptied oyster shells, on the windowsill. She longed to turn the plates over to see if—like those in the Satyricon—they had the weight in silver stamped on the bottom. Beyond the dark window glass, waning moonlight touched patterns of what appeared to be topiary, and like every other room in the downstairs, the little chamber was hung with garish electric Christmas-tree lights mingled with garlands of fresh-smelling evergreen boughs and holly. Emma wondered whose duty it had been to gather and arrange them.

With the door closed, it was at least blessedly quiet.

"A little silence." Emma tried to appear as though the encounter was pure coincidence, and made a move as if to leave. "I'm sorry. If I'm intruding . . ."

"No, no," sighed the older woman. Her features would have been called "strong"—large chin, unfashionable nose—in curious contrast to the uncertain look in her eyes and the droop of the too-wide mouth. Nearly Emma's height, she was soft of flesh and reminded Emma of the overweight spaniel that had belonged to the Warden of New College in her girlhood. "It's the smoke as much as anything else," Mrs. Blair added, shaking her head. "Everyone says that times must change, but I cannot like all these 'new women' puffing on cigarettes like men."

Her voice, with its accent of the American South, had a peevish note that seemed to be permanent, as if life had been a disappointment for decades. "And the men . . . What's gotten into them? Ten years ago, *no* man would have smoked in the presence of a woman! Well, Negroes, maybe, or immigrants." She grimaced. "It's all this radio and films, showing people all these things my mother would have forbidden me even to think about!"

Emma reflected upon the pile of *Police Gazettes* and *Dawn* magazines she'd found below the stables, and wondered if Mr. Blair had concealed them there from his wife. Now that she thought about it, those blue chalk arrows *were* at about eye level for a man of Blair's height.

"I've certainly never understood it." With a sympathetic wince of distress, she turned one of the sleek breakfast-table chairs around so that she could sit close to her companion. "And I think you must be right, ma'am," she added confidingly, "about it all being the fault of films, though I'd never thought of it that way before! The way those people in the film company carry on! I have as little to do with them as I can—mostly, I remain at Miss de la Rose's house and see to the servants. But still, your poor husband must have his work cut out for him. It's as if they don't respect *anything*. And I expect," she added, seeing the tightening of the flesh around the woman's eyes, "that you'll have to have the whole place cleaned afterwards."

"It'll certainly need it!" Relief at being so readily understood relaxed the high, tense shoulders, the corners of the mouth. "Jeff—Mr. Blair—does his best to keep them out of the main house, but honestly, it's like trying to chase mice with a shoe! And whether Rosemary will send anyone to clean, after she was the one who wanted to rent the place out . . . Jeff and I *never* liked the idea. The fuss Jeff put up! But, of course, you can't argue with Rosemary." With a silver spoon, she scooped up and swallowed another broiled oyster with its topping of bread-crumbs and butter, but—presumably because Emma had brought no spoon with her—made no move to offer her any. "Just because the place was never finished," she went on, "doesn't mean it isn't one of the finest mansions on the island!"

"No, indeed!" agreed Emma. "It quite breaks my heart to see it used so!"

"And likely the servants will ask for extra money before they'll turn a hand to cleaning afterwards, too! Are they that way in England, Mrs. Blackstone? I *swear*, back home you could get a crew of darkies to scrub the whole place top to bottom for fifty cents and a case of beer!" She shook her head wonderingly at the avariciousness of the local working men with families to feed, and slurped up another oyster.

Emma produced what she hoped was an expression of understanding and leaned closer. "And—well—Uncle Ambrose told me there was some kind of *frightful* scandal about one of the actresses . . ."

The soft lips pursed as if tightened by a drawstring. "Would you believe it? They actually sent a *police officer* to my sister's house, asking where my nephew was that night? Practically accusing him of . . . *Well!*"

"You're *joking*!" gasped Emma encouragingly.

"Just because he happened to talk to whatever-her-name

was—the girl who was killed . . . I've told Rosemary a *thousand* times that only trouble would come, her letting Floppy have an apartment in town!"

Let him? Emma bit her lip not to exclaim. *He's twenty-four!*

"All he does is visit nightclubs and run about with flappers and chorus girls, and not set foot out here or see his poor mother for six months at a time. She should have put her foot down years ago, when Griswold—Mr. Dexter—would spend half the day at those nasty picture studios in town . . . and take poor Spencer and Floppy with him!" She shook her head. "Of course Floppy had nothing to do with any of it, and so we told that *dreadful* police detective. Besides," she added smugly, "Clark was at Abbottsford—our home, you know—all that night."

Emma managed not to raise her eyebrows at this.

"A beautiful house," enthused the older woman, her square features softening. "An exact copy of Burghley House in Cambridgeshire, England—well, smaller, of course. Nothing like this place . . ." She gestured around her, with a moue of distaste. "And nothing like Willow Run—Daddy's plantation near Charleston. *Ostentatious.*" She sniffed at the poor taste of the man whose oysters Rockefeller she was eating. "My dear sister—and my husband and I—are *perfectly* happy there, without inviting half the riff-raff from town, who only come for the free booze."

"Tcha!" agreed Emma.

"And anyway, aside from Floppy *being at Abbottsford* all Monday night, I told that *nasty* detective Floppy wouldn't have anything to do with a *film actress*! Aside from simply the bounds of good taste, he knows he'll be disinherited without a nickel if he marries without Rosemary's permission. *And* he's engaged to marry a perfectly *lovely* girl—"

Her subsequent ten-minute panegyric of Miss Beatrice Schuyler's modesty, beauty, ancestry (Schermerhorns and Vanderbilts), good manners, and charitable activities (*The Women's Ku Klux Klan?* reflected Emma) was broken into by the appearance of the damsel herself, a reasonably pretty woman of Emma's own age in blue-and-silver silk and enough diamonds to purchase a medium-level Congressman.

"Mrs. Blair, you've *got* to get me out of here!" the lady exclaimed. "A few glasses of champagne I can understand, though *honestly* I can't see why lemonade or a good grenadine punch wouldn't do *just* as well! And it would be better for them . . . But the way they *flock* around those film people just turns my stomach! Excuse me," she added, seeing Emma for the first time.

Mrs. Blair performed the introductions, emphasizing Emma's relationship to Mr. Crain, but not offering to share her oysters Rockefeller. Miss Schuyler simpered, "Well, looks like we're three kindred souls! Like three little birds in a tree! We can have our own little party right here!"

But after another half-hour of conversation with Mrs. Blair and Miss Schuyler—which consisted of mostly listening to Mrs. Blair and Miss Schuyler complain to one another about Italians, Irish, Negroes, Jews, Mexicans, and the Hyde Park Roosevelts, and gossip about people of whom Emma had never heard (". . . and she went to one of those clinics in the city without even *asking* her husband!")—Emma had had enough. They both bid her goodnight politely enough when she said she had to locate "Uncle Ambrose," but were deep in their own critique of their host's servants before she was out the door ("*That* kind of people simply don't know what's best for them! Well, what can you expect of *Catholics*?"). Emma noticed that Aunt Violet quickly wolfed down the four remaining oysters before the "perfectly lovely girl" could ask for one.

At any rate, when Emma left the breakfast room, she saw that Miss Schuyler's review of the party seemed to be accurate. The dance band in the ballroom had been joined by the Cake Damsel—no more warmly clad than she had been an hour ago—dancing on top of the piano, and everyone present was forty-five minutes drunker than they had been. The cigarette smoke was thicker, the talk much louder, and the couples on the dance floor performing the Charleston, the Bunny Hug, and the Black Bottom with Neronian abandon.

As Mr. Crain escorted her out to his car, Emma wondered

if Floppy Dexter knew that he would have been disinherited without a nickel if he had married Darlene Golden (or Kitty, or Gloria Swanson, or anyone else). Or had he, as Sugar-Pie Gilroy had surmised, been drunk when he wrote those letters? Having met Beatrice Schuyler, however, she understood how he might have considered it worth fifty thousand dollars to get out of the match.

But if he had to obtain his mother's consent, Emma wondered, where had he intended to get that money?

Maximilien Robespierre, the "sea-green incorruptible" (as the historian Carlyle had referred to him), sat in the salon that he had taken for his headquarters amid the ruin that his followers had wrought. The gilded swags and exquisite white paneling of the chamber were scarred now and scribbled with the graffiti of rebellion: *À la lanterne*, *À bas les aristos*, *Vive la révolution!* Two smashed chairs lay near his desk, a third overturned by rioters. What had been beautiful Fragonards and Bouchers hung, slashed, in their broken frames . . . Frank Pugh had raged for ten minutes at the cost of duplicating the copies originally rented for this scene, but the alternative had been to call production to a halt until Mila Haley could be located to film the scenes that took place with the salon in its unravaged condition, and that would cost more.

The Jacobin leader stroked his unshaven chin and leered at the woman who stood in chains before him, regal in her satin rags.

"So you're old lady Fairisle, are you?"

"Mr. Blakeney, you cannot allow this travesty of historical fact to proceed!" Just beyond the chalk line that delimited the scene, Devon Kingsley lunged to his feet. "Robespierre would *never* have . . ."

George Blakeney yelled, "CUT!" and Zal, Chip, and New York cameraman Eddie Burger all quit cranking.

Again.

At the same moment, Frank Pugh and Neil Bandog got to *their* feet, yelling that they'd told the author already to keep his mouth shut, and if he didn't like it, he could get off the set, and the doomed Lady Fairisle walked over to Robespierre, righted the tipped-over chair beside the scarred and desecrated desk, and flopped into it. The sea-green incorruptible took a substantial flask from his coat pocket and offered his victim a drink.

At least here at MBQ Studio, there was no Mr. Blair to threaten legal action.

Sitting on the sidelines awaiting her own scene with Robespierre, Kitty produced a cigarette, and Mr. Bandog's willowy chauffeur sprang forward to light it for her.

It was, reflected Emma with a sigh, going to be a long Revolution.

"Duchess?"

The decision to continue filming all scenes that did not urgently demand the presence (or at least a frontal view) of Summer Fairisle had meant that the schedules of all extras had had to be rearranged. Sugar-Pie Gilroy, who had hoped to fill in the next few weeks dancing in the chorus of "The Albertina Rasch Girls," stood beside her, looking decidedly the worse for wear. Since her role required her to be a prisoner in the Temple prison, this was no hardship on-screen, though Emma guessed she would have to take a good deal of care with her make-up before sashaying out onto the stage of the Palace Theater that evening. At the moment, in the torn remains of the court gown she'd worn in scenes 234–250, she did actually look as if she'd come through the September Massacre.

"Can I talk to you for a sec?"

Emma glanced into Buttercreme's wicker carry-box to make sure the shy little dog was resting comfortably—Chang Ming snored on Kitty's lap, and, at the farthest extent of his leash, Black Jasmine watched the growing affray on the set as if ready to step in and referee. Satisfied, she closed her exercise book and followed Sugar-Pie into the shadows away from the glare of the Kliegs. "What is it, dear?"

Sugar-Pie, a strikingly beautiful brunette of nearly Emma's height, with calves that an Olympic runner might envy, often acted as a spokeswoman for the female extras. She glanced over both shoulders to make sure they would not be overheard (not likely, with Mr. Kingsley delivering a lecture on the Paris political scene in 1793 at the top of his voice), and said quietly, "You know what the newspapers said about Miss Golden's murder? How it was done with a thirty-eight Police-model Colt?"

Emma nodded. "I assume you were interviewed by the police about how Miss Golden would have got into the Palace backstage?"

"Oh, yeah." The young woman made a dismissive swipe with her hand. "The cops know all about how keys to that door from the alley get passed around; they must make a century a week looking the other way. Thing is, one of 'em had seen that Leslie Carter tab-show that was running a couple weeks ago at the Palace—"

She paused, seeing Emma's uncertainty, and explained, "A tab-show is kind of a fifteen-minute version of a play. Everybody but the headliner on a vaudeville bill gets about fifteen minutes. This one—Leslie Carter's—was all about the Russian Revolution, and eight of us played some filthy-rich aristocrat's all-girl bodyguard. The management wanted some leg action, because who the hell wants to see a bunch of Russian soldiers in army coats? So we're in the usual get-up—"

Emma had seen enough chorus lines over the past three weeks to guess what a vaudeville revue's costumer would make of a filthy-rich Russian aristocrat's all-girl bodyguard . . .

"—and each of us has a rod with a big satin bow on it. They asked where those guns were kept. They're unloaded, of course, and Deuce—he's the stage manager—took the firing pins out of 'em for good measure. But the thing is, one of 'em was stolen. Deuce reported it stolen, but we said it'd gone missing back in October—when Deuce was out of town, so he wouldn't get in trouble. But it was really swiped on the fifth of December."

About ten days after we arrived. We'd started filming by then . . .

"Nobody would have said anything about it," Sugar-Pie went on, "except I heard from Roxie North—who was in the chorus at the time, but she got a better offer from the Mardi Gras Club—that the cops think Zeppo did it. Zeppo Marx," she added, in case Emma thought that Zeppo was a common name in America. "Roxie's a friend of his. She says he swears he had nothing to do with it, and she believes him—I do, too. Zeppo's a sweetheart."

"But he got into a shouting match with Miss Golden at the El Fey a few days before the murder," finished Emma.

"And," continued Sugar-Pie grimly, "he's still not saying where he was last Monday night."

"But *why*?"

The chorine grimaced. "Honey, I asked him. And he said what I'm pretty sure he said to Chico and the cops and to everybody else—that it wasn't my business or the cops' business or anybody's business, and if they think he's guilty, they're welcome to come up with proof."

Emma thought for a moment. "Which they can probably do. According to Miss de la Rose, he and his brothers played at the Palace last year. His fingerprints must be all over the backstage."

"And all over about six members of the chorus I could name." The girl shrugged. "They were headliners there, on and off, pretty much all through 1920. But if Angel-Eyes has a bunch of his people swearing he was with them, and Bull Moose—that's Bandog's chauffeur—is swearing he took Bandog to midnight mass or some damn thing in Queens, and old Pughie"—she nodded towards the ongoing symposium concerning the personal habits of Maximilien Robespierre—"comes up with *his* crew of witnesses, which you know he's gonna, that leaves Zeppo in the soup."

Emma tore her mind from speculation as to how Bandog's whispy young driver had earned a name like Bull Moose, and recalled Chico's words: *The cops may not know who done it, but they know they gotta nail* some*body*.

"Do you know who took the gun?"

"A reporter for the *Gotham Daily Democrat*. I forget his name, but one of the girls'll remember. That's why I'm asking you."

"Asking me what? And why would a reporter from a New York newspaper steal a—?"

The young woman turned her head as Devon Kingsley stalked past them and down the length of the MBQ filming stage to the outer door, visibly fuming. An assistant cameraman chalked new numbers on the clapperboard, and Margaret Mackenzie took another shot from Robespierre's flask and said, "Thank Christ."

"—Asking you to front for us with the cops if there's trouble. If Pughie doesn't fire all eight of us, the front office at the Palace will, if they find out what was going on backstage at the Palace after midnight on the fifth. We need to come up with a good story that'll get the buttons going after the right guy and quit asking Zeppo where he was and what he was doing on the fifteenth."

"Why?" asked Emma. "What were you doing on the fifth of December, when this reporter stole the gun?"

"We were backstage at the Palace with him." Sugar-Pie regarded her as if she had failed to read the answer chalked on a billboard. "Doing a porn shoot."

THIRTEEN

The porn-peddling reporter's name—according to the red-haired "pony" Ginger Knott—was Skinner. "Ricky or Dicky or Davy . . . I have his card in the dressing room someplace." She scurried off to search, her heels clattering on the metal stair. Emma looked around her at the Palace's backstage under the prosaic glare of electric work lights, narrow behind the width of the proscenium and fire curtain. Above the work lights, an infinite dark cosmos of flats, flies, ropes, and sandbags ascended to an empyrean lost in shadow.

The cleaning crew had already been through this area, and she could hear their voices beyond the fire curtain, preparing the house for the matinee. It was six thirty on Monday morning and still pitch-dark outside. The backstage was freezing, and smelled of bleach and cleaning fluid, overlying dimmer scents of wet wood, mold, fresh plaster and paint, and the echoes of a thousand animal acts. In a few hours, the stage crew would arrive; a bit later, the artists. Singers, actors, Chinese acrobats . . . (*The abstract and brief chronicles of the time*, as Hamlet had described them.)

From a stack of flats leaning against the far wall, an immense poster of Princess Laura and Her Peerless Pachyderms smiled benevolently down.

The Palace, according to Chico, was the crème de la crème of vaudeville houses, not only in New York, but across the United States. If you played the Palace, you had really "arrived." ("Hell, just playing two shows a day instead of six makes it crème de la crème," Chico had said. "And management that cleans the men's room every day—Heaven!" He had kissed his fingers like a French connoisseur discussing a 1904 port.)

Emma wondered if there was still a bloodstain where Darlene's body had been found. And, more morbidly, whether

Darlene Golden was the first person who had died in this cold, echoing cavern.

"Over there." Reading her mind—or at least the direction of her gaze—Sugar-Pie pointed to the flats. Her whisper excluded Ginger and Bunnie, the two young ladies who had accompanied her that morning. "That detective said it looked like the man who did it stood between the flats in the shadows, and waited till she walked past him. This place is like Carlsbad Cave when the lights are out. The only light on would have been that one above the door of the prop room."

She nodded towards the bricks of the wall on the Forty-Seventh Street side. "She wouldn't have seen him. He probably shot her in the back, then stood over her and shot her twice more in the head."

Renowned for her beauty, thought Emma, she'd be buried in a closed coffin, in a cheap cemetery in Brooklyn that afternoon. Even the man who "adored" her enough to demand that her close-ups not be replaced in her final film (and thus her name not removed from the advertising posters) had refused to contribute more than fifty dollars to the cost of her burial.

"She's lucky Bandog didn't let her just go to Hart Island," had said Zal that morning, sourly naming the city's grim and filthy potter's field. Like everyone else at Foremost, Zal had suffered from Darlene's tantrums, demands, and petty gossip. But like almost everyone else of the Hollywood contingent, he would take the El train out to Canarsie at two, to bid her farewell.

Not knowing where Jim lay buried—somewhere in Flanders was all Emma knew—Emma understood. You didn't let even an enemy get on Charon's ferry boat with no one to wave goodbye from the shore.

With the conclusion of Citizen Robespierre's condemnation of Lady Fairisle to the guillotine the previous day, George Blakeney had ruled that Kitty's evil plot with the Committee of Public Safety would need a full day to accomplish. A general mutiny among cast and crew had forced Mr. Pugh into concession. Filming at MBQ, he had ruled, would resume Tuesday. ("Bet me he isn't waiting till her family shows up," grumbled

Chip Thaw, "'cause he doesn't want to pay storage at the morgue over Christmas.")

"Skinner paid each of us three dollars for the shoot," provided Sugar-Pie now, as she led the way to the opposite side of the cavernous backstage. Props for the various acts were grouped on or around a long trestle table, ready to be rushed out during the front-of-curtain acts: quilted felt caps to ease the skulls of the acrobats, couches and chairs for a "dramatic playlet" (*A tab-show*? wondered Emma); the disassembled pieces of a white Greek-revival mansion and a few prop trees draped in Spanish moss, background for a "Minstrel Bunch." A neat cluster of bars, hurdles, and poles that reminded Emma of what children called "monkey bars" or a "jungle gym." *More acrobats?*

"The stuff makes great set-ups." Sugar-Pie thumped the curved arm of an overstuffed, gilded, gaudily upholstered couch. "We brought up a couple of dressing screens from downstairs for a backdrop, and Roxie and Fay both knew how to set up lights. There's everything in the prop room from horse whips to teddy bears."

"Were the guns kept in the prop room?" Zal turned from examining a bizarre piece of furniture that could have been something from an orthopedist's office or a health farm, save for the fact that it was upholstered in crimson brocade and decorated with carved cupids.

"Yeah," agreed Sugar-Pie. "But sometimes the stagehands would forget and just leave them out on one of the tables." She nodded at a pile of ostrich-plume fans. "We have about ten seconds when the scene changes and then the chorus has to be out there when the curtains open. Like I said, the firing pins were taken out of the guns, but they're just in a jar in the prop room. Skinner's lucky he didn't blow his hand off—if that *was* him that shot Darlene with it. Those guns haven't been cleaned or fired in years."

"Can't find it." Ginger trotted back through the door that led to the basement dressing rooms. "But I know his name was Dickie or Davie or Manny or maybe Mel . . ."

"But it was *Skinner*," reported the third girl—Bunnie—fair

and bouncy and a little schoolgirlish. "I know, 'cause my aunt Maisie's last name is Skinner. Little guy with glasses and a beard."

"And honey, was *he* all wet." Sugar-Pie rolled her eyes with an exaggerated sigh. "For a guy who made extra dough shooting naughty pictures, the man had *no* imagination. He damn near *blushed* when we suggested the Shanghai Surprise, which is actually pretty tame."

The other girls nodded. "Or the Cincinnati Special," suggested Ginger.

"Or the Turkish Rodeo. That's the one where two of you . . ."

"*Any*way," continued Sugar-Pie firmly, "you can see why we didn't want to tell the cops—or the manager—that anybody'd been here after the show that night. And it wouldn't have mattered, except the next morning this Skinner guy phones me saying as how he left a box of his photo plates here, and could I let him in before the place opened? Of course I did—I sure didn't want Deuce or any of the cleaning guys finding them—and 'cause it was nearly eleven in the morning by then, and there were people around, I played chickie out here while he went and looked for them in the prop room, which was where he'd opened the new boxes of plates during the shoot. To keep them out of the light from backstage or the hallway, you know. Then, lo and behold, comes the one o'clock matinee and there's eight girl bodyguards and only seven pistols. Bunnie had to run all the way to the Rivoli on Forty-Ninth and borrow a gun—"

"He take the firing pin as well?" asked Zal.

The chorus girls looked at one another, a little blankly.

"Let's go look."

Like the backstage, the prop room—located along the opposite wall of the backstage close to the dressing-room staircase—was organized with the smaller items pertaining to each act grouped together on the long table at one side of the room: a tambourine and a set of wooden "bones" for the minstrels, a beautiful Italian violin in a padded case, a frilly pink parasol. On the shelf above it, props long forgotten, or lent by acts of the previous weeks: a beribboned guitar, sheet music for the

"Pickaninny Blues," a curiously shaped musical instrument, like a deformed clarinet (*designed for a Peerless Pachyderm?*). And, stowed in a cardboard box, eight pistols with large satin bows, in various colors, tied to their grips.

"Well, shit." Sugar-Pie peered through the shadows of the windowless room. "Where'd the friggin' jar go? The jelly jar with the firing pins," she added, when Zal looked puzzled. She snapped the toggle on the light switch near the door. The overhead bulb didn't help much. Emma understood why Mr. Skinner had used the room to open his boxes of photographic plates. It would be easy to carry a red safe-light bulb in one's pocket, to screw into place . . .

"It's usually right there on the table . . ."

Bunnie and Ginger turned to the opposite wall, where more shelves held all manner of "extra" props—or those inadvertently left behind by a thousand acts over the years: "Mexican" sombreros ("You're not gonna see anything south of the border that looks like *those*," remarked Zal); white china plates (for juggling, Emma assumed); an assortment of telephones, vases, and small framed pictures (*to dress domestic sets?*). Dismembered and brightly colored pieces of hurdles, sized for any animal from a mouse to a Peerless Pachyderm. Lamps, candelabra, busts of Caesar and Voltaire. Fake spectacles, small copies of famous sculptures. Barber's poles, a rocking horse, four boxes of crepe hair for fake beards, and the taxidermied heads of several species of large game . . .

Bunnie cried, "Is this it?" at the same moment that Ginger removed a glass jar labeled "Welch's Grapelade" from a shelf just opposite the guns on the table.

The red-head shook the jar: it certainly sounded as if it contained firing pins. But Zal strode quickly down the narrow room to where Bunnie stood, a flat cardboard box in her hands. "Don't open that," he said.

"It was stuck behind that box." The girl pointed to a carton which appeared to hold six or seven human skulls. (*The tab-show version of* Hamlet?)

"It's new." Zal took the flat box and held it where the grimy overhead light would fall on it. Emma saw the label: "Eastman

Plates." It was larger than the single packaged plates she'd seen at Zal's cottage in Venice (*California, not Italy . . .*); evidently, something one could buy in tens or dozens. He shook it gently; by the sound of it, there were several smaller packets within.

From the doorway, Sugar-Pie said, "Fuck all," and Zal looked at her inquiringly.

"Allie," sighed Sugar-Pie in disgust. "Legs that go all the way to next Tuesday but dumb as a bucket of gravel. She's the one in the green costume with the silver flowers." She leaned across to pinch the bow of that description on one of the revolvers. "The bows matched our suits, see. She kept asking during the shoot, if we could see the pictures—she'd screwed up on one shot and got worried about how her hair looked . . . Like anybody buying that print was gonna be looking at her hair. I had to stop her from opening one of the boxes Skinner stashed the exposed plates in. She kept saying she just wanted to take that one out, while he wasn't looking."

Ginger rolled her eyes. "Sugar tried to tell her you can't tell what a picture's going to look like, and Allie kept saying, 'That's stupid—he took the picture, didn't he?' I'll just bet she sneaked in here looking for it, opened the box—"

"With the light on," added Sugar-Pie grimly.

"—and when she saw that no, you couldn't see anything on a plate, she stuffed it back in the box and hid the box. Skinner did complain that one of his boxes with unused plates was missing. Dumb coosie."

"Let me take these." Zal tucked the box under his arm and turned to Sugar-Pie. "You think your friend Skinner's beard was real?"

"Without the work lights on backstage," pointed out the girl, "it was hard to tell. It was a little longer than yours"—she caressed her own chin illustratively—"and dark like his hair. But a lot of guys' beards look fake."

That said, she took the jar from Ginger's hand and opened it, and shook the contents into her palm. It contained seven of the odd little semi-triangular pieces of metal that Emma recognized—both Jim and her brother Miles had disassembled their revolvers to explain how they worked—as "firing pins."

Glancing back at the eight weapons on the table behind her, she saw that one, presumably the replacement, was differently shaped, with a longer barrel and, instead of a big silk bow, a number of fancy tied ribbons in ruby-red. Did all the guns have firing pins?

Why steal a pistol from the Palace Theater when one could buy one at any pawnshop in town? She'd have to ask Detective Smith.

"Thank you." Zal returned the pins to the jar, handed it back to Sugar-Pie. "First thing I'm going to do when I get back to the hotel is to call the *Gotham Daily Democrat* to find out if they really have a Mr. Skinner working for them. And I'll just bet you they don't."

As she unlocked the door to suite 1202 at the Plaza, Emma heard Frank Pugh's harsh, deep voice within, saying, "I don't see why not, Kit. It's not like her family's going to be there or anything."

"All the more reason for me to go, honey! Now, the funeral's at two, so there's plenty of time—"

At the sound of the opening door, Kitty swiveled on the couch, where she'd been cuddled at Pugh's side, and at the sight of Emma cried, "Darling!" She sprang to her feet—a connubial-looking spread of donuts, coffee, and Tootsie Rolls on the low table before the pair spoke of a morning of coziness after Emma had left. "Valentino!" she added, her eyes bright with excitement. "Valentino's coming *here*!"

Emma and Zal halted in the doorway. As Kitty rushed to greet them, Chang Ming and Black Jasmine bounded at her heels, and even Buttercreme scurried from the safety of Emma's bedroom to join the welcome.

"This evening!" went on Kitty breathlessly. "He's in town, and he's looking for backing on a project—he's doing publicity for *Sainted Devil*, and I guess he's not happy with the stuff his wife set him up to do for Ritz-Carlton Pictures . . ."

"He's going to be *here*?" Emma looked around the black-and-cream chic of the suite's living room. Gorgeous, but hardly large enough to accommodate what Hollywood deemed a "party."

"Up in Frank's suite, darling! He's already invited Mr. Bandog, and Mr. Zukor from Paramount, and Chico says he'll bring his brothers along after the show tonight and some of Harpo's writer friends . . . George Whatever-His-Name-Is with the weird hair . . . Oh, and Fishy's in town! He got in last night on the Atlantic Express, with Mr. Spiegelmann—and Mr. Goldman, too, from Chase Bank! So they'll be there—"

"Which is why I need you to stick around this afternoon, sugar." Mr. Pugh heaved himself from the couch and crossed to the group by the door, laying his broad, thick-fingered hand on Kitty's shoulder. "If that funeral's late, or there's some hang-up on the El line getting back . . . I need somebody here who knows how to throw a party. And you throw the best parties in town, honey. You know you do."

He's talking about skipping the funeral of a woman who was his lover, so that someone will be on hand to deal with the salmon sandwiches and devilled eggs. Emma studied the heavy dark face, the thick-lidded green eyes—fatuous now as he leaned down to kiss the nape of Kitty's neck, but, Emma knew, in their usual state, cold as the green jade of their coloring.

Gently, she said, "No one will be surprised if you don't go, Kitty." She didn't add, *Everyone remembers the things she'd say about you*, but it was in her eyes as she met her sister-in-law's gaze. It occurred to her that Kitty didn't know where her brother was buried, either.

"Sure," Pugh exclaimed, "sure! Everybody knows how important it is that things go well this evening!" He gave Kitty's shoulders a hug.

To Pugh's surprise—and a little to Emma's—Kitty replied with quiet firmness in her baby-coo voice. "I'm going, Frank. If I'm late coming back, Fishy can handle it, and you know nobody's going to get here before ten anyway. Please," she added. "You'd want her to do the same for me, wouldn't you?"

Not if it means soggy canapés for Rudolph Valentino! Pugh cleared his throat and rumbled, "No—um—Of course, baby, of course . . ."

At one of the nightclubs earlier that week—Emma couldn't recall which—she had heard a song about how romantic it was for a woman to say no when the man just *knew* she *really* wanted "it."

Pugh's eyes clearly proclaimed what his thick lips denied, and Emma supposed the man deserved credit for the lie.

On the local train out to Canarsie that afternoon, crowded together with Margaret Mackenzie, Marsh Sloane, Ken Elmore, and a rather surprising assortment of the lesser players, the New York crew, and even the aristocratic George Blakeney, Zal said quietly to Emma, "I was right. *Gotham Daily Democrat*'s never heard of anybody named Davie or Dicky or even Adolphus Skinner, and none of their reporters or photographers has glasses and a beard."

"Well, I never thought the beard was real," returned Emma. "And Miss Gilroy was right. Unless you had the work lights on—which you wouldn't want to do because of the nightwatchman—you probably couldn't tell if someone was wearing a full-face Tragedy mask until you were right next to him. I presume the watchman was in the lobby where it was warm?"

"Or where the girls in the chorus paid him to be," said Kitty. In a dark skirt, frumpy shoes, a faded coat that looked as though she'd bought it from one of the hotel cleaning women, no make-up, and a headscarf tied tight over her hair, she looked astonishingly like two-thirds of the Jewish immigrant girls who slaved fourteen hours a day in the sweatshops. Nobody in the El train car gave her a glance.

"A buck for the watchman is still half what even a hot-pillow joint would charge for a room. If Darlene thought she was meeting somebody there—or if Floppy set up the meeting—you know they'd have paid off the flatfoot in advance to take a powder. He only came when he heard the shots."

"And I suppose the watchman wouldn't admit he'd been paid," reflected Emma.

"Not if he wanted to keep his job, he wouldn't." Zal shrugged. "I'm sure he was the first guy our friend Smith talked to. And, hell, the man might've been drunk. For that reason," he went on, "when we're done at Canarsie, I'm going to take the train up to MBQ and see what I can get from those plates.

Two of the packets in that container were still sealed, four had been opened—the box originally held twelve. If Allie with the Legs opened one of them and saw the film was blacked out—and realized Ginger was right—she might have just shut the box and shoved it out of sight. And if Mr. Skinner had more than a couple of plates with him—and wasn't really after naughty pictures of the Cincinnati Special to begin with—he probably wouldn't realize he'd left one behind. Don't you just love Brooklyn?" he added, as the train groaned to a stop across the street from a line of cheap hotels, cheaper eating houses, and souvenir stands, beyond which the rickety scaffolding of a roller coaster and the brightly painted turrets of carousels and funhouses loomed against a gray winter sky.

FOURTEEN

Since the party in Mr. Pugh's suite didn't get going until ten, Kitty had plenty of time to bathe, nap, and play "tug" and "fetch" with the dogs in the Park. (Chang Ming was the only one of the three who would actually release the object tossed for him to chase. Pekinese, Emma had found, tended to be very possessive about their toys.) Then, her make-up completely reapplied, she ascended to the fourteenth floor and her duties as hostess. Emma made herself tea, took the Pekes down to the "feeding room" where the hotel staff saw to their dinner, and had time to reflect on why the youngest Marx brother—despite a string of brushes with the Chicago police—would persist in his refusal to say where he had been on the night of December fifteenth.

"He can't not realize that the police know he's friends with half the bootleggers and gamblers in town," she had said to Kitty, as they'd walked back past the fishing sheds and decaying wharves to the Elevated from Canarsie Cemetery that afternoon. "You've seen him at the High Wire—and Heaven only knows how many other places—with a chorus girl on each arm . . ."

"Chico's ready to slap him." Kitty shook her head. "And Frank's just as bad!"

"Did Mr. Pugh ever tell you where he made his call to Mr. Spiegelmann?" Emma was, in fact, fairly certain that the studio head had never made such a call. Why not simply call from Kitty's suite? He was paying for the telephone there after all, and there was an extension in the bedroom if he wanted privacy. "It doesn't sound like he went back to his own suite."

Kitty heaved an exasperated sigh. "Frank says he called from the lobby—" She wrinkled her nose in agreement at Emma's expression of disbelief (*Why wait for an elevator and then go down twelve floors to a public phone?*). "Frank *said* he went to Lindy's . . . in the rain. Only I asked Shakespeare, who knows all the guys who work at Lindy's late at night, to find a waiter who'd seen him, and nobody had. And Detective Smith looks like the kind of guy who'd *also* know all the guys who work at Lindy's late at night, and you know that's the first thing *he'd* check! So then Tony Ransom—who does the lights at MBQ—phones the Eighteenth Precinct out of the blue and tells Smith he saw Frank at the Cotton Club from ten thirty to one. But only two minutes later, Polly Adler—"

Emma recognized the name of the best-known madam in Manhattan . . .

"—calls Smith at the Eighteenth Precinct and says Frank was at *her* place all evening, and has two girls back up her story, except one of them was in bed with Mr. Murphy from the Vice Squad between eleven thirty and midnight. So after that, Smith didn't really believe the three waiters from Lindy's who each call him up at the station and each swear they served Frank at *their* table at midnight exactly . . . One of them wasn't even on shift that night. You'd think Frank would at least organize his bribes! He's usually smarter than that!"

"He probably got Gordy to do it."

"Hmph." Kitty tucked the collar of her disreputable coat tighter around her neck. "And it isn't fair! Angel-Eyes has at least as many people lying about where he was that night. And Frank has never shot *anybody*—not that I know about, anyway. And why would he shoot Darlene?"

Why indeed? Emma could imagine several reasons.

Up in Suite 1403 that night, she watched the studio chief from the other side of the very crowded room, and was again struck at how jumpy he was. He flinched every time someone knocked at the door, and when the telephone rang—as it did almost constantly—she saw his eyes dart in the direction of the little niche that held the instrument. She realized very quickly that with few breaks, either Mr. Morris or Al Spiegelmann was never more than a few feet from it. No one else ever reached it first.

But for all his nervousness, Pugh stayed close beside his guest of honor, with Kitty at his elbow. Emma had been introduced to Rudolph Valentino in Hollywood earlier in the year and understood his appeal. "Latin Lovers" were not (as Kitty would put it) her "type," but Emma found the man genial and intelligent, and impatient with the demands the studios put on him. When he came into the suite, he greeted her by name, clasped her hand with the polished good manners of a professional gigolo, and asked after her opinions of America and Hollywood, "now that you've been here for a year." But he, too, had his job to do that evening and, with a rueful grin, turned back to the task of interesting Neil Bandog, and Foremost's chief financial backer Irv Goldman, in various projects to follow on after those set up for him by his meddling wife.

Mr. Pugh excused himself for a moment to intercept a thickset stranger who was guided into the room by Conrad Fishbein and introduced as Cabel Smalls ". . . from Smalls and Goussage, Dallas . . ." Over the din of the party, Emma caught the man's Texas accent: ". . . representing Doctor Luke Spitz. Doctor Spitz should be here Saturday, and if we could have a meeting then over his late daughter's affairs . . ."

It was the lawyer employed by Darlene's father.

Mr. Pugh turned in her direction and scanned the crowd as if searching for someone, probably Emma herself. She had meant to bring the packet of "rubies, pearls, diamonds" that evening and had been waiting for a moment to go downstairs and fetch it. But now she wondered if he'd prefer to take delivery in private. Had he even mentioned it to Mr. Bandog—who had presumably paid for at least some of its contents—let alone Mr. Smalls?

And something *tinged* in her memory, like a small bell.

Something that had flickered through her mind at the precinct house for a moment, chased away by the more general reflection of how little any person left behind them.

What was it?

She stepped back quickly through the nearest door and closed it before she turned on the light. It was the small, second bedroom of the suite—in case a guest brought family with him—but it held, for a moment, the same quiet that had blessed the little breakfast room at Cypress Cove on Saturday night. *Come for a little air?* had inquired Mrs. Blair.

The plush-draped bed was piled with dresses, slips, lace-festooned undergarments. *Parsimony on Mr. Pugh's part?* she wondered now.

Or the desire to go through them before the police decided on a more intensive search for clues? To search for something that needed to be hidden?

Neat heaps of silk stockings and négligées: she recognized the robe of gold-stamped blue velvet that Darlene had been wearing on the Chicago Limited, when she'd gone into her private compartment to warn her of what Tom Ince had said.

Stay away from it. Stay away from him.

Δόξει τις αμαθεί σοφά λέγων ουκ ευ φρονεί, Euripedes had written. *A fool will think you're a fool if you talk sense to him.*

Floppy Dexter, drunkenly arguing with a tuxedo-clothed strong-arm at the Mardi Gras Club at midnight. Sixty-some blocks from the Palace Theater . . .

But wealthy enough to hire someone sober.

How much of his fortune does he control now*? On a day-to-day basis? Or is that what's really the issue?*

And why . . .

Always, it came back to that. *Why?*

Because he'd learned of her non-stop merry-go-round of other lovers?

Had she asked him for more than fifty thousand? Or had *she* learned something?

But what could she have learned?

For a time, Emma contemplated those expensive piles of silks, the serried ranks of shoes: green snakeskin, diamanté heels, crimson to go with her crimson Patou frock, black and silver to complement the black-and-silver Erté. Burgundy-and-gold hand-painted French silk at twenty dollars a pair . . .

It's not a lot, she had said, with a brown paper packet of diamonds and rubies, the small gold handbag, filling her hands, and Detective Smith had replied quietly, *It never is.*

Earth and shadows, Euripedes had written.

Even if you were King Tutankhamen, three rooms stuffed with gold was not a lot. You still had to leave it at the door when you passed through.

And yet the same thought tugged at her. *There's something missing . . .*

Something . . . about the dresses, about the shoes, the handbag, the jewels . . .

An explosion of noise in the living room: laughter, shouted greetings, voices. She heard Chico's, doing an explanation in stage-Italian double-talk as to why they were late from the theater ("What's-a you doin' out las' night with my wife?"), and Valentino shooting back a reply in equally thick dialect ("That was-a no you' wife, that was a lady!") to roars of laughter at the decades-old vaudeville routine.

Zeppo's voice chimed in, in the thick Irish bluster of a Yorkville cop: "And what was you doin', bhoy-o, out with a respectable lady? Clear acrost the street I saw youse plottin' robbery—" and Groucho, "That's all you know. That lady was my sister, a woman who can whip her weight in wild caterpillars, I'll have you know, and if you were clear across the street, you couldn't have seen past her with a periscope. Come to think of it, haven't I seen you before? Didn't you used to work at the laundry at Sing Sing? I never forget a face, but in your case, I'll make an exception . . ."

"Oh, yeah?" retorted Zeppo, abandoning the Irish flatfoot for a tone-for-tone duplication of Groucho's own voice and stage delivery. "Say, who let you in here anyway? I think I've been insulted getting an invitation to this shindig, and if the food was any worse, I'd leave. Parties around here aren't what they used to be. Look at the Democrats."

"Oh, yeah?" returned Groucho, and for a few minutes Emma listened, laughing, to the two identical voices trading insults before they were swamped by the general racket of the room.

Surely, she thought, *Zal should be arriving soon—Would he come up here? How long would he have to work, developing plates that had probably been light-damaged when Allie of the Legs had opened the box . . .*

Or would he simply go back to the Bayrose and meet her on the El train to Queens in the morning?

Zal.

* * *

As the grateful principals had boarded the train at Point Jefferson on Sunday afternoon, Zal had promised Emma a late-night visit to Lindy's for cheesecake: "I'm getting off in Brooklyn."

"I should hope so," had said Emma with a smile.

And he'd met her eyes, again a little surprised that she knew why . . . but deeply relieved.

"My husband was Kitty's brother, remember," said Emma gently. "So even if I hadn't heard my father read Second Maccabees in the original Greek, I know all about the Temple lamps and potato pancakes." She had kissed him in the yellow glare of the lights on the train platform, grips and gaffers and extras pushing past them, and a small flaxen-fair Pekinese under her arm. She reached around to her satchel and dug out the little packet she'd brought that morning, in the satchel along with Kitty's gin and astrology magazines. "Can you slip this to your sister without your mother suffering spasms of suspicion?"

"I'll tell her it's from the dogs."

When Zal had stepped through the door of Suite 1202 Sunday evening at about ten, he had been greeted by the warm small light of two candles burning in the silver menorah that Jim had bought her, on the day of their wedding, six years before. "You gotta learn to use this," Jim had cautioned her with a grin. "Maybe it'll convince my papa you're not a daughter of Lilith like my sister." (It hadn't.) With the menorah, they had bought two silver candlesticks ("On the Sabbath, Mama would light one for each member of the household".) She never knew what had happened to the candlesticks, but someone (*Who?* Another thing she never knew) had packed the menorah in the small suitcase they'd brought with her when she'd been carried, delirious with the influenza, to the hospital. After one of Lawrence Pendergast's girlfriends had stolen her engagement ring, it was one of the very few things she owned that Jim had ever touched.

Knowing that Hanukkah would fall during their time in New York, Emma had brought it with her, and candles to mark the return of light to the world.

Lighting them in the quiet of the half-darkened suite, she had recalled how it had felt, looking forward to her first Hanukkah as Jim's wife. The first Hanukkah when they'd have a home together.

And Sunday night, sleeping in Zal's arms (they'd left a little shell earring box as a present for Kitty and a couple of Lindy's potato pancakes), she had dreamed of Jim, lighting the menorah on the first night of the first Hanukkah in their first home. The Hanukkah that had never happened, for he had been dead long before autumn leaves fell. Dreamed of the warmth of his lips on hers. Different from Zal's, just as the strength of his arms was different, the shape of his body and the texture of his skin.

"We stay in different houses, every night we're on the road," Jim said to her. "You be happy in every one of them, Em. Like the man said, in Heaven there isn't any marriage or being given in marriage. But there is love."

Emerging from the spare bedroom of Mr. Pugh's suite, she found the parlor contained at least twice as many people as it had when she'd retreated a few minutes before. (Zeppo was right: the gathering did leave a great deal to be desired . . .) Some she recognized from the nightclubs and MBQ studios; others were total strangers. Trays of—yes, indeed, more oysters Rockefeller. Conrad Fishbein was introducing Harpo's tall "writer friend" to Valentino, and Emma realized that the man was the comic playwright George S. Kaufman—her mind momentarily boggled at the idea of Rudolph Valentino starring in a film of *Beggar on Horseback* . . . (*How would they ever capture that dialog on title-cards?*)

No sign of Zal, though at five foot seven, he could easily have been hidden in the crowd.

The door opened to admit a man whom Emma recognized as the matinee idol John Barrymore, accompanied by a woman who was clearly not his wife and followed by several more young ladies of the chorus-girl type: shrieks of amorous greeting and delight all around. Fishbein looked nonplussed. Mr. Pugh, Emma realized, was nowhere to be found. One of the newcomers was hoisted up to dance on a table, to the accompaniment of a rather pixilated George Blakeney on the piano. Chico and Harpo promptly joined him on either side . . .

Ah, there was Mr. Pugh, deep in conversation with a producer of Broadway revues of the less refined sort . . . Had he disappeared at the sound of newcomers entering the room? She couldn't recall.

Emma winced at the screams of laughter around the danseuse on the table, and an exceedingly drunk Ken Elmore caught her by the arm and commenced a long account of the iniquities of the new Chrysler automobile dealership on Fiftieth Street. (*Is he actually trying to purchase a car in New York? How on earth does he plan to get it home?*) The room was rapidly becoming blue with cigarette smoke, the air unbreathable.

"Oh, look!" cried Emma, pointing in the direction of the suite's kitchen door. "Is that Constance Talmadge?"

Elmore swiveled to look, and Emma disappeared into the crowd.

In the hallway outside the suite, three of the chorus girls were smoking, clustered around Neil Bandog—who seemed to be auditioning Miss Golden's replacement—and a Ziegfeld Follies juggler named Bill was demonstrating bullfighter cloak work—with the tablecloth from a room-service trolley—to a fourth. "Duchess!" cried Gordy Graves, moving to intercept her. "That scene in the town square with Nick and Darlene . . ."

"I'll be right back," Emma promised, raising a finger, and made her escape.

The elevator—*Thank Heavens!*—arrived within minutes of her summons, its operator greeting her with a carefully learned "Goot effnight, Duchess." And smiled when, recognizing his accent, she replied, "Spasibo."

It was one thirty in the morning, and though cars were still passing the glass doors onto Central Park South, relatively quiet. Behind the front desk, a trim little gentleman in a dark suit was in conversation with the only visible bell "boy" (thirty at least, and wearing a carefully painted mask over the lower part of his face to conceal what Emma knew would be hideous mutilation from the war). She caught the words ". . . ever since they sold Ruth to the Yankees, they haven't won shit . . ." and though she knew by this time that "Ruth" was actually a man, could not rid her mind of the image of a biblical damsel peddled on an auction block to a pack of bearded Americans in frock coats.

Other than occasional patrons drifting into the hotel's Fifth Avenue Café, the only other person in the lobby was, of all people, Groucho Marx, curled up in one of the deep leather armchairs near the shut-up lobby newsstand, reading *The Sea Hawk*. (*HUNT CONTINUES FOR SCREEN GODDESS MURDERER*, shrieked the headlines just beyond his shoulder). Out of respect for a fellow refugee, Emma collected a newspaper that someone had left on a table (*GOLDEN SLAIN BY GANGSTERS?*) and scanned the room for somewhere to sit that would not violate his solitude.

But Groucho raised his head, said in his "normal" (non-stage) voice, "Ah, Duchess. Had enough up there?"

"I have been entertained," said Emma, "beyond my capacity to appreciate it," and Groucho laughed.

"I'll ask again: What's a nice girl like you doing in a place like this?" and Emma, smiling, crossed to the chair near his.

"Had you met my previous employer in Manchester, you would have no need to ask, sir. I was a paid companion—and not very well paid."

"Was there a crazy wife locked in the attic?" He sat up, interested. Behind thick spectacle lenses, his gray eyes were bright. "So all those girls you meet in Jane Austen and Charlotte Brontë are real?"

"I'm afraid so—and a crazy wife, or husband, locked in the attic would have been a welcome change from rubbing Mrs. Pendergast's swollen feet every night while she told me how disappointed she was in her partner's performance at bridge."

"I never thought I'd hear of anything worse than split weeks on the Gus Sun circuit in the Texas panhandle, but I think that comes close."

So they traded tales—of worlds that were galaxies apart—shaking their heads over Oxford college propriety and the occasional necessity of romancing boarding-house keepers in order to be fed something other than chili every night ("We drew straws," said Groucho). Marx was a good storyteller, and a good listener, well read and observant, and it was after two in the morning—and people were still arriving for the party up in Mr. Pugh's suite—when, very quietly, a tall, fat man wearing a cap pulled down to hide his face and carrying a plumber's toolbag, slipped through the door of the now-silent Fifth Avenue Café and made his way quickly across the lobby . . .

Emma sat up. "I think that's Mr. Pugh."

Groucho turned his head sharply. "If it ain't, it's his twin brother. Now, there's a scary thought. Running from the cops?"

"From someone, I think." Emma got to her feet as Pugh slipped through the doors and out onto Central Park South. "He's been looking over his shoulder since the night of Miss Golden's murder—"

"If I'd had a humdinger of a fight with her and no alibi, I'd be looking over my shoulder, too." He rose also, crossed the lobby with the unexpectedly lithe walk of a dancer, and disappeared through the archway that led to the offices, returning a moment later with two coats slung over his arm. "Night staff," he explained, handing her one. "They'll never miss 'em."

Emma slid her arms into the garment (*If the owner works here, he can't* possibly *have lice or fleas* . . .) and followed her companion to the door. Pugh—and that tall bulk, that rolling walk, could belong to no one else—had just stepped into a break in the traffic on Central Park South, crossing toward the dark leafy rampart of the park.

"He got a girlfriend in town?" asked Groucho softly.

"Other than Kitty?"

"You tell me."

They stepped off the curb, swiftly crossed the pavement before the swerving yellow eyes of taxis, limousines, drunks on their way to the next party (*Hasn't* anyone *in this town heard about Prohibition?*).

"He was in and out of the party while I was there," said Groucho after a moment. "That's what you could do, if you wanted an alibi for being there all night."

"An alibi for what?"

The man beside her shrugged. "Search me. Or if you don't like that idea, I'll search you. There he goes." He nodded as the pale, heavy shape disappeared into the trees.

And the memory of whatever it was—whatever didn't add up—scratched again at Emma's thoughts . . .

They crossed the wet grass, found the break in the trees where Pugh had disappeared. A gravel path. It needed re-graveling, but still they walked beside it, rather than on the noisier surface. Now and then, they glimpsed their quarry, making his way steadily north. When he reached the drive that looped through the park, he turned along it. Groucho glanced at Emma, and the two of them remained in the shadows of the woods, following as best they could along the silent pavement.

"Meeting someone?" Emma asked softly.

"Someone he's not supposed to be meeting, it looks like." His glasses flashed in the lights of a passing car. "Believe me, I've sneaked away to enough clandestine rendezvouses to make up a Salvation Army orchestra, if that's your idea of a good time. It could be—"

Dark without headlights, a car pulled up a short way beyond them on the drive. At the same moment, two men stepped out of the shrubbery behind them, and the car's door opened.

One of the men gestured briefly, and the thin moonlight glinted on a gun.

"Get in the car, Marx."

Groucho's hand closed hard on Emma's arm. "Now, see here—"

The other man said, "You go back to the hotel, sister, if you know what's good for you." And to Groucho, "Get in the car."

FIFTEEN

As the other man stepped forward, reaching for Groucho's arm, Emma gasped, pressed her hand to her throat (as she had seen Mrs. Pendergast or her friends do hundreds of times), and collapsed. Neatly dodging Groucho's attempt to catch her, she tucked her chin and rolled against the gunman's shins, and as she felt him stagger back, threw her weight in the direction of the second man. Both thugs went down like ninepins. She heard one curse and the thud of something—the gun?—hitting the ground. It must have been the gun because Groucho kicked it, spinning, into the drive, grabbed Emma's arm even as she was scrambling to her feet, and hauled her—fast, as one of the fallen men clutched for her ankle—into the dark of the nearby trees.

"Get rid of the coats," he panted, and Emma stripped off the pale garment without slowing down. When they'd dropped both on the grass—dimly visible in the darkness of the wooded lawn—Groucho reversed directions, walking swiftly in the direction of (Emma thought) the circular roundabout at the western corner of the park . . . *Columbus Circle*?

He stopped, and they heard the swishing of feet in the grass; a man said, "That way," and the swishing continued east—the trajectory of their original flight as marked by the coats.

Groucho's hand was shaking and ice-cold as it closed over hers.

From the circle, they crossed Central Park South quickly, the sidewalk in front of the stylish apartment buildings near the Plaza still relatively busy considering the smallness of the hour of the morning. "Don't look around," whispered Groucho, holding her arm now linked in his, like just another couple of strollers (*Without coats?* Emma wondered, but didn't question the matter). (*They can't get us with every doorman on the street watching . . .*)

As they approached the Plaza, he took a deep breath, and his trembling lessened. "Say, you're pretty good at running away," he remarked. "You done this before?"

"First time." She, too, was shaking, and not entirely with cold. "You?"

"You do a lot of it in vaudeville." And as the doorman bowed them through the Plaza's doors, he added quietly, "Thanks. That was fast thinking."

"It's what comes of working for a fast woman."

Groucho checked his stride for a split second, then laughed, almost helplessly, holding tight to her arm. Emma had to fight not to crumble into hysterical laughter as well.

"There'll be coffee up in Kitty's suite."

There was also Chico's hat and overcoat on the sofa there, and the bedroom door was shut. Emma rolled her eyes, and Groucho said, "Good. He can give me a lift home," and bent down to pat the three sleepy Pekinese who waddled up to greet them. "You buy these, or you knit them yourself?"

"Kitty bought them. I was hired to brush them."

He followed her into the suite's small kitchen, Black Jasmine at their heels to supervise the coffee-making, while Buttercreme and Chang Ming busily sniffed the carpet where alien shoes had trod. Glancing back, Groucho explained, "Ah! They're looking for their noses. You OK?" he added, hearing, perhaps, the hysterical note in her laughter, and she nodded, leaning a little on the kitchen counter.

"What . . . was that about?" she asked at last. "Those were Angel-Eyes Taralla's men. I recognized the one with the gun—Bronco, the tall one with the broken nose."

"Shit. Pardon my French, Duchess. Look—my hands are still shaking." He took off his glasses, wiped his face. "I can't figure out what he'd want with me. If it was Chico, I'd understand—he owes money to every crook in town. If I don't quit shaking, Zeppo's going to have to cover for me on stage—he makes a better Groucho than I do anyway. Can I give you a hand with that?" he added, as Emma brought the coffee grinder forward to the edge of the counter. "Though I don't think either of us is going to be worth a red cent tomorrow, you have to be out at MBQ in the morning, don't you? And it's—" He looked around for a clock, then checked his watch. "It's pretty near four already. I live clear the hell out in Great Neck—"

A noise in the living room made them both spin. But it was only Chico and Kitty in the kitchen doorway, Chico in shirt, trousers, and bare feet, and a tousled (but freshly and immaculately made-up) Kitty in another of her extravagant kimonos. Chico said, "Julie!" (Groucho's real name was Julius). "What the hell you—?"

And Kitty, seeing Emma's face, broke in, "What is it, darling? Are you all right?"

"A couple of Angel-Eyes Taralla's boys tried to take me for a ride," said Groucho. "Only I don't think it was me they were after. I think they wanted Zeppo."

"You coulda got Julie killed," said Chico, three-quarters of an hour and three telephone calls later, when Zeppo finally arrived. "You coulda got the Duchess killed. So what the hell is going on?"

The youngest brother stood for a long moment in the kitchen door, eyes on the floor. But when he raised his head, glanced from his brothers to Kitty and then to Emma, in the harsh electric glare of the kitchen lights, he did, indeed, look a great deal like Groucho.

Particularly, reflected Emma, to men who hadn't seen the two brothers together off-stage and were watching the Plaza Hotel doorways from across the street in poor lighting.

"I'm sorry, Julie," he said at last. "I swear I'm sorry, Duchess. But—" Anger (*At himself?* Emma wondered. *At his brothers for treating him like a child?*) struggled with mortification in his face, and with fear.

Very gently, she asked, "Does this have something to do with what happened at the Palace Theater?"

He looked at her sharply, and she went on, "Whatever you did—or whoever you're screening—you know we won't speak of it."

His shoulders relaxed a little, but it was still a long time before he could bring the words out. Then, turning to Kitty, he said, "You know Cissy McLaren?"

"Dennie McLaren's sister?" she returned in surprise. "I knew her back when I was in the Follies in—well, once upon a time." She made a deprecating gesture, as if she hadn't been old enough to be a chorus girl herself in 1912. "I heard she was dancing in the *Scandals* . . ."

"She was," said Zeppo, as if trying to speak around a garrote. "Then she hooked up with Bronco Burnett last year—"

"Oh, shit!" said Kitty, and Chico said a Yiddish word that neither Jim nor Zal would ever translate for Emma.

"Dennie called me Monday night," Zeppo went on. "I've been friends with her—and Cissy—since before we moved back to New York; I taught her how to deal cards when she was about eleven. When I got to Dennie's . . . he'd beat Cissy up bad. Dennie begged me to help her get Cissy out of town. She said Bronco was already checking the hospitals for her, so she couldn't take her there. Couldn't take her anywhere Bronco would find her."

Chico repeated himself.

"Where'd you take her?" asked Groucho quietly.

"Dennie has a friend in Wilmington. A priest. He said he could get Cissy on a train to St. Louis, where another girl from the Follies, good friend of Dennie's, had married and knew people who could help Cissy get a job. Dennie doesn't drive. I drove them both down to Wilmington that night and drove Dennie back before daylight—"

"No wonder you looked like death on a soda cracker on stage on Tuesday," Groucho remarked, but his voice was gentle.

"Bronco'll kill Cissy if he finds her," said Zeppo after a time. "And he'll kill me if he learns I helped her get out of town. Probably Dennie, too. I'd rather keep my mouth shut and hope to God Smith finds somebody else to pin the rap on for poor Darlene. Even if she was a bitch to Mila—"

"You ever heard why Mila made herself scarce?" asked Kitty. She fetched the coffee pot from the stove, refilled everybody's cup, and got one for Zeppo, who sank down into the place at the table between Emma and Groucho. In the time it took for

Zeppo to arrive, she'd dressed—and Chico had donned his jacket, ascot, and shoes—and had telephoned down to room service for donuts, which so far no one had touched.

Zeppo shook his head. "Nobody I've asked knows," he said. "Which is weird, because . . . I hate to sound cold or anything, but with Miss Golden out of the picture, this would be her chance for a starring job. You did say, didn't you, Kit, that they don't want to do re-shoots?"

Kitty nodded, fished a cigarette from her pocket, and offered others to Zeppo and his brothers. "I thought of that, too. And I bet poor Emma has, having to rewrite all those scenes—"

"Maybe," said Groucho thoughtfully, "she's afraid the police are thinking the same thing. And maybe they are."

The brothers left at six, after a breakfast of donuts and coffee. Groucho and Chico had houses (and wives and children) just beyond Queens on Long Island; Zeppo merely went downstairs and booked himself a room at the Plaza, since there was a good chance that Bronco Burnett might be watching his West Side apartment. "As soon as I know he's awake, I'll phone Shakespeare," said Kitty, returning to the kitchen after closing the door. "I won't say why, but I'll see if I can get him to sort of hint to Bronco that he's barking up the wrong tree."

A hint from Shakespeare Malone, Emma had learned by now, probably had the force of orders at gunpoint elsewhere.

Kitty settled again at the table, delicate hands cradling the coffee cup before her. "And what a pain for you, sweetheart, since I don't have to film anything today . . . but poor Zallie's got to go up to MBQ anyway and shoot all that stuff about what's-his-name—Robertson?"

"Robespierre."

"Yeah, something like that. The one who was giving poor Margaret a hard time the other day . . . About him getting killed—Robertson, I mean. Zal called from the studio last night, right after you left. I came down here looking for you—"

"I was in the lobby." Emma poured herself the last of the tea in the pot and went on to relate the curious preface to the park attack . . .

"I wondered what you two were doing in the park."

"And I feel bad about those two coats we left out there in the woods," said Emma. "They belonged to someone on the hotel staff, but if we hadn't got rid of them, they were light-colored enough to have shown up, at least a little, in the dark under the trees. Has Mr. Pugh returned?"

"Search me." Kitty shrugged. "You want me to go up and check? I have a key."

Emma started to surmise that Mr. Pugh was probably on his way to MBQ, then stopped herself as a thought—several thoughts—crossed her mind. "Would you?" she said. "And if he isn't there—and he's probably not—would you look in the spare bedroom, where he has Miss Golden's things? There's a cardboard box beside the dresses on the bed, with all her make-up things—"

Kitty brightened visibly at the prospect of being able to loot her rival's collection of Dorin de Paris.

"—and probably everything else from her dressing table. If her telephone book is there, could you bring it down?"

With Kitty's departure, Emma tidied the dishes to the sink counter—placing a tip beside them for the maid whose job it was to wash up—and fetched from her small bedroom the packet Detective Smith had given her the day before.

Now, sitting at the kitchen table, she opened it and remembered what it had been that had tweaked her attention in the precinct house when she'd signed for it.

No ten-karat diamond ring.

And . . . Rubies with that gold-and-burgundy Lanvin dress?

Like Kitty, Darlene was very careful about her appearance. Almost obsessively conscious of her clothing and jewelry.

The scarlet of rubies with the deeper hues of burgundy?

Kitty wouldn't have worn such a combination. She called to mind the several times she'd seen Darlene in that dress, and remembered that the blonde actress had a bracelet, necklace, and earrings of garnets that perfectly set off those colors. A few small diamonds for accents, but no pearls . . .

She unfolded the papers and grimaced at the scale and

ostentation of the pieces within. The rubies were, as she'd suspected, completely the wrong color—

The Pekes sprang to their feet as the key clicked in the suite door and Kitty entered the kitchen again. "This was all I could find, honey—Whoa!"

Her sister-in-law sat beside her, picked up the thick band of jewels, and said, "Ew!"

"Those aren't Miss Golden's, are they?"

"Oh, hell, no."

"They're what she was wearing the night she was killed. But they're the wrong color for that Lanvin dress—"

"And they're fakes." Kitty gently rubbed one of the pearls against her front teeth, then carried the bracelet to the kitchen's small ice box and set it inside.

"Fakes?"

"Look at the size of them, honey. You don't get rocks like that all together on one piece unless you're the Queen of England. They're bigger than anything else Bandog gave her—or Frank," she added, with a little scowl. (*Of course Kitty would keep track of that . . .*) "Think about the other jewels you've seen her wear."

She opened the ice box again and removed the bracelet, held it close to her lips, and blew softly on the central medallion of diamonds. The misty ghost of her breath dimmed the sparkle like a frost.

"Breath'll fade from a real diamond almost at once." Kitty turned the jewels toward the overhead light. "Darlene was wearing these?"

"I don't think she was," returned Emma slowly. "Now that I think of it, the shoes she'd wear with that dress are up in Mr. Pugh's room also, with the rest of her things. They're painted silk—"

"Oh, yeah!" Kitty seldom missed a pair of shoes. "Maison Huygen-St-Ouen."

"And she wasn't wearing that monstrous ring Mr. Bandog gave her."

"Well, if she was meeting Floppy Dexter, she wouldn't be. But it isn't with the jewelry that's up in Frank's room, either."

Of course she looked!

"Is it in her handbag?"

Emma took from Smith's packet the gold chain handbag and opened it. Even before she did, Kitty said, "She was carrying *that*? *Phew*," she added, as the whiff of too-sweet cologne puffed into the room. "That's pure Woolworth . . ." She fanned the air as she named the popular five-and-dime store, then reached into the bag. "So's this." She held up the powder compact. "Darlene used Deauville Naturelle. This stuff . . ."

She shook her head. "And there's no gum. She'd have packets of it in her bag. Unless the cops took it . . . You think the cops switched the jewelry? Or kiped the ring? They must get tons of the cheap stuff every week, and with that sour pill Smalls asking for it back—"

"No." Emma picked up the small, rather tattered booklet Kitty had laid on the table beside the heap of counterfeit glory, and flipped open the front cover. In faded ink on the inside was printed, *DORIS DARLING, 607 West 43rd Street—5-H*. ("Hell's Kitchen," Kitty identified it at once. "I had a place not far from there on Eleventh. Hot and cold running cockroaches.") Two other addresses followed, crossed out in pencil like the Forty-Third Street room. In a different color ink, lines were drawn through *DORIS DARLING*, and *DARLENE GOLDEN* replaced it, in the same hue and style of printing, with telephone number. Then another New York address (also with telephone number, also crossed out), one in Chicago, and two more in Los Angeles.

The final Los Angeles address was her current one.

Emma said, "I don't think that was Miss Golden at all."

SIXTEEN

Kitty thought about it for a long time before she said, "Well, shit," in a thoughtful tone. "I always wondered how Darlene could manage to be making arrangements with Floppy Dexter to get married and getting her ashes hauled by that divine Joey Saylor at the same time she was keeping Angel-Eyes on a string. How she could be in two places at once."

"When the answer was looking us in the face," concluded Emma quietly. "She must have paid Mila a lot, to put up with her and go on doubling for her . . ."

"I'd have done it, if Princess Laura looked anything like me at all . . ."

Emma refrained from mentioning that, in a sense, she herself had "doubled" for Kitty, not only driving away from Dias Dorados in an identical red jacket and cloche, but on the nights when Mr. Crain had tickets to the opera and Kitty had just had a peremptory dinner invitation from Mr. Pugh (to say nothing of a more entertaining prospect from Mr. Marx). With poor Zal stuck on Long Island until late in the evening, Kitty had been sure that Emma would keep her elderly beau occupied without worrying that her substitute would usurp first place.

Instead, Emma said, "It didn't really come into focus for me, either, until Chico told Zeppo that he could have got their brother killed, simply for looking like him. And for being in the same place where this Mr. Burnett knew that Zeppo would be last night."

She turned her attention back to the notebook, thumbing the smudgy pages carefully, studying entries that had been crossed out or updated. "Look." She turned the little book around and held it flat on the table.

"Lola Rutter," Kitty read. "Oh, Loïe Lamour! She dances at the High Wire—I didn't know her name was really Rutter! No wonder she changed it—Rutter sounds like a farmer's wife . . . Wait, isn't that Darlene's old address?" She frowned and turned the pages back, to check Miss Lamour's later addresses against Miss Golden's. "Looks like they roomed together until Darlene left town in '16 . . . I was in Chicago by then."

"And Miss Lamour's address and telephone number have been renewed four times since then," pointed out Emma. "So Miss Golden has stayed in touch with her. None of the others have more than one address listed, so it looks like she's the only one in New York that she's stayed in touch with."

Kitty said, "Hmmn," and glanced at the clock.

"Thank God!" exclaimed Miss Lamour, the tinny quality of the telephone receiver seeming to put an extra edge onto an inflection of Texan speech even more pronounced than Darlene Golden's. "I'll get her . . ."

"Now, for God's sake don't pay attention to what my sister says!" exclaimed Darlene's voice in unmistakable—and exaggerated—Texas accents. "Loïe, stop foolin' these nice people, whoever they are . . . Loïe's always foolin' around, ma'am. My name's Dotty and I'm sick of her playin' these kinds of jokes . . ."

"Darlene," said Kitty's voice over the extension, Emma realized, from the bedroom. "We know it's you. We have to talk to you and find out what really happened at the Palace Theater. That was Mila Haley who got killed, wasn't it, and don't you dare hang up and leave town! Frank's been out every night for over a week looking for her in every speak and club in town, and you know he's going to give that up and find somebody else who looks enough like you to finish the picture—anybody. Poor Emma's been rewriting every scene in that silly scenario so they won't *need* you to finish. You know that's just a matter of time."

"Whoever you are"—Miss Golden's voice sounded shaky—"I don't know what the fuck you're talkin' about." She cracked her chewing gum. Emma reflected that that was Miss Golden, all right.

"What I'm talking about is that it's just a matter of time

before Mr. Bandog finds somebody—anybody—else as well. If he fell for you, he'll fall for somebody else."

"Your father's lawyer arrived yesterday," Emma interjected into the long silence that followed these words. "Your father will be in town Saturday, to collect the rest of the money owed on your contract, if he can, and to claim the contents of your bank account—and the deed to your house on Crescent Drive. If nothing else, he's asked for all your jewelry, and all your dresses, which I'm sure he plans to resell—"

Miss Golden's next remark would have brought a blush to the cheek of an Army muleteer. And then, after another silence: "Has Bandog found somebody else already?" And her tone, Emma noted, was not angry, but frightened. "Or asked for any of the stuff he gave me?"

Emma said nothing, understanding suddenly why Kitty's rival had fled to the one friend in New York whose address and telephone number she still kept, and not to her wealthy lover.

And Kitty said, very quietly, "Oh, shit."

"Yeah."

"Do you have any reason," Emma asked after a time, "to think Mr. Bandog might have had something to do with it? Anything you saw, anything he said? He was out on Long Island . . ."

"Honey," sighed Kitty, "men *always* have an alibi. But you can't stay hid, Darlene. You've got to at least tell the cops what you know. What you saw, what Mila was doing there . . . Right now, they're just stumbling around in the dark, and God knows who they'll pin it on. We'll find a place to stash you, that won't drag Loïe into trouble. Besides," she added brightly, "think how it'll piss off your dad!"

Indistinguishable words on the other end of the wire. Then Loïe Lamour's voice: "You be walking along the drive in the park in twenty minutes. I'll pick you up in a cab."

Kitty brought her .32 Special in her handbag, but in fact it wasn't necessary. A Checker cab, with Loïe Lamour in it—a long-legged brunette of about Kitty's age and, like Kitty, exquisitely made-up—cruised past them on the drive in the park not far from where Bronco Burnett had bush-whacked Emma and Groucho twelve hours previously. It dropped them off on West Fifty-Fifth Street, not far from the park, and from there Miss Lamour led them to an apartment building which, though it lacked the expensive gloss of those that flanked the Plaza, still whispered of some very expensive infidelity.

Despite her breathtaking natural beauty and exquisite make-up, Darlene Golden looked drawn, haggard, and scared.

The first thing she said to Emma was, "I'm so sorry, Duchess. You were right. You tried to warn me, and I told you to fuck off, and Jesus, half the poor girl's head was blown off! I'm sorry."

"It's all right," said Emma, reflecting—she had not seen the body—that it was no wonder everyone had assumed the dead woman was Miss Golden.

Darlene produced a "ladies' note"-size envelope which contained a single sheet of folded notepaper. Emma—observing that Darlene still wore Mr. Bandog's diamond paving-stone—took it and opened the sheet.

> 12:00—the Palace. I am longing to hold you in my arms.—Floppy

"Frank was supposed to meet me at eleven," said Darlene, her voice a little hoarse.

Kitty's mouth opened protestingly, outrage snapping in her eyes just as if she hadn't expected Chico Marx at ten thirty-five.

"I always set it up with Mila to meet Floppy backstage at the Palace. He and I both had keys, and I knew it would be like the Tunnel of Love back there: Floppy couldn't have told me from Al Jolson by that dinky little light above the stairway."

"Floppy had a key?"

Darlene shrugged. "The way the kid goes through chorus girls, you think he wouldn't? I told her—like I always do—to find out where he is with the plans for the wedding, and when he's going to get me the money for it—'cause I guess he has to sneak it out from under the noses of that Board that runs Dexter Consolidated—and then find some reason to blow out of there. But Frank phones me at about ten thirty, sayin' he can't make it—"

"Oh!" cried Kitty. "He must have called you from the lobby after dropping me off! The four-flusher!"

"Oh!" exclaimed Darlene, equally indignant.

If he'd been a minute longer on the phone, reflected Emma, *he'd have passed Chico in the lobby . . .*

"The lying tub of—! So I thought, this is my chance to clinch things with Floppy, 'cause all Mila could really do was get the information and scram. So I jump in a cab and head like hell over to Forty-Seventh Street to catch Mila before she goes in. But when I get there, the stage door's half open and I can see the work lights on backstage."

She winced and looked aside. After a time, she swallowed hard and went on, without looking back at them: "I could see her from the door. See the rhinestones sort of glittering on her dress . . . *my* dress. She always wore one of my dresses when she'd meet Floppy. He's pretty near-sighted, and she'd meet him for just short times, in clubs where the light wasn't good. She'd wear my perfume, and she could do my voice real good. And I . . . I could smell the blood from the door. Oskar—the watchman—was stooping over her. I'd paid him that afternoon to stay the hell out of the theater—a lot of the girls do that. I heard him say something in Polish, and then he turned around and vomited. He staggered out around the fire curtain, and I went in and . . . and saw her.

"She was lying next to one of those big stacks of flats, and there was blood . . . Jesus Christ! I knew Oskar had to be calling the cops, and I thought, *Shit, they'll think I did it*. And then I thought, *Shit, whoever did this might still be around!* And looking down at her like that . . . that's when I remembered what you said, Duchess, about Tom warning Kitty."

She looked up then, sickened shock struggling on her face. "But why would Floppy set up the whole wedding thing just to . . . to get me there and kill me? Is he crazy? Or was it somebody else who followed Mila, thinking it was me, somebody who got jealous? Somebody like Angel-Eyes, or—" Her voice faltered. "Or even Mr. Bandog. I'd swear he didn't know about Floppy. He would have made trouble about it before this, if he knew. He's said to me a million times, 'I'll never let you go,' but that's what everybody says . . ."

Emma reflected momentarily on the number of murders she had heard of which had included hindsight justifications to the effect of "We were victims of a love that would not answer to reason."

Kitty said, very quietly, "Or Mrs. Bandog."

Darlene nodded, a tiny movement, as if even now she could barely think of who else might want her dead.

"Is this Mr. Dexter's handwriting?" Emma gestured with the notepaper.

"I think so."

"Do you have other notes from him?"

"I got rid of them. I was afraid Frank would find them. Or that Mila would keep them and then sell them to Frank—or maybe to Mr. Bandog—or back to me."

"Thank you." Emma held up the envelope and the note. "If we take this to the police, they may be able to trace whether it was written by Mr. Dexter or not. I'll see what I can do about getting another sample of his handwriting. The police will want to see you . . ."

Darlene shuddered.

In her most practical voice, Emma added, "And so will your father's lawyer."

At this, the actress sat up, her jaw coming forward. "Oh, I'll look forward to *that*!" She turned to Kitty, held out her hand. "Kitty, sugar, I know we've had our tiffs—you know, like everybody does—"

Emma recalled some of the more graphic expressions Miss Golden had used when Kitty had won the "Goddess of the Silver Screen" contest in *Screen World* earlier that year, and held her peace.

"—but could you do me a great big favor?" She rose from the rather faded plush chair where she'd been sitting—Loïe's apartment had clearly come furnished—and crossed to the little table beside the door where her handbag lay. From it, she took a hotel-room key: "Frank's got all my things in his suite, don't he? Afraid somebody'd steal 'em . . . And I bet he plans to give about two strings of beads to my dad, and say some chambermaid walked off with the rest of it. Could you wait till he's out at MBQ and bring the stuff here?"

She held out the key.

In her sweetest voice, Kitty said, "Oh, I've got one, honey. And I'll be glad to."

From the Plaza, Emma called MBQ and left a message for Zal, asking him to call her when he returned to the city, or after five o'clock, whichever was most convenient. She then telephoned the Eighteenth Precinct, and was told that Detective Smith would be back around three. She and Kitty had lunch, brushed the dogs, and walked them in the park; she could not help looking at the place in the woods where, she estimated, she and Groucho had shucked their raincoats last night. They had disappeared, and she made a mental note to find a way to arrange to pay the staff members for new ones without admitting that she herself was the thief.

Were a couple of down-and-outers currently thanking God that they hadn't frozen to death in the small hours of the morning? Or were those same down-and-outers swilling rot-gut in an alley somewhere while the coats hung in the nearest pawnshop?

Her father, she reflected ruefully—or, for that matter, the emperor Marcus Aurelius—would tell her that it wasn't her business.

The moving finger writes, and having writ, moves on, the Persian sage Omar Khayyam had written, eight hundred years before. The words of the quatrain circled in her mind as they walked in the sharp afternoon chill, Kitty smoking and chattering and watching the Pekes chase one another ecstatically over the grass, and Emma shook her head. The short nap she'd managed to take that morning while waiting for Loïe and Darlene to wake up enough to deal with a telephone call had long since worn off. She definitely needed another.

An hour later, she found Detective Smith brooding over a cup of what looked and smelled like motor oil, at a desk in one corner of the detectives' squad room upstairs at the Eighteenth Precinct; he did not look any perkier than she felt. As had been the case on her previous visit, the heater in the far corner did little to warm the big room, and the voices of the other men there—about a third of the other desks were occupied—hung in the air like the smoke of decades of cheap tobacco.

Snatches of interviews, like fragments of a shattered mosaic, half heard all around them:

"And you say this man lived in your attic for two and a half years without you being aware of it?"

"And there was nothing in that envelope he'd handed me but a bunch of cut-up newspaper!"

"Did you ever have genuine intercourse with this person?"

"What do you mean by 'genuine,' officer?"

"That box was full of ladies' underpants!"

Smith looked up as she came around the partition from the hallway, stubbed out his cigarette, rose, and shook her hand. "Can I get you some coffee, Duchess?" he asked, as he held the chair for her to sit. "Or does the hope in your heart urge you to live on for another day?"

She smiled in spite of herself. "I've had as much as I can stomach for one day, thank you," and the smile he returned was surprisingly human and sweet. From her handbag, she took the envelope Darlene had given her, and held it out to him. "Miss Darlene Golden gave me this letter this morning," she said. "The woman whose body was found at the Palace Theater was her stand-in, Mila Haley—"

"The one Pugh's been scrounging around the speaks all week lookin' for?" He brought a clean handkerchief from his pocket, shielded his fingers with it as he took the envelope from her hand, and sat. There was a magnifying lens on his desk, and with this he studied the envelope, both sides, before using tweezers to open the flap and take out the note.

While he was so engaged, Emma went on, "Miss Golden would send Miss Haley to meet Mr. Dexter—if the encounter would be brief and in poor light—when she had another commitment for that evening. She often did. They did look a great deal alike." And as he slipped a manila folder from beneath the other papers on his desk and took out two or three sheets of what looked like samples of Clark Dexter's handwriting, Emma explained Darlene Golden's complicated love life and the events as described to her that forenoon.

"She's in hiding now with a friend," she finished. "She was certain, when she saw the body, that Miss Haley had been killed in her place, and she was afraid to contact anyone—even Mr. Bandog—perhaps especially Mr. Bandog—for fear that any of them might be the murderer. For that reason, she begged me to set up a meeting with you under whatever circumstances will prevent anyone from learning her whereabouts . . ."

"Well, you can eliminate Bandog." Smith looked up from the sample and Darlene's note. "His alibi stinks like last week's garbage, but it checks out. The place where he and his missus were playing parcheesi until one in the morning is out in Hempstead. That's on Long Island, and you're looking at an hour's drive even at one in the morning. His host's cook saw him there at midnight. There's no way he could have done it. Not personally. The others—"

He gestured with the tweezers. "Miss Golden is wise to lay low. Anybody who'd kill Miss Haley by mistake would still have it in for her, whether it's your boss Pugh or Taralla or even the Marx kid, though I can't really see him being steamed up enough to kill Golden over somebody else's acting job. Not in cold blood that way, sending a fake note and lying in wait. But I been wrong before. People do dumb things if they're in love, but I don't think the kid was in love. Not with Miss Haley, anyway."

"Is the note fake?"

He was silent for a time, studying the writing sample on his desk. "The handwriting's all over the place," he said at length. "That could just mean Floppy was drunk when he wrote it. Thirty people sure say he was drunk at midnight when he got kicked out of the Mardi Gras. By what I hear, he spends a lot of time that way."

He turned over the sample page—Emma cocked her head to read polite bread-and-butter phrases thanking Mrs. Corcoran for her kind hospitality on Tuesday last—in long fingers callused from some past stint at manual labor. "I'll have to send this out to one of the experts, but it doesn't look genuine to me. The paper's the same, and so's the ink. That may just mean our forger's a professional who knows his business. Somebody sure wanted to get her there, but the thing is, it doesn't look like this has anything to do with the Dexter family. Jeff Blair brought in a copy of the Dexter Trust docs last week, to show us who inherits what and how. Killing Floppy's bride wouldn't have made any difference to any one of them. Unless Rosemary Dexter OKs Junior's marriage, the whole shebang goes to a list of charities as long as your arm: A.S.P.C.A., Carnegie libraries, Catholic charities, Esperanto League, Fraternal Order of the Orioles . . . Kid doesn't get the price of a cup of coffee."

("Another wife and three children in Philadelphia," said a woman, leaning earnestly across the desk of the detective next to Mr. Smith's. "And my mother knew about it for ten years!")

"So why harm Miss Golden, if there was no money involved?" asked Emma. "And what would Mr. Ince have known about Mr. Dexter that he felt the need to warn Miss de la Rose?"

"You tell me, ma'am." Smith leaned back a little in his chair. "The attempt on Miss Golden could have nothing to do with Floppy's love life, though I'll sure ask her about it when I see her. And if you'd arrange that for me—this evening, if you can; I'll be here till six thirty—I'd appreciate it. I'm curious about what he told her—or what he might have told Miss Haley, thinking it was her. Will you do that for me?"

"I will," said Emma. "Thank you. Will you do something for me?"

"Depends on what it is."

"Will you call Mila Haley's parents? Or should we wait on that? Miss Golden will probably be safer if her attacker thinks he succeeded, won't she?"

"She will," said Smith. "But as soon as it's safe, yes, I'll give them a call. And in the meantime"—he rose and held her chair as she also got to her feet—"you watch your step. And you tell Miss Golden to keep her head down and stay out of sight for the time being. Right now, we have no idea what this is about. The whole set-up smells fishy, and it could be that Miss Haley was the target all along. Or," he added grimly, "someone else."

SEVENTEEN

"Darling!" Kitty bounced to her feet as Emma opened the suite's door, scattering Pekinese in all directions. Zal, looking like ten miles of bad road, followed her to the door and folded Emma in his arms.

"Pugh wants you to rewrite Scenes seven-hundred to eight thirty-five," he said, between two long kisses.

"Mr. Pugh can go chase himself."

Another long kiss.

"By tomorrow. And we're all going out to Versailles tomorrow to re-shoot the highwaymen sequence."

"You and Mr. Pugh are welcome to chase one another . . ."

"And," declared Kitty, making a triumphant dart back to the little coffee table by the couch, "look what I found!"

Gapstow Hotel, E. 60th Street, was written on a sheet of Plaza notepaper in Kitty's erratic block printing. *Bo Sharpless.*

And beneath it, *National Bank of the Republic* and a string of numbers that was quite clearly a bank account. Beneath this was a second account number, *Bank of Italy*, and a little knot of dollar amounts, arrows, and jotted dates that indicated that Mr. Frank Pugh (Emma recognized the account number from a year of dealing with Kitty's salary) had opened a second account at the National Bank of the Republic, on December fifteenth—the first business day after his arrival the previous Saturday—with a deposit of one thousand dollars taken from the Bank of Italy account. From that account, he had paid one hundred and thirty dollars ("deposit") on the same afternoon, to the Gapstow Hotel.

"The address was on a piece of Gapstow stationery in the pocket of a pair of overalls hidden at the back of Frank's bedroom closet." The childlike triumph faded into anger. "With them was a plumber's toolkit—the bag and the tools were all shiny-new—and a crummy old jacket with MBQ wardrobe department numbers inked on the lining. The overalls were from MBQ, too. And if that chiseler rented a room at the Gapstow so he could sneak off and meet Darlene, I'll—"

"He wouldn't have," pointed out Zal. "If he had, Darlene wouldn't have had to go hide with Loïe Longlegs in Hell's Kitchen. That's if he wasn't the one who set up the murder in the first place."

"At least Miss Golden can now hide in greater comfort," said Emma, and related what Smith had told her about the alibi for both Bandogs—

("I wouldn't put it past Mrs. B to hire it done," groused Kitty.)

—and for whichever members of the Dexter family knew the provisions of the Trust. "Which they might not do," added Emma worriedly. "I certainly don't know the provisions of my uncle David's will, for instance, if he has one. And Mr. Pugh could have set up the murder as easily as Mrs. Bandog could . . ."

"Depending on how many gangsters Mrs. Bandog knows?" Zal raised his brows.

"Well, he sure as hell rented that room for *somebody*!"

"Beau Sharpless," said Emma, a little grimly. "The highwayman hero of *Shining Bright*."

"I knew the man didn't have an imagination," said Zal.

"He sure doesn't," returned Kitty, "if he can't imagine what I'd do to him if I found out he was two-timing me—*and* Darlene at the same time!"

Emma politely swallowed back all reference to Messrs Marx, Malone, and Crain, and asked instead, "I don't suppose there's a chance we can simply go ask at the Gapstow's front desk? Do you have a picture of Mr. Pugh, Kitty?"

"We can just go inquire," said Zal, "if we do it at about one in the morning with a ten-dollar bill. I'll do that part." He followed Kitty to the couch—Kitty detoured to where her handbag lay and dug out a ten-dollar bill—and from the little table picked up half a dozen photographs. Four were clouded with light damage, but on two, figures could be made out.

These two Zal had enlarged to the size of the bigger publicity pictures, twelve inches by eighteen.

One illustrated what Emma assumed to be the Cincinnati Special. Despite marriage, widowhood, and a year in Hollywood, she felt her cheeks get hot.

No wonder they don't want the management finding out about that photo session . . .

The other was of a line of eight lovely young women—as fully clothed as chorus girls ever got on stage (*The shot must have been taken early in the session . . .*)—and brandishing pistols with huge silk bows on their grips.

"I'm not sure what they can tell us," said Zal judiciously. "Except that Sugar-Pie is double-jointed. There's Ginger. That one's probably Bunnie—what you can see of her looks like Bunnie . . ."

"Isn't that girl one of the dancers at the El Fey?" Emma pointed to the clothed picture (not the athletic illustration, which she could not even bring herself to touch). "She's the one Mr. Dexter was trying to steal ostrich plumes from. I recognize that little mole at the corner of her mouth."

"Oh, that's Sylvie Mason," said Kitty. "She's living with the *sweetest* ice-man in Brooklyn . . . Girls come and go from one chorus to another all the time. The dark girl's Roxie North—I think she's over at the Mardi Gras these days."

The costumes were clearly intended to represent a filthy Russian aristocrat's Amazonian bodyguard: high-cut at the neck, skin-tight, and featuring barely more than ballet skirts wrought of beads. Each costume—what there was of each costume—was wrought of different patterned silk brocade, and the bows that decorated their pistols, as Sugar-Pie had said, matched each bodice. Emma estimated that each bow—stripes of assorted widths, several different sizes of Oriental flowers—contained more fabric than the "costumes" themselves.

"Now that the Bandogs are cleared, do you want to call Darlene?" Kitty looked up from sorting out the jewelry that heaped the rest of the coffee table like pirate treasure. "And we should probably tell Frank, just so we can warn him that he and Bandog can't put Darlene back in front of the camera until we get an all-clear from Mr. Smith. I called Frank this afternoon and told him I'd taken Darlene's jewelry. I told him

I heard her father's lawyer was going to hire a private detective to break into his suite and swipe it, so I was going to inventory it. He sort of choked on that, but what could he say?"

"Do we tell Doctor Spitz?" asked Emma.

"Who's gonna blab to who?" finished Kitty. "We better not, though I'd love to see him have a heart attack when he realizes he's not going to get Darlene's money. But he'd probably gripe to his lawyer, and the lawyer would throw a fit, and then the cat would be out of the bag."

"It sounds so cruel not to tell them," said Emma. "But I think you're right. And it means—thank Heavens!—we can go back to the original scenario and stop playing peek-a-boo with the plot. That should please Mr. Kingsley, even if he doesn't know why."

Kitty sniffed. "What makes you think that?"

"You have a point," Emma agreed, trying to think of something that *would* please Mr. Kingsley. "And poor Mr. Blakeney will still have to make adjustments about how to shoot scenes without showing the double's face . . ."

"Not just that," objected Zal quietly. "For one thing—yeah, Spitz is a jerk, and he has only himself to thank if we don't tell him his daughter's alive . . . but we can't tell poor Mila's parents, either, that their daughter is dead. And you and Blakeney can't actually use Darlene, so you have to go on shooting with a double . . . Do we tell Blakeney? I think he can keep his mouth shut. And we still have no idea who pulled that trigger, or who the real target was . . . and no, there's no Skinner working for the *Gotham Daily Democrat*."

He gestured with the more respectable of the enlarged photographs. "We saw from Taralla's alibis that there's lots of people who'd be willing to do a job for him—and who probably wouldn't have the nerve to blackmail him over it afterwards. That's something you can't say about, say, Frank. So who was Skinner—or whoever the hell he is—really working for?"

"But why would Frank want to murder Darlene?" protested Kitty. "Or Bandog either? That's tens of thousands of dollars' worth of re-shoots!"

"And why go to the trouble of stealing a gun from the Palace

Theater?" added Emma. "Any associate of Mr. Taralla would have his own gun."

"Beats me. But that doesn't mean there isn't a reason. We just don't know what it is. It can't be a coincidence that this Skinner guy would steal a gun from the Palace Theater that's the same type and caliber as the gun that was used in a murder at the Palace Theater a week and a half later. And who'd pay him to do it, if there's no way Floppy can inherit if he marries Darlene or anybody else? And . . . what if it turns out Mila really was the original target? You can't tell me old Smith has forgotten Frank threatened a couple of times to can Darlene and run Mila in as a replacement?"

"You mean"—Emma hesitated—"Miss Golden could have been the murderer instead of the victim?" She remembered the sickened look on Darlene's face when she'd spoken of finding her rival's body, the way her voice had choked. "And everything she told us was so much make-believe?"

Well, she's an actress . . .

Is she that good an actress? Emma had seen Kitty, perhaps the worst actress in Hollywood, turn in astonishing performances when gazing up into Mr. Pugh's infatuated eyes.

"You know what the Bible says about handmaidens who pinch what belongs to the lady of the house." Zal mimed pinching his own backside and winked.

"That the earth can't bear them up," affirmed Kitty, a little surprisingly. But then, Emma recalled, her father, for all his poverty in Yorkville, had been a respected scholar back in Łódź. "I always thought it was sort of like what DeMille did in the *Ten Commandments* last year, with the earth shaking and lightning blasting people with leprosy."

"A maidservant who *becomes the heir to her mistress*," said Zal, "goes to hell. My money's on Smith keeping an eye on Darlene."

After an unsuccessful midnight attempt to corrupt the night clerk at the Gapstow, Zal slept most of the way from Penn Station to Port Jefferson the following morning. "Just my luck to get a guy who'd been imported from some Puritan town in

New England—I think from sometime in the seventeenth century. He looked at Kitty's money like Jesus telling off Satan on the mountain top. I'll try earlier in the evening next time," he assured Emma and Kitty as they boarded the Long Island Rail Road in the lightless cold of dawn. "Wake me up when we go through King's Peak."

While Zal slept, and Kitty sat before a make-up mirror in one of the two "private" parlors of the parlor car, Emma rewrote, yet again, the dozen scenes that would permit Summer Fairisle's countenance to appear on-screen once more later in the week. In response to Mr. Pugh's diatribe about budget overruns, the threat of bad weather, and a day already lost for a funeral, Mr. Blakeney had informed him that if he made everyone work on the following day—Christmas—he would be visited by jovial giants in green and silent specters in black. Mr. Pugh had had the good grace to grumble, "A poor excuse for picking a man's pocket every twenty-fifth of December . . ."

"We will be here all the earlier next morning," the director had promised, finishing the quote from *A Christmas Carol*.

Thus Pugh would spend the afternoon stonewalling Dr. Spitz's lawyer without telling him why. Like Detective Smith and Kitty, he put no faith in anyone's willingness to keep their mouths shut if money was involved.

And, Emma guessed, there was a good chance that nobody would be able to get Devon Kingsley thrown off the set that day. Certainly, Gordy Graves was no match for him—("Gordy Graves is no match for *Black Jasmine*," sniffed Kitty)—and since Darlene, reassured by Detective Smith's report on the Bandog alibi, had telephoned her lover to arrange an ecstatic reunion, it was fairly certain Mr. Bandog would not be at Versailles either.

As soon as Mr. Blakeney began running the actors through a repeat of the Emerging from the Woods Scene (to establish that Miss Fairisle was now wearing a large hat which disguised her face—a hat which curiously remained on her head through and after her ambush by the Evil Comtesse's henchmen), Emma made her preparations. She placed exercise books full of old notes and discarded drafts of *Shining Bright*, pens, a copy of the novel, and half a cup of tea on a makeshift desk in Kitty's dressing room in the chateau, arranged the dog carriers close to the heater, and with a pang of regret made her way to the stables, the Pekes trotting hopefully at her heels. (*At least Mr. Blair is safely back at Abbottsford making eggnog!*)

In addition to several clean make-up towels (so Chang Ming, Buttercreme, and Black Jasmine wouldn't have to lie on the freezing bricks of the floors), she carried her latest drafts and notes, and another cup of tea. (*Surely there has to be a tack room or garage above ground that will be habitable for a few hours . . .*)

But actually, there wasn't. After thirty minutes of trying to work in one of the rooms in the main stable block that seemed most protected from the cold breeze of the Sound, Emma gave it up. There was, she knew, an electric heater in the extras' changing tent connected to Foremost Productions' portable generator, and with any luck, she could get Carrie Drebbett to set up a couple of screens for her in the far corner. Carrie, despite her diminutive stature, was as tough as a sergeant of the Marines and could easily prevent Mr. Kingsley from physically searching the tent.

Emma gathered her things, reattached the dogs to their leashes, peered cautiously outside (yes, there was Mr. Kingsley's ginger-mustard coat moving through the woods in the direction of the chateau . . .). Being by now more or less able to get her bearings in the sprawling complex, she made her way down one wing and out a door that opened onto the Sound side of the building and took the long way around towards the set . . .

And came around the corner of the building's east wing to walk smack into Detective Smith.

"Mr. Smith!" she exclaimed, as Chang Ming rushed to prostrate himself at the newcomer's feet, as Black Jasmine perked up his ears and let out a gruff little quack of welcome, and Buttercreme disappeared into the nearest clump of holly.

The detective took a step back, as nonplussed as she. Then he tipped his shabby fedora, nodded at the satchel and notebooks in her arms, and asked, "The management doesn't even give you an office? Yeah, yeah," he added, kneeling to pat Chang Ming, "I know—the Duchess beats you three times a day."

"Regrettably, the location of my office is known to the author of the original novel." Emma stepped off the path to retrieve Buttercreme and held the little dog in her arms. "He doesn't feel that I do justice to his work. I trust you were able to interview Miss Golden yesterday evening?"

"She was packing when I got there." Smith straightened up. "Dressed to kill. Bandog showed up while I was there, and I guess she bought his story that no, he had nothing to do with it. Christ knows what she told him about what she was doing at the Palace. I understand Bandog's got two apartments in town besides the one he lives in with Mrs. B. Not to sublet; just as spares for himself on the nights he doesn't want to spend at home. She say anything to you about who she thought might be after her?"

Emma shook her head. "Unless Mr. Bandog—or his wife—paid someone else to do it. But that wouldn't explain Mr. Ince's warning."

"Yeah. That bothers me, too."

"And a hired killer would surely have taken Mila's jewelry, wouldn't he? And why choose a public place like the backstage at the Palace? It's one thing to steal a gun from there, but . . . Surely having her just disappear would be easier."

"That's what everybody thinks," returned the detective, "until they actually have to get rid of a human body. But you're probably right. I offered her police protection," he went on, "but she turned me down. Said it would just tip off somebody about where she was, which is true."

"To get back to your question," Emma went on, after a moment's thought, "I should think Mr. Taralla is the most likely candidate. I understand he has a jealous nature. But the same argument applies, both about what Mr. Ince knew and about the Palace Theater. And I assume Mr. Taralla—or anyone he hired—*does* know how to dispose of a body, to say nothing of not having to steal a gun. But then again, Mr. Ince was talking—I think—about Mr. Dexter's matrimonial offers, not Miss Golden's jealous sweethearts. There isn't any chance that—well, that this young Mr. Dexter might be . . . unbalanced . . . is there?"

"If he is," said Smith, "he comes by it honestly. He was the man at the wheel in 1920 when his brother's car went into the ditch. He was thrown clear and woke up in the hospital to the news that his brother and two sisters were dead. The car caught fire when it rolled over. From what the medical examiner could tell, the brother cracked his head on the side of the door, and was either unconscious or dead when the fuel tank went up. The girls—probably same story. At least it didn't look like either of 'em tried to climb out of the car while it was burning."

Emma turned her face aside, picturing the scene. Remembering what it was like to wake up in hospital to the news that those she most loved were all dead.

"Of course, old Dexter blamed his son. He loved that older boy like a tiger's mother and never had had a lot of use for the younger. I guess Dexter Junior hasn't drawn a sober breath since."

Emma hesitated, then asked, "And is that what you're doing here?"

"Different case." Smith fished in his pocket, hesitated with a pack of Lucky Strikes in hand.

Emma said, "Please," and gestured her permission, touched by the evidence of good manners in someone who looked like he'd stepped out of the *Police Gazette* himself.

Smith lit up, the sea breeze laying the flame of his lighter a little sideways, like a flag. His lighter, like Jim's, had been hand-made from a bullet. Her brother Miles had said that half the men in the trenches had made them, fuse and naphtha being usually easier to obtain than matches. "When you've been out here, Duchess, you ever see a motorized yacht around these waters? Fifty-footer, fifteen tons displacement—it carries sail, too. It's called the *White Goddess*, but the hull's painted blue these days."

Emma thought for a moment, then shook her head. "Though if the hull is blue, I imagine it would be harder to see."

"I think somebody else imagined that too." He turned his head, studied the Sound, not more than fifty feet from this wing of the stables beyond the edge of the miniature cliff. "Looks like they started to build a boathouse down there"—he gestured toward the shallow drop—"but it was never finished."

Emma tried to calculate whether that old, narrow passageway she'd found the previous week to the sea cave might have led to the prospective boathouse, but recollection failed her between darkness and the confusion of the maze.

"It's Jefferson Blair's boat." From the pocket of his shabby jacket, he took a card, checked to make sure he hadn't written a note to himself on the back, then held it out to her. "If you should see it . . . You got a telephone connection here?"

"I'm afraid not. The closest is in Brookhaven. Mr. Pugh pays a young man who works at the Post Office there to take any incoming calls, and bicycle out here at once to fetch him if there's an emergency of some kind. It's a little under three miles. I've never seen any evidence that anyone tried to put in telephones here."

"Didn't get that far before the money ran out. Same story with the boathouse. Blair managed to hang on to the yacht, though they lost everything else, between the war ending and what he spent on this place." He gestured with the card in the direction of the "chateau" on its lonely cliff, surrounded by the untended knot of overgrown gardens and flanked by the four Foremost out-houses, like maids-in-waiting attending a queen. "If you see that yacht—blue hull, maybe dark sails as well—see where it goes if you can, then give me a call at this number. Only don't let yourself be seen."

Emma slipped the card into her own pocket. "Don't tell me Mr. Blair is bringing in liquor from Canada? You should have seen his face at his son-in-law's birthday celebration . . ."

On the other hand, she reflected, would *she* have agreed to do a little smuggling to get out of Mrs. Pendergast's establishment? *Not anything really harmful like cocaine . . .*

And her father's voice replied, *Dura lex, sed lex . . .*

The law is hard, but it is the law.

How much did rank-and-file bootleggers make, anyway?

"We don't know whether Blair just rents Angel-Eyes Taralla the boat or pilots it himself. But Blair knows these waters. He was a member of the New York Yacht Club and took prizes pretty much all over the world: England and Italy and fu— and Hong Kong"—he hastily omitted an adjective describing Hong Kong—"as well as at every meet on this coast from Havana to Labrador."

Wind hissed in the beach grass by the cliff, and, distantly, distorted by a megaphone, George Blakeney's voice yelled, "Cut!"

"He grew up just over in Eaton's Neck," Smith went on. "I guess during the Revolution, the British held this whole island, and guerrilla fighters would cross the Sound from Jersey and Connecticut to make life difficult for 'em. The story was that Washington and his men would run powder and muskets in for the local partisans, and stash 'em in caves along here somewhere, connected to the sea. The farm that used to stand hereabouts was their headquarters."

His cigarette trailed a line of smoke as he waved, and Emma wondered if anyone had ever written a novel about that aspect of the Revolution. Far more interesting, she reflected, than the blameless Miss Fairisle's romantic tussles with Graignor Barbu and Beau Sharpless.

"And you think Mr. Blair is working for *Angel-Eyes Taralla*?" Surely, compared to the Pendergast household, how bad could the Widow Dexter's ménage be?

"I think Blair'll do pretty much what Taralla tells him," agreed Smith. "See, Griswold Dexter would have made Ebenezar Scrooge look like Santa Claus. The Blairs lost their place at Montrose when Griswold flat-out refused to help him after the bankruptcy. The Dexter place at Abbottsford's nothing but a primped-up farmhouse; they've got seven servants living in the attic and the rest of the staff bunks in what used to be the cow barn."

(*Someday let me tell you about the accommodations at Mrs. Pendergast's house in Manchester, Mr. Smith.*)

"Not the kind of thing Mrs. Blair's used to, and I can just imagine what the tea-party ladies at Oyster Bay have to say about the Blairs."

He shook out another cigarette and lit it from the end of the first.

"So about six weeks after old Griswold died and went to Hell in 1921, Blair tried to borrow a shitload of money from Dexter Consolidated. I don't know if he mentioned it to the other Board members at first, but they shut him down when they heard about it—including Dexter's widow, Rosemary. God knows what it was for. But he got the dough from Angel-Eyes, and then, all of a sudden, the *White Goddess* gets a paint job, and people are seeing her out on the Sound on moonlit nights."

He shrugged. "So if you should ever happen to see Blair—or even Aunt Violet, 'cause weirder things have happened—poking around the place, let me know. Only don't let 'em see you."

"Mr. Blair has been here since we started filming," said Emma slowly. "He's the representative of the owners—presumably the Dexter Trust?—assigned to make sure the chateau sustains no damage. Though it scarcely could, since it's unfinished on the inside. I can't imagine who would buy it, considering how much money it would require to complete and furnish it."

"You'd be surprised."

"I assumed his attitude stemmed from contempt for 'film people,'" she went on, "and mortification that his palace is now being rented to film companies. But if he's working for Mr. Taralla, he may just want to keep everyone from looking the place over too closely. And it would explain why I've seen Mr. Taralla's men here—and Mr. Malone. But why they'd be here if there's no real road to transport liquor back to New York—"

"That wouldn't stop hard cases like Bronco Burnett from stealing a couple crates out of a shipment and hiding them here. You could hide practically anything in those cellars, and nobody'd find it in fifty years. Or they could be doing a little freelance work, even taking money from Waxey Gordon or Lucky Luciano, or even Malone—"

He turned his head sharply, and Emma saw Devon Kingsley striding purposefully through the scrub and beach cabbage towards the stables, his whole bulky tweed body radiating determination. Hastily, she stepped back around the corner of the stables, set Buttercreme down, and gathered up Chang

Ming in her arms, lest he bark and give their position away. Smith raised a reassuring finger and ambled forth to intercept the author and took him by the arm. Kingsley asked him something; Smith glanced back at the stables, shook his head innocently, and pointed, as he did so, at the line of pine woods and laurels that fringed the cliff stretching away eastward.

Kingsley thanked him and set off in that direction like a man in pursuit of his destiny.

Emma wondered how far he'd get before dark.

EIGHTEEN

The following day, like an intermission, was Christmas.

Emma returned to Lord Wellington's camp from her conversation with Detective Smith to find George Blakeney preparing to end the filming early and send everyone home. Mr. Pugh delivered a stern lecture about the weather (it was beautifully cloud-patched sunlight and, as Kitty phrased it, cold as brass underpants) and the cost of renting Versailles per day, then took Kitty off to dinner at the Beaux-Arts Gardens, and a performance of the Music Box Revue.

Emma stayed in Suite 1202, brushed the dogs, and lit seven Hanukkah candles, to welcome anyone who wished to come by.

She had imagined a quiet Christmas Eve with Zal and the Pekes, and it was, up until about eight o'clock. But Kitty had wisely arranged for Lindy's to send several cartons of latkes to the suite, and Margaret Mackenzie turned up with three cheese-cakes from the same source. Everyone else who arrived that evening (Marsh Sloane, Nick Thaxter, Chip Thaw, Gordy Graves, and every single one of the Hollywood contingent including Al Spiegelmann and Mrs. Mackenzie's maid) brought something: meatballs from Giolito's, imported grapes from Gristede's, oranges and dried figs. Brownies, tarts, and cupcakes from every bakery in mid-town. A collection was taken to provide Christmas tips to every hotel employee obliged to work that night, and the Plaza Café kitchen returned the favor with urns of coffee and tea. Zal made eggnog, and Mr. Vaskey the elevator man donated two bottles of excellent grappa. As Mr. Bandog was—naturally—spending Christmas with his wife and her family on Long Island, Darlene Golden arrived chaperoned by Bandog's angel-faced chauffeur. Everyone was sworn to secrecy ("Oh, well," sighed Emma, "we tried . . .") and the greetings Miss Golden received—welcoming embraces, "So glad when I heard you were OK after all!"—brought her to tears.

George Blakeney—his own family being in London—led carol singing to the wailing of Chip Thaw's harmonica. Kitty and Mr. Pugh arrived at midnight, for a holiday toast and a round of good wishes. Then everyone went back to their rooms to bed and returned, by ones and twos, late the following morning for a congenial breakfast—with leftover latkes and cheesecake, and more contributions from everyone—that lasted until just after four. As if, reflected Emma, everyone simply wanted a day to mentally digest the tumult they'd been living in for over a month.

Since there didn't seem to be any further point in hiding it, it was agreed that Detective Smith would call the Haley family the following day. ("Not on Christmas . . .")

I will live in the Past, the Present, and the Future, Mr. Scrooge promises the Spirit of Christmas Yet to Come. *The Spirits of all Three shall strive within me . . .*

Christmas with her parents, her brother, in Oxford: playing the piano while her family sang, walking to church in sunlit, snow-blanketed cold. Four bleak and terrible Christmases in the household of Mrs. Pendergast, who didn't believe in giving her servants the day off while she went to visit her friends ("I *do* so hate coming home to an empty house . . ."). Dodging the drunken attempts of Lawrence Pendergast to corner her alone.

Then last Christmas, making avocado omelets in the weird, sunny brightness of her new home in California. Trading shy presents with Zal and realizing how much she was coming to love him . . .

She looked up at Zal now as he brought her a cup of tea and a little plate of latkes and egg foo yung. God only knew when he had found the time to shop, but she'd found a copy of *A Princess of Mars*—one of her favorites—that morning beside her pillow. *Christmases (and Hanukkahs) yet to come . . .*

He was wearing now, she noticed, the silk shirt she'd bought him at Bendel's when Margaret Mackenzie had taken her shopping. And pausing every time he passed the mantlepiece mirror, infinitesimally, clearly tickled to see how he looked in it.

And what about the Spirit that Dickens never mentioned?

The Spirit of Christmases that Never Were? The Christmases that would not come? Her dream walked gently through her mind again: lighting Hanukkah candles with Jim, on their first Hanukkah in their first home. In the life in which she'd never met Zal.

What about the first Christmas after the war, which she had looked forward to as the reunion of her family, for so many weeks in 1917? What she'd thought would happen, instead of the actual Christmas That Was: herself in stunned mourning for Jim, her parents exhausted with the drudgery and hunger of those first post-war days of rationed food and no money and caring for the eyeless, unspeaking automaton that had been sent home from Flanders, that had been her brother Miles?

We stay in many houses, she heard Jim murmur again in her ear. *Be happy in all of them, Em . . .*

Her father, she recalled, on one of those magical pre-war Christmases, had discoursed learnedly why so many religions celebrated midwinter with light, with candles, with stars. "All agricultural societies celebrate the first visible lengthening of days after the winter solstice, as a reassurance of seed time and harvest to come. *Diffugere nives / Redeunt iam gramina campis / Arboribusque comae*." He had raised his arms as if conducting Handel's *Messiah*. "*Winter has fled; grass has returned to the fields, and leaves to the trees . . .*"

And she and her mother had laughed, knowing that the truth was simpler than that. The candles of the menorah and the Christmas star, like the torches of the Saturnalia and the bonfires of the Greek Haloea, were simply a reminder that darkness was not forever. That light would come again.

Her hand closed over Zal's, and they kissed, their lips tinted with bootlegged champagne.

The next day, everything returned to real life.

Summer Fairisle—now thickly veiled because in the previous scene (to be filmed as soon as the police deemed it safe for Miss Golden to return to camera range), she glimpsed a flirtatious maid (Sugar-Pie Gilroy) stealing forth with an admirer into the woods and feared to be recognized by the light of the full moon—met with her former groom (Fred Bowser, last seen on Broadway playing Zelda Sears's butler in *Lollipop*) to learn whether her beloved Beau Sharpless had indeed been hanged. It was possible, Carrie Drebbett assured Emma, to stuff Betty Cheviot's corset to heighten the illusion of Miss Golden's bosom, so the scene, already filmed twice, was immortalized yet again.

"It's nonsense!" Mr. Kingsley raged, shaking Emma's notes under Mr. Pugh's nose. "No well-bred woman in 1782 would so much as *glance* at her groom, much less sneak out into the woods to kiss him in the moonlight!" ("He's obviously never seen Darlene making goo-goo eyes at Bandog's chauffeur," Zal remarked later.) "And in scene"—he consulted his notes—"ninety-seven, which takes place the previous night, you specify that the moon is on the wane, and yet . . ."

Emma had already consulted with Mr. Blakeney concerning "stock footage" of the moon.

Quickly and discreetly, she gathered the rest of her notes and beat a hasty retreat up the path to the chateau. There she found Kitty—still in powdered wig and panniers—and Marsh Sloane, in highwayman garb, in what would have become the main ballroom, rolling celluloid table-tennis balls the length of the enormous chamber for the Pekes to chase. Mr. Blair evidently had Boxing Day duties back at Abbottsford.

"It looks like they're going to be doing the Meeting in the Woods until sundown," she reported. "Until midnight, the way Mr. Kingsley is going on."

"Nertz," said Kitty. "That means we've got to come out tomorrow, too—"

And Marsh Sloane sighed, "Bugger," in his customary Shakespearean tones.

"Darling . . ." Kitty followed Emma towards her dressing room in the former pantry. "Frank's got another meeting with that *awful* Mr. Smalls, and—would you believe it?—Spitz is arriving tomorrow, with his family, and is asking to be reimbursed for the family's train fare because Darlene's still alive! So Frank sort of begged me to meet him for dinner afterwards because he says he'll really need it—and I just *know* that's not *all* he'll need. And I just *know* if I don't say yes, he'll call Darlene, the two-timing chazer! *I* saw how he was looking at her at your party the other night! Could you stand it? Ambrose says it's an opera called Lower Something, or Louis Something . . ."

"Of course, dear." Emma tried hard not to jump up and down with pleasure at the prospect of one of her favorite works by Wagner.

"Oh, good! And anyway, he'll take you to the Colony or the Breevort or someplace really nice, so the evening won't be a dead loss. I'll send one of the boys back to town to telephone and let him know."

Thus it was that Emma—after walking the Pekes in the park (accompanied by Marsh Sloane—she had never quite gotten over the ambush by Taralla's "boys" on Monday night) and seeing them fed—found herself sharing a box at the Metropolitan Opera House not only with Ambrose Crain but with Mrs. Violet Blair and (as W.S. Gilbert put it) her "daughter-in-law-elect," Beatrice Schuyler.

"Do please forgive me, Mrs. Blackstone," Mr. Crain whispered to her as he conducted her to her seat. "But as soon as I learned you were to be my—I think young people call it my 'date'—for the evening, I asked Violet to join us. To tell you the truth, I've never felt easy about what Kitty has told me of poor Clark's matrimonial offers. And whether the victim of the crime was meant to be Miss Golden or poor Miss Haley, or whether Clark was mixed up in it at all, the fact remains that there is something going on that someone considers worth killing over. I thought that with further conversation, you might be able to gain a little more perspective."

Emma reminded herself of this, firmly, several times, as Aunt Violet proceeded to talk through the exquisite Bridal Chorus and the Act Three Love Duet: about her cousin Heloïse's facelift ("I swear she should sue that doctor of hers! She looks *just* like a Martian!") (*And how would you know what a Martian looks like, ma'am?*), her sister Rosemary's new diet ("You're not supposed to eat 'acid' food and 'alcohol food' at the same meal . . . but I can't see the difference. Her hands are blown up *just* like balloons, and anyway she never drinks alcohol . . ."), and the imbecilic iniquities of last night's bridge partner (". . . kept bidding up and up and *up* on *two clubs*! I kept *trying* to signal her that I had all the hearts, but . . ." "Oh, Mrs. Blair!" cried Miss Schuyler with her shrill laugh, "you just *know* you're lying! I had the queen, and the seven, and the three . . ." "You did *not* have the three because *I* had it . . .").

It was like watching someone pour canned tomato soup over a vase of lilies.

"Forgive me." Mr. Crain handed Emma into his town limousine after bidding the Blair ladies farewell following après-catastrophe ices at Henri's. "I am covered with shame. It seemed to me a good idea at the time."

He patted her hand, gloved fingers thin as chopsticks. "How can I make it up to you, my dear? A ticket to *Così Fan Tutti* at the start of the new year? A new frock to wear to that tea party she invited you to at Abbottsford tomorrow? Which I'm sure will turn your hair gray from boredom . . ."

"Oddly," said Emma, "and much as I would kill even someone I was moderately fond of to see *Così Fan Tutti*, I shall take you up on the offer of a new frock." (*Accepting expensive gifts of clothing from elderly gentlemen . . . Mother would* faint*!*) "I gather Mrs. Dexter's other guests will include Vanderbilts, Roosevelts, Astors, and Goulds, and I don't wish to stand out in any way. Only to listen."

Margaret Mackenzie escorted Emma to Bergdorf Goodman first thing the following morning (she was not scheduled to be beheaded until Tuesday) and supervised the purchase of a deceptively simple, low-waisted afternoon frock of heavy embroidered silk, with hat and shoes and gloves to match: mauve, silver, and black, like a discreet signal of second mourning ("There's none so respectable as a widow, my dear," declared the Scots actress. "'Tis enough to make one murder a husband just to impress the neighbors.")

And indeed, the combination of young widowhood (Chanel prêt-a-porter notwithstanding) and three adorable Pekineses, seasoned with the information that she had first-hand knowledge of some of those *nasty* film persons at Versailles, had its desired effect. Gossip about the schism in the fashionable Roosevelt family ("Darling, what can you expect? She married a *Democrat*—and I daresay she'll be taking care of him for the rest of his life, now he's a cripple . . .") and the prospects of victory when spring yacht racing began, paled to insignificance against a well-bred, ladylike war widow's personal view of the film industry ("Is it true about the solid gold bathtub?"). Admitting to conversations with them (though, of course, as Mr. Crain's goddaughter, not the actual facts) brought out all the reciprocal gossip concerning Griswold Dexter's involvement with Biograph Films, Tom Ince, "those dreadful vaudeville people," and his worthless second son, spread like a Persian carpet before Emma's interested gaze.

"I'm sorry to say the film people were a bad influence on my late husband's life." Rosemary Dexter, after four years still deep in mourning for her children and her husband, tightened her thin lips. As Detective Smith had said, Griswold Dexter had departed this world barely a year after the automobile accident that had claimed the lives of his elder boy and the daughters "who were the treasure of his heart." ("*Treasure* my grandmother's left hind foot," whispered the coolly beautiful Mrs. Longworth to Emma. "Rosemary had to hold him at gunpoint to get poor Myra a proper gown for her own coming-out!")

"I could only be glad of it," the stern-faced Widow Dexter went on, "when that man Ince removed himself to California." She glanced up as a liveried servant entered the sunlit Abbottsford parlor, and gestured to him with the twitch of one bloated finger to set down the silver tray on which he bore the next round of teacakes and salmon sandwiches. Emma wondered whether he was one of the servants privileged to sleep in the attic, or only rated a cot out in the barn.

"Both my sons, as well as poor Griswold, were always at that studio place in town, and I will take oath that it was Mr. Ince who introduced poor Spencer to the sort of women who would have ruined his life—and broken my heart—had not fate intervened." She pressed her black-bordered handkerchief briefly to her lips. "Not that I would *dream* of speaking ill of the dead . . ."

A remark which, in Emma's experience, usually preceded speaking ill of the dead . . .

Though no beauty—and despite last night's relentless torrent of complaint and commentary—upon making the acquaintance of Rosemary Dexter, Emma found Violet the more sympathetic of the sisters. Both were, she guessed, deeply selfish women, with racial prejudices which disgusted her. But the elder had an air of self-righteous coldness that forestalled sympathy, even though Emma recognized in Rosemary's swollen hands—and Aunt Violet's description of her rigidly proscriptive food regimen ("alkaline" foods, not "alcohol" . . .)—the onset of Bright's disease. Even without the pain and exhaustion of her illness, Emma guessed that it would never have occurred to Rosemary Dexter to spontaneously invite an acquaintance to a holiday tea. The woman's chilly glance—both on herself and on Violet—told Emma everything she needed to know about the widow's opinion of "film people"—and of her sister.

Only the joyful exclamations of every one of her guests, Emma deduced, prevented Chang Ming, Black Jasmine, and Buttercreme from being banished to the Abbottsford cellar for the afternoon.

"I don't know how you endured it, Rosemary," exclaimed Aunt Violet, clasping the puffy, lace-mitted hand. "I know *I* could not have borne it, had Jeff behaved as . . . well . . . as Griswold sometimes did . . ."

"Oh, couldn't she?" muttered a Mrs. Frick, gorgeous in three hundred dollars' worth of Belgian lace and cuddling the worshipful Chang Ming on her lap. "It wasn't building that palace up beyond Port Jefferson that bankrupted them—and it isn't so much of a muchness, you know. Nor is this place, for all they're swimming in money."

She gestured around them at the parlor, which was, as Mr. Crain had said, much more old-time farmhouse than an exact copy of a stately British mansion. "Neither can compare with *our* place at Clayton. And the architect Blair worked with was a completely common little man. And it wasn't the way he mismanaged that newspaper Griswold gave him to run, either. It was keeping that Marsh girl—her *and* her sister, I'm told—in apartments in New York."

"He told Violet they were his *models*," added one of the Gould cousins, feeding Black Jasmine a bite of a beef-jelly sandwich. "I think he paid one of the *actual* photographers on the *Democrat* to take the pictures, and then showed them to her as his."

"Oh," said Emma brightly, "is Mr. Blair a photographer?"

Mrs. Longworth snickered. "If you mean, does he know that you point the shiny part of the camera at your target and press the button, you could say so." But she spoke in a whisper, and Aunt Violet turned, her face wreathed in smiles, having heard only Emma's words.

"Oh, yes! *Do* come into the study and see some of his work!"

Mrs. Longworth rolled her eyes. Rosemary Dexter sniffed.

"Study" seemed to be a sort of honorific term applied to what was barely the size of a dressing room in any country house Emma had ever entered in England. It lay at the back of the second floor, tucked in as an afterthought next to the modest—and thickly cluttered—bedroom still occupied by the Blairs in Rosemary Dexter's house. Jefferson Blair being absent that day (*Inspecting Versailles for finger marks on the walls? Running shipments of "hootch" in from Canada?*), Emma pushed open the bedroom door and got a glimpse of what looked like all the disused furniture salvaged from their previous mansion, Montrose, crowded together in the half dark and blanketed with an army of expensive-looking souvenirs. Small bronze reproductions of statues (*There's Michaelangelo's David again . . .*), ships in bottles bearing banners with *Welcome to Hong Kong* at their masts. A replica of the Pavilion at Brighton wrought of a hundred colors of glass.

The clutter in the study was worse—nearly fifty trophy cups in silver and gold, grayed with dust.

No wonder Mr. Blair is ready to collude with bootleggers to get out from under this roof . . .

Expensively framed in gold, Blair's photographs covered every wall.

Mrs. Longworth's silent evaluation of Jefferson Blair's photographic talent was, unfortunately, amply justified. A year's close association with visual imagery had sharpened Emma's understanding of composition and the values of light and shadow. Before making his way to Hollywood, Zal had spent eighteen months while hiding from the Draft Board as an itinerant photographer. Looking at his work—portraits, still lifes, cats sleeping on windowsills, children at play, mansions of the South ruined in the Civil War sixty years before—Emma knew good work when she saw it. And she knew Jefferson Blair's was not good work.

She also knew dry-plate photography when she saw it. It was a rather old-fashioned technique these days, but, as Zal had often said, one that had a particular way of reproducing light and shadow that the newer celluloid films simply did not have.

And the line of family members stretched across the front steps of the half-built Versailles, grinning self-consciously into the camera, rang a bell in her mind.

As did the curious clouded area at the bottom left corner of the print, and the way a flaw of light seemed to be reflected above it.

Every picture Aunt Violet showed her—and Emma asked to see them all—had the same flaws.

"I also asked to see the books she'd kept of Mr. Blair's work on one of Mr. Dexter's newspapers," she told Zal, at one o'clock the following morning on the El train back from Queens. "Dexter Consolidated controls several. Apparently, during the war the senior Mr. Dexter needed an editor on the *Gotham Daily Democrat*, and Mr. Blair convinced him he had the political connections to get decent stories."

From the Port Jefferson station near Abbottsford, Emma had taken the train as far as Queens, then a cab to MBQ Studio, where Zal, she knew, would be shooting the final meeting in the Temple Prison between Summer Fairisle (still heavily veiled and draped in shawls for good measure) and her doomed mother.

She had remained on the premises, sharing the picnic dinner that Becca had brought for Zal ("Mama says it's OK for me to ride the El on the Sabbath if it means an extra day's money from Mrs. Tappan." "Becca, don't tell me you lie to your mother!") and escorting the girl back to the Murray Hill station before it grew dark, the Pekes happily sniffing and barking at everything along the way. From there, she had returned to MBQ.

"I hate to think of waking Kitty," Emma said now, as the train rattled its way into Penn Station, and Zal hooted with laughter.

"You think she'll be home? She has the night off, so we probably won't see her till daylight. And I want another look at those prints."

Kitty was, of course, absent from Suite 1202, and while Emma made tea in the little kitchen, Zal fetched from the cupboard the prints of "Mr. Skinner's" Palace porn shoot, and spread them on the table.

"I thought I remembered that dark area in both pictures." Emma came to sit beside him and studied the larger print. As in Jefferson Blair's photograph of friends and family standing before the half-constructed façade of Versailles, the eight "bodyguard" beauties brandished their guns in a single line. They were used to posing and knew from long practice how to arrange themselves, but there was, Emma could see, no imagination in the placement of the group.

And the inexplicable zone of darker gray, with its odd streak of light, hovered in the same quarter of the print as it had in every print in the Blair bedroom. (Detective Smith had been quite right about the stinginess of Dexter charity towards bankrupt relatives.) Bracing herself a little—and feeling silly for her embarrassment—Emma briefly studied the other print (*There is* no *difference between those eight young women and, say, the female damned depicted by Michelangelo in his Last Judgment* . . . Except, of course, the female damned hadn't been grinning from ear to ear.)

The mysterious areas of dark and light were there, too.

"You get that effect if there's a scratch or a flaw of some kind on the back element of a camera lens," said Zal.

"So these were definitely taken with Jefferson Blair's camera."

"Oh, yeah. And the description of this Skinner fellow fits Blair all right, without the fake beard and glasses."

"But *why*? I can see why Clark wouldn't want to marry Miss Schuyler, but if Mr. Blair is on the Board—and has access to the Trust documents he showed Mr. Smith—they all must know about the provisions of the Trust. Certainly, Mr. Blair—or his wife—would know that if Clark marries anybody *but* Miss Schuyler, he loses all access to the fortune anyway. And even if there *is* collusion of some kind between Miss Schuyler and Mr. Blair, why would he run a risk like stealing a gun from the Palace Theater prop room? There's a quite well-stocked gun room at Abbottsford—I looked into it on the way to the Blairs' bedroom . . ."

"Oh, I can tell you that." Zal tactfully tucked the more lurid of the two prints under the "line-up" of the semi-clothed chorines. "The first thing the cops do, in a headline case like this one, is look at who can get hold of a gun. They've probably already matched the caliber of the slugs they took out of poor Mila with every handgun in that gun room—and with any gat they can trace to Taralla, or Bandog, or Pugh, or Zeppo or any of his brothers. If it was Blair who did the murder, for whatever reason, he'd try to get hold of a gun that would be harder to trace."

He tilted the photograph a little to the electric bulb overhead: eight pretty young girls, Emma reflected, whose only job—if not doing someone's laundry or raising some man's children—was being pretty young girls.

"He may have been trying to frame Clark Dexter for the killing," Zal went on. "Trying to push the Board into changing the terms of the Trust. It's not like there's any other Dexter kids around to object. And there's eight guns, just lying around at the Palace with a jam jar full of firing pins sitting right there in a drawer. Look." He reached over to the counter drawer which contained not only its original quota of Plaza coffee spoons for the suite, but the debris of five weeks of residence: cigarette lighters, a packet of Sobranie cigarettes, several lipsticks (Djer-Kiss Persian Rose, Lanchere Blue Rose, Princess

Pat Pomegranate . . .), and a small jar of Vaseline . . . and a magnifying lens.

This last he took, and Emma followed him back to the table.

"We can even tell which girl's gun he took. See? The bows are made of the same fabric as their dresses, and each color dress had different embroidery." He held the lens over the picture. "Wide stripes here, narrow stripes here, big flowers on this one, little all-over flowers, and fish—and the gun with the red bow on it was the odd one, because it just had plain red ribbon on it. It was the one they had to replace at the last minute. That's the one he took."

Emma studied the face of the girl holding the weapon, the bright whiteness of her smile against the complexion of an Italian or Spaniard. One of the ones, Kitty had said, who was no longer dancing at the Palace . . . *Had the disappearance of her gun gotten her into trouble of some kind?*

Surely not . . .

"But *why*?" she asked again. "Detective Smith saw the Trust document . . ."

"No idea," said Zal. "But I have a good idea of who might know something. Or know how to find it out."

NINETEEN

Kitty exclaimed over Emma's discovery at breakfast the following afternoon, and agreed wholeheartedly when told of Zal's theory about who might know something—or be able to find it out. "We'll go ask him," she said, "as soon as he gets to the High Wire . . . He knows just about *everybody* at City Hall!"

I'll bet he does, reflected Emma, and dabbed a little apricot marmalade on room-service toast.

Owing to Mr. Blakeney's dissatisfaction with a scene in which the heroine's face must remain invisible behind a veil, Sunday would be spent shooting a different version of the Jail Scene on the eve of Lady Fairisle's execution, and Kitty's presence for the long-delayed re-shoot of the Hair-Pulling Scene would yet again not be required that day. Zal had not been so lucky. An hour after Emma woke to the sound of Pekinese toe-nails clattering excitedly from her bedroom—and lay sleepily for a few moments looking at the lights of Fifty-Eighth Street reflected on the ceiling and listening to Kitty's whispered instructions to her celestial angel-muffins not to wake poor Aunt Emma—she'd been waked again by Zal sliding carefully out of her bed, by the soft scratch of his beard as he kissed her shoulder.

She had stirred, and he'd whispered, "Go back to sleep, Em. I've got to be at Penn Station at six." She had heard the water in the bathroom gurgle softly as he washed, but was asleep before the tap turned off.

When she came out to the kitchen at ten thirty, she found the chorus-girl line-up enlargement still on the table, but the Cincinnati Special had been discreetly replaced in the cupboard. By the time she had walked, fed, and brushed the dogs, had taken her own bath and dressed in something more respectable than an old tweed skirt and shirtwaist, and had brushed her hair, Kitty was awake and stirring, and Emma had called down to room service.

Shakespeare Malone, she knew, would not be at the High Wire Club before five.

"He talked to Bronco Burnett, though," Kitty informed her, when she at last emerged from her room, immaculately made-up and in silk Callot Soeurs. "So I could tell Zeppo that everything is all right, though, of course, poor Cissy won't be able to testify that she was with him. But Shakespeare says he'll find someone who will."

Emma sighed. *No wonder Detective Smith doesn't trust us.*

She watched Kitty for a moment as she sorted through the ice box in quest of the last of the Hanukkah leftovers—thinking of Zal, who was going out to Brooklyn again that night, to spend the final hours of the holiday with his family—then asked, "Are they still alive?"

Kitty glanced inquiringly back over her shoulder.

"Your parents." *Jim's parents . . .*

My in-laws.

(*Shiksa. An impure thing* . . . Like a whisper in the back of her mind.)

"Search me. Is there any marmalade left?"

"You haven't even looked them up in the city directory?" There were—Emma had ascertained—at least two dozen Blechsteins in Manhattan alone. *And they might well have moved to some other borough . . .*

Kitty turned and closed the ice box, her beautiful face kind. "Papa was a famous rabbi, back in the Old Country," she explained, and shrugged. "Jimmy must have told you that. So when he came here, he had to be the holiest guy in Yorkville. He had to have students to look up to him. For Jim, that just meant he had to keep his schoolbooks over at a neighbor's, 'cause Papa wouldn't have pictures of anything in the flat. But from the time I was twelve and started having periods, he treated me like I was a bitch in heat. He took me out of school after that, and I had to stay home and help Mama with the housework and her sewing. I couldn't read magazines or newspapers 'cause they were full of 'impure' stuff. He'd beat me if he caught me in the street not wearing a scarf on my hair, or if he saw me talking to a boy. Jimmy tried to stick up for me, but I knew in a couple of years he was going away to college, and Papa was already trying to push me into marrying Myron Wasserman, who was his best student at the synagogue and practically worshipped the water Papa walked on. They finally threw me out when I was fourteen."

Other things—other memories—stirred in the shadows behind her eyes. She closed them for a moment, as if to blot those shadows out; opening them, the memories—whatever they were—were gone.

"So, no, I didn't look them up."

Emma recalled how her parents' neighbor on Holyrood Street back in Oxford—Mrs. Moody—had come over the week before her wedding to Jim for the express purpose of "having a serious talk with Emma about marrying a Jew." "I'm sure he's a perfectly nice young man—for an American—*but* . . ." Her mother had politely shown Mrs. Moody the door. A few days after Jim's death, she had found a note from Mrs. Moody in her mother's waste-basket: *I am, of course, quite sorry for poor Emma, but you must admit that it is all for the best* . . .

"Just wondered," she said.

They reached the High Wire at a little after five, and though it was closed, the maître d'—a doe-eyed Italian with a voice like a truck engine warming up—admitted them without even a glance at the three Pekes in their jeweled collars. Malone turned from chatting with the piano player and crossed the opulent white chamber with his hands held out to the two women. "No combat at the Bastille yet?" He bent to kiss Kitty's cheek.

"Emma has an idea," said Kitty, as the club owner guided them to a table on the edge of the vacant dance floor. The big room with its glass-and-chromium tables was still decorated for the holiday, electric Christmas lights mingling with holly, ivy, pine boughs, and toy balloons as they had at Cypress Cove, a festive medley of color against the chaste walls.

The sherry-brown eyes flickered sidelong at Emma, eyebrows

inquiringly raised. At the same moment, he lifted a finger. "Tea for Mrs. Blackstone, Ben," he instructed the maître d'. "Campari and lime, and—will you have gin, my dear? A gin sling for Miss de la Rose. The Seagram's, please. What is your idea, Mrs. Blackstone?"

She explained to him briefly about the flawed lens in Jefferson Blair's camera, and the certainty that four weeks previously, he had stolen a .38 from the Palace Theater's prop room. "I don't know why he would do that," she said. "And I don't know if it has anything to do with the murder that took place backstage at the theater a week ago Monday night. According to the detective who is working on the case, it doesn't sound as if Blair himself stands to gain anything if his wife's nephew marries or doesn't marry a woman of his sister-in-law's choosing. The way the Dexter Trust seems to be worded, he had no reason that I know of to harm either Miss Golden, or Miss Haley, since by the terms of the trust, young Mr. Dexter cannot inherit if he marries Miss Golden or any of the several women he has offered for over the past two years, at fifty thousand dollars a time."

The club owner paused in the act of lighting Kitty's cigarette, with a lighter of alabaster and gold. (*No hand-modified bullets for* him . . .) "Where did he plan to get the money?"

"I don't know. From what Miss Golden told me before the murder, she was still negotiating about when that money would be handed over to her—it's the reason she sent Miss Haley to the theater in the first place. And given her relationship with Mr. Bandog, I can't see her threatening suit for breach of promise."

"I can." Kitty blew a thin line of very expensive smoke. "She's thirty-two if she's a day. In another"—she paused, mentally calculating her rival's true age against her own true age—"well, in not very many more years, she won't be any use to either Bandog or to Frank, or to any other producer in the business."

Shakespeare Malone clicked his lighter shut. "Age does not wither, nor custom stale, your infinite variety, Cleopatra . . . But yes, it is most curious."

"And I have heard," continued Emma, lowering her voice though the club was empty save for the maître d', a man in a neat white uniform operating a vacuum cleaner between the tables, and two plainly dressed gentlemen quietly smoking near the piano, "that Mr. Blair borrowed a large sum from Mr. Taralla, and seems to be repaying the debt by lending him a yacht."

"Ah." Malone smiled. "The *White Goddess*. Has she been seen in those waters lately?"

"So I hear. I also hear that the money does not appear to have been spent on finishing construction at Versailles, nor in finding the Blairs anyplace to live other than in a single bedroom at the Dexter house at Abbottsford. It may be a curious string of coincidences," finished Emma. "And I may be over-imaginative for feeling that there's a connection there that I can't see."

"Imagination is the foundation of all human civilization, Mrs. Blackstone. I myself imagined all sorts of things when a gentleman named Joe Ladrone—a mechanic in charge of both the camera cranes and the studio vehicles at Famous Players—rather suddenly came into a large sum of money, six weeks after Griswold Dexter's death in the summer of 1921. I gather he journeyed to California—"

"Oh, Joe Ladrone!" cried Kitty. "He bought Crown Studios in Culver City and made Westerns with what's-his-name—Ace Phoenix—and June Ross, who couldn't play *herself* on the best day she ever had. He tried to hire me away from Foremost and made a pass at me every time he came on the lot . . . He tried to get poor Tom Ince to combine their studios. I guess he was good buddies with Tom when they were both at Biograph . . ."

She broke off, her dark eyes going from Malone's to Emma's.

"Were they?" said Emma thoughtfully. Her own glance returned to her host. "I realize it's a terrible imposition, Mr. Malone . . ."

"No imposition whatsoever, Mrs. Blackstone. In fact, it should be a fairly simple matter to trace how Joe happened to acquire a hundred thousand dollars the week after Jefferson Blair borrowed a like sum from my generous friend Mr. Taralla.

I'm only sorry that poor Mr. Ladrone's venture into the film industry did not pan out before his unfortunate death, in connection, I understand, with other sums of money borrowed from various individuals." He lowered his eyes in recognition of an untimely tragedy. "At the time, I simply thought it was all of a piece with the man's record of poor fiscal habits and poorer judgment, and did not pursue my curiosity about how a sum so exactly equivalent to Mr. Blair's loan from Mr. Taralla would have found its way into Mr. Ladrone's bank account the following week. Should I look into the details for you, Mrs. Blackstone?"

"As a favor to me?" Kitty gazed into his eyes like Buttercreme pleading for a morsel of pâté.

"It will be my privilege." He reverently kissed her hand.

The only other thing of note that happened that day took place an hour later, when Mr. Malone—who did not need to return to the High Wire until seven—took Kitty and Emma to an early dinner at the Beaux-Arts. The pre-theater crowd milled around the restaurant's lobby, but Mr. Malone murmured a few words to the maître d', who immediately signaled the table captain to lead the party to a table beside the dance floor. It had a card on it that said *Reserved*, but the man simply pocketed this, and Emma could not help noticing that he did this also with a similar card on a nearby, smaller table, to which he conducted the two plainly dressed gentlemen who'd been seated at the end of the High Wire's bar. Watchful friends, she deduced, of Mr. Malone.

Not surprisingly, a short, sturdy woman in the lobby, resplendent in at least a thousand dollars' worth of Russian sable, and a staggeringly Parisian lavender hat, exclaimed indignantly. The restaurant's manager paused in his expressions of how delighted he would be to host Chang Ming, Black Jasmine, and Buttercreme in his office during their owner's dinner with Mr. Malone, excused himself, and hastened to placate the usurped diner . . .

And turning her head, Emma saw that it was Mrs. Pugh.

* * *

It took two days for Shakespeare Malone to "happen to stumble upon" (as he put it) details of the arrangement between Jefferson Blair, Angel-Eyes Taralla, and the unfortunate late Mr. Ladrone. During those two days, Darlene Golden occupied a handsome apartment on Park Avenue, under the protection of two private detectives (for whom Mr. Bandog rented a much less luxurious "studio apartment" elsewhere in the building) and Mr. Bandog's elfin chauffeur.

In that interval, Mr. Blakeney turned the filming of Ken Elmore's hanging (and rescue) over to Gordy Graves, went to meet Charles and Frieda Haley at Penn Station and take them out to Canarsie to visit their daughter's grave, and to assure them that steps were being taken to change the order for the modest headstone to read *Ludmilla Haley* instead of *Darlene Golden*. He also took them out to lunch.

When he returned to MBQ late on the Monday afternoon, it was to face yet another indignant history lesson by Mr. Kingsley concerning the use of side saddles by well-bred young ladies in 1801 (Graves had not yet gotten a good take of the complex scene), and Mr. Pugh's information that Miss Golden would return to the production on the following day.

"The set'll be closed," commanded Pugh, with Bandog at his shoulder like a pale and exhausted ghost. "We'll have detectives keeping an eye on things."

Emma could only admire the equanimity with which the Englishman received this news—and his restraint in not inquiring why, in that case, they had bothered shooting the Hanging Scene that day at all. Catching sight of Emma, Pugh then descended on her before she could make her escape, with instructions that she rewrite scenes 750–767 and scenes 885–903, by that time, to accommodate Miss Golden's actual presence. "And we'll have to get rid of that whole veil business," he added. "Folks'll want to see Darlene's face. So rewrite those scenes as well."

"You tell Pugh he can take a long walk off a short pier," steamed Zal, when he learned that Emma would be rewriting scenes 750–767 and 885–903 that evening, instead of taking advantage of the first evening off that Zal would have that didn't involve a duty to his family. "You just rewrote—"

"It's all right," said Emma quietly. "Thank you—I'm as annoyed as you are—but I don't think it's an argument we can win. Another home-cooked meal at your mother's won't kill you."

"You say that 'cause you've never had one of my mom's home-cooked meals," returned Zal. "Jackals wouldn't eat her cooking." He relaxed his shoulders, almost physically shaking off his quick-firing anger. "Each meal comes with a free lecture about how food in Los Angeles can't possibly be really kosher." Raising himself slightly on his toes, he kissed her, as the Klieg lights on the market square set snapped back on and Princess Laura—clothed and wigged as Darlene instead of Kitty for the occasion—brought her horse around for yet another carefully plotted plunge through the crowd of extras. (In addition to training five elephants to play the clarinet, the Princess was the equal of any Hollywood cowboy Emma had ever seen in the saddle.) "You're right about not getting on Pugh's bad side right now. I guess I'm not the only one who's tried to get information out of the night man at the Gapstow—"

He sidestepped the two prop men who were righting tipped-over fruit carts yet again, and collecting scattered apples and pumpkins . . .

"—so it looks like Smith isn't buying any of those five stories about who was with him the night poor Mila was shot."

("And get those bananas out of here!" yelled Mr. Kingsley. "They did *not* have bananas in Britain in 1801!")

"I'll see if I can get Mama to go out to Oscar's Deli instead." He picked up an orange, tossed it to the nearest searcher, then straightened his cap and scrambled up onto the crane from which his camera overlooked the market square in such a way that it wasn't obvious that the whole panorama—fifteen thousand square feet of it—was built on a shooting stage. Ken Elmore stubbed out his cigarette and had his hands tied behind him once again at the foot of the gallows. Like a pudgy sheepdog, Gordy Graves began herding the extras back into place.

Smiling, Emma reflected that, in her heart, it didn't really matter to her whether Mama Rokatansky and her daughters accepted her or not. It was Zal who mattered.

The rewritten Ballroom Sequence was, for a wonder, successfully reshot in its entirety the following day (replacing the Terrace Sequence shot at Versailles earlier in the week), and Zal and Emma finally had the leisure of an evening to themselves on Tuesday night. ("I'll be back at eleven, darlings; Chico's picking me up at eleven thirty . . .")

Tomorrow night would be New Year's Eve.

And then it would be 1925.

Time, which seemed to have stopped in June of 1918, had only restarted for Emma with her arrival in Hollywood last year, and she still sometimes had the sensation of emotional pins and needles as life came back to her. Her cheek pillowed on Zal's arm in the reflected glow of the streetlamps far below, she felt as if, for the first time, the Ghost of Christmas Yet to Come had given her a blessing, rather than the shadow of fear.

Room service was later summoned, tea made in the kitchen. A quiet discussion was in progress about the possibility of a post-coital excursion to Lindy's ("By the time we get there, the theaters'll be out . . .") when the telephone rang: "A Mr. Malone to see Miss de la Rose," said the Front Desk.

"Jefferson Blair"—Malone set his attaché case on the kitchen table—"had an appointment with Hiram Abrams at the Famous Players' Lasky Studio in Astoria on the fourth of October, 1920. That was the day Clark Dexter drove his car off the road on Long Island, killing his brother, Spencer, and their sisters, Myra and Claire. Blair's appointment was in the morning, and he left the studio a few hours before the Dexter party arrived there, but there's no record of exactly where he was between his departure and his arrival at Abbottsford that evening, to hear the tragic news. According to police records, the Dexters stopped at a roadhouse called The Old School House just west of Hauppage, which I deeply regret to say served spirituous liquors. It may still. Quite good ones, I understand."

He shook his head sadly at this blatant disregard for the law. "On the way to Versailles, Dexter's car went off the road, and such was the damage from the subsequent fire that it is impossible to determine the cause of the mishap. But it is a fact that Mr. Joseph Ladrone, who worked, as I said, at the Astoria Studio, was the brother-in-law of the owner of The Old School House and lived on the premises. He was at the roadhouse that afternoon, though one can only surmise, at this late date, what he might have seen from the windows of his quarters, which were above the garage and overlooked the yard where customers parked. But shortly after Griswold Dexter's death in June of 1921, Mr. Blair was moved to borrow a hundred thousand dollars from Angel-Eyes Taralla—his bankruptcy over the costs of Versailles having made him ineligible for any more formal sort of loan. A tragic story."

"I can barely restrain my tears," responded Zal politely.

"He first attempted to—um—secure the money by means of his position on the Board of Dexter Consolidated." Emma looked up from her perusal of the top sheet of the stack of papers Malone had withdrawn from his attaché case. It was on the stationery of the Suffolk County Sheriff's Department. Immediately below it was a bank book belonging to Joseph K. Ladrone with a New York Police Department "evidence" tag attached, dated August of 1922.

"Unfortunately, he neglected to let the other Board members know what he was doing. Mrs. Dexter learned of the transaction and prevented it, but I should be surprised to hear the police were informed. Do you happen to know?"

"My dear Mrs. Blackstone"—Malone widened his golden-brown eyes at her—"why should *I* have any need to speak to the police about such matters? Of course, when Miss Golden—as they believed—was found dead in the Palace Theater, the earliest suspect was naturally poor young Mr. Clark Dexter. But his family's oaths notwithstanding, he was seen by dozens of people at the Mardi Gras Club, I am sorry to say, making a spectacle of himself trying to get in to talk to Roxie North. Even if he was sober enough to find a cab at that hour in Harlem—"

"Roxie North?" Emma and Zal spoke at the same time, and Zal immediately followed up with, "Why do I know that name?"

"She was in the Palace chorus line," provided Emma. "The one who was holding the gun that later got stolen. She left to work at the Mardi Gras—"

"And she quit the Mardi Gras Club the night before last"—Malone's voice turned suddenly hard—"to go to work at Lulubelle's—one of the few Harlem nightclubs that actually admits men of color as customers. I had planned to go down there this evening," he went on, "to see if I could lure her back—she really is an extremely good dancer. But this afternoon, I acquired this"—his long fingers touched the stack of papers on the table—"and I thought I had best talk to you."

He shuffled aside the police reports concerning Clark Dexter's automobile accident of October 4th, 1920—and Joe Ladrone's bank book—to uncover a thick, red-covered stack of typescript, headed:

PERSONAL INHERITANCE TRUST and CORPORATE INSTRUCTIONS
Prepared for
GRISWOLD DEXTER
EXECUTED November 18th, 1920

Six weeks, Emma noted, after the death of his favorite son.

"I'm not even going to ask where you got that," said Zal.

TWENTY

Thirty minutes later, Zal and Emma both sat back from perusal of Sections Three, Four, and Seven of the trust document, and Zal whistled softly.

"Didn't trust Junior as far as he could throw him, did he?"

"And no mention," added Emma, "of the A.S.P.C.A. or the . . . what was it? The Esperanto League?"

"As a member of the Board of Directors," pointed out Malone, "Blair would, of course, have a copy of the Trust documents. And since he was not a suspect at the time—and nor, of course, were the A.S.P.C.A. or the Fraternal Order of the Orioles or any of that other very long list—I doubt that the police did more than make a note of the clauses which mandate the senior Mrs. Dexter's approval as a requirement for her son's inheritance under any circumstances. Certainly, as a member of the Board, Blair would not be expected to leave his own copy of the Trust in the hands of the police. But I'm sure if you looked at the clauses in the document that Mr. Blair showed the good Detective Smith, you would see that those sections were typed on a different machine than the one used here—" He patted the red cardboard folder before him.

"Could he get away with that?" asked Zal. "Typing up a couple of fake clauses and slipping those pages in to show the police? I mean, other people have copies of the Trust. When Floppy and his mom and Aunt Violet all drop dead—and Mrs. Floppy, too, if he marries Miss KKK—"

"He won't." Malone looked a little surprised that they'd even entertain the possibility—Emma wondered if he'd made Miss Schuyler's acquaintance. "And I'm sure their deaths will be months, if not years, apart, and will appear perfectly natural—"

"And in his mother's case, I think it might be," said Emma quietly. "From what Aunt Violet told me—all through the Act Three Love Duet of *Lohengrin*—Mrs. Dexter suffers from

Bright's disease: long-term kidney failure. So by the time anything happened to her nephew, Clark, Aunt Violet would almost certainly already have her sister's share of control of the company. Even if Rosemary Dexter were still alive, I doubt that she would be in any condition to take part in the Board of Directors."

"Interesting." Malone stirred the coffee Emma had poured out for him before they'd started reading, now cold. "Interesting and instructive. No, by the time the Trust is wound up by Clark's death—or disappearance—I doubt anyone would even consult the details of notes made on a murder case several years old in which Clark was proven not to be involved. Detective Smith's notes about the Trust would by then be buried in the files at the Eighteenth Precinct—and the deaths of Mrs. Dexter and her son would probably be investigated by the police in Suffolk County."

"Perhaps not even that," added Emma thoughtfully. "Mr. Blair will still be on the Board. As Mrs. Dexter's illness progresses, he might very well institute changes to the Trust itself. Minor ones, to which the other board members probably will not object, but which will require new copies in everyone's files. By the time Clark dies—or 'goes overseas'"—she provided quotation marks with a wry inflection of her voice—"though, of course, he will send letters periodically to Mr. Blair . . ."

"Typed, of course." Malone saluted her with his coffee cup.

"Of course. By the time the Trust itself is wound up, the documents as they were originally framed may have been superseded, withdrawn over the years from the files, and no longer be in existence."

"Very good!" Malone agreed. "All he needs is time. Prior to the accident, Griswold Dexter's will, which I happen to have a copy of here"—he patted his attaché case, with the casual air of one who generally carries the wills of millionaires about with him—"stipulated that in the event of all four children predeceasing their father, his wife Rosemary would inherit all personal property, as well as controlling stock in all the family's various enterprises. This will was made in April of 1918, at the beginning of the Spanish flu epidemic—"

His voice paused for a fraction of a second, as if he saw Emma look quickly aside. Then he continued smoothly, "At the same time, his wife made a will naming her sister, Violet Butler Blair, sole residuary legatee of everything of which she died possessed, should she outlive her husband and four children. This will has not been superseded by anything that I could find in the office of the Dexter family lawyer."

"Gosh," said Zal, who clearly wasn't about to ask what Shakespeare Malone was doing in the office of the Dexter family lawyer. "And I wonder who Aunt Violet names as legatee in *her* will?"

"Not the Fraternal Order of the Orioles, anyway," said Emma. "It was one of the things that made me wonder, even before I saw those photographs. Old Mr. Dexter never sounded to me like the A.S.P.C.A. sort. But how could he be sure—"

"Violet Butler Blair"—Malone touched his attaché case once more—"also made her will in April of 1918—on the same day, in fact—leaving her jewelry and a one-hundred-and-twenty-place set of Limoges china to her daughter Arabella, and the rest to her husband Jefferson, who you will remember was, at that time, quite well-off himself. Financial provision was made for their daughter Arabella only in the event of Jefferson Blair dying before his wife."

"Under the assumption that Jefferson would provide for Arabella in his will." Emma nodded. "Very proper."

Zal said something in Yiddish.

"But after Spencer and the two girls were killed"—she turned the red-covered Trust folder around on the vinyl table-top, and opened it to Section Three again—"Mr. Dexter clearly wasn't about to leave any large sums in his son Clark's hands."

"Would you?" asked Malone quietly. "As I told Mrs. Blackstone, Clark worshipped his brother. He was devastated by his death, and he reacted as many young people have done when faced with tragedy that was arguably of their own making."

"He got drunk," said Zal. "And stayed drunk. I sure would have."

"And since the trust was made after the slump of 1920, Griswold had had several years of watching his brother-in-law's antics with yachts and palaces and enough expensive horseflesh to fill that preposterous stable compound. He'd raised Clark not to get in his older brother's way for control of the family's holdings, and then despised him for his ignorance and inexperience. Thus, he put all the power in his wife Rosemary's hands—recognizing no doubt that she was the smartest person in the family anyway. He knew by then he had cancer," added Malone more quietly. "He relied on his wife to keep things together either until Clark 'snapped out of it,' as I'm sure he put it, or until Clark married a woman who would be able to take control. The kind of woman he could count on Rosemary to choose."

"'Inherit entirely and absolutely at the age of thirty-five,'" read Emma, "'or upon his marriage with the approval of his mother, Rosemary Butler Dexter . . .' Nothing about his being completely disinherited and the money left to charity, which is apparently what Mr. Blair told his wife, as well as inserted into the document he prepared to show to Detective Smith. And in the actual trust documents," she added thoughtfully, "Mr. Dexter, Senior, seems to have neglected to make any stipulations whatsoever about a potential Wife Number Two."

"Would you divorce a guy with eight hundred million dollars? Or risk giving him grounds to divorce *you*?" Zal glanced across at Malone. And, evidently forgetting his early resolution, "Where'd you get all this?"

"I found it on the sidewalk," replied the club owner. "Outside the Club Mardi Gras. I was quite surprised, naturally. It could be that the omission to mention an extremely short first marriage was an accident—due to the pain medications that Griswold Dexter would have been taking by then as his cancer progressed. But I suspect he was counting on his wife to select a bride whose principles would preclude either divorce or adultery."

"Like Beatrice Schuyler," agreed Emma. "And perhaps even one whose conversation practically guarantees her husband's retreat into fantasy and alcohol. In which case, Mr. Blair could continue to control the Board of Directors through his wife—"

"Without the cops getting suspicious," concluded Zal. "He's

on the Board—he can finagle a couple of unscheduled withdrawals. But why kill the girls?"

"Because they might marry men stronger than Clark," said Emma quietly. "Men who might demand places on the Board, and might very well keep a sharper eye on changes proposed to the trust. I assume each of the girls stood to inherit stock as well."

"They did," said Malone, "under the terms of the 1918 will. I gather they were both bright and well educated. Once Jefferson Blair went bankrupt—once he was living under Griswold Dexter's roof—he could play a long game. Had all four of the children been killed, the police would have looked a great deal more closely at the circumstances of the 'accident.' They must have had their suspicions, since the minute Dexter Senior was out of the way, Blair was willing to pay blackmail for *something*—"

"So what did Joe Ladrone see?"

"Probably," Malone guessed, "Jefferson Blair doing something to the engine of Dexter's car—Vauxhall Prince Henry. A mechanic could replace a bolt in the steering coupling with one that was sawn nearly through. It would fail at high speed around the first curve—"

"I believe King Pelops did something of the kind in a chariot race against Oenomaus in ancient Greece."

"Didn't realize Vauxhall made chariots back then," reflected Zal.

"They're an old firm." *I've really been spending too much time in the company of Mr. Marx . . .*

"But the easiest way," continued Malone, whose own grin quickly faded, "would be to plant a small time bomb—like a pencil-bomb—in the engine. Not enough to kill everyone, but enough to put the car into the ditch and stun or knock out the driver and the passengers."

"*Would* a car catch fire under those circumstances?" asked Emma. "When I was being taught to drive ambulances, the instructor told me repeatedly, 'They're not bombs, you know.' Of course, at the time I thought they were . . ."

"Depends on how fast you were going," said Zal. "And what

kind of car. If Blair didn't want it to look like murder—just wanted to make sure whoever survived would be the easiest one for him to manipulate—or croak—later on—he could have hung around near the roadhouse and followed them with a can of gas, a book of matches, and a sap. That puts Clark in charge. Even if poor Mrs. Dexter lives for another thirty years, Blair gets to siphon money out of Dexter Consolidated . . .

"And that's why Clark wanted an actress!" he added, suddenly inspired. "Alternate candidate for Wife Number One! Beatrice'll never divorce him, so he finds somebody who will. Big repentance scene, takes the pledge, gallons of tears for her former way of life . . . Who was it who did that in *Intolerance* . . .? Pleads with Mom to guide her in her new way of living . . . Either Kitty or Darlene could have pulled it off. Gloria Swanson sure could have. Mom's delighted by the change of heart, ditches Beatrice, and gives her consent. Then divorce a week later, leaving Floppy in full possession."

"Precisely," agreed Emma. "Well worth an investment of fifty thousand dollars plus the cost of the dress."

"Excellent!" Malone raised his coffee cup to her again. "You make a very fine criminal, Mrs. Blackstone."

"I work in the film business," retorted Emma drily. "I live surrounded by mentors. I assume, from the conversations I've had with Miss Schuyler, that her interests are limited to minding other people's business for them and keeping undesirables out of America, but if Clark married her, after all—instead of Miss Golden or Gloria Swanson or Kitty—might she not have used her husband's power with the Board of Directors to investigate a money leak? If the police already had their suspicions, Blair wouldn't dare risk killing her, too, surely?"

"He wouldn't need to." Malone looked surprised. "So far as I know, Clark has no intention of marrying Beatrice Schuyler or any woman of his mother's choosing. Not when he'd already met the woman he has loved faithfully for the past four and a half years."

And when Zal and Emma stared at him in surprise . . .

"Roxie North," he said.

* * *

"The girl—" began Zal, after a long pause.

"The gun," said Emma.

"To frame her for killing Darlene?"

"If Blair simply did away with Roxie," the club owner explained, "he would run the risk of his nephew falling in love with someone else . . . or marrying some enterprising damsel from the chorus line while under the influence. Worse, Clark might at that point become suspicious and talk to the police—who, as I said, may very well have some questions of their own. Better to gain unbreakable control over Miss North—of whom Dexter's mother would never approve in a million years because of her race. Blair could order her not to marry Clark, but to keep him on a string, for years, probably . . ."

"Could he do that?" Emma thought back to the box of guns on the shelf in the Palace prop room, the plain blood-red ribbons among the gaudy bows, the different shape of the replacement weapon. "Stage that spectacular murder and then make the police believe that she'd used that gun?"

"Oh, I think he could." Malone gathered the pages of the trust document together, long fingers tidying them like a professional typist. "Completely aside from how easy it is to get the police to suspect even a white chorus girl, to say nothing of a Black one . . . Have you ever heard of ballistics testing?"

Emma frowned. "Doesn't that have to do with working out the range on an artillery piece? How much elevation a gun needs in order to drop shells on enemy trenches?"

"That's what it means now." Zal looked from Emma to Malone. "But that's also what they call the new tests that show that any specific bullet came from a specific gun. A German fellow came up with a double-lensed microscope that lets you see the rifling patterns on two slugs side by side. They used it when they tried Sacco and Vanzetti a couple years ago, if you can call that a trial—"

"Exactly," said Malone. "If Blair has a gun bearing Roxie's fingerprints, which can be proved as the gun that fired the bullets retrieved from Miss Haley's body—"

"He can hold Miss North hostage." Emma felt herself heat

again with rage at the cynical completeness of the manipulation of what was, clearly, a miserable young man trying to fight clear of a trap.

"Which he does," agreed Malone. "The moment he hears the gossip on the set, that a bride has been selected and negotiations have begun, it becomes imperative that he establish absolute control over Miss North with, as you say, a spectacular murder, and with proof that it was she who pulled the trigger. You're very good, Mrs. Blackstone. I may have to hire—that is, I may be moved to recommend your services to . . . er . . . friends."

Zal put an arm around her shoulders. "That's my girl." Rising, he went to the stove, put a hand near the side of the coffee pot, and brought it back to the table. "Ince knew Ladrone, didn't he? They probably met at Biograph, and then Ladrone came out to the coast to work with him at Triangle. Ladrone probably suspected something fishy about that car accident—suspected enough to blackmail Blair, anyway. And his suspicions would be confirmed when Blair paid up. Ladrone must have known Dorothy Dalton when they both worked with Ince, and even if he didn't have proof that Blair killed the other Dexter kids, he'd have warned Dorothy to pass on the Matrimonial Sweepstakes. He guessed Blair was dangerous. And Ince may have asked him why . . ."

"So what do we do?" asked Emma quietly. "Take this to Detective Smith at once, of course—"

"Well . . ." Malone laid his hand on the document. "Actually, suggest that the District Attorney subpoena the Board of Trustees of Dexter Consolidated for a copy of the genuine document—which I will take it upon myself to return to the Board's legal offices tonight." He glanced at the kitchen clock.

"At one in the morning?" asked Zal.

"I have a friend who has the keys," returned the club owner smoothly, like Chico Marx admitting to possession of the key to the Palace's stage door. "This document also contains information concerning the legal status of property mortgaged to Dexter Consolidated—"

Emma opened her mouth to say, *Versailles*? And closed it.

Her eyes met Malone's.

Complete with smuggler tunnels opening on the Long Island Sound? That you'd really rather didn't fall back under the control of someone being blackmailed by Angel-Eyes Taralla?

Malone raised his brows. *Smuggler? I?*

She asked instead, "How long might that take? Because Mr. Blair may very well have heard from some of the extras about the photographs of the backstage Palace shoot by this time. He may even have seen you or Detective Smith at Versailles. He may panic and decide to get rid of Clark Dexter, which would at least put the money into his sister-in-law's hands. Even if Rosemary Dexter lives for several more years, she won't be able to rule the Board—or to control her sister's votes—much longer. And if he kills poor Clark in such a way that the body is not found, he would have access to funds through the Board indefinitely. It's late—"

She glanced again at the clock. (*And where in Heaven's name is Kitty*?)

"My dear Mrs. Blackstone," purred Malone, "I should scarcely describe it as 'late' for Broadway."

"Yes, but goodness only knows where Mr. Dexter is."

"I know exactly where Mr. Dexter is." The club owner rose and strolled out to the parlor, where the phone sat on its marble-topped table. "Or I can guess within a few percentage points of certainty, given that Roxie North is now at Lulubelle's, after refusing to see poor Clark or answer any of the desperate letters he sent her there—"

He reached for the telephone, only to have it ring as he touched it.

He drew his hand back, startled, and Emma got swiftly to her feet and picked it up. She heard Zal explain, "Don't want to shock the Plaza's house dicks."

"Hello?"

"Mrs. Blackstone?" said a woman's velvety contralto. "I'm so sorry to be calling you like this, but I was told Mr. Malone would be there this evening—is he there still? This is . . . This is an emergency. May I come up? Tell him this is Roxie North."

TWENTY-ONE

"They didn't see me." The tall girl had the air of one not easily unsettled, but her slender hands were shaking as Zal handed her a hotel tumbler with two fingers of Seagram's in it. She was if anything more beautiful than the picture taken backstage at the Palace, though in a less conventional style; the trace of African parentage was more obvious than the photograph showed. Her black hair was short, waved, and pomaded tight to a skull like Nefertiti's, her eyes a light, almost silvery hazel-gray with a dark ring around the iris. Her café-crème skin was ashen with shock.

"Clark was at a table right down front for the second show," she said. "I should have known he wouldn't pay any heed to the letter I left him, telling him to leave me alone. And, of course, he'd find out where I was. He had a drink in front of him, but he hardly touched it. If he'd been drunk, he'd have made a scene, but he wasn't. He just watched me . . ." She closed her eyes for a moment, turned her face aside. "Mr. Blair came in—that . . . that uncle of his. I was in the middle of a routine, I couldn't . . . Mr. Blair . . ."

She couldn't go on for a moment, and Emma, beside her at the kitchen table, laid a hand gently on the girl's wrist and said, "I think we all know what Mr. Blair has on you."

Her head jerked up, gray eyes blazing. "It isn't true! He said he could prove it, but it isn't—"

"No," said Emma. "We know that. And we know how it was done."

"You've got to help me." Roxie's hands started to shake again, and her glance went from Emma to Malone. "Please, Mr. Malone! You've got to . . . The next time I looked around at Clark, he'd passed out; he was sagging down on Blair's shoulder like he was drugged. I know Blair put something in his drink. Blair didn't see me—I think he thinks I'm still at the Mardi Gras. He got him up and got him out of there; I dodged back out of the line, ran through the dressing rooms and out the back into the alley. I wanted to scream, but if the cops came, they'd bust Lulubelle and close the club—"

Emma could well imagine upon what grounds . . . and if "Lulubelle's" had a Black owner, the club might very well stay shuttered for good.

"I couldn't do that to her. I came out of the alley, and I swear to God, there was Darlene Golden. I swear it was Darlene Golden—she walked right past me, as Blair was helping Clark out the front door. I swear it was her—"

"It was," said Emma. "Go on."

The younger woman shook her head, her eyes frantic. "There was a car pulled up at the curb, and Bronco Burnett got out, just as Darlene got up to them. There's a streetlight right there near the entrance . . . They shoved Clark into the back of the car, Blair and Bronco—"

Miss Golden would know Bronco, thought Emma, *from Mr. Taralla's retinue . . .*

And Bronco would know her.

"—and Darlene walked up and grabbed Bronco's arm, and he pushed her in too—pushed her in and pulled out a gun. I–I ran back inside to call the police, but Lulubelle said the cops would just say it was Clark's uncle, helping him 'cause he was drunk—"

"They'd finish their coffee before doing anything." Malone was already on his feet and heading for the telephone again. Roxie followed him, camel-hair coat flapping open to reveal the scanty coating of sequins she wore to back Lulubelle's floor-show headliner. "They got tired of chasing after Clark's antics years ago. Benny?" The club owner turned his attention to the phone. "Get Gas-Bomb and the Kid and whoever else you can round up, fast, and meet me at Versailles. Yes, Roxie's here with me. Did you tell her where I was? Good man. Did Ice ever find out how to get into the cellars under the stable? Did anybody?"

"You can get into them from the Italian garden," said Emma. "How do you know that's where . . .?"

"What?" He half turned from the telephone, then turned

back and said, "Get going. We'll meet you there. Get your coat, Mrs. Blackstone—"

"The hell she is." Zal stepped between Malone and Emma as the club owner reached for Emma's arm. "If Blair's working with Angel-Eyes's boys, Emma's not going anywhere near—"

"Mr. Rokatansky—" Malone sighed as he pulled an automatic pistol from inside his stylish ivory-colored jacket. When Emma took a step toward him, he caught her wrist and twisted it, causing her to cry in pain and stumble . . .

"I'm certainly not going to kill you," said Malone to Zal, the barrel of the gun not wavering an inch from its target on his left hip. "But at this distance, I can scarcely miss incapacitating you, and I'd much rather you came with me to protect Mrs. Blackstone—who, believe me, I will leave in the safety of the car once she's shown me how to get into those cellars under the stables. Blair knows the place. Where else would he hide Clark's body? Hide it where it won't be found for fifty years? Especially when he'll have control of the place? Are you coming, Roxie? Any delay is only going to give Blair more time to get Clark—and Miss Golden—down into those cellars. Our timing is already down to minutes."

Roxie stared frantically at Emma, who said, with what calm she could, "I'll come, Mr. Malone, and I won't make trouble . . . Yes, do please come with us, Zal. I–I think I should very much like a bodyguard—"

Malone had released her wrist, and though he kept his eyes on Zal, she knew he was aware of every move she made as she went to fetch her coat from the closet.

"You're not—"

"Zal, please," said Emma. "This is the fastest way, and I would like Mr. Malone to be able to concentrate on his driving. No, Chang, Jazz, you can't come with us . . . Stay here and be good.

"You know they'll kill Miss Golden," she added, as they walked down the hallway to the elevator. "She will have recognized Mr. Burnett, and she'll be able to identify Mr. Blair, and probably whoever else is driving. And if she simply disappears—'goes overseas,' I expect, with Clark . . ."

"After Clark leaves a note—and it sounds like Mr. Blair can forge Clark's signature, at least, convincingly," put in Malone. "Living at Abbottsford, he's had plenty of time to collect handwriting samples to copy."

"Oh, surely he'd invest in a typewriter," argued Emma. "I expect poor Mrs. Dexter, and Aunt Violet, will be receiving letters from 'Clark' for years, from Shanghai or Tahiti or wherever Mr. Blair can get someone to forward them from. And who's going to ask for details? Everyone on the Board knows that Clark is irresponsible . . ."

"While Blair helps himself from the Trust." Zal nodded approvingly. "Or maybe 'Clark' sets up a bank account in Paris and asks for money . . ."

"And I don't want to sound selfish or anything," added Roxie quietly, "but I'm pretty sure *I'll* have to leave town if Blair and Angel-Eyes aren't taken care of. And even that might not help. They didn't see me see them"—she tucked Malone's attaché case of papers, which she'd fetched from the kitchen, tightly under her arm as she tied the sash of her coat—"but Blair knows who I am, and how to find me. And he knows if Clark disappears, I'm not going to be shut up by threats about my fingerprints being on some damn gun."

"I'm afraid I'm going to have to give you the cab fare home, Miss North"—Malone pressed the elevator's call button—"rather than act the gentleman and drop you off at your door. But I wasn't fooling when I said we may have only minutes if we don't overtake Blair on the road. I suggest you find somewhere else to stay—"

"Screw that." Miss North dipped briefly into the pocket of her coat and produced, for a moment, a small pistol, similar to one that Kitty kept among her lingerie. "You're gonna need all the backup you can get, Mr. Malone, if your boys get lost on the way."

"My dear Roxie—"

The elevator arrived then, and both Malone and Roxie discreetly pocketed their weapons as the operator opened the door for them. The prospective rescuers rode down in silence—Malone keeping to a corner of the car and watching both Zal and the operator—but as they stepped into the lobby, Emma asked quietly, "Should we leave a note? Kitty should be returning at some point—"

"And could be asked to call the police?" Malone raised his eyebrows. "Who, if they did come at all—to rescue a drunkard from the benign assistance of his uncle—would probably arrest Gas-Bomb, Benny, and the boys before they even found their way into the cellars. Or do you think their presence would prevent a gunfight if Bronco, and whoever he's got driving Blair's car for him, panic?"

"And if the cops don't feel up to a two-and-a-half-hour drive out to Long Island to rescue a known drunk from a family member," pointed out Zal, "do you really think Kitty's going to say, *Oh, well, if we can't get the cops, I guess Chico and I'll just sit home and play Old Maid*? I don't like this," he added, as the doorman bowed them out onto Central Park South and they crossed the street (*What are all these people doing still out at one in the morning*? wondered Emma). "But since the cavalry has already been called in, I don't think the presence of the cops—or, for God's sake, Kitty with that little thirty-two she's got stashed in her underwear drawer—is going to help the situation any."

He glanced grimly sidelong at Malone. "I just hope to Christ your guys are at Versailles when we get there."

"So do I," returned the club owner, as they reached the long, low Packard Eight that Emma had guessed on sight was Malone's. Malone opened the driver's side door with his left hand and gestured—right hand and gun still politely in his pocket—for Zal to get in. "You drive."

"There's two ways in that I found," whispered Emma, as Zal pulled the Packard off the gravel road and onto the open ground where the Duke of Wellington had camped his army the previous week. "One goes down from one of those ornamental niches in the stable wall in the garden; the other is from the mansion's wine cellar through a tunnel. The garden stairway is more direct. Is that what you were looking for when I saw you here, Mr. Malone?"

"It's how I knew Blair is using the tunnels to hide things in. He's been skimming a crate or two from every cargo he carries for Taralla; he has to be hiding them here, to sell later."

Roxie's voice was tight with dread. "Hurry—"

"They could be parked anywhere." Zal's voice was barely a breath as he opened the door. Above the pine woods that surrounded the mansion called Versailles, the last of the waning moon gave barely any light; Roxie groped in the glove box and drew out a flashlight. "If we checked around for Blair's car, we'd probably still miss it. If there's any trouble"—he handed Emma out—"you go down flat in the nearest bushes and then you head back here. You don't wait to see if anybody's hurt or anybody needs help. You get the hell out of there. That goes for you, too, Roxie. Shakespeare's a professional," he added. "You're not."

"Screw you," said Roxie, and got out the other side of the car, gun in hand.

"There's spare batteries there as well," breathed the club owner, slipping out swiftly behind her. Emma heard the soft clicking of the dry cells as the girl collected them and dropped them in the pocket of her coat.

Emma could not but be grateful for Malone's forethought. It was hand-in-front-of-your-face black among the trees. Only to the west, where a break in the pines showed the dim blur of the stable wall, was there any clue as to which direction to travel. As it was, Emma was constantly tripping on deadfall branches and unexpected dips in the ground as they made their way, cautiously, in that direction. Zal kept his hand firmly under her elbow, to steady her and, she guessed, so that he wouldn't lose track of her in the blackness. Dank cold pierced straight through her coat and gloves. The air breathed of the sea.

None of them spoke. Like prey animals in the woods, Emma understood instinctively that Taralla's henchmen could be anywhere, and that there was no guarantee that Malone's troops had yet arrived. (*And goodness knows what kind of fracas there will be when they do!*) She was aware of the pounding of her own heart, and of being almost sick with terror at an odd level at which she did not really feel anything.

When they reached the edge of the trees, she stepped forward to take the lead, picturing the Hercules statue in her mind and exactly where it stood along the stable wall, at the same time wondering what would happen if she forgot where it was. *We can't stand still in the garden for even a moment . . .*

Are they waiting for us to come out of cover?

There was no way to tell. And every second counted.

Did Jim feel like this going on a night patrol in No Man's Land?

Don't think about Jim. Don't think about forgetting. Don't think about anything . . .

She made a quick, small gesture with one finger and stepped out into the thinner darkness . . .

And don't get yourself caught on a rose bush . . .

The remnant of the gravel path was invisible under the black overhang of feral foliage. Every statue was a pallid blur against the dark niches of the stable wall.

There.

The Nemean Lion made for a larger silhouette. She led the way quickly, her back prickling with fear, waiting for the bark of a gun. The writhing shape of the Lion also provided visual cover, as the two men dragged aside the clawing masses of leafless ivy and juniper, and uncovered the slanted doors. Hands shielding the lens, Malone flicked the flashlight on long enough to scan the masses of wet brown leaves underfoot, then switched it off again. He squeezed Roxie's shoulder, signed to her to remain up top as a guard.

Roxie signed to him an extremely vulgar suggestion in return.

Knowing the rescue would involve more physical conflict than she herself was capable of performing correctly, Emma held out her hand for Roxie's gun—*I'll stay*—and had Zal grab her wrist, shake his head violently.

Not on your tintype, Duchess, you're going back to the car . . .

Before a silent argument could ensue (*Malone will never leave Zal behind him with a gun . . .*), through the half-open door in the pavement echoed the thread of a distant scream.

Zal said, "Shit!" and plunged down the stairs, Malone and

the two women at his heels. The flashlight beam slashed across the brick arch of the tunnel and picked up the white arrows of Emma's chalk marks; the black, wet shapes of two rats whipped ahead of them and out of sight. At the T-junction, they stopped, listening. Darlene (*it has to be Darlene*) screamed again, in the darkness to their right. Things Jim had written to her about men in wartime came back, and Emma felt herself scorch with rage—*Of course, if Taralla's men had a woman witness with them, they won't kill her immediately* . . .

She pounded after them, wishing she had a gun as well. Echoes clawed at the sound, confusing in the tunnel among the tack rooms and storage chambers. Another passageway branched to the left . . . Where was the sound coming from?

Movement in the darkness. In the instant that Zal yanked her into the cross-passage, she saw the running figure of a blonde woman, her arms outstretched to either side, ricocheting off one wall or the other as she ran, screaming.

The flashlight's beam showed no one behind her. At the same instant, Darlene saw the flashlight and plunged into the nearest doorway, screaming again as (presumably) she saw that all she had done was enter a dead-end chamber . . .

How many seconds until Taralla's men show up? Emma raced with the others to the door, wondering if calling out to her would help or hurt the situation. (*If she's been screaming as she ran, the men won't be far behind* . . .)

Zal seemed to share this opinion because he yelled, "Darlene, it's us!" as they reached the door, and in the enclosed dark of the room and the tunnel, the report of a gun was like a thunderclap. Malone, the first to reach the doorway, staggered and fell back into Emma's arms, the flashlight clattering to the floor. Zal yelled again, "Darlene, it's Zal!" as he ducked to the side, and the gun barked twice more. "It's Zal!"

To which Emma added her voice, "It's Emma, Darlene!"

Something metal and heavy clattered on the paving bricks within. Zal ducked past Emma as she lowered Malone to the floor—the club owner's hand convulsively gripping her wrist—and she heard Darlene sobbing hysterically, muffled now against Zal's shoulder. Roxie plunged in after them, while Emma scooped up the flashlight (*Thank Heavens the bulb didn't break!*) and turned the beam, first on the wet spreading hotness under her right hand, then on the wounded man's face. (*High on the left side of the chest near the armpit—axillary artery . . .*) She was already tearing loose Malone's expensive silk tie, raiding his pockets and her own for handkerchiefs—

"Zal, handkerchiefs!" she called, and Roxie brought her out a double handful, some pristine, some crumpled and smelling of the alcohol Zal used to clean his camera lenses. To these, the chorus girl added a small silver flask of expensive imported booze of some kind. "Can you walk?" she asked, as the golden-brown eyes flickered half open.

"I'd rather not," Malone confessed in a whisper.

Inside the brick chamber, she could hear Zal coaxing—and trying to keep the urgency from his voice—"Calm down, Darlene, you're OK. You're OK. But we've got to get the hell out of here—"

And Roxie breaking in with, "Where are they? Is Clark all right?"

"No!" Darlene sobbed hysterically. "No!"

The yellow glare of a flashlight jolted into sight in the darkness around them. Emma called, "It's them!" and tried to get her arm under Malone's, to drag him into the relative cover of the room. "I'm sorry—"

"Think nothing of it, Mrs. Blackstone," returned the club owner kindly. He sat up a little straighter against her, leveled his own gun on the approaching flashlight beam, and fired.

The beam jerked and went out. Emma heard the muffled commotion of something soft and heavy falling, and a man yelled, "Fuck!" By the sound of it, a gun dropped, too.

Roxie came out, helped Emma drag Malone back into the chamber where Darlene clung, weeping, to Zal. A pistol lay on the floor—Emma scooped it up and held it out to Zal.

"Empty," he said.

The chorus girl pressed her finger to her lips, slipped to the side of the door, and waited in silence only broken by Darlene's hysterical sobs. Zal coaxed the actress to the side of the room, sheltered from the immediate line of the door, with Darlene tugging against him and struggling every step of the way. Emma understood her blind terror, and still wanted to shake her. Malone turned his head, observing the scene for a moment: although her lip was puffy and her face bruised where she'd been punched, Darlene still wore her fur-trimmed silk-velvet coat, and the clothing beneath it was neither torn nor disarrayed.

The club owner nodded once, then let out a groan worthy of a dying Romeo, and Emma, obediently, gasped, "Mr. Malone? Mr. Malone!"

Bronco Burnett put his head cautiously through the door, and Roxie shot him immediately through the temple.

Darlene screamed and collapsed into renewed hysterics.

Roxie took the gun from under the late Mr. Burnett's hand, turned to Zal, and said, "You come with me."

TWENTY-TWO

"If Mr. Blair was involved with Mr. Taralla's bootlegging operations," said Emma into the ensuing silence, "he might have taken Mr. Dexter to the padlocked room near the passageway that I think leads to the Revolutionary War smuggler caves. He probably has the key."

"It's what Taralla wants," Malone whispered. "Why he keeps Blair . . . Depot . . . for liquor . . . place to bring it in . . ."

And what you *want as well? With Clark Dexter owning it, and not Jefferson Blair?*

Is that what this valiant rescue is really all about?

It made more sense than a sudden attack of self-sacrificing concern for Roxie and Clark.

"The way is marked by the blue chalk arrows," she went on. "You'll find them down at the end of this passageway to the left, where Mr. Burnett came from. I'll stay here with Mr. Malone and Miss Golden—"

Zal opened his mouth to protest, but glanced from Darlene to Malone, as if counting how many active participants any rescue operation would require.

Malone squeezed Emma's hand again, said, "Come back . . . for us. Roxie, my dear, would you be so good . . . see if Mr. Burnett's flashlight survived? And Mr. . . . Rokatansky, could you haul the—er—casualties out of sight . . . another room . . . nearby? . . . Wish I . . . could assist . . ."

"It's all right," whispered Emma.

"Spare Miss Golden . . . further distress . . ." He shook his head, and his voice sank to a murmur. "Couple of corpses . . . upsetting if . . . not used to them . . ."

Emma heartily agreed. Prior to driving an ambulance from the casualty disembarkation piers in Portsmouth to the hospitals during the war, she had never seen a dead human being. Her experiences since then, shocking as some of them had been, had not completely erased her own uneasiness at being in the same room with a corpse. Had there been no choice, of course, she knew that she could put up with it—much better to be in the same room with Bronco Burnett and his driver dead than with them alive. But when Roxie, returning with the second flashlight, exclaimed, "Oh, just leave them in here! We have to hurry!" Emma said, "Go!"

She took the second flashlight, which promptly went out. "We'll move into the next room along," she added, slapping the cardboard tube until the light flickered back to life again. "If Mr. Malone can—"

"We were in the room where Blair hid the booze." Darlene looked up unexpectedly, her face grotesque with the bruises and the ruin of her make-up, and climbed shakily to her feet. "The stuff he stole from Angel-Eyes—crates of it. Floppy's doped, but he was alive when . . . when Bronco and Knuckles . . ." Unsteadily, she brushed at the dirt on her coat, as if momentarily hypnotized by the small, familiar gesture. Then, like a woman who has gained strength from it, she took a deep breath and went on, "Blair yelled at them to hurry up because he needs them to walk Floppy down some stairs to this other room underneath it."

"Blue arrows." Emma pointed into the darkness. "Go!" And as Zal and Roxie disappeared into the tunnel's blackness: "Can you hold the flashlight for me, dear, while I help Mr. Malone? Can you stand up, Mr. Malone?" She held out the flashlight to Darlene, who turned away from her and stepped to Bronco's body—Knuckles still lay some fifteen feet up the lightless tunnel, barely glimpsed when Emma moved the flashlight's beam. Then, with a scream of hatred, Darlene kicked Bronco in the side (being careful not to get blood on her shoe) and spat in the corpse's still face.

Taking the flashlight from Emma, she walked the ten feet or so along the corridor to the next chamber without looking back.

"I should probably go back to the garden door and see if there's a way to bar it." Emma knelt awkwardly at Malone's side. In the few moments that she'd had the beam trained on

Bronco's face (*He'd beat Cissy up bad*, Zeppo had said . . .), she'd seen the fresh scratches left by Darlene's nails, above and below the eye socket. Now her only thought was, *I hope we don't trip over him . . .*

He's more than welcome to never laugh or love or rape a woman again.

"I observe . . . notebook in your pocket," returned the club owner, in a thread of a voice. "Spare me . . . a few blank pages, Your Grace. Burn them . . . in the next room . . . so Miss Golden and I won't be left in the dark. Benny . . . still looking for a few of my friends. If Angel-Eyes hears . . . he'll send out some of his boys after Blair."

"After *Blair*?" Emma braced one hand on the wall, to ease the wounded man to his feet. She had done this more than once when the incoming wounded at the disembarkation pier had far outnumbered not only the orderlies but the ambulance drivers as well. "I thought Blair worked for him."

"My dear Mrs. Blackstone"—Malone's voice remained steady, though she heard his breath hiss with pain—"Taralla . . . not a man to tolerate a thief. Knows there are tunnels somewhere . . . Wants this place for himself. Knows about . . . underground. Doesn't know where . . . how to get in. Blair swore . . . he didn't know. Blair offloads the *White Goddess* . . . the Wading River beach. Five miles up the Sound."

"Heaven forbid Mr. Taralla's employees are dishonest." Emma set her weight against Malone's and thanked her stars that the man was barely above her own height. "So that's what Bronco and—er—Mr. Knuckles were doing here a few weeks ago." It was still, as she had learned during the war, almost impossible to maneuver the dead weight of a man who has not the strength to balance. "Looking for the tunnels." She steered carefully around Bronco in the doorway, inched along the passageway toward the dim outline of the next opening to their right.

"And that's what you were doing here as well?"

"I?" Even in agony, Malone managed to sound both innocent and aggrieved. "No . . . Just wished to . . . see Kitty . . ."

Her mother, Emma reflected, would have responded to this assertion with the phrase, *In a piggy's little eye . . .*

If Mother didn't go into convulsions at the thought that I'd be tripping over gangster corpses and lugging bootleggers around smuggler tunnels at three in the morning . . .

As sometimes still happened, she felt the flicker of a thought of what Jim's reaction would be when she told him about this . . .

No, she told herself. *No*.

There was a hasp on the inside of the doors back up to the garden, but no lock. With gingerly care, Emma shut off the flashlight, waited for a few moments for her eyes to adjust, then pushed the door open, the free scents of the sea flooding in against the dank stuffiness of the tunnel. In the cold indigo dimness, it was just possible to make out the edges of the niche. Stepping out, she reached for the thick branch of the juniper that she knew would be at the core of that snarl of leaves. With the flashlight under one arm (*Please, God, let it come on again when I shut the doors once more!*), she slipped her pen-knife from her skirt pocket and opened it. *At least I can make a bar through the hasps . . .*

The wind moved its direction a point or two, and she smelled it.

Cigarette smoke.

Then the sharp rustle of bodies in the foliage, and a male voice saying, "Figlio di puttana!" (*Rose thorns?*) In the darkness, and with the movement of the wind, she could see nothing, but the noises sounded close. She stepped back at once, closed the doors, dug in her pocket for her gloves, and stuffed the leather through the hasps by touch in the dark, knotting and double-knotting the fingers, the slit cuffs, around the metal. Then, switching on the flashlight (it took her two tries), she strode back to the room where she'd left Malone and Darlene.

"They're in the garden," she said, making sure to stand to one side of the door as she spoke, lest she startle someone who might still have a gun in hand. Then, stepping around it and into the room, she added, "Are any of your men Italian, Mr. Malone? Someone cursed in Italian outside. I tied the doors shut—there was no bar—but it won't hold long."

He whispered, "Damn it." By the flashlight gleam, she saw

that the torn shoulder of his jacket, where it lay over her makeshift dressing, was reddened with a dollar-sized soak of blood, and his face gleamed with sweat despite the cold. Huddled near the burned remains of most of the pages of Emma's memorandum book, Darlene began to weep again, desperately, hopelessly. She had clearly had as much as she could take.

No help there . . . Malone's silver flask lay beside her, empty, and Emma guessed that without that soothing elixir, she might well have gone into hysterics again.

She stepped back into the passageway, shone the light further down into the darkness, and, yes, as she'd remembered, there was another cross-corridor about thirty feet along. Wincing, she returned to Bronco Burnett's corpse, once more jammed her flashlight under her arm, and took him by the wrists, leaning the whole of her weight into dragging him along the bricks in that direction. *At least they won't know the white arrows are mine*, she thought. *They'll follow the other marks—the pink or the blue . . .*

Bronco had been a big man. It took every ounce of her strength to get him a dozen feet past the door of their current hideout chamber, his head pointing further down the corridor. *And I hope to goodness their flashlights aren't any brighter than this one . . .*

She was panting, stumbling, when she ran back into the chamber, snatched up Malone's empty flask, and raced back up the passageway, a few yards past Bronco and nearly to the corner of the cross-tunnel. There she dropped the silver vessel, hearing the echoes of feet kicking, pounding at the garden doors as she strode.

Malone was nodding, eyes shut and breath hoarse with pain. Emma dropped to Darlene's side, caught her arm. "Not a sound," she breathed. "Not one single sound."

"I want to go home!" wailed Darlene. "I want Moose!"

Who in Heaven's name is Moose? It made Emma wonder—through mounting terror—what Darlene had been up to since her "return to life."

"Be quiet! They're—"

She heard the ruckus of the doors slamming open in a deceptive tangle of echoes, then the drumming of feet. She switched off the flashlight, put her hand over Darlene's mouth, and was hard put not to slap her when she struggled confusedly, still making frantic mewing noises . . .

These stopped when a man's voice fifteen feet up the passage said, "Che palle!" (*I'll have to ask Kitty what that means . . .*) "It's Knucks!"

"What's that?"

Flashlight gleam bounced in the passageway and the shadows of men raced past the door. "Vaffanculo!" "That way—!"

Do we cut back out through the garden? Or wait for Zal? Did they leave someone in the garden? Stay here? Did they find the—?

Was that a noise out there?

Foot falls. The click of a woman's high heels on the passage bricks. A muffled voice mumbled, "Where we goin'? Roxie—"

And a hissed "Shut the fuck up, for God's sake!"

Emma flung herself at the door, flashed the light, once, into the dark, and was immediately answered. By the light, she saw the insectile gleam of two pairs of glasses.

"They went up the passageway," she said, after the first desperate kiss.

"Spence an' me—" Clark Dexter shook an owlish finger at Emma and Zal's second kiss. "Now, you stop that. Stop that an' . . . an' lissen." The young man was weaving on his feet, clinging to Roxie's shoulders. "Pass'gway to the house. Spence an' me used to play here alla time. Hide from Dimble—tutor—had a wart on his nose. Wart'd turn red when he was drunk . . ."

"Where?" asked Zal, and Dexter blinked at him in the gleam of the flashlight.

"Right here." He pointed to his right nostril. "He had another one on his—"

"Where's the passage to the house?"

The young man pointed vaguely back up the passage from which they'd emerged. Emma could see in the dim light that the irises of his blue eyes were pinned down to almost nothing. "Jus' past the ol' well," he said.

Was it the blue marks that led that way? Yes . . .

"Come on. Zal, can you get Mr. Malone? I can spell you—"

The distant echo of voices in the darkness, and then, suddenly, the crack of a gun. In the chamber behind them, Darlene screamed.

Emma could not really blame her, but did. Nevertheless, she reached her side in three long strides, pulled her to her feet, Darlene crying again like an exhausted child. "Blue chalk marks," said Emma, and flashed her light back up the passageway. "Bottom of the stair to the left . . ."

They're in the garden. Can we get around the west side of the house as far as the car without being seen?

Darlene stumbled, wobbled against her like a drunkard, clinging to her arm. Emma switched the flashlight on to get her bearings, then off, keeping her hand to the wall until a turn told her they'd reached the passage to the steps . . .

Did they leave guards there?

They had. She made out what could have been a silhouette against blackness barely lighter than the abysses around them, felt outdoor cold breathe down on her face, and smelled the sea again. But the man or men seemed to be looking outward into the garden—or else the blackness of the tunnel was truly impenetrable—because no one called after them as they crossed past the steps, turned the corner beyond. Emma flashed the light again briefly at the wall, and yes (*Thank Heavens!*), there was the smudged blue chalk mark (*Whose? Blair's? Spencer Dexter's all those years ago?*) on the uneven stone.

She smelled the well before they reached it, the unmistakable pong of wet stone and rank water. Flicked on the flashlight again in time to see the outline of the well-chamber door. Behind her, she heard Clark's voice, less slurred, say, "Straight left, and watch your step. It's narrow and the floor's God-awful."

They stepped into the chamber—and a gun barked to their right, redoubled echoes like cannon fire in the darkness. From the corner of her eye, Emma saw the muzzle flash, and the next instant, a second shot crashed almost at her elbow. Zal said, "Shit!" and Roxie said something a good deal worse; Darlene screamed and grabbed Emma's arm so hard it was a moment before she was able to back up into the cover of the tunnel.

Ahead of her in the dark well chamber, she heard the sobbing of a man in pain.

Zal's hand—even in the dark, she knew it—took the flashlight from hers, and the yellow beam skated across the floor, to pick out the shape of Jefferson Blair lying sprawled in the entrance of one of the other tunnels, writhing in pain and clutching his arm. The next second, Zal and Roxie were both striding to the little man's side (*Zal must have handed Malone off to Dexter . . .*); Zal scooped up Blair's dropped gun, while Roxie stood back with her own weapon leveled on Blair.

"God, I'm hit!" Blair was sobbing. "God, I'm hit!"

"Dump his ass down the well," snapped Roxie.

Blair screamed in terror at the thought, and Emma said, "We need him for the police." In her mind, if not yet in actual fact, she could almost hear the Taralla boys running towards the voices and the shots . . . "If we don't, they may still suspect Clark, or Mr. Pugh, or Heaven knows who else . . ."

"Get him on his feet, then—"

Blair was gasping, his head falling back in a swoon. "Malone still got his flask on him?" asked Zal. "He's going into shock—"

"No," said Emma, and Zal cursed, and ran a quick hand over Blair's mud-spattered coat. No flask, but a pint bottle of Seagram's; Blair coughed, sobbed as the liquor was poured down his throat, clutched at his bloodied arm.

"Get up," ordered Zal, and gave him a second drink. "Come on. If Taralla's boys see the liquor you stole from his deliveries, you're gonna want a nice safe jail cell."

"I didn't do anything!" gasped Blair. "I didn't—"

"Oh, the hell you didn't!" Clark Dexter stumbled a step forward, hampered by Malone clinging to his shoulder for support.

"Argue later." Zal dragged Blair to his feet.

Roxie doubled back for a moment, to pick up Malone's .38, lying on the floor with smoke still whiffing from its barrel.

Men's voices and footsteps echoed in the dark, somewhere in the maze of tack rooms and passageways and places where grooms were supposed to have slept. The walls of the passageway to the house were close enough together that Emma could keep a hand on one, and had to move almost sidelong to keep Darlene on her feet. Behind her in the blackness, she heard the rustle of the others—Blair sobbing, the click of Roxie's heels, Malone's dragging breaths—but dared not switch on the flashlight. The tunnel ran straight, without cross-passages. Pursuit could not help seeing light.

She felt it when the old smuggler tunnel gave way to a more even floor, wider walls, plastered rather than old brick and stone. "There's a door in about twenty feet," came Clark Dexter's voice, and he sounded calmer now, and awake. "That'll get you into the wine cellar—"

"That's the way I found in." Emma spoke back over her shoulder. "How do we get out from there? It isn't under the kitchens where you expect—"

"Here."

She had stopped, her groping hand meeting the wood of the door. She flashed the light onto its handle as Clark came up beside her. In the yellowish glow, he was disheveled and filthy, one lens of his glasses broken and a purpling bruise on his receding chin. It was the first time, Emma realized, she'd seen him sober, his mouth firmly set above that puerile chin and his eyes bright.

"There are men up in the Italian garden," she said, as the young man opened the door and led the way out past the wine racks. "We have to get out the other side of the house, then back around to the far side of the stable."

He looked disconcerted at that, and Zal said, "Once we're out of the house, I can find it. We filmed just about every foot of ground around here. I have dreams about this joint at night."

Stairs, then a narrow hallway—one of the servant wings, Emma thought . . . After that, the echoing space of a ballroom, a pitch-black cavern with all its many windows shuttered.

The scurry of rats across the floor.

A step behind her, Blair stumbled, nearly falling into Zal, who still dragged him along by his good arm. Zal said, "Come on," and the older man clutched his elbow, stumbled again.

"What'd you give me?" Blair demanded, terror in his voice. "That booze—"

"Seagram's finest," returned Zal unfeelingly. "Exactly what your boss is selling to the customers—"

"The stuff *I* had?" His voice squeaked. "Shit, the stuff—"

"The stuff you had in your pocket."

"*Shit!*" screamed Blair. "Oh, shit—oh, for Chrissake, get me out of here! Get me to a hospital—" And bending double as if gut-punched, he vomited a queasy brownish slime.

Zal sprang back and cursed in earnest, as Blair fell to his knees. "Oh, Jesus," Blair gasped. "Oh, Jesus, help me! Get me to a hospital! Get me to a—"

"What the hell?" said Roxie, as Darlene screamed again and went into renewed hysterics.

"Arsenic!" Blair screamed. "Get me to—tell 'em it's arsenic! Tell 'em I–I swallowed accidentally . . . Tell 'em—" He doubled up again, clutching his gut and sobbing.

"It was in the whiskey," said Emma, realizing then Blair's scheme to avoid a second round of blackmail.

And Zal, looking down at the dying man, said, quite quietly, "You bastard."

And when Dexter said, "Huh?" Zal took the pint of liquor from his pocket.

"He planned to give this to Bronco and Knuckles after they'd buried you and Darlene. Nobody'd find their bodies, or yours. Not down there, they wouldn't—"

"Leave him." Roxie's voice was like flint as she caught Clark's arm, pulled him towards the French windows. And when the others stared from her to the man writhing on the floor, howling in pain and terror, "Leave him or shoot him. They'll be here—"

"We can't!" protested Emma, and Zal's hand closed on her elbow, thrust her after Roxie—caught Malone as Clark, in confusion, let his own grip slide.

"We can't do anything for him. Go. They'll be here—"

Clark stared around him in panic, then pulled loose from Roxie long enough to grab Darlene and shove her along with them. He sobbed, "We can't just—"

"Yeah, we can, baby," said Roxie. "Unless you want me to shoot him . . ."

"Don't stand here arguing!" Zal shoved the whole unruly gang towards the windows. "They'll—"

Impatiently, Roxie shook herself loose from Clark's grip and yanked Malone's .38 from her coat pocket. She pointed it back at Blair, still screaming and vomiting on the floor, and pulled the trigger, the hammer clicking on an empty chamber.

Zal's right—Emma pushed Darlene through the French window as Zal pulled it open, and they stepped out into the sudden glare of two flashlight beams.

Zal's hands were in the air before the voice of Angel-Eyes Taralla snapped, "Get 'em up!"

TWENTY-THREE

"And no funny business."

Darlene turned like a hare doubling on its tracks to dive back into the dark of the house, and another flashlight beam glared forth from the ballroom behind them. Footfalls and the stink of cigarette smoke. Emma turned her head for an instant to see three more men come through one of the inner doors, guns leveled.

Darlene screamed and crumpled into Clark's arms.

One of the men flicked the flashlight beam over Blair, still gagging, voiding himself, curling tighter and tighter around his belly. "What the hell?"

"Arsenic." Zal kept his hands in the air, one of them still holding the pint. "He brought it to poison Bronco and Knuckles, after they'd shot and buried Clark Dexter and Miss Golden."

The man said, "Fuck," in a tone of utter disgust.

Angel-Eyes Taralla walked over to Zal, placed the muzzle of his automatic against Zal's forehead while he took the bottle. Then he stepped back, glanced down at Darlene and across at Clark. "Somebody didn't get the job done," he remarked. "And Mr. Malone, of all people!" In the dim yellow glare, he grinned. "And who plugged him?"

Malone's eyelids raised as if weighted. He whispered, "I attempted suicide, from remorse at my sins."

Taralla looked around at his captives. "Which of you knows where he stashed the booze? And how to get there?"

"That's me." Clark's voice was quiet. "Just let the others go. I'll take you down there."

The bootlegger's smile widened. "I'll let them go when you and I get back. How's that?"

"Sure," the young man agreed, and Emma had to bite her lip at this display of naïveté. "Just—"

Somebody out in the foliage said, "Vaffanculo!" at the same

moment headlights swept the side of the house, and three cars ground their way through the ruined garden.

Men leaped out. Emma's eyes widened at the sight of sawed-off shotguns and what had to be—by the descriptions she'd heard—"submachine" guns with their characteristic round magazines. The gravel voice of the High Wire's maître d'—Benny—yelled, "Drop 'em!" and a moment later, Kitty cried, "Darling, are you all right?"

Kitty?

And Chico called out, "Watch it, doll!"

The headlights silhouetted the big, slope-shouldered figure of Detective Smith as he stepped out of one of the cars and crunched through the trampled ruin of box hedge and ivy toward the house, a shotgun in one hand. "So, what do we got here?" he asked.

Amid a great rustling of foliage, Angel-Eyes Taralla—and the henchmen circling the French windows of the ballroom—switched off their flashlights and melted into the darkness. In the chamber behind them, Emma heard the swift shuffle of feet and the closing of the inner door.

Silence then, broken only by Jefferson Blair's groaning sobs.

Smith turned. Against the darkness, Emma saw that most of Malone's men had likewise disappeared, and there wasn't a weapon to be seen. "Benny?" Smith raised his voice. "We're taking this guy to Eastern. You, too, Malone." Two men darted forward, caught Malone under the arms, and carried him down the few shallow brick steps towards the nearest car. A third gently lifted Darlene. "She all right?" asked Smith.

Emma said quietly, "From what she said, it sounds as though she broke free of the two men who dragged her away from Blair—I assume to rape her before they killed her. They followed her and were killed before they caught her."

"Killed?" Smith raised his brows, neither surprised nor particularly upset.

"There was a good deal of gunplay in the tunnels," extemporized Emma, deeming it better not to mention that Darlene had grabbed a gun from one of her would-be rapists. "I'm not sure how many of them were down there."

"I saw four at least," corroborated Zal.

"Mr. Malone was hit right off, and the three of us—Mr. Rokatansky, Miss North, and myself—took refuge in one of those little rooms and switched off the flashlight so we wouldn't be seen."

From the engines of the three dark hulks in the foliage came the roar of ignition. Smith glanced past Emma into the darkness of the house, then back at the men loading Jefferson Blair into one of the vehicles. "You mind coming with me, Duchess? Rokatansky? I'll have to call in the Suffolk County sheriffs to secure and search the house—"

"Darling!" Kitty sprang up the steps, caught Emma in her arms. "Are you all right?"

Am I all right? Emma tracked back in her mind everything that had happened since she and Zal had arisen from bed after a leisured evening of love-making and had discussed whether or not they should go to Lindy's for cheesecake, or settle for room service. Beyond the lattice of the pine trees, the eastern sky was beginning to stain with the late winter dawn. "I'm . . . tired," she said at last. "I think I should like a cup of tea."

Over a cup of tea, in a corner of the nurses' sitting room at Eastern Long Island Hospital—far, far out at the most distant tip of the island—Emma detailed an edited version of the events of the night to Detective Smith, who didn't look as though he'd had any more sleep than she had. "What are you doing here?" she had asked Kitty, on their way up the steps of the original mansion that formed the hospital's core. "And how did you know where we were? Surely Detective Smith wouldn't have—"

"Oh, no, we kidnapped Detective Smith," explained Kitty brightly. Smith, mounting the steps ahead of them, paused for the smallest moment, as if he would have taken exception to this view of the matter, then simply moved on. "He was very good about it," she added. "That is—Chico and I were following Frank, you see. Chico paid one of the clerks at the Gapstow to tell him when 'Bo Sharpless' came or went from his room there—to call him at the theater, I mean. Or for Chico to call him. We missed him a couple of times, but last night I was at the theater when Chico called the Gapstow, and the clerk said, Mr. Sharpless and another man—a workman, he said—had just come in and gone up to Mr. Sharpless's room. We drove down there like Sam Sixty and sort of loitered around outside until Frank came out, all done up in a tuxedo, with—guess who? Mr. Doughty! His wife's lawyer! The one with that silly half-grown mustache, who came to the studio last month about the divorce! That's who Frank was renting the room to meet with! So his wife wouldn't know!

"So we followed them down to the Mardi Gras Club, and guess who was sitting in a quiet corner with the most *gorgeous* young man—Alphonse Prince, Monetta Minot told me . . ."

"Who?"

"Monetta Minot," said Kitty. "You remember—that beautiful girl who played the African harlot in the tavern scene? She sings at Lulubelle's—she has the most amazing voice! She came in looking for Shakespeare, because Lulubelle said Roxie North had rushed in saying that that awful Mr. Blair had kidnapped Floppy—and poor Darlene, who was just trying to talk to him about where he'd been the night Mila Haley had got killed!—and she was trying to find Shakespeare to go after them to Versailles. He wasn't at the High Wire, she said.

"I called the Plaza," she burbled on over Emma's vain attempt to ask who had been sitting with the most gorgeous Alphonse Prince, "and the boy at the desk told me Shakespeare had just left, with what sounded like you and Zal and Roxie, and Chico said, there was usually a crap game going on in the back room of the Club Hot-Cha, which is right across from the Mardi Gras, with a couple of Shakespeare's boys who were supposed to be down at the High Wire and weren't. But this sounded like trouble, so Chico and I went back there and got Rizzo and Gas-Bomb Snyder and Big Louis, and Rizzo suggested we grab Detective Smith, who'd be just on his way home then, because they might need to arrest old Blair to keep Bronco and Knuckles from just shooting him. I mean, we *did* still need to find the real killer so we could clear Frank—"

Emma made another fruitless attempt to inquire about Mr. Pugh's meeting with Mrs. Pugh's lawyer . . .

"—although now I know what Frank was doing that night, and what he was doing sneaking around the Gapstow in disguise! He was meeting with Doughty, trying to get the goods on his wife, so he didn't have to pay alimony . . . He's been paying Doughty all along! That's where he was Monday night two weeks ago when Mila was killed! They were tracking her down because Frank heard from Doughty she was carrying on with Alphonse Prince! And she *was*! There they were at the Mardi Gras, but Frank couldn't tell anybody because . . ."

"And Detective Smith?"

"Detective Smith?" Kitty blinked at her, startled. "Oh, no, darling, he's not her type at *all*! Oh!" she added. "Oh, you mean . . . yes. Well, Chico drove, and Rizzo and Boxcar and Slick Eddie pulled up beside Detective Smith on Forty-First Street and pushed him into the car, and Big Louis and Gas-Bomb Snyder followed us out to Long Island. And where *are* Gas-Bomb and Louis?" she added, looking back from the old mansion's doorway.

But the car bearing the wounded Shakespeare Malone had disappeared. Emma guessed, after her interview with Smith was done, that the second car was en route to some other hospital, which would *not* be visited by the Suffolk County sheriff's department that morning.

Although no charges could be brought against Jefferson Blair for the putative murder of Spencer, Claire, and Myra Dexter in October of 1920, on the testimony of Elizabeth (Sugar-Pie) Gilroy and Roxanne North, Blair was convicted of the murder of Mila Haley on the night of the fifteenth of December, 1924. He was further convicted of attempting to murder Clark Dexter and Dorcas Spitz (Darlene Golden), and of conspiracy to murder Bartholomew (Bronco) Burnett and Pietro (Knuckles) Gracciola. Having survived arsenic poisoning by the skin of his teeth, Blair was sentenced to life imprisonment in the penitentiary at Ossining, New York.

On New Year's Day, 1925, Darlene Golden—suitably coached in appropriate political and social views—wed Clark Dexter, who was then put in absolute control of his inheritance. ("At least she's white," had sniffed his mother and his Aunt Violet, both of whom had in fact been deeply impressed by Miss Golden's repentance and change of heart, and her renunciation—mid-film!—of her movie career.) (Miss Golden's parents were invited, but did not attend.) (Director George Blakeney gave the bride away.)

A week later, the new Mrs. Dexter filed for divorce from her new husband—with a generous settlement. ("A hundred thousand, honey, which is what I'd probably get if I sued for pain and suffering.") Because both parties cheerfully admitted adultery in court, and neither asked for any money, the judgement was granted without delay. Aunt Violet's utter horror at the proceedings did not keep her, a few months later, from leaving for Nevada the day after her husband's departure for Sing Sing, and filing for one of her own.

On the ninth of January, 1925, Clark Dexter further scandalized the entire population of Long Island and put his mother "into spasms" (as she put it) by marrying Roxie North, and they lived happily ever after. Dexter paid for Charles Haley and his wife to transfer to the Ansonia Hotel, reimbursed them for their train fare to New York, and paid not only to have their daughter's name put on the grave in the Canarsie Cemetery, but for a larger and more handsome gravestone.

On the tenth of January, the former Mrs. Clark Dexter married Percival "Bull Moose" Poole, the willowy young man who had formerly been chauffeur to Neil Bandog. (Clark Dexter gave the bride away.) ("Why do they call him Bull Moose?" had asked Emma. "Gosh, I have no idea," replied Kitty, with a reminiscent smile.)

That same day, Sugar-Pie Gilroy married Angel-Eyes Taralla.

Rebecca Rokatansky, severely chaperoned by her elder sister, came to Grand Central Station on the twelfth, to see the stars of such films as *Temptress of Babylon* and *Only the Wicked* as they boarded the Twentieth Century Limited to return to Los Angeles. Porters were loading mountain ranges of trunks, suitcases, crates, and camera equipment into the baggage cars, and still more cases and portmanteaux into the "seven and two" luxury Pullmans, around whose doors reporters clustered like bees in swarming time. The combined scandals of Darlene Golden's two marriages, the arrest of socialite-financier Jefferson Blair, and the lawsuit of best-selling author Devon Kingsley against Foremost Productions seemed to have affected the press like bleeding offal thrown to a school of sharks. Above the sea of journalistic fedoras around the Pullman car's door, a continuous battery of flash powder blazed like an American Fourth of July: Emma smiled at the glimpse of Kitty, waving to the reporters in a cloud of chinchilla and diamonds.

Frank Pugh, at Kitty's side, seemed to be doing most of the talking, assuring them (Emma reflected) that the terrible misfortunes that had stalked the filming of the epic bestseller *Shining Bright* would not delay the production by more than a few weeks. "A complete lie," she said to Becca, who had brought with her the newest issues of *Film Fun* and *Screen World*, which contained features to that effect. "Mr. Bandog is so furious about having to abandon plans for his divorce—after paying I don't know how much to his lawyers in anticipation of marrying Miss Golden, not to mention what he paid for that appalling ring—that he's ordered every frame of Miss Golden's work on the film destroyed."

"Oh, no!" gasped the girl, eyes wide with alarm and delight at this piece of movie news. "You mean they'll scrap the whole picture?"

Emma patted the attaché case under her arm. "They're still arguing over it. I suspect we'll re-shoot, at a smaller budget, on the back lot at Foremost, depending on the outcome of Mr. Kingsley's suit . . ."

Certainly, it wouldn't be filmed at Versailles. It had started raining on the second: winter had definitely set in. Moreover, Shakespeare Malone had taken out a long-term lease on the property, the payment for which enabled Aunt Violet to move into a pleasant apartment in Brooklyn. Since the police could find no evidence that liquor had been hidden at the chateau—the formerly locked room beneath the stables was found to be empty (*So* that's *where Malone's men went when they all disappeared like that* . . .)—Malone had also, apparently, purchased the *White Goddess* from her. ("Smuggler tunnels?" Emma could almost hear him say it. "What smuggler tunnels?")

"Kingsley hasn't got a leg to stand on." Zal came down the platform, from where he and Chip Thaw had been supervising the loading of cameras, and barely stopped himself from putting his arm around Emma's waist.

Becca said, "You can go ahead and kiss her. I won't look."

She added, to Emma's startled glance, "I knew it the first time I saw you together. I've seen enough movies to know what it looks like, when you're in love."

Emma felt herself blush, and Zal put an arm around his sister's shoulders and hugged her. "Don't believe everything you see in the pictures, mayn tayere. It doesn't always look like that in Real Life."

"But it should." Becca glanced down the platform to where Ruthie stood, arms folded, watching them like a Puritan confronted by a chorus line. "I'm glad it looks like that for you." She knelt to ruffle the manes of Black Jasmine and Chang Ming, and to poke a finger through the lattice on Buttercreme's carry-box. "I won't tell Mama."

Emma said, "Thank you, dear," and the girl looked up again, from Emma's face to Zal's.

"You're not going to let Mama . . . well, you know how she is."

"I know how she is." Zal smiled. "And I'll stay out in Hollywood as long as I have to—" His eye caught Emma's, and they traded a smile. On the fringe of the mob of reporters, Emma could see Mr. Kingsley, vainly trying to get the attention of a journalist in a checkered suit with his version of events. The other members of the Press ignored him completely. Emma could have told him that 517 pages of the best prose ever written counted as nothing against Camille de la Rose blowing kisses from the step of a Pullman car.

Becca snuggled her face against Chang Ming's fluffy mane, while Black Jasmine licked her chin. "Can I write to you, Mrs. Blackstone?"

"Please call me Emma." She reached down and helped the girl to her feet. "And I would be delighted if you did. I have no family left in England to write," she added. "Well, one aunt . . . It will be good to get letters again."

"And now we better get on the train," grinned Zal, as Ruthie started towards them, "before I kiss you by mistake and blow the whole act." With a display of disinterested chivalry, he helped Emma up onto the step. ("Wanna see if we can manage the Cincinnati Special in a sleeper bunk?") From that vantage point, she could see, down the length of the platform, the little group of Darlene Golden's father, mother, brother, and white-haired family lawyer climb glumly aboard the second-class car. Trailed by the stoop-shouldered Mr. Doughty (and thirty pieces of luggage), Mrs. Pugh crossed the platform, averting her eyes from the scene around the first-class car's other door.

As Ruthie and Zal shook hands, Becca lifted the Pekes up to Emma, and their eyes met in smiling complicity.

It would indeed be good, reflected Emma, to have family again.

Author's Note

Within a few years, the majority of the film industry moved from New York to Hollywood, a shift accelerated by the advent of sound film technology, and the onset of the Great Depression.

With the coming of sound—and the onset of the Depression—the Marx Brothers also made the move from Broadway to Hollywood, establishing themselves among the top film comedians of the twentieth century. Zeppo Marx retired from the act after five films, and went on to a successful career as an agent and an inventor.

The circumstances surrounding the death of pioneering film maker Thomas Ince—and what really happened on the yacht of newspaperman William Randolph Hearst in November of 1924—remain mysterious to this day.